COLORADO EVENING SKY
By
A J Hawke

Mountain Quest Publishing
COLORADO EVENING SKY
Published by arrangement with the author

Cover art and design by Daniel O'Leary.

ACKNOWLEDGMENTS

Many people have been my encouragers through this process. I love and thank you all. Jeanette and Russell Schoof, Windle and Barbara OTeka Kee, Doyle and Barbara R. Kee, Bill and Jean Ann Edrington, Michelle Jourdan, and the Ladies of Monday evening Bible study group. Editing was provided by Teresa Hanger of www.A-1EditingServices.com.

My goal is not just to write novels about the West, but to recreate the authentic American West in my readers' minds. To do this, I research the facts exhaustively. Sometimes the truth is surprising. For example, a scene in this COLORADO EVENING SKY describes electric lighting at the infamous Yuma Territorial Prison in the late 19th Century. The prison, located on the banks of the Colorado River, was the site of one of the first hydroelectric generating plants in the West. Electricity ran an early fan system and lighted the dark cellblocks, which allowed prison guards to watch prisoners more closely. The story and characters are fictional. But, the descriptions of woodworking machines to weather events to religious observances describe what actually existed and occurred in the True American West.

It is impossible to edit to perfection. If you find an editing problem email me at AJHawkebooks@gmail.com. Your help will be appreciated.

Dedication
To family and friends who have walked the path with me
And
To God the Father, the Lord Jesus Christ, and the Holy Spirit who have been my guides.

TITLES BY A J HAWKE
Cedar Ridge Chronicles
CABIN ON PINTO CREEK, Book 1
JOE STORM NO LONGER A COWBOY, Book 2
COLORADO MORNING SKY, Book 3
COLORADO EVENING SKY, Book 4
Stand-Alone Novels
MOUNTAIN JOURNEY HOME
CAUGHT BETWEEN TWO WORLDS: COWBOY BOOTS AND HIGH HEELS

Table of Contents

Chapter One Catherine

Cedar Ridge, Colorado April 1890

"My boy is coming home!" The excitement and joy in Agnes' voice was contagious.

Catherine O'Malley looked at the beaming face of her dear friend Agnes. "Who is coming home?" Catherine took a sip of tea and watched as older woman slide a slice of pound cake onto the pretty porcelain plate that matched the teacup and saucer that held her tea. Taking a break from her work as owner and operator of the Cedar Ridge Café, Catherine sat at the small table in the small workroom at the back of the mercantile. Catherine could hear Agnes' husband, Milburn Black as he moved about in the large mercantile store while Catherine visited with her friend.

Agnes stirred her tea to let it cool. "I can't wait any longer. I have to tell someone our news."

Catherine took a bite of pound cake and waited for Agnes to continue.

"I don't think I have ever told you much about our son Thomas."

Catherine shook her head. "I know you have a son who lives in Arizona, but nothing else."

Sighing Agnes took a sip of hot tea and then set the cup back on the saucer. With a serious look and folding her hands into her lap, she started. "Thomas is our youngest. The two girls, Bessie and Hope, you know about. I don't talk much about Thomas because he has been in prison in Arizona for the last twelve years. He went to jail for rustling when he was seventeen years old. We had moved to Arizona from here when he was four years old, which was the biggest mistake of our lives. Milburn thought he could do better with a store there and Bessie was having chest problems. The doctor told us the heat and dry air there would help her." Agnes' eyes brimmed over with tears and she pulled a handkerchief from her apron pocket. "After Thomas went to Yuma Prison, Milburn decided to move back here because of the cloud that hung over us in Arizona. Milburn wanted the girls to have a better chance at a good life and finding acceptable husbands. Bessie was doing so much better as she got older." Tears, which she tried to catch with her handkerchief, were flowing now down Agnes' plump cheeks.

Catherine wanted to take her friend into her arms and try to give comfort. However, she sensed that Agnes needed to tell her story. So she ate her cake and sipped her tea and listened.

Agnes sighed deeply. "Leaving Thomas behind in prison was the hardest thing Milburn and I have ever done, but we had to think of the girls, too. Every year Milburn has gone back to visit our son and I have waited for news. Thomas is twenty-nine years old now." Agnes took a big swig of hot tea and squared her shoulders. "Now for the good news. Milburn has been writing the authorities in Arizona Territory and so has Jeremiah Rebourn. They have convinced the judge there to give Thomas early parole from his prison sentence of fifteen years. Instead of serving his last three years in prison, the judge is going to let him work on Jeremiah's ranch. My son is coming home." A look of pure joy shown out past her tears as Agnes made the announcement once again as if she couldn't believe it.

"Oh, Agnes. What wonderful news for you and Milburn. When will Thomas be home?"

"Jeremiah, bless his heart, has agreed to travel on today's train to Santa Fe and then on to Yuma. He will escort Thomas home and should be back by Friday of this week. Of course, Thomas will live on the Rocking JR Ranch with Jeremiah and Emily. That's where he will work for the next three years. I will get to see him and visit any time."

Catherine wasn't surprised to hear that Jeremiah Rebourn and his wife Emily were helping Milburn and Agnes with the return of their son. Jeremiah was well respected. He dealt mostly in horses but had a small herd of cattle. Emily was one of Catherine's best friends from church that they attended along with Milburn and Agnes.

"I need to pick out some clothes to send with Jeremiah for Thomas to wear home. It has been so hard thinking about my boy in that place, wondering if he was sick or hurt and what his life was like." Agnes got up and started gathering the dishes. "But I'm not going to think about all those lost years. God is blessing us by bringing Thomas home and that is all that matters now."

Catherine rose and placed her empty teacup and saucer into the pan of water that set on the counter by the stove. "Let me help you gather the clothes to send for your son. I know you don't need help but I would like to do something. And, thank you for sharing with me about your son. I'll be praying about Jeremiah's trip and for the safe return of both men."

Agnes led the way into the main store, which was empty except for Milburn who sat in a chair by the potbellied stove reading the newspaper.

He glanced up as they entered. "Catherine, you're a sight for sore eyes."

She laughed. "Milburn, what does that even mean?"

The older rotund man scratched his baldhead. "Now that you ask, I'm not sure. I know it means I'm glad to see you but what does it have to do with sore eyes?" He moved behind the counter.

"Here's my supply list. Can you have it delivered as usual?" She slid the list toward him over the worn top of the counter.

"Sure. How quick do you need this?" He pushed his spectacles up his nose as he looked over her list.

"There's no rush. But I will be out of flour and sugar by the end of the day."

Agnes stepped beside her husband. The grayed-haired stocky older woman glowed with good cheer. "It is all right that I told Catherine about Thomas?"

Catherine smiled at the older couple who were about the same height and even seemed to resemble each other. Maybe that's what almost forty years of marriage did.

Milburn put his arm around his wife's shoulders and pulled her close. "Sure, honey. Catherine will keep it close to herself and won't gossip. I know you want to tell someone. We just need to not tell everyone for Thomas' sake, all right?"

She nodded and with a twinkle in her eyes gave him a kiss on his cheek. "I understand."

Milburn turned back to Catherine. "How is business?"

"Business is good as usual for a Monday. Quite a few for breakfast and then I expect a busy dinner and supper crowd."

"That was about the same for us. The ranchers and farmers come into town to get supplies they say." He chuckled. "But I think it's an excuse to stop in and have some of your cooking."

Catherine leaned against the counter to relieve some of the pain from her feet. She had started cooking before daylight. "I don't care why they come as long as they do. Being across the street from you all doesn't hurt my business."

Agnes stepped into the aisle and headed toward the garment section of the store. "We better get the things ready to send with Jeremiah. He will be here soon."

Catherine followed Agnes over to the shelving that held men's pants and shirts. "How many outfits do you want to send?"

Pulling several shirts off the shelf, Agnes said, "Thomas needs one to wear out of the prison and it will take them two to three days by train to get back to Cedar Ridge. I think three shirts, pants, under garments, and socks. Milburn will pick out a pair of boots. He may not need that much for the trip but he will need clothes for the ranch work."

"What about a hat and jacket? Will Thomas have anything?" It seemed strange to Catherine to be talking about clothing a man she had never met.

"Good idea. He will need a hat and jacket and oh yes, handkerchiefs and shaving gear. What do you think about this blue chambray shirt and this striped red and black one. It looks like it would fit Jeremiah and Milburn says that's about Thomas size now."

Catherine nodded and picked up a white percale shirt. "What color hair and eyes does Thomas have? That makes a difference what color looks good on him." All three were typical overshirts with three buttons and an opening that stopped halfway down the front of the shirt. The first two had no collar or cuffs attached but the white percale shirt did, which was a new style for Catherine. "Do you think this is too dressy?"

"No, I want him to have one nice shirt for Sunday wear." Agnes laughed. "If Thomas is like most men, he doesn't worry about what color looks good on him." A look of sadness settled on Agnes' face. "I don't know Thomas and what he likes anymore. He was still a boy when he went to prison, and I don't know what kind of man he has become in that place. I don't even know his clothing size. Milburn said to think about someone Jeremiah's size and height. Thomas was just a thin, scrawny boy no taller than Milburn the last time I saw him. According to Milburn, he has grown several more inches and filled out into a strong looking man. His hair is dark brown with a tendency to curl if it isn't cut often. His eyes are dark brown. When he was a boy and he was trying to wheedle some extra cookies, I would tell him his eyes looked just like a deer, all soft and brown. I'm assuming he looks the same, just older." Agnes laughed and shook her head. "Listen to me going on and on. I'm just so excited."

Catherine tried to envision what Thomas might look like, but never having seen him she couldn't. She felt sad for Agnes that she wasn't even sure what her son looked like. What kind of man would a boy be after all those years in prison? She hoped it would be a good homecoming and not bring more grief to these good people.

Glancing around the store, she asked, "What will Jeremiah use to carry the things for Thomas?"

Agnes put her fisted hand under her chin and looked around. "That's a good question." Turning she called out to her husband. "Milburn, do we still have one of those small valises?"

He put down the newspaper and looked up at them. "A valise? Sure, we have two of them."

Agnes waited for him to continue. He stood and put down the newspaper. "Oh, you want me to find one. Is that for Thomas' things?"

Slightly rolling her eyes and glancing over at Catherine, she said in a sweet voice. "Yes, dear, if you would please, and then pick out a pair of boots. We've got the clothes ready to pack and Jeremiah will be here in a few minutes to catch the 10 o'clock train to Denver."

Milburn walked toward the back of the store. "Is it that late already?"

Catherine helped Agnes fold the shirts and pants and roll up the undergarments and socks. She understood Agnes' wanting to do something for her son so that he would be nicely dressed for the trip home. How she must yearn to see her son. And Milburn and Thomas—what were they feeling? Catherine said a silent prayer for her friends and for their son.

Milburn came back with a small dark brown canvas valise with a leather handle and straps. "What about this one?" He handed it off to Agnes.

"Perfect, dear and now please pick out a pair of boots. Do you have any idea of Thomas' size?"

Milburn scratched his head. "I'm thinking he wears a size or two larger than me. Maybe about the size that Jeremiah bought last week." He strolled on down the aisle of the large store and stopped by a display of boots and men's shoes. Soon he came back to where Agnes and Catherine were packing the valise carrying a dark brown pair of leather boots. "These should do both for traveling and for working out at the ranch. The heels are not too tall and they are not fancy but should be comfortable. If the size isn't a fit then when Thomas gets here, we'll get him another pair."

"Those should do fine. They will fit here on top of the other things." Agnes placed the boots into the valise, and Catherine helped her buckle the straps.

The bell over the door gave its clang and Catherine turned to see Jeremiah Rebourn entering the mercantile. She had always thought he was a fine looking man and even though he was often quiet at church, he was always friendly and polite.

Jeremiah walked up to them. "Morning, folks. You have the things for your son ready? And Milburn, I'd like to take that letter from the judge saying he's going to release Thomas."

Milburn nodded his agreement. "I'll go get it from the back. I'm glad you thought about it. Maybe it will keep the judge from changing his mind."

Agnes gave a small sound of distress. "Oh, Milburn, he wouldn't do that."

Milburn patted her shoulder. "Now calm down, honey. That's why Jeremiah is taking the letter. So the judge won't be able to change his mind." He headed toward the back of the store.

Jeremiah took Agnes' hand. "Don't worry. I'll do everything I can to bring your son home to you." He glanced over at Catherine as if needing help.

She moved beside Agnes and put her arm around her shoulders. "We can be praying the whole time Jeremiah is gone. That will be our part in getting Thomas home."

Agnes straightened her shoulders. "You're right. I need to trust that God's will is being done. I don't have the words to thank you enough for going to pick Thomas up and for bringing him home, Jeremiah. It is so good of you."

Jeremiah looked at the floor and Catherine was surprised to see that he was blushing. "It's something I can do for you and Milburn. You've been real good friends to Emily and me."

Milburn came back waving an envelope. "I had to look for this. It was in my Bible." He handed it over to Jeremiah who then put it in an inside pocket of his jacket like an item of great value.

Milburn cleared his throat. "Jeremiah, would you mind if I said a prayer asking God's blessings on your journey and safe return?"

"I would appreciate that, Milburn." Jeremiah sat his hat on the counter and then took Catherine and Agnes' hands. Milburn took his wife's hand and then he and Jeremiah joined hands completing the circle.

Bowing his head and closing his eyes, he began to pray. "Heavenly Father, bless Jeremiah and keep him safe. Bring him back to his family as quickly as possible. Be with Thomas and give us wisdom to help him in this new beginning for his life. We ask that your will be done in all things. In Jesus name, Amen."

Jeremiah hugged Agnes and shook Milburn's hand. He put on his hat and touched the brim in a nod at Catherine. "I better get on my way. I want to be ready when the train pulls into the station. I plan to see you all either Thursday or Friday. If I have any difficulty, I'll send a telegram." He took the valise filled with clothes for Thomas and left the store.

In the quiet after the mercantile door closed, Agnes gave a little sniffle. Milburn patted her on the shoulder again. "There now, he'll be back with Thomas before you can turn around. In the meantime, we need to get some work done and keep praying."

Catherine gave Agnes a hug. "Thanks for letting me help and for sharing your news. Now I know what to pray about for you all, Jeremiah, and Thomas. I am so eager to meet your son and it won't be long until he's here."

Agnes gave a small smile and worked to keep the tears at bay. "I'm glad you know, dear. It's a comfort to have someone to share something like this with." Milburn nodded his agreement.

Turning briskly, Catherine walked toward the back of the store. "I must get my things and get back to the café. Beryl will quit on me if I leave her to face the supper crowd alone." Carefully pinning on her hat, she walked back the length of the store. "So long, I'll see you tomorrow. And in the meantime, I'll be praying."

"Bye, dear." Agnes and Milburn waved as Catherine closed the door of the mercantile and stepped to the boardwalk.

The sun shown bright and the spring air refreshed her. She felt a sense of something important about to happen. Catherine carefully crossed the dusty rutted road to the café with a bounce in her steps and a prayer on her heart.

~

Catherine dropped small chunks of beef into the large pot of water simmering on the wood cook stove in the kitchen of the Cedar Ridge Café. Nodding her head at the sound of scraping chairs on the wood floor from the dining room, she hoped the last of the mid-day crowd was leaving. Maybe she could take an hour off before the supper crowd brought the next rush of the day. Sighing, with her feet hurting from standing on them since before daybreak, she reminded herself to be thankful that she had honest work, even if being the owner and cook for the café left little time for anything else in her life.

The bell on the front door tinkled letting her know someone had entered the café. She wiped her hands on the dishcloth, and then went into the dining room.

"Hello, Catherine." Myles McKinley sat down at one of the tables facing the kitchen.

"Myles, how goes the banking business?" She kept a distance from the table where he sat as she waited for his order.

"Fine, fine. I want a cup of coffee and a piece of pie. Get some for yourself and sit with me." He was a big, stocky blonde haired man in his forties and he acted as if she was his to order around.

Catherine's chest tightened with anger. "I'll get some for you, but I have no time to sit and talk. I have dinner to finish and supper to start preparing." She returned to the kitchen before he could respond.

She put the smaller of the two pieces of apple pie left in the baking tin on a plate and poured a cup of the strong coffee. She then returned to the table where Myles waited and placed the dishes in front of him.

He caught her wrist and pulled her toward him. "Have a seat for a minute."

Shocked that he would behave so, she pulled loose and stepped back. "Now behave yourself, Myles. I told you. I have work to do."

"Maybe that is something we need to talk about. Have dinner with me at the hotel after church on Sunday?"

"I'd rather not plan something for Sunday. It's my only day off." How was she going to get him to leave the café? Why didn't the man eat his pie and leave?

"Then you'll have time to come out with me for Sunday dinner. You can eat someone else's cooking for a change. I won't take no for an answer. Or, we could go for a buggy ride and take a picnic."

"Now, Myles, you have asked me before and my answer is the same. It is not appropriate for us to go for a buggy ride, just the two of us. What would folks say?" How many times had she told the man no? In a way, his attention was flattering as he owned the biggest ranch around and owned the only bank in the town of Cedar Ridge. But, as much as she tried, she had no interest in the man.

Myles's face hardened into a look that was frightening. "I don't care what they would say. It's not their business."

"Well, I care." The busybodies in town would love a little gossip. She wasn't about to give them ammunition. As a single woman running a business alone, she was the object of enough gossip as it was. The nosey women around the small Colorado town seemed to think it was their business to encourage her to find a husband and raise a passel of children. As if, she could pluck a husband out of the air. Catherine sighed. Finding a husband was something she would love to do. However, not just any man would do, and so far, Myles McKinley was not even in the consideration.

"Then go to lunch with me after church on Sunday. That should be appropriate." He looked ready to sit there all day.

Wanting to throw the wet cloth at him to get him to leave her alone, she looked up at him. "All right, I'll go to lunch with you, but only lunch. Now, will you leave so I can get my work done?" Maybe if she went to the hotel dining room on Sunday, he would be satisfied, and in a public place, it should be safe.

He smiled causing his pale blue eyes almost to disappear and take on a squinty look. "I knew you would finally see it my way. That's all I want. I'll look forward to lunch next Sunday."

Catherine noted that the smile did not touch his eyes, which were hard and unreadable. It was as if he looked out onto a hard world but wasn't going to let anyone see into his soul. Some of the young women in town seemed to think he was a handsome man but as Catherine watched him leave the café, she shook her head. He seemed too hard and stiff even though he had a veneer of manners and dressed better than most of the men in the area.

Catherine went to the door and closed it firmly. She turned the sign hanging on the window to show the café was closed until her assistant Beryl opened it at 4 o'clock. Catherine had plans for the afternoon. With the big pot of stew starting to simmer on the stove and dried apple pies made for the supper customers, she could take a couple of hours for herself. She would only need to make cornbread later in the afternoon if Beryl didn't get to it first.

Catherine peeled the potatoes for the stew with quick, precise strokes. She'd had more than enough practice working with her mother and now on her own at the Cedar Ridge Café. She caught herself chopping the potatoes into chunks with angry whacks and then tossing them into the stewpot with a splash. Why had she agreed to have lunch with Myles McKinley on Sunday? She wasn't even sure she liked the man. He was so demanding of his way.

After peeling the last potato and dropping the quartered pieces into the big iron pot which already had carrots, peppers, and onions cooking, Catherine checked the fire and added a couple of pieces of wood. She positioned the pot to keep the contents at a slow simmer so the stew would be done before the supper crowd arrived at the café. The ever present huge pot of pinto beans simmered at the back of the stovetop.

Beryl Potter sauntered through the open back door of the café kitchen. "Good day to you, Catherine. Beautiful spring day."

Catherine smiled at the cheery greeting from her helper. No matter her circumstance, Beryl managed to find something to be optimistic about. "Beryl, I haven't been out enough to see what kind of day we have. Now that you're here, I'll go see for myself."

The heavy-set, gray-haired widow nodded her agreement as she prepared to wash up the dishes from the noon customers. "You go on and take your time. I'll take care of things here. What are we serving for supper?"

"We'll have stew and cornbread and the dried apple pies I baked this morning. Of course, the pinto beans are always on the menu. After you clear the dishes, please sweep the dining room. I have wiped the tables clean once but give them a swipe after you sweep. And, go ahead and make the cornbread for supper. I'll be back in time to do it if you don't have time." Catherine stretched her back that was aching from being on her feet since five that morning.

Beryl tied her large bib white apron over her faded gray dress. "Don't worry. I'll get the cornbread baked. Also, I'll make tea and coffee."

Catherine took off her apron and hung it on the peg by the back door. "Thanks, Beryl. I may walk down by the river and sit awhile. I may be gone a couple of hours."

"You take whatever time you want. You've been at it since before sunup. You need a break. I can handle the afternoon crowd." Beryl laughed. "Course three or four men wanting coffee may not really be a crowd."

Smiling at Beryl's humor, Catherine pinned on her hat and grabbed her supply list. "Well, if it gets too much send someone to find me. See you later." Catherine walked through the café and out the front door onto the boardwalk. She took a deep breath of the cool spring air flowing down from the mountains to the west of town, and even though the afternoon air had a bit of chill, she was so glad to be done with the winter snows.

Herman Jones, the owner of the livery and wagon yard, drove past in a big work wagon drawn by four horses. "Afternoon, Miss Catherine," he yelled over the noise of the horses and wagon.

She waved and waited a moment for the dust to settle before stepping off the boardwalk and with care crossing the dusty, rutted road to reach the path that led down to the bank of the river. Settling on her favorite large rock, she gazed out over the beautiful flowing river with the high mountains beyond. She said a silent prayer for Jeremiah's trip and the safety of both men. What would Milburn and Agnes' son be like after so long in prison? She brushed the tentacles of hair that had escaped her hairnet away from her face. What would the next couple of weeks bring with the advent of Thomas Black to Cedar Ridge?

Chapter Two Thomas

Yuma Territorial Prison, Arizona 1890

"Thomas Black, on your feet."

Even through the fog of sleep, he knew better than to ignore the summons and the hard poke of the baton in his ribs. The new electric light in the corridor outside the small cell silhouetted the two guards as they waited with impatience for him to wake up and respond to their command. Thomas tried to straighten his back. His bones ached with exhaustion from fourteen hours of wielding a sledgehammer. Another day of work had come too soon, but a guard's demanding voice wasn't to be ignored.

"Move it, Black. On your feet. Now." Ed, one of Thomas's least favorite of the prison guards, towered over the hard metal bunk with the straw-filled tick pad so thin it could hardly be called a mattress.

He again felt the hard nagging poke in his ribs from the baton as he groggily staggered to his feet, trying to understand the purpose of the predawn awakening. He couldn't remember any infraction that warranted the hoisting out of his bunk. Since he had three more years to freedom on his fifteen-year sentence, Thomas followed the rules of Yuma Territorial Prison. He had learned some hard lessons. When not to argue with the guards was one of the first. The guards would have to dish out a lot of misery before he would fight back now.

George, the shorter of the two guards, unlocked the shackles from Thomas' feet and unwound the chain from the iron ring on the floor. The guard made no effort to do it quietly. The five men chained to the three-tiered, metal bunks in the narrow cell kept still. Whatever was going on, they wanted no part of it. George slung the shackles and chains over his arm, and Ed prodded Thomas with his baton into the corridor.

Thomas asked no questions. Over the years, he had learned that ignorance was sometimes safer.

"Into the yard and to the bathing room." Ed gave him another agonizing prod in the back. Three bruises were bound to come from this peculiar awakening.

"Yes, sir." Thomas obediently shuffled in front of the two guards into the yard that was surrounded by sixteen-foot high, five-foot wide stone walls. Away from the snoring prisoners, the air no longer smelled of unwashed bodies. He took a deep breath and inhaled the cold early dawn desert air. The primitive bathing room was in the far corner of the prison yard. How a place intended for cleaning the body could always smell so bad was something Thomas couldn't figure out.

When they approached the door, Ed reached in front of Thomas, and opened it. "Take a shower and put those clothes on. Be quick about it." He pointed to a stack of clean clothes on the bench just inside the room. Ed then shoved him into the bathing room, but left the door open so they could keep an eye on him. Trust wasn't a part of this world.

Thomas didn't understand what was going on. His chest tightened with apprehension, as he obeyed Ed's orders.

A cistern on top of the bathing room caught what little rainwater there was. When no rain fell the prisoners had to muster buckets of water from the reservoir under the main guard tower that was filled by the Colorado River. They carried them up the rickety ladder to fill the cistern.

He took off the dirty stripped prison uniform and showered in the lukewarm water, using the piece of lye soap tied to a string. He wanted to linger as it had been over a week since he had had shower privilege. He hurried having experienced Ed's displeasure in the past. The guard knew where to hit the lower back with his baton.

With no towel in sight, Thomas used his prison garb to dry off and put on the new clean cotton undershirt, drawers, blue overshirt, dark brown cotton worsted pants, socks, and leather stockman boots he found placed on the dirty bench. Amazingly, everything fit. He wished for a razor to shave but prisoners were only allowed to shave once a week under the watchful eye of an armed guard.

Clean and dressed in civilian clothes for the first time in twelve years, Thomas stepped back into the prison yard. Ed and George looked put out and annoyed as they waited with the shackles. Whether it was at him, or just at life in general, he had no way of knowing.

After securely attaching the heavy shackles and chains to Thomas' wrists and ankles, they pointed toward the warden's office. Just before reaching the heavy office door, Ed said, "Stop there by the wall."

Thomas listened to the clanging of the chain attached to the shackles on his wrists as George threaded it through an iron ring a couple of feet from the door. Against the quiet of the early morning, the sound was jarring.

"Stand here. The warden wants to see you." Ed slammed him against the wall causing his arms to stretch awkwardly because of the chain around his wrists. Leaving George to guard him, Ed entered the building that housed the prison administration.

Instead of protesting, Thomas savored the outside air and let the cold desert breeze blow through his wet hair. He didn't even mind the chill, as he closed his eyes and took in the feel of the early morning. In the distance, was the pleasant sound of doves cooing.

Thomas could only guess what he was waiting for. There was no reason for what was happening that he could see. The new clothes must have come from his folks who owned a mercantile in Colorado. It had been twelve years since he had seen Ma, and it had been over a year since Pa's last visit. Thomas had to give him credit. Pa had made the long trip at least once every year to visit him a few hours, and then make the long trip home.

Was Pa here for his yearly visit? Never had Thomas been given street clothes on his father's previous visits, only the gray stripped cotton shirt and pants of the prison uniform.

The door of the warden's office whisked open and Ed hustled out. He unlocked the chain attached to the iron ring and jerked on it, pulling Thomas none too gently toward the office door.

He shuffled into the warden's office with the new boots feeling strange on his feet. It was only the second time he had been there. The last time had been twelve years ago when he had first come to the prison. He recognized Warden Henry Devise standing next to the large desk with a commanding star. A man he didn't recognize sat in the chair behind the desk.

"Judge Horton, this is the man." Warden Henry Devise pointed at Thomas with his chin.

"You're Thomas Black, serving a fifteen year sentence for cattle rustling?" Judge Horton was a little man with a baldhead, a pointed goatee, and the most piercing black eyes he had ever seen. The judge was dressed in a black suit that had seen much use, but Thomas could tell the suit used to be very fine before years of wear. The judge's collar, white and starched high, seemed too big for such a skinny neck.

"Yes, sir." Thomas stood still. This man held power over him.

"Listen carefully. I'm going to say this once. According to your record, this one charge of rustling is all that's against you. Although you had some problems when you first got here, you've been a good prisoner for the last ten years. No black marks of any kind. The governor of the territory has decided to give early parole to a few select prisoners. You've been chosen, but with certain restrictions. You understand what I am saying?"

His arrogant voice had a demanding, abrupt tone that got Thomas's jaw to clenching.

"Yes, sir." What else could he say? His hands sweated and his knees trembled. Early release? His mind whirled with the possibilities, and a faint hope.

"Now, here are the conditions and there's no negotiating. You'll swear on the Bible that you'll follow these conditions, or there's no deal. First condition, I place you on parole for three years and you get a release paper after that time. That means if you get into any trouble, you'll be right back here. The three years start again and you'll serve your full sentence. Second condition, I'm paroling you into the keeping of Jeremiah Rebourn of Cedar Ridge, Colorado. You're to work on his ranch under his supervision for the next three years. He's agreed to take responsibility for you, and he'll be in charge of your parole, but he doesn't have to pay you. Do you understand?"

Thomas could only nod. "Yes, sir." Cedar Ridge sounded familiar, as that was where his folks lived. And more than that, Colorado was a long way from here. Three years on a ranch sounded glorious after twelve years of Yuma Prison.

The judge picked up a Bible from the desk and placed it in front of him. "Place your hand on the Bible and repeat after me."

He placed his sweaty palm lightly on the Bible.

The judge's voice was almost a whine, which, unlike his collar, did seem to fit his skinny neck. "I, Thomas Black, do swear that I will keep the conditions of the parole and understand each of its conditions, so help me God."

Thomas swore in a low, soft voice on the Bible to keep the conditions of the parole. He had no idea if he could, or would do it or not, but anything was better than what he had.

The judge set the Bible back down on the desk, then slid a piece of paper toward Thomas. "Sign this here at the bottom and mark the date." He pointed a fountain pen at him.

Thomas scratched his name for the first time in years, but the habit ingrained by the various teachers in school carried through. Then he hesitated and glanced toward the judge, as he didn't know the date.

The judge coldly said, "Today is Monday, April 7, 1890."

"Thank you, sir." Thomas filled out the date carefully then laid the pen down on the desk.

"Jeremiah Rebourn is waiting outside the gate. You're to go with him and leave the territory as soon as possible. Good luck young man, make the most of this break you've been given. And if I ever see you back here again, it'll not go easy on you." The judge folded his hands on the desk and sat back in the chair. He didn't stand or offer to shake hands. But his black piercing eyes never left Thomas' face.

"Thank you, sir. You won't be seeing me again." And he meant it. He had had enough of Yuma Prison.

Ed and George slowly escorted him out of the office building and through a smaller side door next to the big iron bars of the front gate and ushered him out into the road. He had no personal belongings so there was no need even to go back to the cell. He walked out of the prison as he had walked in twelve years ago, with the clothes on his back.

A man who looked to be about his own age waited with two valises at his feet, and held folded over his arm, an extra black jacket and in his hand an extra black felt hat of a type worn by most cowhands. A tall strong looking man with unusually broad shoulders, Thomas guessed the ladies would say he was also handsome with dark brown eyes that held him in a stare.

Ed stepped toward the man. "You Jeremiah Rebourn?"

"Yes."

Ed handed him a piece of paper. "Here's the parole agreement. It gives you the right to take Tom here with you. You can keep the shackles on him or not."

"We won't need the shackles." Rebourn took the parole agreement, folded it, and put it in his jacket pocket.

"Suit yourself but watch out. Tom has been in jail here for twelve years. Give me a moment and I'll get them shackles off him." Ed and George released Thomas' hands and feet. They gathered up the iron shackles and chains, then turned back toward the prison door, and disappeared inside without a word.

Thomas stood there waiting to be told what to do. It had happened too fast and he couldn't take it in. He rubbed his wrists where the iron shackles always bruised them. Outside the prison with no shackles, he was free, almost.

The man put out his hand and Thomas shook it slowly. "I'm Jeremiah Rebourn. You can call me Jeremiah."

"I'm Thomas Black. I prefer to be called Thomas but some people call me Tom." It felt strange to shake hands. This new life was going to take some getting used to.

"Here, these are for you, plus extra clothes in this valise." Rebourn handed him the jacket and hat, which Thomas put on since it was still chilly in the early morning desert air. The tall man picked up the other valise. "Grab your stuff and follow me. I want to catch the seven o'clock train to Santa Fe and we've just enough time to make it." He turned and walked quickly down the incline toward town.

The eyes of the prison guards seemed to be boring into Thomas' back. Was he free to walk away with this man? He followed him. He didn't know what else to do. It took them almost twenty minutes of fast walking to get to the train station. By then Thomas' feet hurt from the new boots, but he kept up with the man.

At the station, he followed Rebourn aboard the train. Rebourn stowed their valises under the seats and gestured for Thomas to sit next to the window. Then he sat next to him with their shoulders touching from the small width of the seat. There were three other people in the train car and the seat facing them was empty, but Thomas didn't argue. All he knew to do was what he was told. Within minutes, the train pulled out of the station.

Rebourn stared straight ahead.

As Thomas glanced at the stone-faced man, he noticed Rebourn's hands shook. Could it be the man was afraid of him or was it something else? He was dressed in the garb of a rancher with black corduroy pants, white cotton overshirt, over the hips gray coat, black Stetson hat, and black rancher's boots. Thomas couldn't see whether Jeremiah had a revolver or not. It could be in a holster hidden by his coat.

Chapter Three Thomas

Thomas realized that Rebourn had spoken. "Sir? Did you say something?" The noise of the train seemed extra loud after so many years of relative quiet in the prison cells. He strained to hear.

"I asked if you had ridden a train before, and you don't have to sir me, I'm just Jeremiah."

He glanced at Jeremiah, then looked ahead. "Yes, sir...I mean Jeremiah. I mean, no, I ain't ever been on a train before." He felt like a stammering fool.

"Well, we got us a long trip ahead. We'll stay on the train for the next day and half straight until we get to Santa Fe. Then catch the train from Santa Fe to Cheyenne, getting off at Cedar Ridge, of course." Jeremiah's lips twitched as if almost a smile but not quite making it. "You're not going to give me any problems are you?"

"No sir. Kin I ask a question?" Thomas was curious as all get out but also fearful of doing something to make this man angry. His gut clenched at the thought of going back to Yuma Prison. Keeping Jeremiah Rebourn pleased was a necessity until he could figure out what he was going to do.

"What do you want to know?" There was an edginess to Rebourn's voice, as if he didn't like questions.

It reminded Thomas of the guards. "Exactly who are you?" He stared at the man. Was Jeremiah just going be a different kind of jailor? Thomas knew what slave labor was from working on the road gangs in prison. Had he been handed over to someone who would make his life more miserable than it had been? His safest route might be to get as far away from this man as possible.

Rebourn glanced at Thomas, then looked away. "What did they tell you?"

"Nothing. I got woke up this morning, told to dress in these clothes, swear on a Bible, and follow you." That was a short version, but it was what happened.

Rebourn looked out the train window at the passing desert. "I'm a rancher from Colorado. I own the Rocking JR Ranch. The judge would only release you to someone with a job for you." He paused and looked over at Thomas. "I have a ranch and we can always use another hand."

"I don't know what to say. This is the first I've heard about an early release." He couldn't understand why this man was willing to do this.

Jeremiah Rebourn had traveled a long way to meet him. Was Rebourn what he claimed to be, a rancher willing to give a man a second chance?

Jeremiah said, "You understand I also had to swear to abide by the parole agreement. I intend to honor that. You don't have a choice, but to work with me for the next three years. You may not like it, but there it is."

"I don't mind the working for you. Anything is better than what I've been doing." Would it be better to go along with this release and work off the rest of his sentence? Three more years wasn't that long after the twelve years of hard time he had just served.

"What work have you been doing?"

"For the last couple of years it's been building a road with a shovel and making bricks by hand." Thomas' calloused hands were proof of his hard physical labor. It has been back breaking work day after day, month after month, and year after year. He was weary to the bone.

"I guess you haven't done ranch work, or ridden a horse much?" Rebourn asked.

"I haven't ridden a horse in twelve years. And I'll be honest with you. Don't know how to do much. There wasn't opportunity for learning a trade at Yuma."

"How old were you when you got there?"

For some reason he didn't mind telling Rebourn about himself. In prison, he had learned to keep his private matters to himself. He could never know how someone might use it against him. "I was seventeen when I was sent there."

"I imagine you're right about not knowing how to do much. Well, we'll have to see about teaching you some things." He shifted his legs and pulled down on his shirtsleeves. "Your parents are friends of my family. We go to church together. Your father asked me to fetch you and give you a job on my ranch. After things get settled, they'll come out and visit with you. Your mother is anxious to see you."

"My folks sent you? Did my father arrange the early release?" It had to be Pa that had accomplished such a thing. If they went to church together maybe this man was what he claimed.

"Yes, Milburn corresponded with the governor of the territory and made the arrangements."

So, he not only owed Jeremiah Rebourn a big thanks but also Pa. Times had been hard between he and Pa before he went to prison. He knew it all from the time he was twelve or so he thought. His two older sisters were obedient children. Their folks weren't ready for Thomas. If Pa said the sky was blue, Thomas swore it was green. He thought Pa stupid and Ma didn't understand anything. It only took a couple of weeks in Yuma Prison for Thomas to discover how wrong he had been.

Rebourn tipped his hat down and closed his eyes. Soon he was softly snoring. Thomas' body ached for rest but his brain was too busy taking in the sight of the tan and red countryside of the Arizona desert. As he stared out the train window at the far horizon and enormous clear blue sky, he tried to twist his mind around being free from the dark, smelly cramped prison. He hadn't left any friends behind as he had kept himself apart from the other prisoners. That had been his only protection against the brutality of the place. The first month he had cried in the dark but soon realized there would be no rescue.

The train slowed as it struggled up a slight incline in the rolling desert country. Thomas could step outside the train car and drop off the train. Be free for real. He eyed the sleeping man beside him. Yeah, he could do it, escape and make a run for it. But to where? And what kind of life would that be? No, he'd give this new jail a chance first. He gripped his hands in his lap and stayed seated.

The door of the coach banged open and two men with bandanas tied over the lower part of their faces entered carrying pistols pointed at the passengers.

One of them yelled, "Hands up. This is a holdup."

Not original but effective, Thomas raised his hands above his head. Rebourn sat up with a jerk, then in a movement that Thomas barely saw, removed a wallet from his jacket, and dropped it on the floor. Without looking, the rancher pushed it out of sight under the seat with the heel of his boot, as he raised his hands.

The two bandits moved from traveler to traveler. "Your money and valuables. Be quick about it," the taller of the two men yelled.

Thomas tensed as he recognized the voice. Yancy Smith. They had shared a cell for a couple of years at Yuma Prison.

"You, hand me your money." The man pointed his revolver at Rebourn.

The rancher reached into the pocket of his pants, pulled out a watch and paper money, and handed them over.

Yancy turned to Thomas. "You next. Give me your mo…" He stopped in mid-sentence, staring. "Is that you, Tom?"

Thomas didn't want to identify himself and be associated with these men but didn't know how to get out of it. "Yeah. It's me. I ain't got no money. I just got out of Yuma this morning."

"That's all right. I don't want your money, Tom. I still owe you for a couple of good turns you did me. Where you going? You got plans? You can come with us if ya want."

The other man stepped up. "What's the hold up? We got to get going."

"Hold your horses, this is a friend from Yuma. I offered for him to come with us if he wants."

"He knows you?" There was something sinister in the other man's tone.

Thomas felt a clenching in his gut. This was not good. He could sense Rebourn tense seated next to him.

The second man pointed his gun at Thomas' head. "I'm not leaving no witnesses behind who knows us."

Without questioning the wisdom of his actions, Thomas threw himself at the man as he fired the weapon. Thomas felt a burning, searing pain along his left ribs. Hitting the man square in the chest with his shoulder he shoved with all his strength and the man hurled back against a wooden train seat with a resounding clunk of his head. The gun clattered to the floor. A shuffle was going on behind him and he turned to see Rebourn land a punch on Yancy's chin that dropped him where he stood.

Thomas reached down and picked up the pistol off the floor. He looked up into the eyes of Rebourn who was contemplating him with an impassive face. Glancing at the weapon in his hand, Thomas shook his head and handed it over to Rebourn.

"I gave my word I'd abide by the parole. This ain't my doing."

Rebourn took the pistol. "I know that."

The train conductor hurried into the train car carrying a rifle. Stumbling to a stop by the two unconscious men he asked, "What's going on in here?"

An older man who looked to be a salesman spoke up. "Them two cowboys knocked those bandits out. They took my wallet and I want it back."

Rebourn reached down and retrieved the things that had been taken from the other passengers and handed them back to their owners. He turned to the conductor. "You got a place we can tie these two up until you can turn them over to the authorities?"

"Sure, we can put them in the baggage car. We'll soon be at Tucson and we'll turn them over to the sheriff there. You men give me a hand."

Rebourn turned to Thomas. "You stay here. I'll help get these two to the baggage car."

Thomas picked up his hat, shoved it on his head, and sat down in the corner of the seat. He kept his arm pressed against his side where the bullet had struck. Rebourn, the conductor, and two other men carried the two unconscious train robbers toward the baggage car. Thomas wondered where their horses were and if there had been a third outlaw. The train was picking up speed now it was past the upgrade that had allowed the outlaws to board.

Not wanting to bleed all over his new clothes, he pulled his valise from under the wooden seat to find something to make a bandage. Thomas spotted Rebourn's wallet on the floor under the seat. He picked it up and without opening it, put it into his coat pocket. In the valise, he found a couple of handkerchiefs. Wadding them up, he pressed them against the bleeding wound. He sighed with relief that his side had only been grazed. The wound didn't appear deep nor bleeding over much, but it still hurt. Returning the valise under the seat, he leaned back against the wood seat and tried to settle his nerves. Had he missed a chance to be free? His hands shook and his heart pounded. What effort had it taken his folks to get him early release? No, after all the hurt he had given them he owed them at least to try to finish his sentence and truly be a free man. Escaping the ranch might be easier and he could make preparations. Out here in the Arizona desert, he had no place to go and no way to get there.

Rebourn came back from delivering the prisoners to the baggage car and resumed his seat. He glanced at Thomas. "You're bleeding. I thought he missed you. Where're you hit?"

Opening his coat, Thomas let Rebourn examine the slice along his ribs. "It's only bleeding a bit now. I'm all right. It was just a graze. Unfortunately it messed up my new shirt and left a bullet hole in the back of my new jacket." He grinned.

Rebourn remained somber. "I'm glad it's not worse. Do we need to get off the train at Tucson and hunt a doctor?"

Thomas shook his head. "I've had worse. I'll manage. Let's just get out of Arizona."

"Amen to that." Rebourn glanced out the train window and then looked intently back at Thomas. "If we need to get a doctor, we will, but I'd like to keep going. I hope that they won't need a statement from us at the sheriff's office in Tucson. It might not be too helpful so soon after getting out of prison to talk much with the law."

"I appreciate that. But I'm fine." The pain was there but not any worse than several injuries he had had over the course of the years.

"Would you have gone with them?"

Rebourn's question caught him off guard. Taking a moment before answering, he shook his head. "No. What would it have gotten me? I'll take my chances on working with you."

Rebourn grunted as if satisfied. "Good choice."

Thomas remembered Jeremiah's wallet and handed it to him.

~

The train stopped several times in the next twenty-eight hours. They were able to get off at a couple stops with enough time to eat at the train stations. Rebourn was cautious not to let him out of his sight.

Thomas couldn't help watching as people got on and off the train. Men in broadcloth suits that indicated that they were prosperous, men in outfits that told of work on the range, miners recognizable by their boots and hats, and then several women and children were all among the ebb and flow of people boarding and departing the train. Thomas had to work at not staring especially at the women. He had seen some of the women prisoners at Yuma but never up close and they had been in prison garb. One young woman with a young man that looked like a rancher got on at Tucson with two small children. As Thomas watched the interaction of the little family and heard the laughter of the children and the young woman, an ache settled in his chest. What would it be like to have a family and a normal life? Something he would probably never have. Surprised by the wetness of his eyes, Thomas turned and stared out the train window. Would the regret at his foolish decisions as a kid never end?

~

As they approached Santa Fe the next afternoon, Rebourn sat in the seat across from Thomas with his legs stretched out. He seemed more relaxed now that they had crossed into New Mexico. Thomas didn't know why, but Rebourn obviously didn't like Arizona. He had a nervous habit of pulling down his shirtsleeves and making sure the bandana was secure around his neck. Except for that first conversation, they hadn't talked much. He didn't have anything to say and Rebourn didn't seem to be a big talker. Thomas had questions but didn't want to badger him. And Thomas slept a lot. It was the first day off from hard physical work that he had had in years. Even on Sundays he had chores within the prison.

After the train pulled into Santa Fe station, it felt good to get off and walk up the street, carrying their valises, toward the hotel to eat a meal before catching the next train. Thomas' bones ached from the constant vibration of the ride and he guessed Jeremiah Rebourn felt the same way.

They passed a barbershop and Thomas was wishful he could have a decent haircut, but he couldn't afford it. He not only couldn't afford a haircut, he couldn't afford anything. He didn't have a dime to his name, which was shameful for a twenty-nine-year old man to realize. Twelve years and absolutely nothing to show for them except a prison record.

Rebourn stopped and looked back at the barbershop. "We got time. Come on." He pushed open the door and entered the shop.

The barber was a stout, bald older Mexican man with a handlebar mustache. "How can I help you *señor?*"

Rebourn sat in the barber chair. "Give us a haircut and a close shave. We need to catch the 3:30 train to Denver and want to eat, so we need to hurry."

The man tied a towel around Jeremiah's neck. "*Si señor*. No problem. I can do this quickly." He waved Thomas to an empty chair. He wrapped a warm, wet towel around Thomas' face. "You relax and I cut the hair of your friend."

Thomas almost went to sleep it was so relaxing. It felt wonderful to have someone else shave him and cut his hair.

After Jeremiah paid the man, they left the barbershop and walked toward the hotel. Thomas, like a kid, couldn't seem to keep from staring at the people and shops along the main street. He hadn't seen many women and children in the last years. Wanting to stop and look, he kept walking in the direction Rebourn had pointed.

Rebourn stayed behind Thomas and when they entered the hotel dining room, he chose a table in a corner.

He pointed toward the chair against the wall. "You can sit there." It effectively hemmed Thomas into the corner with no way out but by Rebourn.

Thomas didn't blame him for not trusting him. He wouldn't have.

"Don't worry about the cost of the meal. You work for me now and the ranch will take care of your expenses." Rebourn spoke casually as if it was a small matter. He ordered a full meal of roast beef off the menu board.

Thomas ordered the same thing. They ate in silence, then walked back to the train station to catch the next train going north to Denver.

The train from Santa Fe to Cedar Ridge was much slower than from Yuma to Santa Fe, as it meandered through and around the mountains. Thomas didn't mind that Rebourn didn't talk much. It was beautiful country, and he found himself glued to the window as he stared out hour after hour upon a free, green, and brownish-red land. His soul thirsted for color and beauty of nature after the barrenness of his life the last twelve years. Out the train window, he could see a vast expanse of blue sky. As he watched white fluffy clouds march across the sky, he tried to drink it all in, as if it would disappear and he would be back in his cell.

As they traveled another thirty hours, Thomas became more nervous about what lay ahead. He finally couldn't stand it and turned to Rebourn, "What do I do when we get there? Will I go straight to your place? Or, will I stay in the local jail?"

Rebourn lifted his eyebrows as if startled. "Guess I sort of thought you knew. You have to stay out at the ranch. I promised the judge that you would be under supervision at all times for the next three years. You can't go anywhere without someone from the ranch being with you. You'll do whatever I decide for you to do. The judge was clear about that. When we get to Cedar Ridge, we'll go directly to the ranch."

"So it's like I'm your prisoner now." Thomas blurted it out before he thought, then wished he hadn't said it. No need to get Rebourn's hackles up.

He stared at Thomas with a hard look. "In a way, I guess you are. I hope we don't have to treat you that way. In fact, I'd like to have your word that you won't try to leave the ranch, but will go by what the judge has ordered. It'll make it easier on everyone."

Rebourn appeared to be taking it seriously and Thomas better be thinking that way, too. "All right, I can promise to go by the judge's orders and not try to leave." He hoped he was telling Rebourn the truth, but wasn't sure. Thomas didn't know this man nor what it would be like working on his ranch. If it got too bad was he a man of his word? Thomas liked to think he was.

Rebourn nodded. "Good."

Thomas hoped he was telling Rebourn the truth. Thomas neither knew this man nor what it would be like working on his ranch. If it got too bad, would be a man of his word? He liked to think he was. After leaving Denver, the train tracks took them closer to the mountains, although they had been in view most of the way. The ride from Santa Fe to Cedar Ridge passed quickly enough as Thomas sat glued to the window. After twelve years of nothing but the walls of the prison with occasional times out on the roads to work, everything seemed bright and clean. Surely, this could be a new beginning for him.

Chapter Four Thomas

In the early afternoon, the train drew up to the platform at the little train station in Cedar Ridge and stopped with a blast of steam and noise. Thomas had traveled two days and two nights on that train. He ached all the way to his bones and his side burned where the bullet graced him. He wanted to find a place to lie down. But his curiosity about the town kept his eyes darting as he tried to look at everything at once out the train window. Cedar Ridge was larger than he expected with several streets.

Rebourn led the way off the train, down the platform, and onto the street.

"Hey, boss." A tall, lithe black-haired cowhand with long, muscular legs propelled himself from a bench where he sat by the side of the train station.

"Hey, Bob. Glad to see you. You got the wagon or horses?" Rebourn turned. "This is Bob Fife, the ranch foreman. Bob, this is Thomas Black."

Bob held out his hand, "Glad to meet you."

Thomas liked the look of the black-haired, dark-eyed man with the square-jawed face. Wrinkles spread out from the edge of his eyes toward his temples in the deeply tanned face. He looked to be in his mid-thirties and fit enough to take on anything. This was someone Thomas would be working with for the next three years.

"You, too." He awkwardly gripped Bob's hand.

"I got the wagon packed with supplies and ready to go." Bob strolled down the street to a big wagon loaded with supplies and four horses hitched to it.

"Climb up on the back there, Thomas." Rebourn threw his valise on the load, then climbed onto the wagon seat next to Bob.

Thomas climbed onto the back of the heavily loaded wagon to sit on hundred-pound sacks of flour, dried beans, rice, corn meal, and sugar. Crates held Arbuckle coffee in ten-pound bags, canned goods, and other supplies.

Bob yelled, "Giddy up." The four horses stepped out pulling the wagon down the street.

Trying not to look too obvious, Thomas gazed at the different businesses and people walking along the boardwalks. They passed Black's General Mercantile and he stretched his neck to get a better look inside.

He assumed that was his folks' store and that they still lived above it in the second story where he could see curtains on the windows. It seemed bigger than he thought it would be. It gave him a small comfort that he had not made a complete mess of their lives with his behavior when he had run away back in Arizona and joined up with the wrong crowd. In a way, Thomas wanted to stop and greet his folks, but he was hesitant, ashamed to see them. He also wanted to go in and tell them how sorry he was for the past. But, what could he say to make up for the twelve years of pain he had put them through? Thomas swallowed hard and pulled his hat down to hide his face. Too many memories were flooding back.

Bob and Rebourn talked about the work on the ranch. Evidently, Rebourn had no problem talking to Bob.

"Anything happen while I was gone?" Rebourn asked.

Bob slapped the reins to encourage the prodding horses. "I don't know what to think of it, but Arkenstone lost some cattle. He's sure it's rustlers. The sheriff isn't so sure. He thinks they may have pushed a fence over and wandered off."

Rebourn pushed his hat on more snugly, as there was a breeze. "I hope they wandered off. We don't need to worry about rustlers. How are the mares?"

Bob waved at a horseman riding by. "We've had fifteen foals this week while you were gone. Everything went fine."

"You wrote everything down?"

"Sure did. We'll know just when to have the mares covered. I've been watching the stallions, and they all seem in good form."

"Good, we can start organizing for next year's crop." Rebourn took his hat off, ran his hand through his hair, and then put the hat back on. "How are my boys?"

Bob chuckled. "I only chased them out of the horse barn twice. I don't know what else they got into."

"Did Emily seem to be doing all right with them?" Rebourn asked with a chuckle in his voice.

"I only saw them at meals and they were fine, but then Jacob was there and you know how the boys listen to him."

"Right, if they don't listen, he won't let them hang out at his workshop." Rebourn turned and looked back at Thomas. "You all right back there?"

"Yes, sir." He bit his lip. Rebourn had told him not to sir him.

"We're going to stop up here at the café and eat."

Thomas was hungry and wouldn't mind eating, but he wondered why they didn't ride the four miles out to the ranch. Wasn't his place to question, just to do as he was told.

Bob pulled on the reins. "Whoa."

The horses stopped by a hitching rail down the street from a small white washed clapboard building with curtains on the windows and a sign proclaiming it the Cedar Ridge Café. Thomas scooted off the back of the wagon and joined Bob and Rebourn to walk to the entrance to the café.

Bob held the screen door open and Thomas followed Rebourn into the café. Rebourn stopped at a table and turned to him. "This one all right?"

It took Thomas a moment to understand. He wasn't used to anyone asking his opinion, so he just nodded and sat at the small square table that had four chairs around it.

Rebourn pointed to a chalkboard menu. "Choose what you want."

Thomas looked around at the café. It was clean and bright. All the walls were painted white and the table and chairs were made of pine. The windows hung with yellow curtains were open allowing a breeze that felt good on his bare head. Toward the back of the room was a counter with a vase of wildflowers on it and couple of pieces of cake under a glass dome. How to go about getting a piece? He hadn't tasted cake in over twelve years.

Behind the counter was a doorway. Thomas could see into what looked to be a kitchen. They were the only customers, as it was long past the noon hour. Thomas tried to identify the smells that had hit him on entering the café: fried chicken, bread baking, coffee brewing, and cinnamon. The combined aromas brought back the memory of Ma's kitchen. His jaw went to hurting with the sudden release of saliva.

Just then a young woman hurried through the doorway from the kitchen. Her petite form and pretty face captured his attention as did the light brown hair done up in braids and wound around her head like a crown. Thomas admired how fresh she looked in a full white bibbed apron covering a light blue dress. The light swishing sound of her long skirt reached his ears as she approached the table. He stared. She was the prettiest thing he had seen in years.

"Jeremiah, Bob, I didn't hear you come in. What can I get for you?" She looked expectantly at them, then at Thomas.

Her eyes were a deep dark blue with long lashes. He could have stared all day into their depth. He felt his cheeks burning. However, he couldn't take his eyes off her.

"Hey, Catherine. You still have some of that fried chicken, potatoes, and gravy?" Bob greeted her like a longtime friend as he squinted up at the menu board.

"Sure, how many pieces of chicken do you want?" The young woman looked from Bob to Rebourn to Thomas.

"I'll take three pieces of chicken and pile on the potatoes and gravy." Bob nodded. "And bring me some coffee, please."

"I'll have the same." Rebourn spoke up. "What about you Thomas?"

"That'll be fine for me." He looked at the table to give himself a chance to breathe. It had been twelve years since he had been this close to a girl and one so lovely.

"By the way, Catherine, this is Thomas Black. He's going to work out at the ranch with us," Rebourn said.

Thomas looked up to find the girl nodding her head in greeting.

"Hello, Mr. Black. You've chosen a good ranch to work on and good people to work with." She smiled at him and her whole face lit up. Her voice was warm and mellow and she seemed to be speaking to him almost as if she knew him.

"Pleased to meet you, ma'am." He felt like a stammering fool. He didn't have any idea what to say next, and could feel that his face was bright red. He'd almost forgotten that girls made him blush so.

"I'll get your coffee, then have your food out." She turned and strode through the doorway at the back of the café.

Rebourn and Bob talked of the ranch and stock.

Thomas waited to see her again. Soon she returned with three cups and a coffeepot, which she set on the table.

"Thanks, Catherine." Bob and Rebourn said almost at the same moment.

"You're welcome. Let me know if you need another pot of coffee."

She was gone back through the doorway before it finally registered on Thomas that he should have also said a word of thanks. Normal conversation didn't roll off his tongue yet. But when she returned with three plates full of hot food, he was ready.

As she set the plate of food in front of him, he glanced up. "Thank you, Miss Catherine."

She smiled. "You're welcome, Mr. Thomas." Her voice was so lilting that he wanted her to go on talking, but after serving Bob and Rebourn she disappeared into the back of the café again.

"Let's pray." Rebourn said and he thanked the Lord for the food and for their safe journey.

God and Thomas hadn't been talking much the last few years. Remembering when Pa had prayed at the dinner table, Thomas gladly bowed his head and silently thanked God for delivering him out of Yuma Prison. So far this new prison looked good.

When they finished eating, Rebourn paid Catherine for the meals. They left the café, then climbed back on the wagon, and headed out of town. Every bump on the trail stung the wound on his side, but he was used to pain.

"Thomas," Rebourn called back to him.

He sat up on the flour sacks where he had been leaning. "Yes, sir?" There he went again with the sir.

"We're almost to the ranch. When we get there, Bob will drive up to the kitchen door so we can get the wagon unloaded. After that, you can help him unhitch the wagon and then he'll help you get settled. And no need to sir me."

Thomas nodded at him, fearful of forgetting his admonition. Helping unload the wagon was no problem, and he had handled teams with work details at the prison. Jeremiah seemed to have forgotten about the wound on his side and Thomas intended to do the same, no matter how it pained him. For some reason Rebourn's neutral manner made Thomas nervous, as if he waited for the man to begin to shout and poke with the baton the prison guards had all carried. At least Thomas had known what to expect from the guards. Rebourn's quiet manner left him wondering.

Bob guided the horses into a lane with rail fences and ponderosa pines lining each side. The lane led to a large wood plank house with a deep front porch and to its left, a large barn with a huge corral behind it. Thomas liked the look of the prosperous and well-tended ranch with green pastures spreading out in all directions. It sure was nothing like Yuma Prison.

Chapter Five Catherine

Catherine's thoughts kept coming back to the handsome young man with dark brown hair and sad brown eyes who came in with Bob and Jeremiah. Catherine set about cleaning the café after the men from the Rocking JR left. Sweeping allowed her mind to drift to thoughts of the day and different customers who had been in for a meal. Most had been regulars that she saw every day.

The sweeping done, she went into the kitchen and checked on the stew bubbling on the stove and the chicken boiling in another pot. Chicken and dumplings, stew, cornbread, and beans made up the menu for supper. The beans were available every meal. For a nickel, a hungry cowhand could get a big bowl of beans with ham hocks and cornbread. Even if they didn't have the nickel, it was on the house until they could pay. She never turned anyone away hungry, and it wasn't unusual to find an extra nickel on a table after some cowhand left the café.

She stirred up the dumpling dough ready to drop into the boiling chicken broth. As she prepared the chicken and dumplings, her thoughts wandered back to the man who had come in with Bob and Jeremiah.

Thomas Black, so that was Milburn and Agnes' son. In the last couple of years, since her mother died, Milburn and Agnes had become close friends and had talked occasionally of their son so far away in Arizona. She had not known he was in prison. They were such good solid church-going people. It was hard to imagine their son had spent the last twelve years in prison for rustling.

Supper was busy and the clean up its usual drudgery, but finally she finished her workday. She grabbed a shawl and her embroidery and walked across the street to the mercantile.

Milburn stood behind the counter writing in a ledger. "Catherine, it's good to see you. Did you have a busy day?"

Catherine gave him a peck on the cheek. "Just the usual coming and going, although I did get to meet your son, Thomas. Bob and Jeremiah came in about two this afternoon and had dinner. Thomas was with them."

"Oh my, Agnes will want to hear all about it. We haven't seen him yet. Although, Jeremiah said he would try to be back today. We agreed that we would let Thomas get settled at the ranch and go out on Saturday to visit with him." Milburn rubbed his eyes as if he had something in them.

Catherine was about to say more when she heard footsteps entering the store. She turned and saw a couple of cowhands from one of the ranches stopping to look at some boots. With her back to the cowhands, she patted Milburn on the arm. "I'll go up and visit with Agnes. After you close up I'll tell you about Thomas."

"All right, go on up. She needs to hear about Thomas more than I do." He turned and walked toward his customers.

She went to the back of the store and up a flight of stairs to the living quarters. After she tapped on the screen door, she opened it and stepped into the cozy, homey kitchen.

The gray haired woman with a round kind face greeted her. "Come on in, dear. How are you this evening?" She put down her dishtowel and gave Catherine a hug and kiss on the cheek.

"I'm tired and glad the day is over. I needed to get out of the café." Catherine hung her shawl and hat on their usual hooks by the door. "You still busy?"

"No, just getting the kitchen straightened up. Milburn will be up soon for his usual bowl of soup." Agnes poured a couple of glasses of tea and carried them into the small parlor. "I remember when we first married how he wanted three full meals a day. Now he eats breakfast and dinner but very little for supper. I guess it's his age."

Catherine sat in the gliding rocker beside the couch. "It might be all those crackers he snatches out of the cracker barrel through the afternoon."

Agnes laughed. "Or those bits of candy he sucks on when he thinks I'm not looking." She settled into her spot on the couch and took a sip of tea.

Catherine searched the face of the kindly woman who had come to mean so much to her. Agnes had been her mother's best friend and had helped see her through the dying. She reached out and took Agnes' hand. "I met Thomas this afternoon."

Agnes put her hand to her mouth and with the other gripped Catherine's hand tightly. "Oh my, how is he? What did he look like? What did he say?"

Catherine smiled. "He looked fine. Of course, since it was the first time I have seen him I have nothing to compare him with."

Agnes let go of Catherine's hand and sat back against the cushion on the couch. "Tell me absolutely everything about him."

"Shouldn't we wait for Milburn?"

"No, I'll repeat everything to him later. I need to hear it now."

"Well, he's about as tall as Jeremiah, maybe a little taller than six feet, thin as a rail. He looks like he's spent time outdoors, and he was dressed in that shirt, pants, and boots I helped you pick out to send with Jeremiah. He recently had a haircut and he was clean shaven." Catherine took a sip of her tea. What could she say that would give Agnes comfort? "He was shy. I mean, he turned bright red and got all tongue-tied when I spoke to him as men often do when they come into the café. But he was courteous and soft spoken."

Agnes nodded. "He always blushed around the girls. How did he look, really?"

Catherine thought for a moment. "I know you told me that he is twenty-nine years old, but I would have guessed he was younger in a way. Yet his face shows tough living, and his eyes are watchful as if he is on his guard all the time. He looked sad. I stood in the kitchen and watched him for a while. He has a nice smile, but I don't think he has used it much lately." She shook her head. "I don't know if that is what you wanted to hear."

"Yes, it is. Did he seem well? Does he have scars on his face?"

"He seemed healthy enough although he needs some meat on his bones. He's too thin. And no, there were no scars on his face. Just a stillness in how he held himself and looked around, as if he didn't feel free to relax." Catherine smiled. "You know how Bob and Jeremiah are with talking about horses all the time. Thomas just sat and listened. Other than telling me what he wanted to eat and thanking me for serving him, I didn't hear him say anything."

Agnes dabbed at the tears in her eyes, with her lace-trimmed handkerchief. "I have no idea what he's gone through. Twelve years, I still can't believe that Milburn and Jeremiah were able to get him out of that place. I want him home, but the judge thought it would be better for him to finish his sentence on the ranch with Jeremiah."

"He's with good folks. I can't think of a better place than the Rocking JR Ranch."

"I know you're right, and I need to be thankful that the Lord has blessed me to have him just four miles out of town." Agnes dabbed again at her eyes. "We made such a mistake when we left Cedar Ridge and moved to Arizona when Thomas was four. Our daughter's health demanded we get her to a warmer, dryer climate. After Thomas got in trouble people wouldn't let us forget it, so Milburn decided to move back here and it was like coming home. Even though he was born here Thomas doesn't remember living here."

Catherine nodded at the older woman. "I can't imagine how much you want to see him after all these years. Only a couple more days and you'll get to be with him." She stood and gathered her embroidery, which had not been touched. "I need to go home and get my bread dough rising. Tomorrow is another busy day."

"Bless you for coming over and telling me about Thomas. You understood that I needed to hear. You're a good girl, Catherine, and I love you very much." Agnes gave her a warm hug and a kiss on the cheek.

~

Catherine lay in her bed in the small bedroom behind the café and tried to go to sleep. Her thoughts kept turning to the quiet young man whose eyes had spoken much more than his words. She remembered how he stared at her when she first walked up to the table, and then ducked his head and turned so red. When she served them, he looked directly into her eyes and smiled. Something about that captured her attention. She wanted to see him again. Turning over in the bed, she punched her pillow. What was she thinking? The man had just been released from jail. He was a convicted rustler. On the other hand, Myles McKinley never captured her attention like that. And Myles would never be as handsome as Thomas Black.

Chapter Six Thomas

The wagon lumbered between the house and barn. A woman, who looked to Thomas as if she was expecting a child, came out onto the front porch. She was an attractive petite woman with brown hair so light that it looked like it had streaks of gold.

Rebourn jumped down from the wagon to meet her. He was embracing the woman when two identical little boys who looked to be four or five years old came running up. They dove for Rebourn and each grabbed a leg and hung on. Laughing, Rebourn staggered to stay upright. A lump formed in Thomas' throat and he had to blink to keep tears from forming just watching the reunion. He wasn't sure why the sight affected him so.

"Whoa." Bob brought the wagon to a stop outside the back door and a stocky man several inches shorter than Thomas came out of the house.

"Hey, Bob. Who have you got there? Is that Thomas Black?" The man undid the back hinged gate of the wagon. "I am Jacob Blunfeld." There was a foreign accent in his voice.

After climbing off the wagon, Thomas shook the hand the man offered. "Glad to meet you."

Thomas towered over the short man who looked to be in his late thirties or early forties. Thick set with broad shoulders, Jacob looked strong, which he proved by picking up a hundred pound sack of flour and hoisting it over his shoulder with ease.

Grabbing the next sack of flour, Thomas followed Jacob into the house. With the three men unloading it, the wagon was soon empty and the supplies packed in a storage room.

Bob picked up Thomas' valise. "Follow me, and I'll show you where to stow your things."

Thomas followed him across the hall from the kitchen into a large room filled with six single bunks each with a small bedside table holding a lamp. At one end of the large room was a box woodstove with a coffeepot on one of the two burners. In the middle of the room was a plain wooden table with four chairs around it. Windows on one side of the room were without curtains and let in the daylight. Thomas was relieved to see there was a door that led to the yard between the house and barn. Although rustic, it was much larger and brighter than the jail cells he was used to sleeping in and there were real mattresses on the beds.

"Just pick a bunk that's not made up." Bob handed the valise to Thomas. "We have three other riders that you'll share the bunkroom with. My room is down the hall. Jacob has his own place out by his workshop at the back of the barn. Besides working on the ranch, he builds fine pieces of furniture and sells them."

Thomas chose one in a corner of the room away from the three bunks already made up. He was so tired of having to be in the close quarters of the crowded prison that he wanted as far from the other cowhands as possible. He slid his valise under the bunk. To be allowed even that small choice felt good.

"I'll let the ladies know we need bedding and get your bunk made up before night. For now let's get the wagon unhitched, take care of the horses, and finish up in the horse barn."

"Yes, sir." Thomas followed Bob out to the yard. Jacob was already leading the horses pulling the now empty wagon toward the barn.

Thomas helped Bob and Jacob take care of the horses, and followed as they walked about a quarter of a mile back behind the ranch house to a second barn, the biggest Thomas had ever seen. Inside in several stalls were mares that looked ready to foal. In a huge fenced pasture next to the horse barn were more mares and young foals. He had been puzzled when Bob spoke of a horse barn but now it was clear. As he looked out over the pastures from the horse barn, he could see hundreds of horses in the distant green pastures.

"Does Mr. Rebourn raise only horses?" he asked Bob.

Bob turned and looked toward the pastures. "Mostly, but he also has cattle. He grows feed for the horses. The ranch goes for about ten miles back into the hills and is about fifteen miles wide in places which is about ten thousand acres." Bob grinned. "Don't worry. You'll soon get to know every foot of it."

Bob pointed toward a wheelbarrow and pitchfork. "You take the stalls on this side of the barn and muck them out. I'll go up into the loft and pitch down some clean hay for you to spread out in each stall."

Three hours later Thomas finally made it to the last stall. His back hurt, the wound on his side burned, and he was beyond tired. Pitching the dirty straw and manure onto the muckheap had taken his last bit of energy.

Bob brought clean straw and helped Thomas spread it out in the stall where a bay mare kept an eye on a foal that appeared to have been born within the last day or so. The only thing the foal seemed interested in was getting dinner from its momma. He rubbed the little foal along its smooth neck and felt a delight at the sensation. It had been years since he had seen any animals except the worn out horses and mules at the prison.

Bob picked up the pitchfork. "You did a good job. Let's put the wheelbarrow and pitchfork away and head to the house for supper."

Thomas pushed the wheelbarrow back to a corner of the barn. He saw some riders coming toward the barn by the house. The crew would gather for supper, and he would meet them. How would they accept someone just out of prison? He didn't want any trouble, but he also wouldn't take any guff off anyone. The prison guards had been mean sometimes, and Thomas let it slide. He knew when to fight and when to let it alone. Looking at the ranch foreman, Thomas had to make every effort to be at peace with the other riders.

Bob showed him a room across the hall from the bunkroom that was for washing up. Thomas had never seen anything like it. It had a zinc-lined bathtub big enough you could lower your whole body into it, a sink with a water pump that had its own drain to the outside, and a stove to heat a reservoir of water. After Bob washed up, he left Thomas there to finish.

Thomas wasted no time. He didn't worry about heating the water and pumped cold water over his head. Just as he finished scrubbing his arms, Bob came back with a towel made out of flour sacking and threw it at him.

"Here, use this and keep it with you. We try to use one for several days to save the women so much washing."

Thomas had seen Rebourn's wife but didn't know there were other women at the ranch. This was sure a different place than the prison.

He ran his fingers through his hair and wished he had a comb. As he put the towel on a hook by his bunk, which now had blankets and a pillow, he heard a bell and looked at Bob who waited at the door of the bunkroom.

Bob grinned. "That's the supper bell, and I'm ready for it."

He followed Bob into a large kitchen with a huge cook stove against one wall, a sink and cabinets on another wall, a large dry safe, and in the middle of the room, a long table with twelve places set. It reminded him of the kitchen from his childhood home. As he looked at the dry safe, he remembered the times Ma had told him to close it tight to keep the flies and mice out of the food.

Two women were busy putting bowls and platters of food on the table.

Bob took his hat off and put it on one of several hooks just inside the door of the kitchen. He waved at the two women. "This is Mildred and Sally, our wonderful cooks. Ladies, this is Thomas Black, our new hand."

"Hello, Thomas. Let me welcome you to the Rocking JR. Go ahead and sit down." Mildred, the older of the two women, had a pleasant face with her gray hair pulled back into a bun covered with a hairnet.

Sally was much younger and smaller with a dour expression. She was a plain looking girl with mousey brown hair. He didn't know if she was shy or simply unfriendly. She barely looked at him.

He deposited his hat on a hook and pulled out a chair next to Bob.

Rebourn came through the doorway from the main part of the house with the woman he had seen him embrace on the porch.

"This is Thomas Black. This is my wife, Emily."

Thomas stood and shook the hand she held out. "Ma'am."

"Call me Emily. I'm so glad to meet you and to know that you're going to be with us. I hope you enjoy your stay here." She held onto his hand a moment and smiled. Her greeting was one he expected for any new hand, not one just released from prison. Perhaps she didn't know.

"Thank you, I'm sure I will." He didn't know what else to say to this beautiful, friendly woman.

Four men came trooping in from the hallway and two little boys ran in through the other doorway.

"Whoa, slow down." Jeremiah caught the two boys by their shoulders. "I want you to meet someone. This is Thomas. He's going to be working with us. This is Elisha and Joseph. They're five-years-old."

The two boys came up to Thomas, and he shook their hands. He looked at them carefully and couldn't see any difference between them. He sat back in the chair next to Bob.

"That's Harlan, next is Cal, and that's Barney." Bob pointed at each cowhand. "You met Jacob earlier. Fellows, this is Thomas Black, our newest hand. Be sure and welcome him to the Rocking JR."

They all nodded and gave a word of welcome.

He nodded back, curious about these men he would be working with for the next three years.

No one took any food and everyone watched Rebourn. As Thomas looked down the table, he saw Rebourn take Emily's hand and one of the twins, who took the other twin's hand. Rebourn bowed his head and began to pray.

Thomas watched him until he realized that everyone in the room had bowed their head. He bowed his head, heard Rebourn asking God to bless the newest member of their family, and realized he meant him.

He had stopped praying after three years in Yuma Prison. God didn't hear his prayers. He didn't think God would ever listen to him again.

After the amen, Bob took a platter of biscuits, put two on his plate, then passed it on to Thomas. He followed Bob's example, and handed the platter off to Jacob. Roast beef, potatoes, gravy, carrots, and sliced tomatoes made their way around the table. By the time Thomas was passed the sliced tomatoes, his plate was close to overflowing. It was a banquet compared to prison food.

There wasn't a lot of conversation around the table except between the two boys and their parents. Everyone else dug in and ate. Just as Thomas cleaned his plate, Mildred got up from the table and went to the stove. She took a large pan out of the oven and set an apple cobbler on the table.

Thomas could smell the cinnamon and apples. He thought he was full but as he smelled the aroma of the cobbler, he found he had space for a little more.

"Hand me your plate, Thomas. Since this is your first day here, you get first serving." Mildred proceeded to pile a big serving of the cobbler onto his plate.

"Thank you, Miss Mildred." He took the plate from her. He cautiously took a small bite, which was wise as it was still hot from the oven. The flavors mixed in his mouth and he slowly chewed and swallowed, taking delight in each spoonful of pie as he closed his eyes and savored the sweet taste. This was the first dessert in twelve years.

After supper, everyone started leaving the kitchen until only the two cooks, Rebourn and his wife, and Thomas were left.

Rebourn glanced at Thomas and then at Emily. "Thomas, I want Emily to look at that bullet wound on your side."

He was surprised, as he had tried his best to ignore it. "Huh ... all right."

Emily smiled at him. "I do most of the doctoring of the small stuff around here. Jeremiah told me what you did to protect him. Although why he didn't have a doctor look at it in Tucson, I don't know."

Rebourn ducked his head and murmured, "I just wanted to get out of Arizona."

Emily patted his shoulder. "I know, dear."

Looking up at her and then over at Thomas, he shrugged, "And he didn't complain, not once."

As usual, Thomas remained silent.

Emily pulled a small box out of a cabinet and sat it on the table. "Sit in the chair here and take your shirt off. Let's see what it looks like."

Thomas could feel the heat rising on his neck as he slipped out of the shirt. The handkerchiefs were still pressed against the wound held on by the dried blood. Lifting his arm out of the way, he sat quiet as Emily gently soaked the cloth and removed it from the wound. He sucked in his breath as she finally got it off. The last bit really stung.

"Sorry Thomas. It looks like it's healing but still too red and there is some fever around the wound. I'm amazed it didn't get infected with you two men neglecting it. Let me clean it with this carbonic acid and then I'll spread honey over it and put on a clean bandage." Emily worked quickly but with a gentle touch that reminded Thomas of his Ma taking care of scrapes and cuts. He had his share of scars from fights and beatings at Yuma but none tended like this.

Rebourn sat and watched. "Does he need to see Doc and does he need to take it easy for a few days?"

Emily finished tying on the bandage around Thomas' chest and stepped back to survey her handiwork. "We'll watch it for a few days. If it gets infected we'll call the doctor. You helped Bob in the barn earlier, Thomas. How did it feel?"

"It's all right as long as I don't bump into anything." He didn't want Rebourn thinking he couldn't do his work. After all that was why the rancher had taken him from Yuma Prison.

Emily nodded. "It should be all right, but if it gets to bothering you let me know." She put the medicine box away. "I'll see you in the morning."

"Thank you, ma'am." Thomas pulled his shirt back on. The wound did feel better.

The two little boys came running in from the front room. "Come Pa, Uncle Jacob is going to tell a story."

Thomas stood by the chair and wondered if he had to go to the bunkroom and stay until morning. Rebourn must have noticed his indecision.

"You can go on to bed if you want or, some of us will probably sit on the front porch and enjoy the cool of the evening for a while. Do what you want." Rebourn had a hand on the shoulder of each of his boys, and they seemed content to lean their backs against his legs.

"If you don't mind, I'd like to walk a bit and watch the sunset." Thomas couldn't remember the last time he had walked across a meadow and enjoyed the evening sky.

"Sure, do what you want. If you go toward the west, you come to a creek with a large meadow beyond. It's a good place to watch the sunset." He looked down at the boys. "Let's sit on the porch. I'll tell you about the train ride and we'll listen to Uncle Jacob's story."

Thomas slid quietly out the back door at the end of the hallway and followed a path west toward some trees. He soon discovered they were on the banks of a small creek. Past the gurgling of running water, he heard birds chirping and in the distance the lowing of cattle. The smell of new cut hay hung in the air. He sat on a large boulder and watched the sun as it began to set behind the hills to the west.

As he gazed out over the green hills, he wanted to weep. To walk off alone and enjoy the evening sky was so strange, and it shouldn't have been. Thinking of Yuma Prison, his heart filled with regret at the wasted years. He had no one to blame but himself.

~

The next few days went by quickly, and Thomas fell into a pattern of work. Keeping the horse barn mucked out was his primary duty. He also helped Bob with the mares in foal. When he had a little time he chopped wood and carried it into the house for the cook stove.

He saw that Rebourn and Bob knew what they were doing in helping the mares in foal and didn't mind teaching Thomas. The work was hard but not brutal, and the food was plentiful. And after supper he was free to do what he wanted. Not a bad prison, he could do the time.

Jacob, Rebourn, or Bob were with him throughout the day. He had not been allowed to ride a horse yet. Thomas didn't find that unexpected. If they hadn't been watching him closely, he would have been surprised. He was used to being watched by the prison guards. Jeremiah and the others didn't know him and weren't yet ready to trust him, even on the ranch.

Saturday morning Thomas cleaned his breakfast plate and was about to head to the horse barn to continue his day of work.

Jeremiah stood at the doorway leading from the kitchen to the front room. "Thomas, I need to talk to you. Come into the front room."

"Yes, sir." Why couldn't he remember not to say that? Jeremiah didn't seem to notice. Had Thomas done something to displease Jeremiah? Was he already in trouble? Ever since he had arrived at the ranch, he'd done exactly what he was told to do with no back talk, even though it was obvious that he was being given the worst of the work. His stomach lurched and he felt his face tighten as he walked into the front room behind Jeremiah. He had started to think of him as Jeremiah rather Rebourn.

Chapter Seven Thomas

Thomas gazed around the front room, partly to relieve his tension. Bob had told him that Jacob made all the furniture in the house. He followed as Jeremiah strolled to the cherry wood desk and chair. The bright room also held two couches, two overstuffed chairs, and several small tables. Braided rugs covered the floor. He was interested in the quality of the woodwork of the bookshelves and Jacob's showpiece, the elaborately carved mantel over the fireplace. He couldn't help but be impressed with the impact the room had. It exuded an aura of comfort and permanence.

"Sit down." Jeremiah waved at one of the overstuffed chairs in front of his desk.

Thomas sat and waited.

"How are you settling in?" Jeremiah sat with his elbows on his desk.

"Fine. I hope I haven't done anything wrong." What else could he say?

"No, you haven't done anything wrong. You're a good worker. I have no complaints." Jeremiah pulled down on the cuffs of his shirtsleeves, a habit Thomas had noticed on the train. "You haven't asked about seeing your folks."

"Sir?"

"I'd have thought you'd want to see your folks."

"I would, but I don't know that I have that right." Thomas shifted in the chair. What was Jeremiah getting at?

"Of course, you have a right to see your folks." Jeremiah sat back and rested his hands on the arms of the chair.

"I haven't seen or heard from my folks since Pa came to visit last year. He didn't want me to write even if the prison had allowed me to. They were trying to start fresh after the mess I made of their lives in Arizona. My father didn't want to let everyone know he had a rustler for a son. He reckoned it might hurt his business. That's why they moved back here. He did the right thing." Thomas drew in a breath. Sharing so much wasn't easy. Twelve years of trying to hide his every thought was too ingrained.

"I'm sorry, Thomas, I didn't realize." Jeremiah ran his hand through his hair. "I'm not always good at explaining things. I should have told you. They're coming out for dinner today and to spend the afternoon with you. I just wanted to make sure you wanted to see them."

Thomas leaned forward and tried to think what to say. "How are they?"

"Oh, they're doing well. We see them every Sunday at church, and of course, when we go into the mercantile. I've known your folks for eight or nine years. They're good people." Jeremiah sat much more relaxed and leaned forward with his hands resting on his desk. "We thought it might be easier for them to come here to see you."

"Thanks. I really do want to see them." Yet, Thomas was uneasy about the visit. He rubbed his sweaty hands on the legs of his pants. He needed to say so much to them. But he didn't want to do it in front of others.

Jeremiah's voice broke into his thoughts. "I know we've given you some of the worst jobs around the ranch. It's nothing personal. The work needs doing, and as the new hand, you're low man and get the dirty jobs."

Thomas appreciated Jeremiah letting him know that it wasn't personal. He had wondered. "I don't mind. It's no worse than what I did at Yuma."

Jeremiah rubbed his chin. "Would you want to learn more about dealing with the horses? Bob told me you had helped him out, and he thinks you might be a good worker with horses. Course that means we've got to get you to riding."

"I'd like that." He'd muck out all the horse stalls every day to be out of Yuma Prison. But to get on a horse and ride out across the range—that would be a fulfillment of a desire he had been afraid to dream could come true.

"There's one other thing. I hadn't planned to tell people where you've been the last twelve years. I figure you've done your time and have a right to start fresh. But the judge sent Sheriff Grant a letter explaining the parole." Jeremiah leaned back and rubbed the back of his neck. "The sheriff saw no reason to keep it a secret and so, everyone knows. They also now know that you're Milburn and Agnes Black's son."

Thomas spread his hands where they rested on his knees and looked Jeremiah in the eyes. "I stole cattle and deserve to be punished. But, I don't want it to hurt my folks any more than I already have."

Jeremiah smiled. "I suspect your folks are so happy to have you close by that they aren't worried about what people might say. Why don't you go spruce up and put on a clean shirt if you want. I expect your folks to arrive in about an hour. Plan to take the day off and visit with them."

Thomas stopped by the bunkroom for some clean clothes and then went down to the creek. The washroom was open to him, but he preferred to bathe in the creek. The water was cold but it felt good, as the day was warm. He swam for a while, washed his hair, toweled off, and put on clean clothes.

He waited for his folks on the front porch of the ranch house and hoped to greet them before others on the ranch knew they had arrived. As he sat in a rocking chair, he thought about the last time he had seen Ma. Still in the skinny stage of boyhood, he remembered trying not to cry as through the barred window of the jail house he watched her walk away knowing the next morning he'd be sent to Yuma Prison. Now several inches taller and considerably filled out, he assumed his face showed what he had been through over the last years. What would his folks think of him now?

He watched as a buggy pulled by a sorrel horse came slowly up the half mile of lane from the main road. He stood and walked toward the buggy. Her hair was gray and her face wrinkled, but he would have recognized her anywhere.

"Thomas, oh Thomas, is that really you?" Ma scrambled out of the buggy and caught him in a fierce hug, which he eagerly returned.

Thomas fought not to weep. "Ma, I'm so glad to see you. I'm so sorry."

"Hush, we aren't going to worry about being sorry. It was a long time ago. I'm so happy God has brought you back to us." She stepped back, still holding on, and studied his face. "You're older ... and you've suffered."

"Now Agnes, let the boy go. You have all day to visit." Pa held out his hand, and Thomas took it, then his pa pulled him into a hug. "It's mighty good to see you, son. It's an answer to prayer."

"Thanks, Pa, for getting me out of Yuma." Thomas strove to keep his voice from wavering. Pa could have no idea how glad he was to be out of that place.

Pa patted him on the shoulder. "God arranged that, son. I just went along with the idea."

His father might believe it was God's doing, but Thomas knew God had given up on him years ago. Why would God bother about him now?

Jeremiah and Emily came out onto the porch. "Welcome, come on in." Jeremiah shook hands with Pa and gave Ma a kiss on the cheek.

Emily also greeted them. "Mildred and Sally will have dinner ready in a little while. Come on into the front room and get out of the sun."

Jacob came up and took the reins of the horse and buggy. "I take care of horse, Milburn. You visit."

"Thanks, Jacob," Pa handed off the reins.

Thomas followed his folks across the porch and into the front room. Ma took his arm and guided him toward a couch to sit by her. Pa sat in a chair close by facing him.

"You folks want to visit alone with Thomas?" Jeremiah asked.

Thomas had noticed that Jeremiah sometimes had a way of speaking directly to the point that other folks usually danced around. He preferred that Jeremiah and Emily stay, but sat quietly and left it up to his folks.

Ma waved at the other couch. "No, sit down, you two. We don't have anything to talk to Thomas about that we wouldn't want you two to hear. Please."

"We do want to thank you, Jeremiah, for going to Arizona and giving Thomas a place here." Pa reached over and put his hand on Jeremiah's arm. "We feel sure he'll be a good worker for you, and you all can teach him a lot."

Emily looked at Thomas and grinned. "If eating is any indication, I will testify that he works very hard indeed."

Thomas nodded at her, thankful she had lightened the tone of the conversation. "With Miss Mildred's cooking there's no way but to eat hardy."

"Well, I hope you can put on some weight. You're way too thin, son. Taller than I remember but still so thin." Ma hugged his arm tighter like she never wanted to let go.

"Give us some time and we'll fatten him up." Jeremiah looked over at Emily who smiled at his words. "I remember when I arrived at my friend, Elisha Evans's place. All I heard from the women for a year was how thin I was. I felt obligated to eat just to please them."

Ma patted Thomas' arm. "Let me tell you about your sisters."

For the next half hour, they talked about his two older sisters and their families. They both lived on a ranch up close to Cheyenne and came to visit once or twice a year. His oldest sister Bessie had married Hank Smith and had four children. Hope was married to Bill Oliver and had three children. They worked a ranch together and his sisters lived next door to each other. As his folks spoke about his sisters and their families, Thomas saw the pride and joy they had in their daughters. It made him wishful they could one day speak about him with such pride. So far, he had done nothing to make them proud.

Sally appeared at the kitchen door. "Dinner is ready."

"Thank you, Sally. We'll be right there." Emily stood and turned to Jeremiah. "Do you know where the boys are?"

"Nope. Do we want to know?" He grinned at her. "I'll go find them."

"Let's see if they come in after Mildred rings the bell." Emily led the way into the kitchen.

Thomas took Ma's arm, escorted her into the kitchen, and guided her to a chair at the table, which was laden with food.

Jacob and Bob came in the back door followed by Elisha and Joseph. They all greeted Milburn and Agnes as old friends.

Bob pulled out a chair and sat at the table. "Jeremiah, it being Saturday, I gave the hands the rest of the day off after they got the horse barn mucked out. They headed into town."

"Good." Jeremiah turned to Pa. "Will you say grace for us?"

As Thomas looked around the table, he noticed everyone held hands, even Bob and Jacob. He took Ma's hand and then Pa's hand. His father's prayer was short and to the point. He prayed for the food, for Jeremiah and Emily, and he thanked God for the return of Thomas. When Pa said the amen, he squeezed his son's hand tight as if emphasizing his words. For a brief time, the terrible sense of aloneness and worthlessness receded a bit from the center of Thomas' being.

They spent the rest of the visit talking about the store, the town, the church, and even stories about Thomas as a little boy. What no one talked about was the last twelve years, as if everyone had agreed to pretend those years had never happened. He couldn't decide if he wanted to tell his folks what life had been like at Yuma Prison, or if he, too, just wanted to pretend it hadn't happened. Compared to the normal events in a small town, he had nothing to tell that wasn't ugly and brutal.

Late in the afternoon, when his folks climbed into the buggy for the ride back to town, tears marred Ma's rosy wrinkled cheeks as she clutched his arm tight.

Thomas leaned in the buggy and gave her a kiss on the cheek. "It's all right, Ma. We'll see each other in the morning at church."

She wiped her eyes. "I know son, I want to take you home with me."

Pa patted her shoulder and she finally let go of Thomas' arm. "Now, Ma, the time will pass then Thomas will come home with us."

Thomas watched his folks depart down the lane and then turn onto the road until he could no longer see them. The visit had been a good one. He had worried about it for nothing. For the first time, he looked forward to the three years being up so he could get on with his life.

Even though Jeremiah had given him the day off, he walked back to the horse barn to find work to do. If he simply sat around, he would dwell on things, and he would rather be doing something. He began to muck out the stalls of the broodmares.

Chapter Eight Thomas

When Thomas returned from his walk after supper, he was pleased to find the bunkroom empty. The other cowhands had not returned from their day off in town so he had it to himself. The Cedar Ridge Weekly newspaper lay on the table. He sat on one of the wooden chairs and began to read. It had been years since he had the luxury of sitting and reading a newspaper.

The thunder of horses' hoofs announced the return of his bunkmates and the end of his time of peace. Within minutes Harlan, Barney, and Cal tromped into the bunkroom.

"Well, there he is. The famous Thomas Black from Yuma Prison." Harlan's voice was a little slurred.

Thomas sighed as he recognized the bullying tone. Before their trip to town, the three cowhands had not known about his time in prison and had treated him with detached friendliness.

Harlan staggered up to the table and grabbed the newspaper out of Thomas' hands. "I didn't tell you that you could read my newspaper."

Thomas stood and then spread his hands out palm down. "Sorry, Harlan, I thought it belonged to the ranch." He might as well try to placate the man who reeked of alcohol.

Harlan stepped toward him and got in his face. "You watch yourself, Black. We don't take kindly to having a prisoner working with us. If I had my way, you'd be in town in the jail. I don't know what Rebourn is thinking."

Thomas held back from stepping away from the foul smell of the man. He could squash this drunk like a bug. He clenched and unclenched his fists. Finish it now or let it rest? Experience had taught Thomas that men like Harlan would take it as a sign of weakness if he backed down. But, standing up didn't mean he had to punch the man. So, he held his ground and stared back at the drunken cowhand.

Cal stepped up and took Harlan by the arm. "Leave him be. He's not hurting anything. Come on, you said we was going to play some cards before bedtime."

Thomas appreciated Cal's effort to dissipate the situation, but he didn't take his eyes off Harlan.

Harlan blinked a couple of times and stepped back, muttering to himself. "Nothing but a good for nothing rustler. They should have hung you and been done with it." He staggered over to one of the chairs by the table and Barney and Cal joined him. They soon had a card game going.

Thomas took a deep breath and retreated to his bunk. All he needed was a fight with Harlan. Provoked or not, it could get him sent back to Yuma. Staying clear of Harlan had just become his second job.

He pulled off his boots and lay on his bunk willing himself to relax. The hot anger still rushed through his body and his breathing was rugged. Harlan probably had no clue what a fight with a jailhouse brawler would be like. And Thomas had sense enough to know that Jeremiah wouldn't want to see that kind of fight in his bunkroom. The cowhands had probably heard about him while in town and Thomas hated that he was the topic of gossip. What effect would it have on his folks and their business? And what would the pretty girl at the café think of him now?

He couldn't really blame Harlan. It was just how he was, but Thomas blamed himself. If only he could go back in time and stop his fifteen-year-old self from making that first of many dumb decisions. Then he wouldn't have to keep remembering his own part in his downfall. He turned over on his bunk and faced the wall, wanting to hit something.

~

Sunday morning was clear, sunny, and promised a hot day to come.

Jeremiah stood at the door of the kitchen as Thomas finished his breakfast. "Thomas, we'll be leaving for church about nine. You'll ride with me and the family in the buggy."

"Yes, sir." Thomas would do what he was told and he didn't mind going to church. His folks and perhaps the pretty girl from the café would be there. But what ate at him was riding in a buggy while the rest of the men rode horses. Only three years, then he could do as he wanted and no longer be treated like the prisoner that he was.

He helped Jeremiah hitch the team of horses to the two-seater buggy.

Emily came out of the house dressed in a light blue dress with a lace collar. Her straw hat had a matching bow and ribbon. "Beautiful morning, Thomas. I'm glad you're riding with us. If the twins get to be a problem you tell us."

"The twins won't be a problem." He hoped they won't be a problem. He had never been around children much.

The twins came running from around the corner of the house.

"Boys, where have you been? We're ready to leave for church. Climb into the back of the buggy with Thomas and be quick about it." Jeremiah offered a hand to Emily as she stepped into the front of the buggy to take her seat.

Thomas climbed into the back seat of the buggy and the twins quickly decided that they should sit one on each side of him.

Jacob drove Mildred and Sally in a smaller spring buggy. All the other ranch hands rode horses into town. Was it the rule of the ranch that everyone who worked there had to attend church? Thomas wasn't sure. Jeremiah had not given him a choice, just told him when to be ready to leave for town.

Jeremiah still kept a watchful eye on him. Thomas didn't blame him, as it had only been a week since they left Yuma. It seemed longer. This was such a world apart from that life.

Thomas followed Jeremiah and the family into the small wooden church building and ignored the other people. They weren't ignoring him though. His face heated up from all the staring eyes. Jeremiah motioned him to go ahead and sit with his folks in the wooden pew toward the front. Ma scooted over and Thomas sat between his folks. He would rather have been at the end of the pew as he felt hemmed in, but he didn't argue.

Just before the service started, the pretty girl from the café came and took a seat at the other end of the pew next to Ma. She greeted his folks with a smile and handshake and then offered her hand to him.

Thomas took her small hand and nodded in greeting. "Miss Catherine."

"Mr. Thomas." Her lips clamped shut as if she repressed a giggle.

Thomas grinned at her and kept on grinning but not sure why. Her dress was light green cotton and a straw hat with a ribbon to match her dress perched atop light brown hair. At the café she seemed younger, but dressed up with a hat, she looked to be about twenty-five. He glanced down. No ring graced her left hand. So maybe no husband?

Fifteen years had passed since Thomas had attended a church service. In his rebellion as a kid, by the time he was fourteen, he refused to go with his parents. Funny, he couldn't remember what he was so angry about back then.

He held the songbook for Ma, but he didn't sing, as he didn't know the songs. Catherine's strong sweet soprano voice rang out with words of faith and joy. When the preacher rose to give his lesson, Thomas sighed. Catherine was no longer singing.

The preacher seemed to speak another language as he talked about "being made worthy by the blood of Christ" and "accepting forgiveness." Thomas couldn't see how any of it applied to him.

At the end of the church service, he stepped into the aisle and turned to let Ma go ahead.

She turned and put her hand on his arm. "Thomas, this is Catherine O'Malley."

"Oh, remember we've met, Miss Agnes. Your son came into the café with Jeremiah and Bob on Thursday of last week."

"Oh, yes. That was the day Thomas arrived."

Thomas kept his gaze on Catherine and barely glanced at Ma. "Yes, ma'am. We stopped to eat after we got off the train."

Catherine tilted her head and glanced at him from the corner of her eyes. "You're looking more rested today." That brilliant smile came out again.

He didn't know how to respond. His ability at small talk was rusty.

"Catherine! There you are." A big, stocky, well-dressed blond headed man who appeared to be in his late thirties walked up and pulled Catherine's arm around the crock of his elbow.

"Hello, Myles, have you met Thomas? He's new in town and working for Jeremiah." Catherine smiled as she looked from Myles to Thomas. "This is Myles McKinley. He has a ranch east of town and owns the bank."

McKinley didn't put his hand out, so Thomas waited to see what he would do. Hostility exuded from the man.

"So you're the prisoner working for Rebourn. I heard he went all the way to Arizona to pick you up. I hope you realize what a good deal you got." His gaze was hard, and neither his voice nor his face held any warmth.

Before he could respond, McKinley turned to Catherine. "They're holding a table for us at the hotel dining room. Are you ready to go?"

Catherine glanced at Thomas. "Yes, I'm ready." She turned and allowed McKinley to escort her out of the church building. The building seemed to darken with her exit.

Thomas decided that he didn't like Myles McKinley. He didn't like him at all.

Pa frowned and shook his head as he looked at the man's retreating back. "I'm sorry. McKinley has always been arrogant."

"Don't worry, Pa. He only spoke the truth. I am the prisoner working for Jeremiah." He had begun to feel as if he was free. In one sentence, McKinley had taken that away. Thomas was still a prisoner.

He kissed Ma's cheek and received a hug from Pa. He climbed into the buggy with Jeremiah and family and returned to the ranch. Emily and the boys went into the house to change out of Sunday clothes.

Jeremiah and Thomas took the horses and buggy to the barn. While he unhitched the horses, Jeremiah came over and helped. Together, they turned the horses into the pasture.

"You want to tell me what McKinley said to you?" Jeremiah asked.

He glanced over at him, surprised that he had noticed. "Nothing I can't handle."

"I'm sure of that, but I do business with the man. I would like to know what he said. I'm asking, I'm not ordering."

"It really wasn't nothing much, just that he said it in front of—well, Miss Catherine and my folks." Thomas shrugged his shoulders. "And what he said is true. Said I was the prisoner you'd gone to Arizona to get to work for you."

Jeremiah nodded. "Yes, it is true, but it didn't have to be said and especially in the church building like that." Jeremiah slapped him on the shoulder. "You're right to not let it bother you, but just watch out for him."

Thomas nodded. He hadn't said it didn't bother him. And he would watch out for McKinley.

~

The next morning at the breakfast table, Bob handed out assignments for the workday. "Cal and Barney, finish up the horse barn and then ride out to check the cattle. Jacob and I will work with the mares and foals." He took a swig of coffee. "Harlan and Thomas, I want you all to load up the fertilizer wagon from the old muckheap and spread the dried manure over the east field where we cut the hay last week. Thomas, Jeremiah has a wagon with a fertilizer spreader on the back. It takes one man to drive and another man to shovel the dried manure into the spreader. You and Harlan work it out between you as to who does what."

Thomas followed the men to the horse barn and grabbed a shovel. He had never even heard of a fertilizer spreader much less seen one. Harlan and Thomas hitched up a team of horses to the wagon with an odd machine on the back and pulled it up next to the old muckheap.

Harlan scowled and muttered to himself. But Bob stood by the barn door. As Thomas shoveled the manure up into the wagon, Harlan barely moved. When he threw only a half a shovel load into the wagon, Thomas fought the urge to yell at him to make an effort. The job would take all day if Harlan kept moving so slow. What could he do? He wasn't Harlan's boss.

Harlan, Cal, and Barney had been friendly enough the first week, but Thomas had seen a real change in their attitude toward him after their return from town on Saturday night. Sunday evening had been another round of Harlan making comments about how they should hang all rustlers with Barney joining in. Cal hadn't said much. But Thomas had twelve years of experience at ignoring those around him.

Chapter Nine Thomas

When they arrived at the east pasture with the wagonload of dried manure, Harlan grabbed the reins from Thomas' hands. "I'll drive the wagon. You shovel the fertilizer."

"Why should you drive?" Thomas challenged. Shoveling the manure into the spreader took much more work and the sun was hot.

"Because I'm not the prisoner. You don't want me telling tales to Bob about how you wouldn't work. Who do you think he'll believe, you or me?" Harlan's smirk boded no good.

Without a word, Thomas climbed over the wagon seat. After he pulled the lever to start the spreader, he began shoveling the dried composted manure through. He clenched his fists around the handle of the shovel he wanted to land in the middle of Harlan's grin.

Thomas struggled for balance in the slowly moving wagon, pitching shovel after shovel of dried manure into the spinning spreader. The heat of the sun burned through his thin shirt. As the morning progressed, it got hotter, at least 100 degrees. His thirst got the better of him. He turned just as Harlan tipped a jug up to his mouth for a long pull of water.

"Pass that jug back here." Thomas reached out his hand.

Harlan shook his head then placed the jug back at his feet. "That's my water and I only brought enough for me. If you wanted water you should have brought your own."

The temptation to bash him pushed at Thomas. Maybe it'd be worth returning to Yuma. No!

He should have thought to bring water, but at Yuma the guards had always had prisoners load up water for the day. Thomas had to start thinking differently.

Picking up the shovel, he went back to work. As the morning continued, he wasn't sweating anymore. The sun beat down, and the day got hotter. All Thomas could think about was to get the wagon emptied so they could head back to water. Soon his throat and mouth were so dry that he had trouble swallowing.

Thomas pulled his hat down to just above his eyes trying to keep the sun at bay as it got close to noon. He had been shoveling for about three hours. In another hour, he could get the big wagon emptied. Dizziness and nausea overwhelmed him as he leaned over the side of the wagon and threw up. After wiping his mouth on his shirtsleeve, he tried to keep shoveling. But he couldn't lift the shovel full enough to make much difference. Thomas heard a horse trotting up to the wagon and swung his head to see who it was. He was so dizzy he lost his balance, tumbled out of the wagon, and hit the ground.

Bob's face floated in front of him. "Thomas, can you hear me? My goodness, you're burning up! Harlan, hand me my canteen."

Cool, refreshing water. Thomas drank in great gulps. But he still couldn't move. What was wrong with him?

"I got to get you back to the house. Harlan, help me get him into the saddle, and I'll ride behind. You finish up this job."

Thomas felt hands lifting him up on the horse and then nothing.

~

He opened his eyes and looked up into the face of Emily. He was naked in his bunk with just a sheet over him. She laid a cold wet towel over his bare chest and then placed another one over his forehead, covering his eyes. He couldn't seem to move, and the top of his head felt as if it would burst from the pain.

He heard Jacob's voice. "He starts to cool now."

A hand lifted the cloth, felt his forehead, and pushed the hair back. "Thomas? Can you hear me?" Emily's voice was soothing.

"Miss Emily?" He struggled to sit up. Why was she so blurry?

"Be still, Thomas." Jacob pushed him back on the bunk. "You too hot and got sick."

He tried to swallow. "Some water ... please."

Jacob's face swam into view and his hand, which held a cup of water. Thomas couldn't figure out why everything kept moving.

He closed his eyes and his mind drifted. As if from down a long tunnel he heard voices.

He heard Jeremiah speaking. "You sure he's going to be all right, Doc?"

"Yes, but he needs to stay out of the sun and not get hot like this again. No working out in the fields under the sun, and really, he should take it easy for a few days. You know that people can die of heatstroke. And have him drink a lot of water."

Was this voice talking about him? What would Jeremiah do if he didn't work? He could only hope he wouldn't send him back to Yuma.

"Just keep him quiet and cool, and bring him to my office in a few days."

"We'll do that, Doc," Jeremiah said.

"I'll see you then."

Thomas heard footsteps leaving the room.

"Thomas, you awake?" He opened his eyes to see Jeremiah sitting in a chair by his bunk.

"What's happening?" The effort to speak seemed to use too much energy.

"You had a heatstroke. You're going to be all right, but you need to rest for now."

"I can get back to work. I just need to rest a bit." Thomas didn't feel like getting up, but his fear of what Jeremiah would do if he couldn't work was there, a clenching, gnawing thing in his gut.

"I'm ordering you to stay right here in this bunk. No more work for you today, or tomorrow." He took the towel off Thomas chest and soaked it in water. When Jeremiah laid it across Thomas' bare chest it felt good, cold and wet.

Thomas drifted in and out the rest of day. Emily or Jacob came in every little while and soaked the towel in the cool water. Each time they roused him to drink some water.

Emily brought some cold tomato soup for his supper. She helped him sit up, and he was able to feed himself. He wasn't hungry, but he didn't say anything.

Later in the evening, Thomas felt something bump his bunk and looked up to see Harlan walk past with his smirkey grin. What did Harlan have against him? Thomas had been careful not to cross any of the riders. Harlan was just a bully. If Jeremiah let him stay after this, he would have to fight his urge to crush Harlan. What he wanted to do was stake Harlan out under the sun with no water.

The next morning, Thomas dragged himself out of bed and took a bath in the wash up room. By the time he made it to the kitchen, everyone had eaten breakfast and headed out for work, except for Jeremiah and Emily who sat at the table drinking coffee and talking.

"Morning, Thomas. How are you feeling?" Emily rose to fetch him a plate of food.

"I'm fine." He would have said that no matter how he felt.

Jeremiah laughed and ran his fingers through his hair. "Then you haven't looked in the mirror. You're pale and look like you could collapse any minute."

"I'll leave you two to talk and go start my sewing." Emily came over to Thomas and surprised him by kissing him on the forehead as if he was one of her little boys. "I'm so thankful you're all right."

"Thank you, ma'am." He didn't know what else to say, not being used to such attention.

Emily left the kitchen disappearing into the front room.

"Tell me what happened yesterday morning." Jeremiah took a sip of his coffee and waited for Thomas to speak.

He decided to tell Jeremiah the truth. He didn't try to make Harlan sound any worse, but he didn't try to protect him. When Thomas finished, he waited for Jeremiah to speak.

Jeremiah looked at him over his cup of coffee. "That's not the story Harlan tells."

There it was, his word against Harlan's. "You going to send me back?"

Jeremiah looked startled. "Send you back to Yuma?"

"Yes, sir." He held his breath and felt he was going to be sick.

"No, I'm not sending you back to Yuma. In this case, I believe you, and not Harlan. But try not to get into it with him. It won't help your case."

His relief was so great that Thomas found himself trembling. "Thanks. I'll do the best I can."

"Do what you want today. Borrow a book out of the front room and read, or do nothing. Just don't get out into the sun and heat." He got up and put his cup into the basin in the sink. "Well, I better start my work day. I'll see you at dinner."

Thomas sat at the table and finished eating his breakfast. Then he wandered into the front room, looked through the books on the shelves on either side of the fireplace, and found a book to read called *Treasure Island* by Robert Louis Stevenson. There was a slight breeze on the front porch so he went out, sat in a rocker, and read the morning away. He really didn't feel like doing anything more energetic than hold a book. After picking at his noon meal, he went and slept through the afternoon. When he woke, guilt settled over him like a blanket. He couldn't remember a time since he was a child that he had drifted through a day like he was doing. He should be at work, not lazing around.

The next morning, he awoke weak and shaky, but felt that he could start back to work.

Jeremiah insisted that they go into town to see Doc Ford. Mildred and Emily had lists of things they wanted from the mercantile so they took the wagon. Another hot day beat down upon them, and even with his hat on Thomas felt peaked by the time they got to town. Jeremiah pulled the wagon up in front of Doc's place first.

Doc looked Thomas over and listened to his heart through the stethoscope. "You're drinking a lot of water?"

"Yes, sir." He was drinking more water than he had in years. Emily and Jacob saw to that.

"Any dizziness?" Doc asked.

"Some but less than yesterday."

"Good." Doc put his stethoscope away.

"When should I let him go back to work?" Jeremiah asked.

"Well, you might let him take it easy for another day or so, and then start back to work as he feels like it. Don't overdo it, only a few hours in the sun at a time and if you feel like you're going to be sick or pass out, go sit in the shade."

From Doc's place, Jeremiah drove the wagon up to the mercantile. Thomas could see into the store through the open double doors that his folks were busy with customers.

Jeremiah pushed his hat back. "What would you say to going over to the café and eating, then see your folks this afternoon when they aren't so busy? It's past noon and I'm hungry."

"That sounds like a good plan." Thomas wasn't so much hungry for food as he hungered for another glimpse of Catherine.

"Go on over to the café and I'll leave my lists with your folks. I'll tell them that we'll be over in an hour or so."

Thomas slowly walked across the road and up the boardwalk to the café. It was the first time he had been on his own in the town. When he pushed open the door of the café, he saw that several of the tables were full of customers. Taking his hat off, he walked over to an empty table against the wall hearing his boots on the wood floor in the silence that his entrance had caused. As he glanced around at the customers, most were looking at their plates of food. A few stared at him, as if demanding to know what he thought he was doing there. Thomas wished he had waited in the wagon for Jeremiah.

Catherine hurried over with a glass of water. "Hello, Thomas. How are you? I heard that you weren't feeling well."

He looked up into her deep blue eyes and could feel the heat rising on his face. "I'm doing all right. How's your day?"

She smiled and pushed some loose curls back under the hairnet she had holding her thick hair under control. "Busy as usual. What can I get you?"

"Jeremiah will be here soon and we'll order some dinner." He had barely gotten the words out of his mouth when Jeremiah came through the café door. He spoke to several of the customers as he made his way to the table, not seeming to notice the silence in the café.

"Hey, Catherine. What's the special today?" He dropped his hat next to Thomas' as he sat down.

"We have cold roast beef, sliced cantaloupe, sliced tomatoes, and fresh made bread. It's too hot to serve much else."

"That sound all right for you, Thomas?"

"Yes, sir." He barely glanced at Jeremiah as he was too busy taking in the beauty that was Catherine. Why she mesmerized him so he didn't know but whenever he was in her presence she filled the whole room.

"Then bring us two plates of the special. Do you have any ice for tea?"

"No, but I can bring you tea at room temperature." Catherine pushed a curl back from her face. "I ran out of ice about thirty minutes ago and more won't be delivered until later today."

"Guess that will have to do." Jeremiah pulled out his handkerchief and wiped his face.

Thomas watched as Catherine made her way back to the kitchen.

He wasn't sure whether he enjoyed the food or getting to watch Catherine as she served her other customers. Jeremiah and he each finished off their meal with a piece of cherry pie.

Catherine came to collect for the meal and remove the dirty dishes.

"That was good. Did you make the pie?" Thomas asked.

"Yes, I do all the cooking and baking." Catherine took the money that Jeremiah laid on the table.

"Well, that was the best cherry pie I've eaten in years, Miss Catherine." Thomas smiled at her hoping to get one back.

She cocked her head and smiled back. "Are you trying to flatter me, Mr. Thomas?"

Jeremiah grinned.

Thomas could feel the heat rising on his neck and face. "Probably. Is it working?"

Catherine let out a giggle. "I do believe it is."

He didn't know what to say next, but Jeremiah spoke up. "I'm going to the bank and will meet you at the store."

He rose with Jeremiah and said to Catherine, "Thanks for the good meal. I'll look forward to seeing you at church Sunday."

"Yes, I'll see you then." Catherine then turned and walked over to another one of her customers.

As they walked across the road Jeremiah said, "Catherine is a pretty girl."

"Yes, sir, she is."

"And she's a good girl, works hard, and made a success of the café." Jeremiah sidestepped some horse manure in the street.

"What do you want to say to me?" Thomas might as well get it out into the open.

"There's nothing wrong with you and Catherine being friends. Just be fair to her and remember you have three years before you can think of the future." Jeremiah looked over at him and then pulled on the cuffs of his sleeves.

"Thanks for the reminder. There's nothing between Catherine and me. Maybe we'll be friends someday, but I doubt if anything else. I'm not much of a catch for a pretty girl."

"Is that what you really think? You might be surprised what that pretty girl is thinking."

Thomas didn't agree with him that she might have thoughts for him, but he didn't want to argue.

Jeremiah departed for the bank.

Thomas entered the general store and visited with his folks for a couple of hours before they headed back to the ranch with a wagonload full of supplies.

On the ride back to the ranch, Thomas found himself thinking of Catherine and how she looked pushing back the curls that escaped her hairnet. He pulled his thoughts back. There was no benefit in letting his mind go in that direction. Other than a friendly hello occasionally, he had nothing to offer her. Knowing that didn't stop his thinking about her most of the ride back to the ranch.

Chapter Ten Thomas

"You will work with me today?"

Thomas looked up from his breakfast and realized Jacob had spoken to him. "Sir?"

Jeremiah put down his cup of coffee. "I told Jacob that you would help him for a few days in his workshop. That way you'll stay out of the sun like the doctor said. Is that all right with you?"

He nodded. "Yes, sir." He hadn't been inside Jacob's workshop, but he had heard Jacob made furniture and sold it in Denver. What did Jeremiah expect him to be able to do? Thomas knew nothing about working with wood.

After they finished breakfast, he followed Jacob to the back of the barn. There were windows all along the outer wall and a door three-fourths glass. Once inside the workshop, the light flooding in brightened every corner. After so many years in dark cells, Thomas craved the light.

Thomas listened to the soft-spoken man. He could understand him with no problem but there was something different. "Why do you talk different?" Was he being too forward? "Hope you don't mind me asking?"

Jacob looked intently at him. "I first learned to speak German in Germany, my country. Then I come to America twenty year ago and learn English. I come west to be cowhand, but not very good. Not ride good. I get job at ranch of Elisha Evans, up in the mountains. I speak good English but never perfect." Jacob motioned for him to come over to a long work counter set up in the middle of the shop. "I meet Jeremiah in the mountains. When he come here, I come."

Thomas gazed around the workshop walls hung with all sorts of tools.

Jacob stood by a workbench and stroked the long pieces of wood stacked on it. "Today you help me make tall wardrobe. It will be beautiful. Cherry wood is good wood for such furniture. I teach you how to take care of the wood, and it will make a beautiful furniture. If you do not take care it will be ugly." Thomas saw the carpenter's love for the wood in his gentle touch.

"Yes, sir. Just tell me what to do." Maybe he could learn something from this man. "I saw the furniture in the house and the mantelpiece they said you had crafted. They are carved like works of art."

"Thank you. God has blessed me. Now, first, you turn the saw wheel, and I will guide the wood through. We must first make the pieces and then put together. The finish is important but first we must have *gut* design, *gut* wood, and careful work."

He showed Thomas the design for the wardrobe. "It will be six feet tall. Here is a compartment on one side for clothes to hang. This side, four drawers under a mirror."

"How do you know how to cut the wood so it all fits together?' Thomas asked.

Jacob scratched his head. "I just draw and measure and it works. Here I show you."

After a short time, Jacob had measured and marked the pieces of wood, but soon was so absorbed in his work that he no longer explained what he was doing.

Thomas stayed out of the way by wandering around the workshop looking at the tools and stacks of wood. Some of it he recognized, but some of the wood he had never seen before. How could he help when he had no skills?

Every type of tool hung on hooks on the wall. On a side counter were several larger tools he recognized as saws and polishers. The whole workshop impressed him with how clean and orderly it was.

"Thomas, ready for help?" Jacob's voice brought him back to the purpose of his being there.

"Yes, sir." He strolled back to the counter where Jacob had several boards stacked.

"You stand here by the circular saw and turn this wheel just so, no faster and no slower. You turn it that way even when I put board against the saw." He turned the wheel and the pulley turned the saw.

As Thomas inspected it, he had a feeling it might be harder to do than Jacob indicated.

"Here, we wear goggles so if wood flies up, it does not get into eye." He handed Thomas a pair of what looked like spectacles, except they had wire screen around them and a cord to fasten them onto the head. When he put them on he could see all right and they protected his eyes. He had never seen anything like them before, but they made sense. Such a protection would have helped back in Yuma when the small chips of rock had flown up and hit his face as he had broken up boulders with a sledgehammer. There no one had cared about injuries to a prisoner.

"Thanks." Jacob's concern for his safety was unsettling.

He turned the wheel with the hand crank and once it was turning at a certain speed, Jacob put the first piece of board where he had marked it against the saw. As it began to cut into the wood, Thomas understood what Jacob meant about making an effort to keep it whirling around at an even speed. It wasn't easy. The noise, flying wood chips, and smell of sawdust disturbed the former quiet of the workshop. After they had cut several boards, Jacob motioned above the noise for him to stop.

"We rest a moment. There is no hurry and no need to get too hot." He took the boards they had cut and placed them on another counter.

Thomas was hot, trembling, and sweating. Had Jacob noticed and called for the rest period for Thomas' sake? He pulled out his handkerchief and wiped the sweat from his face. How could he be in such a state? Jacob had yet to break a sweat and didn't look like he had even started to work yet. Thomas sighed. He should be in better shape. Maybe the heatstroke had affected him more than he realized.

Jacob brought over a jug of water and two cups. He poured the cups full and handed one to Thomas. "Drink up. Is good water from the well."

Gratefully, he accepted the cup. "Thanks."

"Now we use different saw, a band saw, and cut smaller pieces of wood. This time you sit in chair and peddle. Here I show you." He moved over to a band saw and sat in a wooden chair. The stand had two peddles attached to a pulley on the saw. As Jacob began to peddle, the band saw vibrated up and down.

Thomas had never seen such a machine. "How will I know how fast to peddle?"

Jacob got up from the chair and scratched his head. "I not sure. Maybe you just get a feel."

Thomas peddled and the saw worked with ease. Then Jacob placed his first piece of wood against the blade. The peddling was much harder, but Thomas could do it. Soon he had a rhythm going.

Jacob fed the boards and the pieces of wood became scrolls for the top of the wardrobe.

When the dinner bell sounded, Thomas was tired and ready to eat. The morning had passed swiftly and he enjoyed the work. After washing up they headed to the house.

"You good help this morning. We are now ready to make the wood all smooth, then we put together to make wardrobe. Tomorrow we put first coat of varnish."

Jacob talked as if Thomas would be helping him for several days. He didn't mind as he was enjoying the company of the friendly German. It was better work than cleaning out the horse barn. Thomas had no doubt that by next week he would be back at work shoveling manure.

They spent the afternoon sanding the pieces of wood until they were smooth. Jacob was slow and steady. He never seemed to hurry. Thomas noted the patient, calm way Jacob responded when he messed up and they had to cut another board. He wasn't used to that.

Thomas set himself to Jacob's pace and worked the wood as Jacob showed him, working with the grain. It took longer to do all the pieces of wood than he thought it would, but they had everything ready to put together by suppertime.

After eating, Jacob headed back to the workshop. His living quarters occupied one end. Thomas had noticed at the north section of the workroom the comfortable bedroom-sitting room area that was as nice as any in the main ranch house.

He soon followed Jacob back to the workshop and found him cleaning up.

"You do not have to work now. We start again in the morning." Jacob wiped the counter and saws clean of sawdust.

"I don't have anything to do this evening. Let me help clean up." Thomas picked up the larger pieces of wood that had fallen to the floor as they had sawed the boards and pitched them into a barrel half-full of wood scraps. Then he grabbed the broom while Jacob restacked some of the wood. They had the place clean and orderly by the time the sun set.

"Well, if there's nothing else to do, I'll turn in and see you in the morning." He put the broom back on its hook.

"Thank you, I hope you sleep well and feel God's blessings, Thomas."

He walked back to the bunkroom thinking about Jacob's last words. *Feel God's blessings.* He liked the sound of it, but wasn't sure how one did that.

The next day they fitted the wardrobe together and Jacob showed him how to brush on the first of several coats of varnish. In the two days of working with Jacob, he learned to appreciate the feel of working with wood and wanted to learn more. As Thomas crawled into bed that night, he was tired but was pleased with the help he had given Jacob. The wardrobe was a fine piece of furniture. Thomas tried to remember when he last felt a pride in something he had done and couldn't think of a time. Fitfully he turned over in the bunk. If he wanted any kind of life, he needed to learn to do for himself and be able to take pride in his accomplishments.

~

Saturday morning as Thomas finished breakfast, Jeremiah said, "I'm going to ride out to look over the cattle. I want you to go with me. So go on out with Bob and choose a horse to ride."

Thomas looked at Jeremiah and then at Bob. To ride a horse again, his heart suddenly beat fast and hard at the thought. All he could say to Jeremiah was, "Yes, sir."

Bob led the way to the big corral by the barn where fifteen horses were munching hay. "Which one do you want to ride?" Bob leaned against the rail fence and chewed on a stalk of grass.

Thomas looked over the horses but had no idea which to choose. He had sense enough to know he needed a slow gentle horse that he could hang on to. After twelve years of not riding, he wasn't sure he still knew how.

"You choose for me, Bob. I trust your judgment."

Bob grinned and threw the piece of grass away. "All right then, let's take a look see." He stepped up over the railings and into the corral. "Let me have that rope, Harlan. You go get one of the extra saddles and bridles out of the tack room and bring it back here."

Harlan threw Thomas a scowl and slouched off toward the barn.

Bob shushed the horses into a trot around the corral, then suddenly his rope snaked out and settled around the neck of a brown mare. He worked his way up the rope hand over hand until she slowed to a walk and stopped. Bob patted the neck of the mare and she ducked her head, evidently liking the attention from Bob.

Harlan came out of the barn carrying a horse blanket, saddle, and bridle. He helped Bob saddle the mare.

Bob grinned at Thomas. "Come on and mount. Let's see if you can ride."

Thomas slowly walked up to the horse on the left side. Bob handed him the reins and he mounted the horse on the first try. The mare looked around at him with sleepy eyes. Bob opened the corral gate and Thomas urged the mare forward with his knees to a slow walk. All the riding he had done as a youngster came back to forgotten muscles and he felt at home in the saddle.

Jeremiah came out of the barn leading a big black stallion already saddled. He mounted and said to Bob, "We'll be back by noon."

They rode toward the south and southwest. It was a cool, clear morning and Thomas felt great to be sitting on a horse again. His fear of forgetting how to ride disappeared as the familiar moves of holding the reins threaded through his fingers and guiding the horse as much by the muscles in his thighs as with the reins returned with little effort. Thomas grinned. He could still ride.

Jeremiah slowed and let the mare catch up to him. He had two canteens tied to his saddle and handed one to Thomas. "You left the house without a canteen of water. Not a good idea in this heat."

"Thanks." Thomas took the canteen, swallowed a deep drink of water still cool from the well, and then tied the canteen onto his saddle horn. He needed to think more and not depend on others remembering for him. How was he ever going to be respected as a grown man if he couldn't remember the simplest things? During his time in prison, he hadn't been required to think at all. Every decision had been made for him.

Jeremiah talked about the land and the cattle they saw. He didn't seem to expect an answer from Thomas. He didn't mind listening to the rancher talk. Thomas was eager to learn everything he could about ranching. After they had ridden about an hour according to the movement of the sun, Jeremiah guided the stallion into a stand of quaking aspen trees by a creek with Thomas following.

Jeremiah dismounted. "Let's stop and give the horses a breather." He led his horse down to the creek.

Thomas dismounted, led the mare to the creek, and let her drink. Then he tied her to a low tree branch so she could munch on the grass. He didn't know whether the horses really needed a breather or if Jeremiah wanted to give him one. Either way Thomas was glad for the chance to stop. Parts of his anatomy were already talking to him. He could look forward to being sore after this ride. Flopping down on the grass and moss under the aspen trees along the creek, he opened the lid to the canteen and drank several gulps of water.

"How are you feeling?" Jeremiah put the lid back on his canteen.

"I'm feeling all right. Just get a little dizzy after being in the sun so much." He glanced over at Jeremiah. Was there a purpose to his questions? Or, was he just having conversation?

"Any more trouble out of Harlan?"

"Not anything I can't handle. Ever since he found out I just got out of Yuma Prison, he's made comments. But like I said, nothing I can't handle." Thomas didn't want to tell Jeremiah the effort it took not to bash Harlan. He wanted to see that smirk disappear from Harlan's face.

"I appreciate the way you're choosing to deal with it. Most men would have hit him by now. But with someone like Harlan that wouldn't solve anything. If it comes to a point that you need to protect yourself from getting hurt, you let him have it. Of course, within reason." Jeremiah gazed at him with a serious look.

"I'll try not to get into it with him." Thomas couldn't promise more. If Harlan came at him, he planned to protect himself.

"Did you do much fighting at Yuma? Can you hold your own with your fists?" Jeremiah's voice was calm and steady.

Thomas answered in the same calm way. "When I first got there, I had to fight every day. But as time went on the other prisoners let me be. They learned that I wouldn't take any guff off anyone, even if I was young. Course I got beat up a lot that first year. I learned to end the fight as quick as possible, as fiercely as possible. Hurt them worse than they hurt me. As I got older, my reputation did it for me. I have no doubt I can beat Harlan in a fist fight." He didn't tell Jeremiah that each time he got into a fight he then paid for it with a beating from the guards, and being put on bread and water for a week. It had been worth it to keep the prisoners from bedeviling him all the time, especially those first years. Every minute of the day, he had kept his defenses up and walked a tight rope.

"But, should you fight him?" Jeremiah had a way of getting to the heart of the matter.

"No, I need to try to avoid him and that's what I'll do if I can."

"That's a wise decision."

Thomas glanced at Jeremiah to see if he was being sarcastic, but he calmly looking out over the creek. A small surge of pride welled up in his chest. He wanted to be making wise decisions, and Jeremiah's opinion of him mattered more each day.

"Well, we best get going if we're to make it back to the ranch at noon." Jeremiah stood and put on his hat. "By the way, we've invited your folks and Catherine for dinner after church tomorrow."

Thomas swung back into the saddle and sat tall He couldn't keep a grin from spreading across his face. Catherine was coming to spend several hours at the ranch! That was something to look forward to.

The ride back was quiet. Jeremiah made a circular route over a portion of the land. They saw several herds of healthy looking cattle with Jeremiah's brand, the letter J and an E at each end of a rocker. The grass was adequate and the creeks and ponds had plenty of water in spite of the heat. The spring rains had been plentiful. Thomas hoped the summer would continue to bring occasional showers.

Thomas enjoyed the ride. He longed for the time he would be free to come and go as he wished. His thoughts kept returning to Catherine and the visit the coming day. Of course, he would be happy to visit with his folks, too.

Chapter Eleven Thomas

Sunday morning Thomas woke early before the other men in the bunkroom. He eased his way slowly out of his bunk and into his clothes. His bottom, inner thighs, and lower back were sore from riding the horse the day before. He slowly made his way to the horse barn. There he found Jeremiah, Bob, and Jacob all at work cleaning out the stalls. All the stalls were full of either mares about to foal or had foaled within the last couple of days.

"You sure you're up to the work?" Jeremiah leaned on a pitchfork.

"Yes, sir. If I get too hot, I'll stop and rest."

"All right. We can use the help. We'll let Cal, Barney, and Harlan do the evening chores."

Thomas grabbed a pitchfork and helped Jacob fill a wheelbarrow with the muck from a stall. Two hours later, they had all the stalls cleaned with fresh straw laid out. All the horses had been fed and watered. Thomas was ready to stop. All the men were hot and sweaty from the work.

Jeremiah put his pitchfork away. "I have first choice at the bathtub. You fellows will have to either go down to the creek to wash up, or wait on me to finish."

Bob hung his pitchfork up next to the one Jeremiah had hung up on the hooks on the wall of the horse barn. "I'm heading for the creek just as soon as I can grab some clean clothes."

"Me too." Jacob put his wheelbarrow back in the corner.

"And me." Thomas didn't mind the cold water of the creek even in the cool of the morning.

"Okay, then I can take a long soaking bath." Jeremiah grinned.

~

After a refreshing swim and a vigorous scrubbing with a bar of lye soap, Thomas felt better as he made his way into the kitchen for breakfast. He was eager to get to the church building and see Catherine. Probably not the best reason for looking forward to a church service but it was the truth.

Elisha and Joseph assumed that Thomas would be riding with them and insisted that he sit in the middle. Never having been around children before, he found the boys fascinating. They were so open and uninhibited. At times, he had trouble following their conversations, as they could go from one topic to another without any warning. Their questions were continuous.

By the time Jeremiah pulled up the horses in front of the church building, Thomas was caught up in the antics of the two little five-year-olds. Scampering out of the buggy, the boys quickly found some of their friends.

Thomas followed Jeremiah and Emily into the church building.

His folks were already in their pew, and he went to sit with them. Only this time Ma didn't scoot over but motioned for him to sit by her side while she sat next to Pa who was at the end of the pew by the center aisle.

"Morning, son." Pa held out his hand and he shook it.

"Morning, Pa." Thomas leaned over and kissed his mother on the cheek. "You doing all right, Ma?"

She smiled and patted his arm. "I need to sit by your pa so I can poke him when he falls asleep during the sermon."

Thomas couldn't help but laugh. "You may need to poke me, too. I got up early this morning."

Pa grinned at him and winked. "Your ma has been keeping me awake in church for forty years now. I have a permanent bruise where she pokes me."

"Oh, Milburn, that's not true." Ma patted Pa's arm.

"Well, almost. What got you up so early this morning, son?"

"I helped Jeremiah, Bob, and Jacob muck out the horse barn. With all of us working together, we got it done before breakfast. Unless some of the mares go into foal, we'll have the rest of the day off work." He smiled at his folks. "Therefore, I can enjoy you all coming out for dinner."

"That's nice. Oh, here's Catherine. Sit down by Thomas if you don't mind dear." Ma motioned for Catherine to sit in the pew next to him.

Thomas started to rise, but she slipped into the pew before he could stand. She reached across him and gave his mother a kiss on the cheek. She then held out her hand and he shook it. "Morning, Thomas."

"Morning, Miss Catherine." He didn't try to hold on to her hand, although that was what he wanted to do.

There was plenty of space on the pew and she sat about a foot away. Thomas sat close to Ma, as she held onto his arm.

The song leader rose and stood at the front of the congregation. He announced which song number to turn to in the songbooks and then motioned for the congregation to stand to sing the song. Thomas' father held the songbook for his mother, so he held one for Catherine. As the song was *Amazing Grace*, he knew it well enough to try to sing. He sang softly so he could hear Catherine's voice.

As they got to the last verse, Myles McKinley walked up to the pew and stood by Catherine. Thomas noticed that she didn't look at McKinley. When the song was over they sat down and the foot of space between Catherine and Thomas was gone. He had the distinct impression that she wasn't pleased that McKinley had sat next to her.

Thomas tried to pay attention to the services, but his thoughts kept coming back to the presence of the beautiful girl sitting so close to him that their arms touched. She left space between herself and McKinley. Thomas noticed that McKinley glared at the space between himself and Catherine and a stormy look gathered on his face. Thomas managed not to grin.

As soon as the service was over, Catherine turned to Thomas' folks. "May I ride with you all?"

"Of course you may Catherine. It is so nice of them to invite us out for Sunday dinner." Ma seemed unaware of the thundercloud that stared at Catherine's back.

Thomas didn't look at McKinley. Whatever was going on between McKinley and Catherine didn't need to involve him.

"Catherine, I thought we would go to the hotel and dine today." Myles spoke in an abrupt way.

"I'm sorry Myles, but I accepted an invitation for dinner. Perhaps another time." Catherine was polite to him, even gracious. Thomas sensed she wasn't at all sorry to have other plans.

He followed his folks out of the building so as not to be drawn into the conversation between Catherine and McKinley. "I'll see you all out at the ranch."

"All right, son. We'll wait for Catherine and be there shortly," Pa said.

Thomas sauntered over to Jeremiah's buggy and helped Emily up into the front seat. He then climbed into the back seat.

Jeremiah walked up with a small giggling and squirming boy on each hip. Soon he had the boys situated one on each side of Thomas and they started for the ranch.

Thomas looked back at the church building and saw Catherine come out with a frown on her face and Myles behind her still talking.

After letting Emily and the boys off at the house, Jeremiah drove the buggy into the barn.

"I can take care of these horses and look after my pa's when they get here." Thomas would rather be taking care of horses than pacing in the house waiting for his folks and Catherine to arrive.

"I appreciate that. I need to go check some of the mares before dinner." Jeremiah threw him the reins and strolled out of the barn. Thomas unhitched the team of horses, put them into stalls, fed them some oats in a feedbag, and put out a bucket of water for each one. Then he climbed into the loft to pitch down some hay.

He heard the sound of a horse and buggy and looked out the loft toward the lane. Pa's buggy was halfway down the lane from the road headed for the house. At the junction of the road and the lane, Thomas noticed a rider on a horse. From the distance, he couldn't make out the face, but he recognized the build of the man. It was Myles McKinley. What was he doing following his folks and Catherine? As Thomas watched, the rider turned the horse abruptly, and headed back toward town.

Thomas climbed down from the loft and walked out to take the horse and buggy from Pa. The women had already entered the house.

"I'll take care of your horses, Pa."

"Thanks, son. I'll go with you so I don't have to sit and make small talk with the women. Emily said Jeremiah had gone up to the horse barn."

"I understand, Pa. Why do you think I volunteered to take care of the horses?" With Pa helping, they soon had the horses in the stalls, fed, and watered. "Since we're out here and have a few minutes, let me show you what I've helped Jacob do this week."

"Sure, son, I'd like to see what you have been doing. How are you feeling? About over your heatstroke?"

"I'm doing all right, Pa. If I get too hot, I still get dizzy. Jacob says the answer to that is not do anything to get hot. Of course with this being an unusually hot spring, almost as hot as the end of June, anything I do I get hot." He tapped on the screen door for he could see Jacob in the workshop.

"Come in. You do not knock, Thomas." Jacob rubbed the finished wardrobe with a cloth soaked in linseed oil from the smell of it. "Milburn, you come to see my workshop, *ja*?"

"I can't believe I've never been to see it before. Look at the tools you have here." Pa glanced around with a look of wonder.

"Well, you should know my tools. I bought all from you." Jacob stepped back from the tall wardrobe, which gleamed from the oil.

"Pa, this is the piece of furniture that Jacob let me help him make. We started with the pieces of wood and a design, and look at it now." He was proud of the work. Of course, it was Jacob that had the know-how. Thomas simply followed his orders.

Pa walked all around the wardrobe and then nodded. "As fine a piece of workmanship as I've ever seen."

"*Ja*, Thomas has the gift in his hands. He understands the wood. Maybe this winter when not so much work with horses, he will work with me to make beautiful things."

Thomas felt his face heat up and a sense of pride spread from the center of his being at Jacob's words of praise. Thomas began to understand how much he had missed in the last twelve years. How much he longed to have the praise of men rather than the condemnation.

"I know my son appreciates your willingness to teach him how to work with wood. You know I always wanted to have a workshop, but it never worked out."

Thomas stared at his father. He had had dreams and wishes just like everyone else. How many of those dreams had Thomas helped to crush by his irresponsible behavior through the years? Another layer of guilt settled on his shoulders.

They all looked toward the house as the dinner bell sounded. Thomas led the way to the wash up room where they met the twins running out with dripping hands.

Mildred and Sally had prepared a banquet. As Thomas passed the platters and bowls of baked chicken, baked ham, gravy, biscuits, corn, green beans, and applesauce, his plate was soon too small to hold the food. He sat across the table from Catherine and noticed that she served herself small portions compared to his. However, he had worked off and on all morning and was hungry.

Harlan, Cal, and Barney kept staring at Catherine. Thomas had to admit she was the prettiest one there. Course Jeremiah would have argued that and Thomas could see where he would think Emily was the prettiest.

Catherine looked up from her eating, glanced at Thomas, and smiled several times, but she never once turned her gaze in the direction of the three cowhands. He wanted to tell them to quit leering at her. It would only create more of a problem. It was Jeremiah's responsibility, but he didn't seem to notice.

After the meal, Emily invited Catherine and Ma to come see what she was sewing for the baby that was due in the fall.

Jeremiah, Pa, and Thomas went into the front room. It didn't take long until Jeremiah and Pa were both asleep, each in one of the big easy chairs.

Thomas heard the women talking out under the big oak tree at the other side of the house. He wandered out there and found them all seated around a wooden table busy with hand sewing. He pulled up a camp chair and sat down next to Ma. She was sewing a tiny garment with the smallest stitches he had ever seen.

"Thomas, would you like to help us?" Emily asked. There was a definite hint of laughter in her voice.

He held up his big rough hands palm out. "Look at these hands, Emily. The first piece of that flimsy cloth I touched would be snagged to death. No, I'll just watch if that's all right."

"I fear you're right, so maybe you better just watch. What happened to your pa and Jeremiah?" Emily was crocheting something tiny. She didn't even seem to be looking at it.

Ma bit off the thread from her last stitch, then looked with satisfaction at the garment she had finished. "I know where they are. They're both sound asleep would be my guess."

Emily laughed. "I suspect you're right. Thomas, make yourself useful and go ask Mildred to prepare something for us to drink."

"Sure." He looked at Catherine who had not said anything, but gazed down at the piece of fabric as she sewed. As he walked back to the house, he realized she had not spoken to him since she got to the house. Had he done something to upset her?

Mildred had anticipated what the ladies would want and had a pitcher of tea and several glasses on a tray with a plate of sugar cookies. She handed the tray over to him to take out to the ladies. "Now you be careful and don't spill it. I've had that pitcher of tea soaking in well water for thirty minutes. It should be nice and cold."

"Yes, ma'am." He carefully carried the tray out to the table.

"Thank you, Thomas. Now you can pour everyone a glass of tea including yourself. I love cold sweet tea sitting out under this old white oak tree on a hot spring afternoon." Emily rubbed her rounded stomach with a quiet smile. He noticed that she did that often and wondered if it was something women expecting a child did.

As he sat there about to doze off himself, sipping on the cold tea, Emily said, "Thomas, why don't you take Catherine down by the creek where it's cooler. Catherine, you seem tired."

Thomas glanced at Catherine who didn't seem overjoyed with the idea if the solemn look on her face was any indication. "I'll be glad to walk with Catherine if that's what she'd like to do."

She put her sewing down on the table and stood. "Yes, I would like to walk a bit."

He followed her toward the creek, picking up a canteen that hung by the back door. He was getting used to not going anywhere without a way to carry water. He wouldn't say that they walked together to the creek as much as he followed her. She walked quickly and soon he panted to keep up.

"Catherine, we can take our time, especially in this heat." He finally offered.

She stopped and turned around. "I'm sorry, Thomas. I didn't think. You shouldn't be in this heat at all so soon after suffering heatstroke."

"I'm fine, just so long as we don't have to run." He grinned at her.

After that, she set a more leisurely pace and they soon came to the creek. He led the way to the area where he usually swam. Lined with trees on both sides of the creek, the area was shady. Several fallen logs offered a place to sit. One log was across a little eddy. Thomas took off his boots and socks, carefully scooted along the log, then let his feet dangle in the cool water.

Catherine seemed undecided at first, but she soon followed his example. She slipped behind a tree and took off her shoes and stockings. Her hat was off and she let her hair flow loose. He also noticed that she had unbuttoned the top two buttons on her dress. She looked free and relaxed.

He tried not to stare at her trim ankles and the little bit of her legs that showed as she tried to keep her skirt from getting wet. He watched the creek water flowing past and felt the coolness of the water on his feet. This prison was definitely not Yuma but, he needed to remind himself that he was still a prisoner.

"What are you thinking, Thomas? You suddenly looked so serious."

He gazed at her seated so close to him on the log and decided to tell her the truth. "It's only been a short time ago that I was in Yuma Prison. And, I have three more years on my sentence. Sitting out here with you and with the creek and all, I have to remind myself of the reality of my situation and not go getting ideas."

"What sort of ideas?" Catherine looked at her feet that were making circles in the water.

"The idea that I'm like other men and free. The truth is I'm not free for three more years. It would be easy for me to start wanting things that I can't have. It's not wise to put that burden on myself or on anyone else." He sat still and waited for her response, worried he had said too much.

She splashed the water with her foot and pulled her dress up another inch to keep it dry. It wasn't to tease him, as there was no indication she was thinking that way.

Catherine glanced up at him from underneath her long lashes. Her expression was serious. "I appreciate your honesty, Thomas. It must not be easy to be in your situation. As I see you at church and then here on the ranch, I tend to forget, as you say, the reality."

"I do want to be honest with you. When I was a kid and got into trouble, it was because I wasn't honest. I want my life to be different now. As the preacher said this morning, it's in the little things that our true character shows up. I'm still trying to find mine."

Catherine smiled. "I think you're doing well toward finding your character. More than most men I know."

"Thank you for saying that. It means a lot to me."

"Let's agree that we'll be friends and both of us will work on doing the small things toward finding the character God would want us to have." Catherine held out her hand and he took it in his.

"I can agree to that, but I have a problem." He kept hold of her hand.

"What is that?" She didn't pull her hand away.

"I don't know what God wants me to have in the way of character. I'm just now learning some things about God. I'm not real sure about a lot of things about Him."

"There you go, being honest again. I do like that. Don't worry, Thomas, God has placed you in the right place for learning about Him. Some of the godliest men and women I know live right here on this ranch. Watch Jeremiah, Jacob, Bob, and especially Emily and you will see godly character at work." Catherine gently pulled her hand away.

"I will. We probably need to think about getting back to the house." He said it, but he didn't make a move. "Since I'm being honest, can I ask you a question?"

"Sure."

"Myles McKinley . . .?"

"You want to know my relationship with him?" She glanced at him with a quizzical look. She didn't seem to mind the question. "Myles and I have known each other for several years. We have sort of kept company. Myles is persistent and takes things for granted. Why do you ask?"

"I noticed that he seemed upset after church service today, then he followed you out here."

"He did what?" She sat upright and turned toward him.

"I was up in the barn loft pitching some hay down when you all turned into the lane. I noticed him following you all to the turn off. He sat there on his horse a few minutes and then turned back toward town. I thought it sort of strange."

"Don't worry about Myles. But, stay away from him, as he can be mean."

"Since I'm not allowed to leave the ranch without someone with me, I doubt that I'll see much of him."

Catherine watched out over the creek and then gazed back at him. "I didn't realize it was like that. You really are still a prisoner here."

He grinned at her. "Not a bad prison compared to Yuma."

She peered at him with a serious expression. "Someday I'll get you to tell me about Yuma."

"But not today, we need to start back." He didn't want to tell her about Yuma. He didn't want such ugliness to touch the beauty that was Catherine.

"Yes, we probably should, but it's cooler here by the creek with our feet dangling in the water." Catherine closed her eyes and tilted her face up to feel the slight breeze that stirred. It also caught some of her hair that had gotten loose around her face and it gently waved in the breeze.

All Thomas wanted to do was put his hands through her hair and stroke her soft skin. Instead, he scooted down the log and stepped back on firm ground. He dried his feet with his socks, put them on, and then pulled on his boots.

When Catherine saw what he was doing, she followed suit.

They slowly walked back to the house. They saw Mildred step out onto the back porch and ring the bell for supper.

After supper, his folks and Catherine prepared to drive into town. Ma cried again as she left. Again, Thomas couldn't understand why. This time Catherine put her arm around Ma to comfort her.

He felt a little down himself as he watched them leave. It had been a good day and he hadn't wanted it to end. He put his hands in his pockets, kicked a rock, and slowly walked back to the creek. He sat on a large boulder and watched the Colorado evening sky as the sun set behind the mountains in the distance, thinking of a pretty girl and her soft laughter.

Chapter Twelve Thomas

Jeremiah assigned him to work with Bob the next morning. Thomas began learning more about the horse breeding business. Working in the horse barn, he already had helped with some of the mares as they dropped their foals.

Bob had a room in the horse barn that he used as an office. He took the stack of papers off one of the chairs and motioned for Thomas to sit in front of the desk.

"What do you know about horses, Thomas?"

"Not much really. I know that I would rather ride a horse than walk."

Bob grinned. "Now that I will agree with. Well, let me tell you some things so you'll understand what we need to do here." He pushed his hat back and shifted to get comfortable. "A mare's gestation time is about 340 days as you know and they have to be covered by a stallion at about twenty days after dropping a foal. What that means is we have to keep good records of when a mare drops her foal so we can get her with a stallion at the right time to have a crop of foals the next year. Sometimes it takes a couple of times with a stallion."

As he listened to Bob, he had several questions. "How do you know which stallion to put with which mare?"

Bob nodded. "That's a good question. Jeremiah will help you learn which stallion needs to cover which mare to get the color of horse we want. For example, for the army contract they prefer a brown or dark tan horse as they blend into the countryside better. We've got some books and we have Jeremiah's written records for the last ten years. You need to be reading those."

"Sure, I'd like that." Thomas shifted in the wooden chair. His bottom was still sore from Saturday's ride.

"For the next two or three weeks, I want you to follow me around and help out. I expect you to be learning so that one day you can work by yourself. Now let's get going."

Thomas spent the morning following Bob as he checked the mares about to drop their foals.

Bob stood in front of a stall where a mare had dropped her foal the night before. "When a mare is within a week of her time, we put her into a stall so she will drop the foal there instead of out in the pasture. If the mare gets into trouble, it's easier to help her. Jeremiah figured out a way to nick the mare's ear so we can know which mare is which."

Thomas nodded. "I wondered how you could tell the mares apart when several look exactly alike."

Bob walked on down the line of stalls. "You'll soon understand the system of nicks on their ears and the books are always in my office for you to check what's going on with each mare."

Thomas followed Bob out of the horse barn and over to a large wall-less shed.

"This is the breeding shed where we have the stallions cover the mares. Jeremiah has it all organized and done according to a plan." Bob glanced over to Thomas. "Even with that, it's a lot of work. We have to be on watch constantly when we're working with such a large horse herd."

Thomas enjoyed working with the horses, especially the little foals. It amazed him to watch the small animals awkwardly walking only 30 minutes after birth. One of Thomas' jobs was to train the foal to be respectful and learn to be comfortable when handled. He routinely lifted their hooves to get them used to having the hoof care they would need. He also put little halters on the foals and gave them lessons in leading so they could learn to walk quietly beside him. He never left the halter on unless he was with the foal. Even though it was part of his work, Thomas almost felt like he was playing with the little foals.

Harlan, Barney, and Cal weren't interested in Thomas being part of their doings. They usually played cards in the evenings. It didn't bother him, as he was used to keeping to himself. He read everything he could get his hands on about raising horses and Jeremiah's ledgers filled with his detailed notes. Cal and Barney let Thomas be and didn't say much. But, Harlan couldn't let it alone with his sarcastic comments.

~

Jeremiah, Bob, and Thomas had been up most of the night with a mare having a difficult birth. It was hard to get enough sleep when several mares foaled within a week or two as they usually dropped their foals at night. They saved both the mare and the foal. After Jeremiah headed back to the house, Bob and Thomas stood outside the stall watching the mare encouraging the little foal onto his feet.

Assigned to muck out the horse barn, Harlan couldn't pass Thomas without a harsh look or word. Harlan made sure Bob wasn't within hearing distance.

As Harlan passed Thomas with a full wheelbarrow of fresh manure, he tripped and dumped the load onto Thomas' legs and feet.

"Oh, sorry there, Thomas. I must have tripped." Harlan wasn't sorry judging from the wicked gleam in his eyes.

Bob picked up some straw and wiped his boots where some of the splatter had landed. "Well, watch what you're doing. Get a shovel and get this cleaned up."

There was so much muck on Thomas' pants and boots that there was no wiping it off with just a little straw.

Bob looked at Thomas' boots and shook his head. "Go on down to the bunkroom and get some clean pants. You better go on down to the creek and take a swim if you want to get the smell off you."

"All right. It may take a bit of time to get my boots cleaned up." He only had one pair. Afraid of what he would do if he looked at Harlan, Thomas left the barn before he pushed Harlan's face into the muck. One of these days, he'd go too far and Thomas would let go at him, even if it meant going back to Yuma. A man could only take so much.

He heard Bob yell at Harlan, "You get to finish the horse barn and don't stop until it is done."

Harlan whined. "But, Bob, I can't get this done by the time breakfast is served."

"Well, you should have thought of that before being so careless and clumsy. If this isn't done by breakfast you will just have to miss it for making more work." Anger laced Bob's voice.

He left and caught up with Thomas.

"Sorry, Thomas, you shouldn't have to put up with such foolishness."

"I can handle Harlan. I don't want to track this muck into the bunkroom. Mind getting me some pants, soap, and a towel?" He looked with disgust at his pants legs and boots.

"Sure. Hold here a minute." Bob went into the bunkroom.

Thomas waited for him outside the door and noticed two little dark-headed boys staring at him from around the corner of the house. "Hey boys, what you doing?"

They edged around the corner and slowly walked over to inspect Thomas' boots.

One of the boys edged over and sniffed the air. "You smell bad, Thomas."

The other boy stood in front of Thomas looking down at his legs and feet. "Aren't you going to wash that off your boots?"

The other one spoke up, which one Thomas had no idea, as he couldn't tell them apart. "I've stepped in a fresh cow pad before, but I never would have thought to go wading in it."

"Yeah, Thomas. Why did you do that for?"

"Well, boys, it's like this. I dropped my magic rock into the muck pile, and I had to find it. There weren't no other way but to go wading."

"A magic rock? Where'd you find a magic rock?"

"That's a secret. Maybe someday when you're older I can tell you." Thomas grinned.

Bob came out of the bunkroom with Thomas' one pair of clean pants, a towel, and soap. "Here you go. Take your time and then come on in for breakfast."

One of the twins pulled on Bob's sleeve. "Uncle Bob, Thomas went wading in the muck pile looking for a magic rock. Will we get into trouble if we do the same thing?"

Bob tried to keep a straight face. "Yes, you will Elisha. You better not try that. Only Thomas is allowed to wade in the muck pile. Now, you boys go on in and wash up for breakfast and leave Thomas alone."

"Bye, Thomas." Two voices said in unison as they ran into the house.

Bob could hardly talk for laughing. "Wading in the muck pile are you now?"

"I had to tell them something." Chuckling himself, he headed for the creek.

It took him a while to clean his boots and pants. The pants would have to be washed a second time to get them clean. He didn't know how, but Harlan would pay. When he got back to the house, he left his wet boots at the door of the bunkroom.

As he padded toward the kitchen door for some breakfast, Jeremiah's voice carried from inside. "We have a problem with Harlan. If he keeps this up one of two things is going to happen. Either we fire Harlan or Thomas is going to run out of patience and beat him up."

The next voice was Bob's, "If it had been me, Harlan would have already run out of luck. The problem is Harlan is sneaky. If he did something outright, we could fire him."

Jeremiah said, "We don't know what else has happened. Thomas doesn't complain."

"I like that about him. He works hard, does what he is asked to do, and doesn't complain. I can't say the same about Harlan," Bob said.

Thomas knew he shouldn't listen to others' conversations, but since it was about him, he wanted to hear what they said.

Jeremiah said, "If Thomas and Harlan get into it, I'm going to let it ride. I should report to the judge any fighting on Thomas' part, but not if it's because of a bully like Harlan."

Thomas decided to let them know he was there. He walked back down the hallway to the screen door and let it bang, then he entered into the kitchen.

Bob grinned. "You sure do smell better."

Thomas nodded back. "Thanks, Bob, I wouldn't want you to be offended."

Mildred came in from the front room. "Thomas, you missed breakfast, but I saved you a plate. Sit down and I'll get it for you."

"Thanks, Miss Mildred. I appreciate that." He poured himself a cup of coffee from the pot at the back of the stove, then sat at the table across from Bob and Jeremiah. The effects of being up most of the night showed in the dark circles under their eyes. Thomas guessed he looked about as bad they did.

Jeremiah rubbed his face and yawned. "After you eat, go get some shut-eye. We'll probably have another long night. I'm predicting we'll have at least three foals to deliver."

Mildred put a plate of eggs, ham, gravy, and biscuits in front of Thomas. He only waited long enough to thank her before he dug in.

"I'm going to go find my bed for a couple of hours. See you fellows later." Bob strolled out of the kitchen.

Jeremiah emptied his cup of coffee. "Bob told me what happened. Watch yourself. If need be, you protect yourself."

"I will. You mind if I ask you a question?" He swallowed some of the hot coffee.

"Ask whatever you like."

"How do you know when the mares are going to foal?"

Jeremiah shrugged and got up to pour another cup of coffee. "I don't know. I just have a feeling." He sat back at the table. "Twelve years ago I arrived at Elisha Evans's Rocking ES Ranch up in the mountains not knowing a thing about horses except how to ride one. I met Joe Weathers and he taught me. Both he and I have this special feel for the horses. You'll meet Joe and Elisha this fall when they bring the rest of the horse herd down from the mountains."

"I'll look forward to that. Well, I think I'm going to follow Bob's example and go get some shut-eye if that's all right." Thomas handed his empty plate and cup to Mildred.

"Sure, sleep as much as you need. Like I said, we'll be up most of tonight."

~

Jeremiah was right and for the next week, they were up most nights. In the month Thomas had been at the ranch, forty mares had dropped their foals. He found it exciting and satisfying work.

Moreover, he had time with Catherine to look forward to each Sunday. It became a regular routine for Catherine and his folks to come out to the ranch on Sunday and spend the afternoon. Jeremiah and Pa managed to get a nap. They also enjoyed each other's company. The talk of cattle, rangeland, weather conditions, and new tools kept them busy. They also enjoyed talking scriptures. Jeremiah seemed to know every verse in the Bible. He and Pa would discuss some point of theology and it wouldn't take too long until they left Thomas behind. It made him want to read the Bible so he could understand.

Emily and Ma were forever planning for the new baby, talking recipes, and other things women got on about.

This left Catherine and Thomas walking down to the creek in the summer heat. Usually Elisha and Joseph were with them, which neither Thomas nor Catherine minded.

After the Sunday Myles McKinley had followed Catherine out to the ranch, he hadn't sat by her at church services. If Thomas looked over at him, McKinley always gave him a stare that told Thomas he didn't want to meet the man some place alone at night. Catherine didn't mention him so Thomas assumed McKinley left her alone.

~

The July morning started out hot. Jeremiah sent Jacob and Thomas into town to pick up a load of supplies.

"While we wait to get the wagon loaded, I go to the wagon yard and see wood they have." Jacob put his feet up on the front of the wagon and leaned back relaxing as Thomas drove the team. "You do what you want. You can visit with folks, or go to the café and get some pie, just so you stay on main road."

Thomas glanced over at Jacob who looked straight ahead. "How long do you think it'll take you?"

"I do not know. Herman Jones and I get to talking wood. It can be long time." Jacob's face brightened at the thought.

"Well, I'll be at the café or the mercantile. I won't go anywhere else. I may not make it to the café as I didn't bring any money with me." He didn't bring any because he didn't have any.

Jacob reached into his pocket and pulled out a dollar. "Here, you take. You do not come into town and not get piece of Miss Catherine's pie."

Thomas hated to take it, as he didn't like to owe anyone, but his desire to see Catherine was stronger. "Thanks, I'll pay you back."

"No worry. You think of it as a little pay for help with building furniture." Jacob pushed his hat back. "Drive up to back of store so it will be easier to load."

He guided the team and they pulled up to a loading dock at the back of the store.

Jacob jumped down with a bucket, and filled it at a nearby pump.. He let each of the horses drink a half a bucket of water. "They will be all right to wait for us. We give them more water before we leave town."

Pa came out of the store and greeted them. Jacob waved to him. "Thomas has list. I go see Herman."

After giving him the list of supplies for the ranch, Thomas followed Pa into the store and greeted Ma.

"This is a happy surprise. Can you stay long?" She beamed at him.

He kissed Ma on the cheek. "Jacob and I are here to get supplies. He has business with Herman Jones. I should have two or three hours to visit."

"I'm so glad. Does Catherine know you're in town?"

"Not unless she saw us drive in. Maybe after awhile I'll go over and say howdy to her." He really wanted to go immediately, but he owed it to his folks to visit a bit.

"Pa, you want help gathering up the ranch supplies?"

"No, son, you just visit with your mother." Pa was soon busy stacking supplies onto the dock at the back of the store.

"Let me read you the letter I got this morning from Bessie." She reached under the counter and pulled out the letter. As Ma read aloud, he pictured his sister Bessie as a pretty, young girl, but then he caught himself. She was a thirty-four-years old woman with a husband and four children that Thomas didn't even know. The same was true of Hope, his younger sister, who was thirty-two-years-old, also with a husband and three children. In the twelve years he had been away, their lives had continued.

Bessie's letter was full of the everyday activities on a ranch and tales of the children. Then Ma read the last part of the letter.

"Your letter telling of Thomas' release was such wonderful news that Hope and I sat down and cried. The children had a hard time understanding that we would take on so about their Uncle Thomas being home or that we would cry for joy. Give him a hug and kiss from both of us. We long for the day we can come and visit.

"Frank told me that he believes we can come home for Christmas, and that you would be wise to start baking now.

"Please kiss Thomas for every one of us, and tell him that we long for the day when we will all be together again. We will continue to pray for Thomas daily, as we have done for these twelve long years.

Most affectionately your loving daughter,

Bessie."

Thomas wiped his eyes with his shirtsleeve and noticed that Ma also had tears. "Thanks for reading that to me. I never thought about them praying for me every day. I regret the trouble I got into at the prison the first month I was there. It never entered my head that the warden would take away my privilege to receive letters and never give it back. I could have written them and known what was going on in their lives." He dropped his head and closed his eyes. He had too many regrets.

"Yes, not being able to write or get letters from you through those years was so hard. I never told your father but when he would leave for the yearly visits I was always sick with worry until he got back. I was always fearful he would come back and tell me something had happened to you in that terrible place." She dabbed at her eyes with a handkerchief. "Then he would come back and I would be so relieved. But then it was the long wait of another year to get any news."

No wonder she was so gray headed. Another wave of guilt as he understood more fully the hurt and pain he had caused his folks. Why couldn't he go back and undo the foolish acts of youth? He had to try to make it up to them now. Their kind faces always looked at him with such love, he had to stay close to them in the years to come. They deserved it.

A couple of ladies came into the store. Thomas gave Ma a hug and kiss on the cheek. "I'm going to the café to say hello to Catherine. I'll be back after while."

"Take all the time you want, son. I'll have some dinner ready for you and Jacob before you head back to the ranch."

"Thanks, Ma." He strolled toward the front door of the general store with a wave to Pa.

Thomas heard one of the women ask, "Isn't that your son, Agnes?"

"Yes, it is. Isn't he handsome?" The pride in Ma's voice made him grin. Someday he was going to be worthy of his mother being proud of him.

As he entered the café, the first thing he noticed was Myles McKinley seated alone with a coffee cup in front of him. There were three rough looking cowhands at another table but otherwise the café was empty. Thomas sat close by the door to the kitchen with his back to McKinley and several tables away. He didn't want to look up and have to see the man's hateful stare.

Catherine came from the kitchen carrying plates with pieces of pie. She smiled, nodded, and walked on to the three cowhands. "Here's your fresh apple pie, boys. Hope you enjoy it."

She then stopped at his table. "Hello, Thomas. It's rare to see you in town the middle of the week." She was just too pretty for him to take his eyes off her. Her hair was done up in a hairnet and she had a smidge of flour on her cheek.

"Hey, Catherine. Jacob and I came in for supplies. I thought I'd get some coffee and pie while I waited for the wagon to get loaded." He heard Myles McKinley shifting in his chair and wished he would leave.

"Give me a minute and I'll have it out to you. We have apple pie today." With a brilliant smile, she disappeared into the kitchen.

Suddenly, Thomas sensed someone behind him.

"You take warning, Black. She's my woman. You try to hone in and you'll pay dearly." Myles voice was low and harsh.

Thomas sat still not wanting to start something in Catherine's place of business. Instead of anger, he felt cold, as if someone had walked across his grave. He believed McKinley meant what he said. What he didn't believe was that Catherine was his woman. He heard the sound of chairs scraping on the wooden floor, coins dropping on a table, and then the door closing to the outside. He looked around and the café was empty. His breath started up again. He had not even realized he was holding it.

Catherine came back with a cup of coffee and a piece that must have been the fourth of a pie . The aroma of the apples and cinnamon filled the room.

"Thanks, Catherine. This looks delicious. Did you bake it this morning?" Thomas slowly put a fork full of apple pie into his mouth. The flavor was even better than the aroma. He ate deliberately so he could enjoy every morsel.

Catherine sat down at the table with him, and smiled. "Yes, I got up at four o'clock this morning to take advantage of the coolness. I had ten pies baked by eight o'clock."

They spent the next fifteen minutes talking of the ranch and the business of the café. Catherine's mother had started the café when Catherine was a young girl. With her mother's death the year before, Catherine continued the business. "My mother always had me cooking with her. She didn't seem to be teaching me. I was just being with her.

Then one day I realized I could cook as well as she could. Of course, that had been her plan all along."

He smiled at her and raised his fork. "Here's to your mother who raised a wonderful daughter and taught her how to make the best apple pie in the world."

Catherine smiled back. "She would have appreciated that."

Thomas hated to do it, but he needed to return to the general store. "I have to go. Ma is preparing dinner for Jacob and me. Then we head back to the ranch."

"I'm glad you came in and had some pie. It's good to see you."

"It is good to see you too. And I look forward as always to seeing you on Sunday." He took out the dollar to pay her.

She pushed his hand back down to his pocket. The feel of her soft, warm hand was like a spark of electrical static. "The coffee and pie are on the house."

"Thanks. That's nice of you." Thomas put his hat on and walked out of the café. All he could think about was how one of her curls had escaped from the hairnet, just like the first time he had seen her.

He walked down the boardwalk before crossing the road to give time for a wagon being pulled by four horses to pass. As he passed a gap in the buildings, an arm came out, grabbed him around the neck, and jerked him into the ally. Before Thomas knew what happened, the three men threw him against the brick wall of the building hard enough that his head bounced against the stone and his eyes wouldn't focus. Then he doubled over as hard punches from several fists landed in his stomach and abdomen. Before he could get his head cleared, another fist hit his chin and he slammed up against the wall again. He tried to hit back, but they were too quick and too many. Things got hazy, but he could still feel the fists repeatedly pounding on his body. Thomas fell to the ground and then it was boots kicking his ribs, stomach, legs, and head. The fire of pain spread through his whole body.

Someone grabbed his hair and lifted his bloodied face. "Mr. McKinley wanted to make sure you got the message."

The message? Then he heard a familiar voice shouting, as he drifted on a sea of pain.

"What you men do? Stop hitting that man." Jacob. He would help him.

Thomas heard men running away. For some reason he couldn't see.

"It is you, Thomas? I will get help."

Relaxing, knowing that Jacob would take charge, he welcomed the void that pulled him away from the pain.

Chapter Thirteen Catherine

Catherine heard running boots on the boardwalk and shouting. Curious to see what was happening, she stepped out of the café in time to see Jacob run into the alley by the side of the café. Loud shouting came from down the alleyway. She hurried to see what the commotion was about. As she looked down the alleyway, she saw Thomas lying in the dirt with Jacob kneeling beside him.

"Thomas! What happened? He's bleeding." He seemed to be covered with blood, from his scalp and face to his chest, arms, and legs. She tore off her apron and handed it to Jacob. "Use this to stop the blood. It is fairly clean."

She turned to Beryl who had followed her out of the café. "Run back into the kitchen and grab some towels."

Beryl pushed back through the crowd of men gathering at the alley entrance.

Jacob took the apron from Catherine and pressed it to the cuts on Thomas' face.

Other men were crowding into the alleyway and then Milburn pressed through. "I heard that something happened to Thomas. What's going on?"

Jacob looked up. "Three men beat Thomas bad. I yelled and they ran off toward the back of the café. He is hurt but we do not know how much." Jacob shook his head. "The doctor is out at the Thurman ranch delivering a baby. He may not be back until tomorrow."

Catherine managed to take a deep enough breathe to ask, "Is it safe to move him? Does he have any broken bones?"

Jacob gently pressed along Thomas' sides. "*Ja*, I think his ribs are broke. We need door to move him on."

Jacob sat back on his heels and looked at the crowd gathered in the alleyway. "With Doc out of town, I think best thing to do is put mattress in the wagon and take him to the ranch for Emily and Mildred to take care of him. They know more about doctoring than most of us."

Catherine pressed her hand against the apron, which was quickly turning red, held to the cuts on Thomas' face. "I'll stay here with Thomas while you go get the wagon ready."

Herman Jones spoke up, "I've got a door at the wagon yard you can use to carry him."

Jacob put a hand on Milburn's elbow and encouraged him to stand. "Milburn, would you go tell Agnes what is going on. I go pull the wagon around. Do you have blankets we can use?"

Catherine felt her heart constrict with the thought of Agnes. "Go ahead, Milburn, go tell Agnes. We'll take care of Thomas."

He took a last look at Thomas lying so still and pale in spite of the blood that seemed to cover him. Catherine could sense that he hated to leave his son lying in the dirt, but didn't want someone else telling Agnes. As he stepped off the boardwalk to cross the street, Sheriff Grant came running up.

"What's going on?" he asked breathing heavy. "I heard Thomas Black has been fighting."

Milburn turned a worried face to the sheriff. "I don't know how much Thomas was able to fight with three men beating on him. In the alley, some men beat up Thomas bad. I'm going to go tell Agnes and get some blankets. Jacob is taking him back to the ranch so they can take care of him. Doc is out of town."

Grant started pushing his way past the men clogging the alleyway. "You men move back out of the way. Give us some room."

Catherine held the apron pressed against the side of Thomas' cheek and the side of his scalp. Soon it was more red than white. There were other cuts on his face and his lip was slit with blood trickling down the side of his mouth. She reminded herself to breathe as her concern caused her to hold her breath. It would not do anyone any good for her to pass out.

Beryl returned with the towels and knelt down to try to help stop some of the blood flow. "You all right, Catherine? You're white as a sheet."

Catherine straightened her shoulders. "I'm fine, just a little shaken at Thomas getting hurt. He had just left the café not two minutes before I heard the shouting."

Soon Jacob and Herman were back with the ranch wagon and the door. Somewhere Jacob had found a mattress and had put it into the bed of the wagon. The two men positioned the wooden door beside Thomas and gently slid him onto it. Then they, along with Sheriff Grant, each took a corner and carried Thomas to the waiting wagon.

Catherine climbed into the wagon bed to keep pressure with a towel on the gash in Thomas' head to stop the bleeding.

Agnes ran across the road with Milburn following carrying a stack of blankets. "Let me through. It's my boy that's hurt." The men surrounding the wagon made way for Agnes and Milburn who was right behind her. She gasped when she saw Thomas and the amount of blood soaking through his clothes and the towels. "What happened to him?"

Sheriff Grant placed a hand under her elbow to help her climb into the wagon bed to kneel beside her son. "He's been beat up bad. I think most of the cuts are not too deep but we don't know if bones are broke or what damage was done internally. The cuts and bruises were probably caused from being kicked by pointed toed boots."

Agnes looked around at the crowd. "Where are the men who did this?"

The sheriff shook his head. "We don't know but that's my job to find out. Once we get you all started toward the Rocking JR, I start investigating."

Catherine took the blankets from Milburn and helped Agnes spread them over Thomas.

Milburn reached up and patted one of Thomas' ankles, one of the few areas on his body that didn't seem damaged. "I'm going to hitch my buggy up and drive out to the ranch behind you, Jacob. Agnes wants to ride in the wagon with Thomas."

Catherine folded a quilt and placed it under Thomas' head. "I'll ride in the back to steady Thomas' head."

Jacob nodded. "I drive the wagon slowly, but we need to get him to help as soon as we can."

Sheriff Grant looked around at the crowd that had gathered. "Could one of you men ride out to the Rocking JR and alert them an injured man is coming?"

Hank Edwards, a cowboy from one of the ranches out beyond the Rocking JR spoke up. "I'll go. I have to go by there on my way back to the ranch anyway."

Sheriff Grant nodded. "Get going then, Hank. Did anyone besides Jacob see anything?"

Catherine waited a moment for someone else to speak up, but realized no one else was going to. "I think I saw the men who might have done this. There were three rough looking men who left the café a couple of minutes before Thomas. They were dressed like ordinary cowhands. I don't remember anything specific about them except I hadn't seen them before."

Jacob climbed up on the wagon seat and picked up the reins. "*Ja*, three men who dress like cowhands run off down the alleyway. I did not see their faces. They had hats on and bandanas around faces."

Sheriff Grant pushed his hat back. "Would you recognize these men, Catherine?"

She shook her head. "I don't think so. I can tell you what they ordered but I didn't pay attention to what they looked like."

Grant nodded. "I'll check the back alley to see if they had horses there and whatever else I can spot. Take Black to the ranch and have the women take care of him. I'll come out after I do some checking here. Maybe then Black will be conscious and can tell me who he riled enough to deserve a beating like this."

Catherine held her tongue with difficulty. Sheriff Grant acted as if this was Thomas' fault rather than the men who had beat him up.

The ride to the ranch was slow and jarring. It seemed to take forever. Catherine sat in the back of the wagon with her hands cradling Thomas' head in an attempt to keep it still. Agnes sat holding his hand and praying aloud for God to help her son.

The road was rutted and potholed. Catherine worried about the effect on Thomas' condition. It concerned her that he was not regaining consciousness. The bruising and swelling of his face increased her fears for how badly he was hurt. By the time they reached the turn off to the ranch, she could hardly recognize him.

After Jacob turned the team of horses onto the lane, Catherine saw Jeremiah and Bob waiting. Jeremiah waved for Jacob to pull the wagon up to the front of the house.

As the wagon came to a stop, Jeremiah and Bob stepped to the tailgate. "How is he, Catherine?"

Catherine struggled to hold back tears. "He's hurt bad. His face and the area around the worse cut on his head are swelling. He hasn't moved nor opened his eyes. I'm afraid of how bad he's hurt here on his head."

Jacob joined them at the tailgate just as Cal came running up to hold the horses. "His ribs are broken, maybe."

Jeremiah's face was a grim mask. "The women are getting a room ready in the house. Let's be careful carrying him in. Slide the door out of the wagon. Cal, you and Bob take a corner at Thomas' feet. Jacob and I will get the other end. Slow and easy."

Soon, the men had Thomas in the bedroom where Emily and Mildred waited with basins of warm water and the ranch medical kit.

Jeremiah glanced from Thomas to Emily. "You need me to stay and help?"

Emily shook her head. "No, the four of us can take care of him. Will you be close by if we need any help?"

Jeremiah patted Agnes on the shoulder. "I'm going to be in the kitchen getting Milburn a cup of coffee. I'm sure he will be here shortly. I'll let you know if we leave the house. I want to talk to Jacob to find out exactly what happened."

Agnes looked up at him. "Thank you, Jeremiah, for thinking of Milburn. He was going to get the buggy."

Catherine began to help cut the clothes from Thomas' body so Emily could start sewing up the cuts. She fought to keep the tears back as she saw the extent of his injuries.

Chapter Fourteen Thomas

The light waved on the wall. It took Thomas a moment to realize he was staring at shadows and sunlight playing across the white wall of a room. He struggled to wrap his mind around where he was and why he lay in the middle of a big bed instead of his narrow bunk. He turned his head to get a better look at the source of the light and shadows. Pain hit his mind from every part of his body. He squeezed his eyes closed and tried to breathe as little as possible as the agony increased.

Voices drifted in from somewhere and then silence. Then he sensed someone close by the bed. He opened his eyes and saw Emily seated in a chair.

"Thomas, can you hear me?" She placed a cool hand on his forehead. "Are you really awake?"

"Emily? Where am I? What happened?" Just the effort to whisper was painful.

"Do you remember anything about getting beat up?" She got a cup from the small table by the bed and lifted it to his lips.

The cool water flowed down his throat. When she took the cup away, he answered her question. "The last I remember...in Catherine's café. I think I ....left it, but then I don't remember."

"Don't worry about it. You're safe and will get better now." She wiped his face with a damp cloth, but he pulled back from it as his face hurt.

"What's wrong...with me?" His voice was a little stronger.

"You have some injuries to your head and face. We feel sure you have several broken ribs. Your stomach and legs are all bruised from being kicked with boots. What else we're not sure. I don't think you have any broken bones except the ribs, but you are badly bruised all over." Her voice was quiet and soothing as she recited his injuries.

"I got beat up...?" He had no memory of it.

"Yes, Jacob saw three men running away down the alleyway. He got your father and a couple of other men to help him load you into the ranch wagon and drove you back to the ranch. The doctor is out of town for the week. Jacob and your folks decided you would be better off if they brought you back to the ranch to heal. Your mother has stayed with you."

"How long...?"

"You got hurt on Thursday. Today is Sunday. We were so worried because you didn't wake up." She sat holding his hand.

"Is it church time?" He thought of the voices he had heard and then the silence.

"Yes, everyone has gone into town to church services except your mother. I talked her into sleeping some as she sat up all night with you. I offered to stay home also. I wanted to help you but also with the heat and the coming baby, it's getting harder to sit through services. So you gave me a good reason to stay home." She smiled at him as if he had actually done something for her.

"Whose room is this?" He looked around at the light and airy room with the furniture that looked to have been made by Jacob. He would recognize his workmanship anywhere. On the windows were light yellow curtains of some sort of flimsy material. The slight breeze was blowing the curtains and causing the light and shadow effect on the wall. On the small table by the bed was a large oil lamp with a glass shade and on the dresser was a bowl and pitcher set. It was without a doubt the nicest room he had ever slept in.

Emily looked around the bedroom. "It's the guest bedroom and for now it's your room. Until you get well, you'll stay right here."

"Thank you, but I need....work. Jeremiah expects me to work." Without thinking, he made an effort to sit up, but the sudden spasm of raw pain forced out a moan.

"Lay still, Thomas. You aren't going back to work for some time, and Jeremiah is fine with that." She gently pushed him back on the pillow with a hand on his forehead. Then she smoothed back his hair from his face. "If I heated some broth do you think you could eat a little?"

"I can try." He didn't want to eat or even move again. That pain had been bad and was still bad.

Emily left the room and he tried to think. Who had beaten him up and why? More than that, why couldn't he remember? He squeezed his eyes shut. Trying to think only made his head hurt worse than ever.

Emily was back with a cup and spoon. "I only brought you a little. We'll start out slow on any food." She sat the cup on the table and picked up another pillow. She slid it gently under his head.

He tried to not show the pain it caused but wasn't successful.

"I'm sorry, Thomas. Let me help you eat a little then I'll give you something for the pain." She lifted a spoonful of beef broth to his lips and he swallowed it. After only a few more spoonfuls, he had had enough.

"Thanks...all I can do."

"You did well. Now swallow this medicine and I warn you, it's bitter." She held the spoon to his mouth and he tried to swallow the bitter stuff.

He gagged, coughed, and ended with a moan, as he felt like he was being stabbed in his chest.

"Here, drink some water to get the taste out of your mouth." Emily had the cup against his lips and he managed a gulp.

Trying not to breathe too deep, he lay in misery.

Emily laid a damp cloth on his forehead, then wiped his face trying to avoid the bruises and cuts. He could feel the sweat all over his body. He didn't know if it was that hot or if it was a reaction to the beating. Slowly he sensed the pain diminishing. Thomas embraced it with relief as sleep overtook him.

~

He heard a humming that reminded him of Ma. As he opened his eyes, he saw it was her.

"Mama." He hadn't called her that since he was a little boy.

"Yes, Thomas. I'm here" She leaned over and kissed him lightly on the forehead. Her kind face had deep lines of worry. He was always getting into something that caused his folks pain.

"I'm sorry, Mama." He wanted the worry lines on his mother's face to go away. His guilt was already too heavy for what he had done to them.

"Shush, my son. You're here and that's all that matters." She sat and rubbed his arm.

He lay there with his eyes closed and yearned for healing. As whatever the medicine was that Emily had given him wore off, the pain returned.

He heard his mother soft voice say, "Come on in,. honey. Here, sit in this chair. If you don't mind I'll go and get a cup of tea since you're here."

Thomas had intended to open his eyes to see who was there, but he drifted a while. He came abruptly back into focus as he started to cough and the knife of pain in his chest tore at him. The deep groan escaped before he could stop it.

"Oh, Thomas. What can I do to help?" Catherine's voice? What was she doing here?

He opened his eyes and looked into her lovely blue eyes filled with tears of concern. He lifted his hand and stroked her face. "Catherine, why are you crying?" He intertwined his fingers into her hair that cascaded down to tickle his bare chest.

"Because I can't help you stop hurting." She sniffled and gulped down her tears.

"Just looking at your beautiful face is a help." He started to cough again and had to take his hand away from her hair to try to hold his ribs together. "Some water." He managed to choke out.

"Here." Catherine slid her hand under his head and placed the cup to his lips.

He swallowed some water and the coughing stopped. "How long have you been here?"

"I came back with your father from church, about two hours ago. I've been here every day, but you were always sleeping."

"Thanks for coming. Do you know what happened to me? I can't remember."

She sat the cup down and held his hand. "I only know that you left the café and about two minutes later I heard Jacob yell for help. You lay in the dirt in the alley by my café all beat up. I feared you would die." She looked as if she were about to cry again.

"It may take a little doing to get back on my feet, but I think I'll live. I'm too ornery to die on you."

"Well, if being ornery is what it takes to get better, then you be as ornery as you want." She laid her hand on his cheek and gently stroked it.

Pa and Jeremiah walked into the room and stood by the other side of the bed.

"How are you feeling Thomas?" Jeremiah asked.

"Like one of the stallions rolled on me." It was the best way he could explain it.

"Ouch." Jeremiah smiled. "That you're feeling anything encourages me you're getting better."

Pa reached over and took Thomas' hand. "For a couple of days we weren't sure whether you would make it or not. Do you remember anything about who beat you up?"

"I remember being in the café with Catherine." He looked into her blue eyes. "Then I woke up here. I don't remember anything in between."

"If you do remember anything be sure and tell us. We need to find the three men that did this to you. Jacob saw them running away but couldn't recognize them." Pa's voice sounded stern. Thomas had never thought of his father being a man of violence, but he saw at that moment that if he had the men in front of him who had attacked his son, he would do violence.

"I will, Pa. But I don't even remember for sure there were three of them." He felt better knowing he was jumped by three men instead of one. If he couldn't hold his own against one, he was really in trouble.

However, to hold out against three men when they have the element of surprise would be hard for anyone. How did he know they had surprised him?

"I have to get back to the store tonight. Your mother will stay a few more days to help Emily care for you. We just want you to get well."

Suddenly Thomas started to cough again and couldn't keep from groaning. All he could do was hold his ribs and try to hang on until the pain subsided. As the coughing died down, he opened his eyes to see almost a look of horror on both Jeremiah and Pa's faces.

Thomas smiled weakly and whispered, "I really will survive this, I promise."

Emily came into the room carrying a little brown bottle and a cup. Jeremiah took one look at it and turned white.

"Emily, do you have to give him that stuff?" Jeremiah groaned.

"Don't worry, Jeremiah. We'll use it only until the worst of the pain is over."

"It goes down better mixed in a cup of hot tea." Jeremiah rubbed his face.

"That's what I thought. I forgot earlier and gave it to Thomas straight. I thought he was going to throw it back up at me." Emily smiled at Thomas.

She wasn't far wrong. He started to say something but instead started coughing. This time it was bad. He hated that everyone was seeing him so out of control, but he couldn't stop the groans of pain. It was all he could do to keep from screaming at the knife slicing through his chest. When the spasm of coughing finally stopped, he lay there spent and gasping for breath.

"Here Thomas, drink this." Catherine had the cup of tea against his lips and he swallowed it as quickly as he could. It was bitter but nothing like the raw medicine. Catherine stroked the hair back from his forehead, and he lay with his eyes closed enjoying the feel of it. In a very short time, he felt the pain free sleep descending.

He heard Jeremiah say, "He's relaxing. The drug is taking hold. He'll sleep for hours now."

As Thomas let himself fall into the black hole of pain free sleep, he wondered how Jeremiah knew that.

~

The next three weeks passed slowly and painfully. Gradually Thomas could get up and sit in a chair for a short time. The doctor came out every couple of days. He told Thomas he figured he had at least six cracked ribs, a concussion, and a broken collarbone. Thomas was thankful none were broken so badly that a lung had been punctured as he didn't cough up any blood. The dizziness and pain from the concussion was still there but was less each day. His head hurt constantly and each breath brought pain from the ribs. The rest of his body just ached.

After the second week, Ma went back into town. She worried about Pa taking care of himself.

Catherine came out when she could after the work at the café.

Thomas stopped taking the medicine after the second week. There was still pain but nothing as bad as the first couple of weeks and he was tired of the foggy state of his mind while taking the medicine.

Sheriff Grant came and asked him questions, which he couldn't answer. Thomas still had no memory of the attack. From the sheriff's questions, Thomas sensed that the sheriff thought he had caused the attack.

The fourth week after the attack, Thomas moved back into the bunkroom. Cal didn't say much but Harlan and Barney kept saying things to indicate that they weren't surprised he got beat up, as he was so weak anyway. Keeping his mouth shut and not answering back took some doing. Thomas had sense enough to know it wouldn't help.

He still couldn't lift much or do a full days' work so Jacob asked him to work some with him. Thomas didn't mind at all. Jacob was a patient, good teacher. By the end of a week, Thomas couldn't believe all that he learned about designing and making furniture. For some reason he kept envisioning furniture he would like to make for Catherine.

"Jacob, what do you do with the wood in the scrap barrel?"

"I use for firewood in winter. Why are you asking?" Jacob came over and looked in the scrap barrel.

"Do you think I could make a little box out of some of it?" Thomas couldn't buy Catherine anything as he didn't have any money, but maybe he could make something.

"Show me what you make." Jacob moved over to the counter and found a clean piece of paper and a pencil.

Thomas took the pencil and thought a minute before he drew a design. "That's what I would like to make."

Jacob examined the design, then nodded his head. "*Ja,* that will work." He placed the design back on the counter and went back to the scrap barrel. "What do you think? Cherry wood?"

"That would make a nice look. Is there enough left?" They began to search through the barrel and soon had a nice stack of various sizes of cherry wood.

Jacob looked at the wood pieces and examined the design again. "This should be enough but will need to be careful with cutting. You mark wood and show where to cut."

He grinned at Jacob. "You think I can do that? You got more belief in my abilities than I do, but I'll try." He spent the next hour carefully measuring the wood and marking with the pencil. When he had all the pieces marked he ambled over to where Jacob sat in his easy chair reading the newspaper.

"You ready to cut?" Jacob put the paper down. "I will peddle and you guide wood."

It took two hours to cut the little pieces out of the scraps of wood. Then Jacob showed him how to use elastic cement to hold the pieces together. Thomas set it aside to work on the next day, as he needed to give the elastic cement time to dry.

The next day, in between helping Jacob with his projects, Thomas varnished the little box. After dinner, he asked Emily if he could speak to her.

"Of course, what can I do for you?" She sat at the kitchen table rubbing her stomach that seemed bigger every time Thomas saw her. Her baby had to be coming soon. She was so big.

"I'm making a little keepsake box for Catherine. I wondered if you might have a small scrap of cloth that would look all right to line the bottom." He kept his voice steady, but he could feel the heat of a blush rising.

"May I see the box?" Emily leaned forward and her face brightened with interest.

"Sure, if you don't mind coming out to the workshop. I just put another coat of varnish on it. I can't touch it for several hours."

Emily, with an effort, got to her feet. They walked slowly out to the back of the barn and entered the workroom.

"Miss Emily, you visit workshop." Jacob's round face was a light from his wide smile.

"Yes, Jacob, I wanted to see the box Thomas is making."

"Here is box but do not touch. Is wet from varnish. Thomas, he is good at working with his hands. He makes a fine worker of wood." Jacob pointed out the little box sitting on a rag on the counter. Thomas had to admit it was a pretty, little thing, especially since Jacob had carved flowers on the sides and top for him.

"Oh Thomas, it's lovely. Catherine is sure to like it." Emily walked around the counter and looked at the keepsake box from all directions. "Maybe you could make me one someday."

He smiled and nodded. Jacob and he were already working on some things for the new baby.

"Let me go back to the house and look through my stacks of fabrics. I'm sure I have something that'll work."

Emily came back a little later with a piece of red velvet cloth.

Cutting carefully and using the elastic cement to fix it in the bottom, the box began to take on a look of elegance. As Thomas looked at the little box, he envisioned Catherine using it for her keepsakes.

~

August was a hot month of work and Thomas constantly checked the sky for clouds. The land needed rain and nerves became more and more frayed, as the heat was oppressive. He made use of the creek both morning and evening to get the sweat off and to feel cool if only for a few minutes.

All of the mares had foaled and been covered by a stallion. There would be another crop of foals next year. The horses were out in the pastures unless hurt or ill. It made for less work if they could keep the horse barn as empty as possible. Finally, toward the end of the month they had several thundershowers come through giving the earth much needed relief. It helped his nerves for the heat to lessen, also.

His body was much stronger, but he still could not remember the attack.

Thomas looked forward to September, as Emily's baby was due. Toward the end of the month, the horse herd from the mountain ranch would arrive, and he would meet the men who worked on that ranch.

Catherine's birthday was the last Sunday in August and she and his folks were coming out to the ranch. Thomas rose early to help with the work in the barn and went down to the creek to bathe. He dressed in clean clothes that were frayed. As he only had three sets of pants and shirts and one pair of boots, the four months at the ranch had been hard on them. He didn't want to ask his folks for more, but he would have to by winter. To do his work he would have to have a winter coat for sure.

When he went to breakfast, he carried the little box wrapped in brown paper and tied with some string. With the breakfast dishes cleared away, Sally set the table for dinner. Thomas placed his gift for Catherine at the place she normally sat. Before they left for the drive into town for the church service, there were several other packages sitting alongside Thomas' gift.

Elisha and Joseph were excited on the ride into town because they were having a birthday dinner for Catherine. They kept asking him what he had as a gift for her. He told them ridiculous things that had them laughing.

He went into the church building behind Jeremiah and family and sat at his usual place next to his parents. Just as services began, Catherine hurried in and slid into the pew next to him. Thomas relaxed, feeling all was well, now Catherine was there.

In the sermon, the preacher spoke of the names and descriptions for God. Thomas had read the scriptures but he never thought of God having several names. Then the preacher showed how each of the names for God in the Old Testament was also a name or description for the Christ. By the end of the sermon, Thomas had more questions than answers. One day he wanted to sit down with the preacher and ask all the questions he was collecting.

Thomas was ready for the service to be done. He was hot, hungry, and ready to get back to the ranch.

James Guinn, the preacher, stood up at the pulpit again. "I want to announce a church fellowship for next Saturday afternoon out at Jeremiah and Emily's place. Everyone is invited. Now this is a special fellowship for raising money for a new roof for the church building. We're having a box supper social, and will auction off all the ladies' box suppers." He stopped and beamed at the congregation. "I know we have some mighty fine cooks out there. You men get ready to bid. And by the way, Emily has offered to feed all the youngsters so the box supper will only be for us grown-ups."

Thomas wanted to glance at Catherine to see what she thought of a box supper. It didn't sound like anything he would enjoy and mainly because he had no money, and no way of getting any. As the preacher dismissed the congregation there was a buzz of talk. Thomas left Catherine talking to some ladies and made his way to the buggy. He waited longer than usual for Jeremiah and Emily to come with the twins, as it seemed everyone wanted to say something to them.

Finally, they were headed to the ranch.

"Oh Jeremiah, I'm so glad we offered to have the box supper at our place. Everyone is excited about it." Emily spoke with excited animation.

Seated between the twins in the back seat of the buggy, Thomas wanted to raise his hand and offer that he wasn't excited about it, but wisely kept his mouth shut.

"Now I'm going to need help getting ready. Thomas, you mind helping this week?" She turned to him from where she sat in the front seat of the buggy next to Jeremiah.

"Glad to do anything I can to help. But, what needs doing for a social?"

"That's a good question. Could you and Jacob make me some rough tables and benches? And some taller tables to serve the food and drinks from would help. Then we need to have it organized to take care of the horses when people arrive. Maybe Bob will do that. I better start a list when I get to the house."

Thomas realized she was no longer talking to him, but thinking aloud. Jacob and he could handle making tables and benches and gladly because it would keep them out of Emily's way. He sensed that the coming week was going to be busy.

The gathering at the Sunday dinner table was festive with the twins trying to get Catherine to tell them how old she was. Thomas was curious himself, but he wasn't about to ask.

She finally gave in and whispered loudly to the twins. "I'm twenty-one years old today."

Elisha looked at Joseph. "That's almost old but not as old as Mama."

Joseph nodded wisely. "And Papa is much older than Mama so he is way older than you Catherine."

Everyone started laughing and Emily punched Jeremiah's arm. "How does it feel to be an old man?"

Jeremiah looked puzzled for a moment and then smiled. "Not bad really especially since I have you as my old lady."

Thomas grinned at their teasing. Catherine was smiling and looking as happy as he had ever seen her. Anything that made her smile was a good thing.

Mildred and Sally had prepared all of Catherine's favorites. They had fried chicken, mashed potatoes, green beans, fried okra, sliced tomatoes, and tea with ice. Where they had gotten the ice, Thomas didn't know for sure. He assumed that Jeremiah had it delivered from town where it came in on the train. Thomas did know where the fresh vegetables had come from as he helped to tend the garden. He mostly helped carry water in the evenings during the dry spell. Harlan and Barney also helped to keep the big garden watered and complained about it when they were back in the bunkroom. Thomas noticed they ate their share of the produce. Cal also helped with the work, but he didn't complain like the other two.

Catherine seemed touched by the attention at lunch. Thomas hadn't heard her mention any family now that her mother had died. He guessed his folks, Jeremiah, and Emily were her family now.

When she opened her presents, she had tears in her eyes even when she was talking and laughing. Jeremiah and Emily gave her fabric for a couple of dresses. Bob and Jacob gave her a frame for hanging a quilt. His folks gave her squares of fabric to make a quilt. Mildred and Sally gave her a book containing their best recipes. The twins gave her a game, *Across the Continent.*

And she opened his gift last. By the time she got to it, he was sweating. It had been a dumb idea, and he was sure she wouldn't like it.

She smiled her brilliant smile and looked over at him. "Oh Thomas, this is lovely. I've never had a keepsake box before. Thank you, thank you all. This has been a wonderful birthday." Catherine wiped a couple of tears away.

One of the twins said, "Can we play the game?"

"Now Elisha, that's Catherine's gift. She gets to decide when the game gets played." Emily patted one of the twins on the head. Thomas assumed that was Elisha.

Catherine took pity on the little boy. "We can play later this afternoon, if you want to."

"That'll be fun." The other twin responded.

Jeremiah shifted in his seat and leaned forward. "Why don't you boys go play for a while and let us adults allow our dinner to settle."

The two boys jumped down from their chairs and ran out the back door.

Catherine talked with Emily about what style of dress pattern would go best with each piece of fabric.

Thomas leaned back in his chair and watched her, satisfied that his gift had made Catherine happy.

Chapter Fifteen Catherine

After dinner Emily, Catherine, and his mother sat at the kitchen table and started planning what needed to be done for the social.

As Thomas sat and listened, he began to understand that it was a grand occasion, especially for the women. There would be as many as a hundred people coming to the ranch. Cowhands from the ranches as far as fifty miles away would come for the chance of bidding on a pretty girl's box supper. The idea of some other fellow bidding on Catherine's box supper, then spending the rest of the evening with her was enough to depress Thomas. But, he couldn't see any way to get the money to bid. He would try to borrow it, but that wasn't something he would do when he had no way to pay it back.

Toward the middle of the afternoon, Catherine and he slowly ambled down to the creek. The twins had already jumped into the water. Catherine sat on a stump while he sat on the ground and pulled his boots and socks off. After he dangled his feet in the water and watched the boys play, she went behind some bushes and removed her shoes and stockings. He resisted turning around and watching her climb up on the log and sit down by him. It was tempting as her ankles were so enticing and the thought of the rest of her legs left him with the feeling of rising heat in his face. He hoped if she noticed she thought it was because it was a hot afternoon.

"This feels wonderful. It has been so warm all week." Catherine brushed some curls back from her face, as she splashed water with her bare feet.

"It was a hot week but not as hot as July and the first part of August. I can almost feel the autumn in the air." He was ready for some fall weather, although it was at least six weeks away.

Catherine watched as Elisha and Joseph splashed water on each other. "Next Saturday will be so much fun. What is your favorite pie?" She looked sideways at him with a smile.

"I like all kinds of pie, but if I had to choose just one it would be peach."

"Peach, I like peach also."

As they sat there splashing their feet in the cool water, Catherine kept talking about food and asking him questions of his favorites. Thomas told himself it was because she had a café and cooking was such a part of her world.

Thomas and Catherine put their shoes back on and then convinced the twins to get out of the water. They walked slowly back to the house. Catherine seemed content. Thomas was. It had been a good day.

~

The week was as busy as Thomas had thought it would be. Between the normal work of the ranch and making all the tables and benches that Emily wanted, he hardly had time to think. He and Jacob put up poles and strung rope to hang lanterns. He wondered how late the social would go. Thomas vaguely remembered going to a few with his folks when he was a child, but it had been over twenty years ago. He barely remembered them.

Harlan, Barney, and Cal all bathed on Friday evening down at the creek. They had gotten haircuts and brushed their boots off. Thomas wondered which girl's box supper they were planning to bid on.

He put on clean clothes and brushed his boots after he swam in the creek on Saturday morning. It wouldn't really do much good because by the time he helped set everything up, then helped put the visitors' horses in the corral, he would be hot and sweaty.

His folks closed the store early and arrived to help. Catherine came with them.

Thomas volunteered to take care of the horses when the guests arrived. For some reason he felt he could deal with the evening better if he didn't spend too much time with Catherine.

Families and riders started arriving by two o'clock in the afternoon. Bob and Jacob seemed to know most of the single cowhands, but Thomas didn't know any of them. Some had started out the day before in order to attend the social. By four o'clock, they had the large corral full of horses and buggies lining the lane all the way to the main road. With over a hundred people at the ranch, they had close to a hundred extra horses.

West of the house and around the old oak tree, Jacob and Thomas had placed all the tables and benches they had built through the week. Lanterns hung ready to light at dark. The porch on that side of the house was set aside for women with babies and small children. All the rest of the children ran free, playing, and hollering at the top of their lungs. The men stood or sat around talking horses, cattle, and weather. It seemed like bedlam to Thomas, but he had to admit everyone seemed happy to be together.

Jacob and Emily were in charge of auctioning off the box suppers. Emily told him that Catherine's box would be about the middle one auctioned off, and that it would have a large red and white bow on it.

They started the bidding at five o'clock.

Thomas helped Mildred and Sally serve the fried chicken, corn on the cob, and biscuits to the children. This left the parents free to enjoy the bidding. As he served the chicken and biscuits, he listened to the bidding. Jacob really knew how to do an auction and how to liven up the bidding. He poked fun, cajoled, and generally got the men to bid more than they had planned. Thomas found himself laughing along with everyone else. After they finished feeding the children, he wandered over next to some trees at the back of the crowd to watch.

Catherine's box supper came up next for bid. Thomas felt sick that he couldn't bid. It started out lively and several of the single riders tried to outbid each other. Just when it looked as if a redheaded rider from a ranch to the north was going to win, a new voice raised the bid out of his reach. Thomas saw that it was Myles McKinley. He made himself stand still and kept his fists clenched to his sides.

Thomas looked over at Catherine and she stared in his direction. He sensed that she was imploring him to bid and not understanding why he was so silent. When her boxed supper went to Myles McKinley for fifty dollars, everyone gasped as it was the highest bid for any of the boxed suppers. Catherine gave Thomas a last glance of such coldness and then turned her back.

Thomas stumbled his way down to the creek and just kept walking. What did she expect him to do? He had no money. Nobody had mentioned it. They probably had been so busy with all the preparation to even think. Or was it that he just didn't enter their consideration?

His heart thumped against his ribs and he wanted to throw up. Catherine sitting with Myles, talking and laughing as they ate the food she had prepared made him want to hit something.

How long Thomas walked he didn't know, but it had gotten dark and he made his way back to the house by moonlight. He would need to help with the horses, as people got ready to leave. When he got back to the corral, Bob was there helping hitch up some of the buggies for the families with babies and small children. From the other side of the house came the sound of hymns as the guests were enjoying a good old-fashioned songfest.

"Here, help me hitch up these horses." Bob threw the harness to Thomas. "Where you been? Jeremiah was looking for you."

"I went for a walk down by the creek. Do you know what Jeremiah wanted? Should I go look for him?" He helped back the two horses between the shafts of the buggy and they quickly had the horses hitched up.

"No, I don't think he really wanted anything except to know where you were." Bob helped the family whose buggy it was to climb in and they started down the lane.

"I didn't think about telling him." The only thing he had thought about was Catherine. Things had been going so well that he hadn't thought much about still being a prisoner. Jeremiah took it seriously. For Thomas to be gone for two or three hours without Jeremiah knowing where Thomas was, would bother him.

"Well, don't worry about it. He'll probably be coming round in a while to see someone off. You just stay here and help folks."

"Yes, sir." Fully reminded of his status at the ranch as a prisoner, he dutifully helped hitch up buggy after buggy.

Finally, his folks came around the house carrying empty dishes in wooden Arbuckle coffee crates.

"There you are, son. We missed you. Have you been taking care of the horses the whole time?" Pa sat the box he carried carefully in the floorboard of the buggy, then turned and took the box Ma carried.

"I brought enough food to share and thought, since you didn't bid on a box, you might eat with us." Ma came up, hugged him, and kissed his cheek.

Thomas hated that she had a look of concern and again he had put it there. "I took a walk down the creek, then came back, and helped hitch up the buggies."

"Are you all right, son?" Pa helped him back his horse between the shafts and hitch it up to the buggy.

"I'm fine, Pa. I'm just not used to all these people and such."

"We forget that it's been a lot of years since you had a chance to be at a social. It must seem strange with so much going on." He patted Thomas' back, which was Pa's way of showing he cared.

Their concern made him feel guilty. Would he ever be at a place in his life where he wasn't a concern for his folks? It was almost as if their goodness left him feeling sad, as he couldn't live up to it.

As he stood watching them drive down the lane toward the main road, Jeremiah came up to him and put his hand on Thomas' shoulder.

"Thomas, where did you get to this evening? I looked for you but you weren't anywhere to be found."

Thomas turned so he could see Jeremiah's face to try to gage his thoughts. "I took a long walk down the creek, then helped hitch up for folks. I should have told you before I took off, but I didn't think about it."

"Why didn't you at least try to bid on Catherine's box supper?" Jeremiah always said what he thought.

Usually Thomas appreciated his forthrightness, but he was embarrassed to confess why he hadn't bid. He would be thirty his next birthday, but he didn't even have enough money to bid on a box supper. But this was Jeremiah and Thomas owed him an explanation.

Thomas ducked his head, kicked a small rock out of the way, then looked Jeremiah in the eye. "I wanted to bid on Catherine's box in the worst way. But, to do that I had to have money and I don't have any. I couldn't stand to watch her and Myles sitting together, so I took off walking."

Jeremiah didn't look angry, but thoughtful. "I never thought about it, but I suppose you don't have any money. The judge told me I had to have you work for free. He said I wasn't allowed to pay you. I gave my word." He almost looked embarrassed himself.

"I understand. Just being able to work here and not be at Yuma is plenty of pay. I got a place to sleep and good food. I'm grateful to you for getting me out of that place."

"Was Yuma that bad?" He seemed to want to know. "You don't have to talk about it if you don't want to."

Thomas didn't want to talk about it. Those twelve years in Yuma were something he just wanted to forget, but he couldn't. "Yes, sir. It was bad. I know I deserved it. I was a rustler and am grateful I wasn't hanged. But as a kid, it was bad and never got any better."

"You mind telling me what made it so bad?" Jeremiah's voice was quiet.

Thomas thought for a moment. What had made it so bad? He looked out past the barn into the darkness. "Of course, not having freedom, no choices, I had to do what was ordered. Being chained at times in a small cell with six to ten other men was hard to take. The smells, dirt, bad food, monotony, the beatings, having always to be ready to fight to survive, all made it bad. The worst was knowing I done it to myself and deserved what I got. Knowing what I had done to my folks and that I lost twelve years out of my life, maybe some of my best years. It was all bad." He had never said those things to anyone before.

Jeremiah stood staring out into the darkness. For a moment, Thomas thought maybe he had forgotten he was there. "How old were you when you went to jail?" he asked.

"I had just turned seventeen. I thought I was a grown man but it took only one night in jail for me to know different." He remembered the hours in the dark listening to men groan, cry out, and snore. He had been afraid to sleep because of the nightmares and afraid to be awake because of his fear until he finally cried himself to sleep. Yes, it had been a bad time, and as he remembered back on it, he didn't want to return to Yuma Prison.

Jeremiah turned and looked at him for a moment. "I understand. It's not easy to talk about. If taking long walks helps you to deal with the memories then you take them. If you're going to be gone more than an hour, I'd appreciate it if you would tell someone." He yawned and rubbed his eyes. "It's getting late. Go on to bed. Tomorrow we get to worship God. He's the one that'll help us deal with all of this."

It was a long conversation for Jeremiah. And, what was strange to Thomas was that he did seem to understand. But, how could he? How could anyone who had not been in prison? After Thomas crawled into his bunk, it took a long time to finally fall asleep. The talk with Jeremiah had stirred up too many memories. And, how was God supposed to help him deal with all of it?

The next morning he felt good when he went into the kitchen for breakfast. He had helped muck out the horse barn, then bathed in the creek, and put on clean jeans and shirt. Now he was ready to eat a good meal before the ride into town for the church service.

Catherine had slept over, as it was so late when the women had gotten all the dishes washed up after the last family had left the social. She was at her usual place at the table with everyone else when Bob and Thomas arrived together for breakfast.

As he walked toward the table, she looked up at him with a cold glare. Thomas almost stumbled he was so surprised. After Bob and Thomas sat down, Jeremiah immediately gave the blessing for the food.

During the prayer, Thomas glanced over at Catherine. Was she mad at him for not bidding on her box supper? The rest of the meal was quiet, as no one seemed inclined to talk. He wanted to say something to Catherine, but he was all tongue-tied. What could he say to her?

When they climbed into the buggy for the ride to church services, Jeremiah asked Elisha and Thomas to sit in the front seat with him. Emily and Catherine sat in the back seat with Joseph sitting between them. The twins kept up a lively chatter back and forth on the drive to the church building.

Thomas sat there conscious that this morning Catherine had not spoken to him at all.

The church building was filling up by the time they arrived. Thomas let Catherine take the lead and she sat in her usual place on the pew with his folks. He stepped carefully across her and sat by Ma. There was a good foot and half of empty pew between Catherine and him.

He was sure James Guinn preached a good lesson, but he didn't hear it. All he could think about was how to make peace with Catherine. The church service wasn't the place to try to talk with her. After dinner would have to be the time when they walked down to the creek, he just hoped she would go with him.

When services were over he halfway expected her to stay in town, but she came out of the church building and made her way to his parents' buggy. He saw Myles McKinley make his way over to talk to her. Whatever he said to her wasn't something she wanted to hear. After shaking her head "No" several times, she climbed into the buggy and sat next to Ma.

Harlan, Barney, and Cal stayed in town. They had the afternoon off because of having worked late the evening before.

The twins were quieter than usual on the ride back to the ranch. Thomas was just as glad because he wasn't in a mood to respond to them. Maybe they were all tired from the activities the evening before. Even Jeremiah and Emily were quiet.

When they got to the ranch, Bob met them. "One of the mares is down and in a bad way. I think it's colic."

"Thomas, you take care of the buggy and horses, then come on up to the horse barn. It may take all three of us to keep her on her feet. Emily, you all go ahead and eat. We'll eat when we can."

Thomas put the buggy away and let the horses loose in the pasture behind the barn. By the time he had that done, Pa had his team unhitched. Thomas helped him put the two horses in the corral with some fresh hay.

"Will it be all right if I watch you all work with the mare?" Pa asked.

"Sure, Pa, Jeremiah won't mind, but you better be ready to pitch in and help. It can get messy."

"Don't you worry about me, son. I've done my share of messy jobs before."

They walked to the horse barn together. When they got there, they saw a brown mare laying on her side rolling back and forth.

Bob had hold of the halter and encouraged the horse to get up.

The horse finally stood, then tried to nip at her flanks, a sure sign of pain in her abdomen.

Jeremiah stood watching. "She has colic, but whether there is something we can do to help or not only time will tell. She's only six years old and I'd like to save her if possible."

"What can you do?" Pa asked.

"We can walk her, get her to drink water, and put oil in the rectum. Let's start by walking her for fifteen to twenty minutes every hour." Jeremiah walked up to the mare making cooing sounds, then gently stroking her neck. He put his ear against her belly and listened. Straightening up he patted her rump. "The belly sounds are too quiet."

Jeremiah took the halter from Bob and handed it to Thomas. "Walk her for the next twenty minutes, then bring her some water. I'll go get some oil warmed up and get my long gloves. Bob, you can walk her the next hour. For now you and Milburn might as well go eat."

Thomas took the halter and led the mare out of the barn and into the back pasture. She followed him without any problem. The mare's big brown eyes seemed to look at him with trust that he could do something to help relieve her pain. He hated the thought that they might not be able to do anything for her.

After a while, Jeremiah returned with the warm oil. Thomas walked the mare into the shade of the barn and held the mare quiet so Jeremiah could administer it. Then they let the mare rest for half an hour. She drank about half a bucket of water.

By the time Bob and Pa returned from eating dinner, Thomas was again leading the mare around the pasture with Jeremiah watching from the shade of the horse barn. It was hot out in the sun and Thomas sweated, but he didn't care. He wanted to help the mare.

As he led the horse back to the barn for more water, she started dropping large piles of manure.

"Don't stop, keep walking her for another ten minutes," Jeremiah said, "I think maybe she's going to be all right."

Thomas led her back around the pasture for another round of walking. The mare lifted her head and seemed to perk up. She followed him into the barn and drank the rest of the water from the bucket. She was no longer trying to nip at her flanks nor did she seem to want to lie down.

Jeremiah rubbed the mare's head between her eyes. "Yes, sir, I think she's going to be all right. But, we need to keep walking her for fifteen minutes every hour for about the next six hours. Also, let's not let her eat for several hours and then only a small amount, but keep her drinking water."

Bob took the halter rope from his hand. "Thomas and I can take turns walking her. I'll watch her for the next couple of hours. You and Thomas go eat some dinner."

"I'll go eat and then come right back to help," Thomas said.

"No, don't hurry. You can take over later this afternoon." Bob pulled up a stool and sat down to watch the mare.

Jeremiah, Pa, and Thomas walked back to the house. It was close to three o'clock and he was hungry. In addition, he was also hot, sweaty, and smelled like horses.

After washing up they entered the kitchen where they found Mildred seated at the table snapping beans. "Your food is in the warmer." She pointed with a string bean over toward the stove.

Jeremiah went over to the stove and opened the warmer. He took out two plates of fried chicken, potatoes, carrots, and gravy and set them on the table. There was a plate of biscuits and a pitcher of tea on the table already.

It didn't take Thomas long to dig into the food after Jeremiah had said a blessing. Jeremiah wasn't inclined to talk and neither was Thomas.

Pa took a glass from the cabinet and poured a glass of tea. He had eaten earlier.

Mildred got up and put a pan of blackberry cobbler on the table. Most of the pan was empty but there was enough for Jeremiah and Thomas to each have a good-sized helping.

"Emily went to lie down and so did Agnes." Mildred sat at the table and returned to snapping the beans. "I think Catherine is on the front porch reading a book."

Jeremiah licked the last of the cobbler off his spoon. "Where are the boys?"

Mildred smiled. "Jacob has them out at the workshop making something or other."

Jeremiah pushed back from the table and stood up. "I'm going to check on Emily. Why don't you go keep Catherine company and rest for an hour before going back to the horse barn?"

Thomas nodded although he wasn't sure she wanted him to keep her company.

"Well, I'm going to go find Agnes and maybe take a nap myself." Pa rose from the table, then he and Jeremiah left the kitchen.

Wishing he wasn't so sweaty, Thomas made his way to the front porch.

Catherine looked up from her book. "How is the horse?"

Sitting down in a rocking chair downwind from her, he relaxed his legs. "The mare is doing much better. If we can get past the next day or so with no more problems, she ought to be all right."

"I'm glad." She went back to reading her book.

"Catherine." She was avoiding him, but he wanted to smooth things out.

She looked up at him without a word.

"Are you mad at me?" He might as well get it into the open.

"Why should I be mad at you?" She wasn't going to make it easy.

"I didn't bid on your box supper. I thought maybe you were mad at me."

In a voice he could only call cold she said, "It makes no difference whether you bid on my box supper or not. You were under no obligation."

"I wanted to bid on it. I couldn't." For some reason he didn't want to admit he hadn't bid because he was broke.

"That was your decision and it doesn't matter." She closed her book and stood. "I need to check on Emily, she's not feeling well."

He watched her go into the house without looking back. For someone who had such few friends, it hurt to lose one. And that's what he felt, like he had lost Catherine as a friend. As he looked down the lane at the heat waves shimmering in the summer afternoon, he felt a cold emptiness.

Chapter Sixteen Thomas

After Catherine and his folks left for town after supper, restlessness was upon him. He asked Jeremiah if he could take a horse and ride for a while. Jeremiah looked at him with a searching glance, then nodded. Thomas hadn't asked before for the privilege of riding out alone.

He saddled a mare out of the corral and rode toward the ridge. With two hours left before sundown, he guided the mare up the trail to the top of the ridge. He dismounted, tied the reins where the horse could reach the grass. There were several large boulders and he chose one to sit on and looked out over the rolling hills. It was a beautiful view that should have soothed him, but he was anything but calm.

Had he lost any chance with Catherine? Had he ever had a chance? He had been foolish to let his feelings get ahead of his reality. What did he have to offer anyone much less someone as wonderful as Catherine? He had nothing. Even though he had been at the Rocking JR for almost six months, he was still a prisoner for the next two and half years. Then what would he do, work as a cowhand? That wouldn't give him much to offer a woman. Perhaps it was just as well that Catherine had let him know he had no chance. At least now he knew how it was going to be. His life stretched out before him and he saw himself alone.

Sighing he mounted the mare and started back. He didn't want to worry Jeremiah by being gone too long. And he didn't want to do anything to cause more pain for Pa and Ma. He owed them too much. As he rode back to the barn, he made a decision. If he couldn't have Catherine, then he would at least try to do something good for his folks.

When Thomas arrived at the house, he went through the kitchen and into the front room. He hoped that Jeremiah would still be up so he could let him know he was back. A couple of lamps still gave light to the front room, but it was empty. Thomas stood in the middle of the room not sure what to do. Shrugging his shoulders, he walked to Jeremiah and Emily's bedroom door and tapped lightly. He stepped back from the door and waited with his hat in his hands.

Jeremiah opened the bedroom door. "Yes, Thomas?"

"I wanted to let you know I was back. I'm heading to bed now." He felt like a kid standing there reporting to a parent.

"Thanks for letting me know. I appreciate it." Jeremiah started closing the door.

"Good night, sir."

"Good night." He closed the door.

Thomas headed to the bunkroom. He was relieved that he had done the right thing in letting Jeremiah know he was back. Nevertheless, he couldn't help longing for the day when he could come and go as he liked.

The next morning they started to work on a long list of chores Jeremiah had drawn up. The horse herd from the mountain ranch of Elisha Evans was due within the next two weeks. Thomas had learned that Jeremiah, Elisha Evans, and Joe Weathers had a partnership. They bred horses for the army. During the summer, except for the breeding mares, the horses went to the mountain ranch of Elisha Evans where Joe Weathers was responsible for breaking as many of them as he could for riding. Then toward the end of September, they brought the horse herd back down to the Rocking JR for the winter months. Through the winter, Jeremiah broke the rest of the horses and rode the ones that Joe had broken to keep them used to the saddle.

Jeremiah had worked for Elisha for four years before he came to Cedar Ridge and bought the Rocking JR. He had been at the ranch two years when he met Emily at church.

One of the chores Jeremiah wanted completed before the horse herd arrived was a section of rail fencing. He assigned Cal, Jacob, and Thomas to work on it together so they could get it done quicker.

Cal didn't seem to mind working with them and it gave Thomas a chance to get to know him without the presence of Harlan and Barney.

They first had to drive the wagon into the hills west of the ranch house to cut trees to make the fence poles. Fortunately, for Cal and Thomas, Jacob knew which trees to cut. He also knew how to trim the trees into logs for the fencing. Jeremiah wouldn't use barbed wire, as he feared the horses would get cut. It was more work, but he wanted only rail fencing. Thomas had to admit that he liked the look of it much better than the barbed wire fencing.

Mildred prepared a lunch for them to take along, and they took a small keg of water. Each morning they started from the ranch house at first light and didn't return until just before dark. They spent five days chopping down trees, cutting them into the right lengths, and splitting the logs. The work reminded Thomas too much of how hard he had worked at the prison. Preparing to build the fence helped make the work with the horses seem easy. On Saturday, they took the cut logs and dropped them off along the line the fence would take. By the time they got back to the ranch house, Thomas was as tired as he had ever been.

After eating supper, he headed down to the creek to swim. When he got back to the bunkhouse, he barely noticed Harlan and Barney playing cards. Thomas did notice that Cal was already in his bunk sound asleep. When he stretched out on his bunk it only took a couple of minutes for him to drop off into a dark pool of sound sleep. He woke briefly as heavy thunderstorms rolled through the countryside. Since Bob didn't roust him out to go check on the cattle and horses, he dropped back off to sleep.

Sunday morning was clear and cool. As Thomas walked up to the horse barn at first light to help with the mucking out, he looked out over trees and grass glistening with rain drops left over from showers that had passed through during the night. Yesterday had been hot summertime, and this morning was the coolness of autumn. He breathed deeply of the clean fresh smelling air. It was the first fall in over twelve years that he was free to enjoy being out among the fall foliage.

But he didn't feel like enjoying it. He kept seeing Catherine's cold glare when he hadn't bid on her box supper. In a few hours, he'd be sitting at the church service next to her. But if it was like last Sunday, she would be far from him. He needed to get himself to a point where he didn't care. That would be best, but he wasn't there yet. He did care.

As he entered the horse barn, he saw that Bob was there ahead of him.

"Hey, I didn't expect you this morning. I figured you'd sleep in after a week of cutting down trees. You boys must have really been working to get all the fence posts and rails done." Bob leaned on the pitchfork.

Thomas took a pitchfork off the wall by the door. "I'm too used to waking at daylight. Which stalls need done?"

"We only have six to muck out. You take those three and we'll get done quick." Bob started to fill the wheelbarrow with the dirty straw and muck from the stall where a sick mare stood with head drooping.

Thomas began with a stall where a small weanling foal with a swollen tendon in its foreleg stood watching him. The foal kept nuzzling his hand. He guessed that someone had been feeding the foal sugar lumps. He didn't have any to give but that didn't stop it from trying to find one.

"Sorry little fellow. I can't help you today. Maybe this afternoon I'll come back with some sugar." He spread fresh hay out in the stall, rubbed the foal's neck, then closed the door to the stall as he moved on to the next one.

Bob and Thomas strolled back to the house together when they finished in the horse barn.

Mildred and Sally arranged the big platters of fried eggs, ham, fried potatoes, gravy, and biscuits on the table.

"Go ahead and help yourself boys. Sally, please go ring the bell for breakfast." Mildred poured two cups of coffee and handed them to the two men.

"Thanks Miss Mildred. This looks great as always." Thomas filled his plate until it would not hold any more. He thought of the men still at Yuma Prison having a bowl of lukewarm watery mush and a rock hard biscuit with weevils. To spend the last three years of his prison sentence at the Rocking JR was a blessing. No matter how impatient he felt, he was determined not to mess it up.

Emily wasn't feeling well enough to go to church services. Jeremiah decided that he would take the boys anyway. He asked Mildred if she and Sally would mind staying with Emily. Her time of birthing was any day and Thomas sensed a worry on the part of Jeremiah.

"Thomas, we won't take the buggy this morning. If you don't mind, we'll each ride a horse with one of the twins riding with us."

"I don't mind at all. But, you sure Elisha and Joseph can sit the saddle well enough not to fall off?" They could but he was sure to get a rise out of them.

"Of course we can." "You know we can." Both boys spoke at once and then they realized he was teasing as all the adults were grinning at them.

"You're just teasing us, Thomas," Elisha said, "You know we can ride a saddle."

"Yeah, Thomas. We can ride a saddle." Joseph turned to his father. "Pa, why can't we ride a pony by ourselves?"

"If it were here on the ranch, I'd let you, but not riding into town. Go on, wash up, and comb your hair. Then don't forget to say good-bye to your mother."

Thomas went to the barn and saddled Jeremiah's gray gelding and the brown mare for himself. The ride into town with the small boy seated in front of him in the saddle was fun as the two boys asked questions non-stop. It amazed him how patient Jeremiah was with the boys. He never seemed to get tired of their questions.

Again, Catherine sat in the pew with a distance between them. He held the songbook for her, but she didn't acknowledge him except for a small nod. Ma kept patting his arm as if she were trying to make up for Catherine's coldness.

During the prayers, everyone included a prayer for Emily and the coming birth of the baby. Thomas wondered if that was normal or if there was something specifically wrong.

It wasn't helping his attention to James Guinn's sermon to be sitting on the pew next to Catherine, but not really sitting with her. As soon as services were over, he made his way out to the horses. By the time Jeremiah came out of the building with the twins, Thomas had the cinches tightened on both horses.

Dinner was a subdued affair because of everyone's concern for Emily. Even the twins were quiet. Thomas noticed that Jeremiah hardly ate anything.

Catherine had stayed with Emily in her bedroom and wasn't at the table.

Bob and the three cowhands left soon after lunch to ride out to the cattle herd. They would camp out and start gathering the cattle for the fall round-up.

Jeremiah wanted Jacob and Thomas to complete the fencing. Then they would join Bob and the other riders.

Thomas sat with Pa and Jeremiah in the front room. They talked some in a quiet voice. He let his thoughts roam. He wished Emily could just go ahead and have the baby, as the tension of waiting was getting harder to deal with.

The twins came in and quietly sat close to their father. That bothered Thomas as much as anything. He hated that the two little boys seemed confused and worried as to what was bothering the adults.

Thomas asked, "Jeremiah, you mind if I watch after the boys this afternoon."

Jeremiah looked up with a frown. "That's a good idea if you don't mind."

Thomas stood up and signaled for the boys to follow him outside. "You boys want to go to the swimming hole with me?"

Elisha looked at Joseph and then at him. "Sure. Do you think it's all right with Mama sick?"

"I think she would want you to go. That way you can play and make noise, but it won't bother her." He felt a small hand from each boy slide into his, as they walked down to the creek. It told him as much as anything how concerned they were.

They spent several hours swimming and playing. Thomas tried to think of any games they could play that might help take their minds off their concern for their mother.

Everyone except Ma was sitting down to supper when they got back to the house. Jeremiah asked Pa to say the blessing.

He prayed for Emily and Jeremiah and almost as an afterthought thanked God for the food.

Jeremiah reached over and tousled the hair of the twins. "Did you boys have a good afternoon?"

"Yes, Pa." "Sure did, Pa." Both boys spoke at once as they often did.

"Thomas showed us some new games to play in the water. We swam until we almost couldn't swim anymore." Elisha said just before he shoved half a biscuit into his mouth.

"Yeah, Pa. Thomas said it was all right for us to play even if Mama wasn't feeling well. Was that right?" Joseph looked inquiring at his father.

"Of course, it was all right. And we need to thank Thomas for spending the whole afternoon playing with you two." Jeremiah looked down the table at him and nodded.

"Thank you." Two little boy voices said in union.

"You're welcome, boys. It was a fun afternoon for me too." And it had been, but it also made him think about the possibility of having children of his own some day.

"Your mother is doing all right. She just needs to rest as she waits for the new baby to come." Jeremiah said.

"Where is the new baby coming from, Pa?" Elisha asked.

Jeremiah looked around the table as if looking for help.

Jacob leaned toward the boys. "I tell you all about it after supper."

Jeremiah looked relieved. "Thanks, Jacob. I would appreciate that. First thing, you two go in and say hello to your mother, and then you can go with Jacob to the workshop."

Catherine took a tray that Mildred prepared into Emily.

Jeremiah followed her.

Thomas sat at the table and talked with Pa. In a short time, Ma and Catherine came into the kitchen carrying their hats and gloves.

"Milburn, we're ready to head back to town. Jeremiah is spending the evening with Emily. Catherine and I are both tired."

"Sure, I'm ready." Pa stood.

"I'll go hitch up the buggy." Thomas wanted to say something to Catherine, but she hadn't talked to him all day. He didn't know what to say to her.

Pa followed him out to the corral and they hitched up the buggy together.

"I'm praying that baby comes this week. This waiting is as bad as when I had to wait for you to be born." Pa grumbled.

"Not remembering that time, I can't say anything about it." He grinned at Pa.

"No, I suppose you don't, but I remember your birthing as being a real troublesome time."

"I hope it's not so bad for Emily." He didn't know a lot about babies being born, just horses.

Ma and Catherine came out and climbed into the buggy.

"You take care, son." Ma hugged him and kissed him on the cheek.

He hugged her back. "I will, Ma. You take care of Pa. Don't let him work too hard."

Pa did his usual hug of mostly slapping his back. "See you next week. Love you, son." He climbed up on the seat.

"Good-bye Catherine. Hope your week goes well." He held out his hand.

She slowly took it. "Good-bye, Thomas."

Pa lifted the reins to start the horses to moving, but then he turned to Thomas. "I plumb forgot something I wanted to tell you. Jeremiah explained to me that he couldn't pay you anything because of his promise to the judge. He felt bad he hadn't realized you didn't have any money to bid on a box supper. Your mother and I do, too."

Ma reached out and took Thomas' hand. He stood by the buggy not knowing where Pa was going with his talk.

Catherine sat still looking at her hands.

"Anyway, I asked Jeremiah to write the judge and see if it was all right for us to give you some money so you aren't walking around dead broke. We don't want to do anything to mess up the parole."

"Pa, I don't want you to give me money. I'm doing all right. I've a place to stay, food to eat, and I enjoy the work. It's so much better than being back at Yuma. I don't mind not having any money. I've cost you all too much as it is."

Ma patted his hand. "Now, don't you argue with your pa. If the judge says that it's all right, we plan to give you some money."

"I won't argue with you two. You better get started if you want to make it home before dark." It would take a couple of weeks to get a reply from Yuma. He could argue with them then.

After they left, he went to the bunkroom and lit a lamp. With Bob and the others out starting the round-up of the cattle, he had the bunkroom to himself for the first time. Even though it was early, he got ready for bed and laid back to read from his Bible. He only read for little while when he started to nod off. Putting the book away, he turned the lamp off. As he settled into his bed, he thought about how pretty Catherine had looked in her light lavender dress with the white lace collar. He regretted that he hadn't seen her smile in his direction the whole day.

~

"Thomas, wake up." Someone shook his shoulder and a light shone into his eyes.

Jeremiah held a lamp and stood by his bunk.

Thomas sat up and rubbed his eyes. "What is it?"

"It's Emily. We got to get the doctor." Jeremiah was shaking and the oil in the lamp was sloshing about.

Thomas pulled on his pants, shirt, and then his boots. "What can I do to help?"

Jeremiah sat the lamp on the table. "I hate to ask you to do this, but I can't leave Emily. We need the doctor, now. I want you to take my stallion and ride into town as fast as you can. Go to Doc's place and get him started out here. Then go tell Catherine and your folks. After that you get back here as fast as you can." He rubbed his face. "I'd send Jacob, but he can't ride well enough to do more than a trot. I want you to gallop all the way."

"Sure, I'll ride for the doc." He reached for his jacket and hat.

"Thomas, I know this violates your parole. So don't stop for anything. You get to town, get the doc, tell Catherine and your folks, and get back here without anyone seeing you. You think you can do that?"

"I'll do my best. You go back and help Emily. Where are the boys?"

"Jacob is taking them out to the workshop. I don't want them in the house. I'm afraid this is going to be a difficult birth."

Jeremiah trembled.

Thomas wanted to reassure him that Emily would be all right. "Jeremiah, don't forget who you told me helps us get through these things."

Jeremiah looked at him with a frown, and then nodded. "You're right. I had almost forgotten to pray. Do your best to get the doc here as soon as possible." His voice was calmer.

Thomas took a lantern from the wall by the door and lit it. It was a dark night but with some moonlight. It only took a few minutes to saddle the black stallion. He was a powerful horse and as Thomas galloped down the lane, he could feel the movements of the horse's muscles as he ate up the half mile to the road. Thomas slowed the stallion to turn onto the road toward town and then urged him back to a gallop. As with all horses broken by Jeremiah, the stallion was easy to ride.

It only took Thomas a short time to reach town. The street was dark with no lights. If it had not been for the moonlight, it would have been difficult to see. Thomas rode to the doc's house first. Breathing heavy, the stallion stopped. He jumped off the stallion, tied the reins to the post by the doc's house, and then banged on the door.

In a couple of minutes, a light appeared from the back of the house, then the door opened. "Who is it?"

"It's Thomas Black. Jeremiah Rebourn sent me. Emily needs you now."

Doc thrust the lantern into Thomas' hands, then he lit a lamp on a table by the door. "Go out back to my barn and hitch up the buggy for me. I'll dress, get my coat and bag, and meet you there."

"Sure, Doc." He grabbed the reins for the stallion and hurried to the barn. He hitched the horse in the barn to the little buggy and then watered the stallion. By the time Doc made it out, he was ready to go.

"Thanks. I forgot your name, but it doesn't matter." Doc climbed up on the seat of the buggy and started out at a fast trot.

Thomas got the stallion and walked over to the back of the general store. An outside stairway led up to the second floor where his folks lived above the store. He climbed the stairs two at a time, then knocked sharply on the door.

Pa opened it. "Son, what is it? Is it Emily?"

"Yes, sir. I just got Doc started for the ranch. I'm going now to tell Catherine. Can you bring her and Ma to the ranch?"

"I'll wake your ma right now. Tell Catherine to give us about ten minutes to get ready." He stepped out onto the landing and looked around. "You shouldn't be in town by yourself."

"I know. But Jeremiah didn't have anyone else to send. As soon as I tell Catherine, I'll head back to the ranch. Otherwise, I would offer to hitch your buggy for you."

"No, you go tell Catherine and get on back to the ranch. And for sure don't let the sheriff or Myles McKinney see you." Pa pushed him toward the stairs.

"All right Pa, I'll see you at the ranch." He ran down the stairs and grabbed the reins of the stallion. As it was only a short distance to Catherine's place, he walked him quickly around to the street. He couldn't see anyone on the street and crossed it with the horse following him.

The easiest way to get Catherine's attention was to go to the back door to the café. He knocked on the door lightly, then said, "Catherine, it's me, Thomas."

A light came on and the door opened an inch. "Is that you, Thomas?"

"Yes, Jeremiah sent me to get the doctor. Emily is having the baby. My folks will pick you up in about ten minutes."

The door opened wide and Catherine stood there pretty as could be in a pink robe with her hair falling all around her face and shoulders. She was barefoot. "Come in while I get dressed."

"I can't. I have to get back. I'm not supposed to be in town without someone from the ranch." He was getting more nervous about it by the minute.

"I had forgotten about that. You go on. I'll be ready when your folks come."

"I'll see you at the ranch." He mounted the black stallion and started for the road. He heard a door slam somewhere and someone yelled. He didn't stop to see who it was. Within moments, he was lost in the darkness of the night.

He passed Doc's buggy on the road with a wave. When he rode into the yard between the house and the barn, Jacob met him with a lantern in his hand.

"Is doctor coming?" He took hold of the stallion's bridle.

Thomas dismounted. "Yes, he's about five minutes behind me. How's Emily?"

"I do not know. Jeremiah and Mildred seem worried. I am glad doctor comes."

After unsaddling the stallion, Thomas rubbed him down, threw a horse blanket on him, and gave him some water. He had ridden him hard, but the stallion was in good shape. The ride into town and back hadn't even winded him too badly although he had worked up a good sweat.

"I wait for the doctor. I take care of his horse. You go in and talk to Jeremiah."

"The doc ought to be here shortly." Thomas walked into the kitchen.

Jeremiah came in from the front room. "I thought you were Doc arriving. Is he on his way?" Jeremiah's hair was sticking up as if he had been running his fingers through it, his shirt was buttoned up crooked, and he was waving his arms around as if agitated, which was very unlike him.

"He's about five minutes behind me. My folks and Catherine are about ten minutes behind." He moved over to the stove and poured himself a cup of coffee.

"Did anyone see you?" Jeremiah paced back and forth, not really seeing him.

"I'm not sure. Someone yelled at me, but I kept riding. I don't think they could have recognized me, it was so dark." Thomas sipped on the strong black coffee enjoying the aroma as much as anything.

"What did they yell?" Jeremiah stopped his pacing and turned toward him.

"I couldn't tell you if it was really a word or just like ... hey." He finished the coffee and sat the cup at the back of the counter. He figured that he would want more coffee later and would use the same cup. "What can I do for you?"

"Just pray for Emily. She seems to be having a harder time than with the twins. I asked Jacob if you and he could take the boys tomorrow with you to work on the fence."

"Sure, we can do that. Where are Elisha and Joseph now?"

"Jacob bedded them down over at his place." Jeremiah rubbed his hand over his face.

The doctor came through the door from the yard.

Jeremiah immediately headed toward the bedroom. "Follow me, Doc. You need to see Emily."

Doc chuckled. "Sure, Jeremiah. That's why I'm here. Howdy, Thomas. Now I remember your name."

Thomas smiled at the backs of Jeremiah and Doc heading through the front room for the bedroom. Doc's nonchalant attitude was a marked contrast to Jeremiah's near panic. Of course, Doc had delivered most of the babies in the area for the last several years.

Thomas waited for Catherine and his folks to arrive. The coffee pot was almost empty so he rinsed it out and put on a new pot to brew. Stoking up the stove, he noticed that the woodbin was low. That was something he could do. He didn't know of anything he could do to help Emily except stay out of the way and keep an eye for ways to help around the house. He was washing up some dishes that had accumulated in and around the sink when his folks and Catherine arrived.

"So you made it back safe." Pa gave him one of his sideway hugs as Thomas had his hands in the soapy water.

"What are you doing, Thomas?" Ma took her shawl and hat off, then placed them on a hook by the back door.

Catherine hung hers beside them. "He looks like he knows what he's doing."

"I never taught him how to wash dishes. How is Emily?" Ma asked.

He dried his hands on the dishtowel. "Doc just got here and Jeremiah seems worried."

"I'll go on back to the bedroom. Milburn, it may be a long night. Why don't you find a place to get some sleep?" Ma went into the front room heading for the bedroom.

"I smell fresh coffee." Pa pulled out a chair and sat at the table.

"Let me get you some. You want a cup, Thomas?" Catherine stepped up to the counter where the cups were stored.

"No, thank you. I just finished one." He sat at the table across from Pa.

"Do you know where Mildred and Sally are?" Catherine sat the hot cup of coffee in front of Pa.

"My guess is Mildred is in with Emily and Sally is asleep." He sat with his hands folded on the table and watched Catherine as she moved about the kitchen.

"Then I better get some water boiling." Catherine pulled several pots from the cabinet.

He remembered the almost empty woodbin. "Pa, if you could help Catherine fill the pots with water, I'll bring in some wood."

Catherine looked over at the woodbin. "Thanks that will be helpful. Then I suggest you men get some rest. This is going to be a long night."

Thomas made several trips and filled the woodbins, the one in the kitchen, as well as the one in the wash-up room. Then he showed Pa the extra bunks in the bunkroom. He refused to take Thomas' bunk even though he offered it. As Thomas lay down, he hoped to be able to sleep.

Chapter Seventeen Thomas

"Thomas, you must wake up now."

He groggily lifted his head to see Jacob standing by his bed. "Is it morning?"

"The sun will come up in a few minutes. We take twins and go work on fence."

"All right, I'm awake." He pulled his pants on, then grabbed his shirt. "How is Emily?"

"The doctor says she have hard time. That it will take many hours yet. So Jeremiah said we go on to work." Jacob scratched his head and yawned. "Catherine has breakfast ready."

Thomas rubbed his jaw. Not that it mattered, but with Catherine here he wanted a shave. "You go eat. I'll wash up a bit. We need to take extra water and food for the boys."

"I will ask Miss Catherine what we can take." Jacob left the bunkroom.

Stomping into his boots, Thomas finished dressing. He gathered his towel and shaving gear and stumbled into the wash-up room. Someone had left a lantern on and there was hot water on the little box stove. Quickly he washed up, shaved, and combed his hair. Looking at himself in the mirror, he saw a thin-bronzed face with straight eyebrows above dark brown eyes. His dark brown hair was too long and starting to curl making it harder to control. The face that looked back at him from the mirror was just a regular one. He didn't figure it was anything special although Ma thought him handsome. He grinned at his thoughts. He didn't know if he could count Ma as being very objective. What Catherine thought about how he looked he had no idea.

After eating the breakfast Catherine prepared, he and Jacob started out. They were seated on the wagon seat with the two boys riding in the back of the wagon with the tools. They had a long but fun day with the carrying's on of the boys, plus getting about a quarter-mile of fencing up. With the terrible heat of summer letting up, the work wasn't so hard. The boys tried to help, but in reality, they just slowed them down. Of course, they didn't tell Elisha and Joseph who were proud of having done what they called grown-up work.

By the time they made it back to the house, both boys were so tired they were sound asleep in the back of the wagon. Thomas and Jacob carried them into Jacob's place and put them to bed on a pallet on the

floor. They had let them eat what Catherine had packed for them plus wild blackberries. Thomas didn't know what Emily would say about the state of their faces, hands, and front of their shirts from the blackberry juice.

After making sure the boys were sleeping soundly, he and Jacob made their way to the wash-up room. After washing the grime of the workday off, they headed for the kitchen and something to eat.

As they walked into the kitchen, Thomas could tell that the word wasn't good. They were the last to arrive. Seated around the table were Mildred, Sally, Catherine, Pa, and Ma. Jeremiah and Doctor Ford were absent. The table seemed empty with Bob and the other riders still out on the range gathering cattle for the round up.

Jacob and Thomas took their places at the table as everyone sat in silence. Thomas sat between his folks and across from Catherine.

"Let's hold hands while we pray." Pa prayed for Emily and the baby. He blessed each one who was trying to help, especially the doctor. Then he thanked the Lord for the food.

Thomas passed platters of food. What did Pa expect God to do for Emily? Thomas didn't have much faith God concerned Himself with the folks down on earth. At least at Yuma he had never sensed His presence. As Thomas looked at calm faces around the table, he felt an outsider. They had faith that the prayer of his father would actually help Emily.

Everyone talked little at the table and when they did, it was in hushed tones. Thomas wanted to ask what the latest word from the doctor was and when they expected the baby to be born. But he was afraid to ask because of the possible answer.

"Thomas."

"Yes, sir?" He turned toward Pa.

"Your mother wants to stay until the baby is born. I'm going to drive back to town so I can open up the store early in the morning. I'll come back out after I close up. If it's not too busy I'll probably close up early." He rubbed his hand over his face.

Ma spoke up. "I think the baby will be born in the next few hours. The doctor hasn't said so but I have a feeling. Emily is so weak that we need to keep praying." Ma put her hand on Thomas' arm as if she were trying to find something to hold on to. "I want your pa to go on to town and get some rest. There's not much he can do here he can't do at home."

"How are you doing, Ma?" He looked at her tired face and knew she needed rest, too. But, until the baby was born and Emily was all right, Ma wouldn't sleep.

"I'm all right, son. It was a help for you and Jacob to take the boys today."

"Jacob and I enjoyed it. Tomorrow we can take them out again." He glanced over at Jacob.

"Ja, it is no problem to care for boys. But Thomas, we must take fishing poles tomorrow."

"That's a good idea and maybe put a pallet in the wagon for them to nap on. They were sure tired out by the time we started back."

Pa stood and stretched his back. "If I'm going back to town later, I better get the buggy hitched now. Then I won't have to do it after dark."

Thomas got up and pulled the chair back for Ma to stand. "I'll hitch up the buggy. You stay with Ma."

After he hitched up the horse to the buggy, he tied it up to the hitching post by the front porch. He looked to the west. They had about two more hours of sun before dark. He debated saddling a horse and riding to the top of the ridge. Better to stroll down to the creek. He wanted to ask Catherine to come with him, but he didn't want to face her turning him down.

As he passed the back of the house, Catherine stepped out of the back door.

"You mind if I walk along with you?" She looked uncertain as if he might refuse her.

"Of course not, I'd enjoy some company." He shortened his stride to walk in pace with Catherine.

She had a shawl folded across her arm. "I'm glad the heat of last week has let up."

"Yes, fall will be here in a few weeks." He didn't mind talking about the weather. He didn't care what they talked about as long as they were talking.

"I hope I'm here at the ranch when the horse herd arrives. It really is a lovely sight to watch the horses all spreading out on the range." She glanced up at him and caught him staring down at her beautiful hair all braided and crowning her head.

He looked away and felt the heat rising on his neck and face. The Lord had really found some funny ways to keep a man humble when he couldn't even control a blush. "I look forward to the herd's arrival so I can meet these men I've heard so much about. Although, if they bring as many horses as Jeremiah says they're bringing, we will have some work to do this winter."

"How many horses will be in the herd?"

He pushed his hat back and glanced at her. "Jeremiah said anywhere from three to four hundred. We already have over two hundred with all the new foals."

Catherine sat on a log facing the western sky. "Are you enjoying your work here?"

He bravely sat next to her on the log. "Yes, I'm learning something every day. Course there is some work I enjoy more. The last week of chopping down trees and then today digging postholes is not exactly my favorite. It has to be done, and I can dig a proper posthole now that I have all this experience."

She gave him a small smile. "I want to apologize to you for the way I've acted."

Surprised, he turned to look at her. "It's all right. It was my fault."

"How can it be your fault? I'm the one who has acted like a pouting child for two weeks. I didn't understand why you didn't bid on my box supper." She sighed.

He wanted to take her hand but resisted. "That's why it's my fault. I should have spoken up and told you I couldn't bid on it."

"I'm confused. How did you get the money to buy that beautiful little keepsake box for my birthday?" She fixed her gaze on his face and waited for his answer.

The answer was so simple if he had only told her at the time. Would he ever get to the place he could interact with people without making mistakes? "Jacob helped me make that box for you. We made it from wood left over from other pieces of furniture. Emily gave me the red velvet to put in the bottom of it. It didn't cost anything."

"You made it? But it's so beautiful. I would never have guessed. I thought it must have cost a lot of money."

"I wanted it to be a beautiful keepsake box for a beautiful girl. Jacob and I made it in between other work. It was enjoyable."

"Do you think I'm beautiful?" Her blue eyes locked on his and her eyebrows arched up, as if in surprise.

He was amazed she didn't know. "Yes, you're the most beautiful girl I've ever seen. Surely you know that."

She gave him the smile that left him breathless. "I've never had anyone tell me that before. Thank you."

What did Myles McKinley say to her? Surely, he told her how lovely she was.

"If it isn't too bold of me to say, I find you're not bad looking yourself," Catherine said. For the first time, he saw her blush.

She shivered slightly and he took the shawl from her lap and draped it around her shoulders. He allowed his arm and hand to rest briefly across her shoulder. She didn't pull away but leaned slightly toward him. It was all he could do not to take her into his arms, but he remembered what Jeremiah had said about being fair to her.

"We better head back to the house because if we sit here much longer I'm going to try to kiss you. With two and half more years to go before I'm free, I want to be fair to you." He held his breath afraid he'd been presumptuous.

Her gaze was serious as she looked deep into his eyes, but her brilliant blue eyes were sparkling. "Only a good man would be that kind. We can be friends and enjoy each other's company. Then we will see what God has in mind." She worried her lower lip with her teeth.

"You got something else on your mind?" Thomas sensed she had something she was hesitating to say.

"Thomas, do you believe in God?"

The question took him by surprise. "Yes, I believe in God and in the Lord Jesus Christ."

"So do I. My belief is very important to me. Are you a Christian?" She spoke in a quiet voice with a seriousness that told Thomas she really wanted to know.

Thomas looked her in the eyes as he thought what to say. "I think I am."

"You're not sure?" she responded with surprise.

"Well, when I was thirteen I asked God to forgive me and I was baptized by Pa. I remember that I was so relieved after I came up out of the water that I no longer had any sins. But it didn't last long, especially as I started hanging out with the wrong crowd. God and me, we haven't been on the best of terms since. When I first got to prison, I begged God to rescue me but he didn't. I kinda lost hope that God even cared about me." He glanced across the creek and sighed. He had never shared anything like this. "Since being here and attending church, listening to the sermons, I've been reading the Bible that Ma gave me. I want to be alright with God but I'm just not sure."

Catherine had listened attentively. "Did you ever stop believing?"

"No, I've always known God is real, even when I lost hope of him listening to me. But, here lately I've felt as if he is back with me." Thomas smiled. "Or, maybe I'm back with him."

"I think you're right. It sounds to me as if you truly became a Christian at your baptism. Even though you drifted away, you still held on to your belief. Read the story of the prodigal son and you will see God's response to your return to him over these last few months."

"How did you become a Christian, Catherine?"

She smiled. "Yes, turn about is fair play. My mother and I always attended church but she taught me that becoming a Christian wasn't automatic just because I had been surrounded by Christians all my life. It had to be a decision I made when I became old enough to be aware of sinning against God. That happened when I was also thirteen. I had told some lies and felt so bad. I knew God wasn't pleased. It got me to thinking and asking questions. I was baptized in the river just outside of town by the preacher at that time. I've never regretted it."

"So you think I'm alright with God and that he has forgiven me for those years that I turned my back on him?"

"Yes, I do. God wants to forgive us. We just have to ask him."

Thomas took a deep breath and slowly let it out. It was as if a dark hole within himself was filling up with the light of God's blessings. "Thanks for telling me that." He stood and put his hand out to help her rise from the log. "We really do need to start back to the house."

She put her hand into his and left it there. They walked slowly back to the house in silence holding hands. He wanted the walk to last forever.

When they went into the kitchen, Thomas sensed that something was different. Pa stood behind Ma, who sat at the table weeping.

Jeremiah wasn't there.

Mildred and Sally sat looking at Ma.

Jacob sat with his head in his hands.

Thomas heard Catherine catch her breath. "What's happened?" Her voice wavered.

Mildred took a deep breath. "We have a beautiful baby girl. She's perfect. Emily is very weak. Doc is still with her."

Catherine looked at Ma, and then back to Mildred. "She's going to be all right. She has to be all right."

Mildred got up, came over to Catherine, and hugged her. "All we know is that it was a hard delivery. So we pray and hope. And we thank the Lord for a baby girl." Mildred guided Catherine to a couple of chairs and they both sat down at the table.

Thomas moved over by Pa and put his hand on Ma's shoulder. "Do we know what the baby will be named?"

Ma wiped her face with her apron. "I don't think they've decided yet." She blew her nose and put her handkerchief into the pocket of the apron.

"You all forgive me for breaking down like that. It was such a relief when that baby girl was finally born. I'm all right now."

Pa patted her arm. "That's all right, Agnes. You've been working hard at getting that baby here. Now we pray for Emily." Pa put his arm around Thomas' shoulders and the other around Ma. "Let's pray.

"Our heavenly Father, we thank you for this baby girl that has entered your world. Give us all wisdom to know how to be a blessing to this infant. Be with Emily and help her to have the strength to live, not only for this child, but for Jeremiah, Elisha, and Joseph. Just as you answered our many prayers to bring Thomas home safe to us, we believe in your power to answer our prayers. But in all things, your will be done. In the name of your Son, Jesus the Christ, Amen."

Thomas kept his head bowed trying to get a handle on his emotions. He couldn't imagine God would put the prayers to bring him home safely equal to the prayers for the life of someone like Emily. His life was so worthless compared to hers. If he knew a way, he would give his life so that she might live. The depth of his feelings surprised him. When had he come to care for these people so deeply? He finally lifted his head and found himself looking into the deep blue of Catherine's eyes. She had tears running down her cheeks, as did the other women.

Pa sat down next to Ma. "Now we don't want Jeremiah to come in here and find us all so droopy. Mildred, do you think there might be some coffee and cake?"

"There sure is some cake left. Sally, you go get some plates and forks. I'll get the coffee going." Mildred seemed relieved to have something to do.

Thomas didn't want any cake, but he took a cup of coffee. He was slowly sipping it when Doc came into the kitchen.

He sat at the end of the table and Mildred put a cup of coffee in front of him. Doc cleared his throat and said, "Well, folks, it's been a hard birthing, but your prayers are being answered. I think Emily is going to make it."

"Thank the Lord." Ma was reaching for her handkerchief again as tears flowed down her cheeks.

Doc took a swallow of the hot coffee and sighed. "Emily is going to have to take it easy for some time. I know you will do what is needed to help her and Jeremiah. Mrs. Black, if you could go sit with Emily and try to get Jeremiah to come eat something. He hasn't eaten or slept in a couple of days."

"Of course." Ma suddenly seemed revived. She stood and quickly went toward the bedroom.

"I better head to town if I'm going in tonight." Pa said his good-bye and went out to the buggy.

Thomas followed him and untied the horse. Then he lit the lantern hanging at the front of the buggy. "Will this give you enough light to make it into town?"

"Sure it will, son. Old Betsy here could find her way to the barn with her eyes closed."

"We'll see you tomorrow evening at supper?"

"Yes, I may even close the store early. Don't worry, son, it's going to be all right now."

Thomas stood and watched him drive the buggy down the lane until all he could see was a faint glimmer of light.

When he went back into the kitchen, Jeremiah sat at the table. He looked terrible, but in spite of that, he had a grin on his face.

Jeremiah glanced over at him as he sat at the table. "Thomas, did you know we have a baby girl?"

"Yes, Jeremiah. I heard." Thomas grinned at his boss.

"And Emily is going to be all right." He looked down at the plate of food as if he just realized it was there. After he put the first fork full of potatoes into his mouth, he began to eat like a hungry man.

Doc looked around. "Is there a place we can bed Jeremiah down? And for that matter I would like a bed. I'll stay until morning to make sure Emily is on the mend."

"I'm the only one using the bunkroom right now. All the hands are out with Bob at the round-up." Thomas didn't know what other beds might be available.

Jeremiah stared at his plate seemingly unaware of the rest of the people around the table.

Doc stood up. "Let's get him into a bed before he falls asleep in his plate."

Between the two of them, they guided Jeremiah into the bunkroom and let him tumble onto the bunk where Pa had slept. Jeremiah was almost asleep before his head touched the pillow.

Thomas pulled Jeremiah's boots off and pulled the blanket over him.

Mildred had followed them into the bunkroom carrying a pillow and a couple of blankets. She quickly made up a bunk for Doc. "You men sleep-in. If we need you, we'll holler. Agnes, Catherine, and I will take turns sitting with Emily and caring for the baby."

Thomas turned toward her. "I'm surprised that Catherine doesn't need to get back to town to open the café."

"She said Beryl would be taking care of the café tomorrow," she responded.

"Mildred, I'm almost as tired as Jeremiah. You call me if you need me." Doc patted her shoulder, then closed the door after she left.

Thomas was glad to undress and stretch out on his bunk for a couple of hours sleep before it would be time to get up.

Jacob had the twins out in the workshop. What they would think of a little sister?

~

Thomas woke with a start. The light of dawn was just breaking, and he could make out the forms of Jeremiah and Doc asleep on their bunks. He didn't feel fully rested but knew there was work to do. After slipping into his clothes, he picked up his boots with his socks in them and softly padded across to the kitchen. Before he got to the kitchen door, he could smell the fresh coffee and meat cooking.

Jacob was busy at the stove frying bacon. "Good morning, Thomas. You wake early."

Thomas sat at a chair by the table to put his socks and boots on. "I just woke up and started thinking about all the work that needs doing."

Jacob poured a cup of coffee and put it in front of him. "Ja, with Emily so sick we need to do Jeremiah's work. I think maybe you and me must muck out the horse barn and look at horses. Then we go finish fence."

"Thanks for the coffee." Thomas swallowed some, then sat the cup on the table. "We need to watch the boys, too. You think they will sleep a while yet?"

"I think so. Here is breakfast. I did not eat supper much. I am hungry." Jacob set a plate of fried eggs, bacon, and biscuits in front of Thomas, then a plate for himself. "We pray.

"Lord, bless this household. Thank you for new baby. Thank you for food. Help Thomas and me to be good servants today. In the name of Jesus the Christ, Amen."

It didn't take Thomas long to clean his plate and to drink another cup of coffee. He sat his dirty plate and cup by the sink. "I'll go get started at the horse barn."

"I come soon. But I will look in at the boys." Jacob sopped up the last of his fried eggs.

Jacob and Thomas worked as fast as they could to clean out the six stalls and checked on the horses in the barn. Jacob knew a lot more than

Thomas did about the condition of the horses. Thomas got the wagon hitched up and made sure they had all the tools they needed and a big jug of water. When he went back into the kitchen, Mildred was there.

"Why didn't you wake me? I would have fixed your breakfast." Mildred pointed the spoon she was using to stir a pan of gravy at him, but he could tell she wasn't upset.

"Jacob did the cooking. I just did the eating. We need to put some sandwiches together for us and the twins. If you'll tell me what to do I'll make them myself." He picked up the cup that was still sitting by the sink and poured another cup of coffee. Usually he stopped at two cups in the morning but this was a three- or four-cup morning.

"You'll do no such thing. Sit down and drink your coffee. I'll prepare some food for you all to take for your dinner." Catherine had come into the kitchen without him seeing her.

"All right. I'll sit right here and watch you make sandwiches." He grinned at her. He hadn't made a sandwich since he was a kid. Her taking over was just fine with him. "How is Emily?"

Catherine took a loaf of bread and starting cutting big slices. "She's much better, although she's still weak. She lost a lot of blood." She must have noticed his face. "I'm sorry. I shouldn't have said that."

"No, I want to know how she is. I'm not used to talking about someone else bleeding." He hurried to take another sip of his coffee.

Mildred chuckled. "Thomas, you're like most men. You go out and doctor animals on the range without blinking an eye. But talk about a woman being sick and you go to pieces."

Two little tousled headed boys came stumbling into the kitchen, yawning and rubbing their eyes.

"Morning, boys. You ready for breakfast?" Catherine asked as she gave them each a hug.

"Yes, ma'am. Where's our ma and pa?" Elisha asked.

Thomas looked at Catherine and she nodded at him, so he answered. "Your pa is in the bunkroom asleep. Your ma is resting in her bedroom with your little sister."

Joseph looked at Elisha and then at Thomas. "A sister, we don't have a sister."

He couldn't help laughing. Reaching over, he tousled their hair some more. "You do now. You boys are coming with Jacob and me today, aren't you? We're taking the fishing poles."

Both boys grinned and nodded. But then Joseph was serious again. "Is Ma all right? Can we see her?"

Catherine nodded. "I think it would be a good idea for you to visit your mama and meet your little sister. But, you'll have to be real quiet and not stay very long."

Just then Jeremiah came in from the bunkroom followed by Doc. They both looked rumpled. Jeremiah stopped in the kitchen long enough to kiss both the boys on the top of their heads, then headed for the bedroom to check on Emily.

When the boys had eaten their breakfast, Thomas took them to the wash-up room. He washed their faces and hands, then slicked back their hair with a comb.

"All right, boys. You remember what Miss Catherine said. You be real quiet and gentle. Think you can do that?"

Two little solemn faces nodded up at him. They also looked scared. They didn't really understand what had gone on for the last few days. Thomas reached down and gave them each a hug. He wanted to pick them up and carry them to the bedroom, but his ribs were still too tender for that. So instead, he took each one by the hand and they walked to the bedroom.

The door was open and Emily was propped up with pillows with Jeremiah sitting on the bed next to her.

"My little boys, come to Mama." Emily held out her arms to the boys and they tugged at his hands wanting to run to their mother. He kept hold because Emily looked as fragile as a porcelain vase.

"Easy boys. Remember what I said." He turned the boys loose and they slowly walked up to the bed and snuggled up as close as they could to their mother.

Jeremiah was holding a tiny little bundle that suddenly gave a sound almost like a cat crying. He held the baby where the boys could see the little squeezed up face as the baby started to cry in earnest. "Meet your little sister, Charity."

Elisha put out his hand to pat the tiny little fingers. The baby naturally grabbed hold of the finger. The look of wonder on his face was something to behold. "Look Joseph, she's holding my finger."

Joseph put his hand out and the infant grabbed his finger.

"Well, what do you think boys?" Jeremiah smiled at his three children.

"She's awfully small. What can she do?" Elisha asked.

"Yeah, Pa, she don't look like she would be much fun to play with." Joseph stepped closer to examine this strange new creature. "When will she walk?"

"Not for another year or so." Emily stroked the boys' heads.

"A foal can walk as soon as he's born. What's wrong with her?" Joseph asked.

Thomas struggled not to laugh and Jeremiah seemed to be having the same problem.

Emily took it in as a normal thing to ask. "You must remember that little people babies aren't like horses. You boys were nine months old when you first walked. She will probably do the same." Emily's voice sounded tired.

Thomas held out his hands to the boys. "We need to get going if we're going to get any fishing done."

"Thanks, Thomas, we appreciate you and Jacob looking out for the boys." Jeremiah gave the baby to Emily. He knelt on the floor and gave each of his little sons a kiss on the forehead and a long hug. "Thanks for visiting your mother. You can come back this evening. Go on with Thomas now."

"Jacob and I finished the horse barn and will try to get the fence completed today."

"Thanks to you both. I was wondering how I was going to get the horse barn done." Jeremiah sat on the side of the bed and then rubbed his hand over his face. "Do we have any mares close to foaling?"

Thomas shook his head. "Jacob says not for a day or so, but we will keep an eye out."

Jeremiah nodded. "I'll check the mares in the horse barn later this morning. You men go on and get your work done."

"Come on boys." Thomas took them by the hands and led them out of the bedroom. He looked back and saw that Emily was lying with her eyes closed looking fragile and Jeremiah held a tiny bundle gently with his strong hands.

Chapter Eighteen Thomas

It took Jacob and Thomas three more days to finish the fence. They could have worked much faster, but they took time to entertain the twins. Elisha and Joseph were not really a problem; but they were normal, active five-year-old boys.

The boys seemed content with a short visit each morning with their mother and then spent some time with their father in the evenings. They moved back to their own room to sleep after spending several nights with Jacob.

Toward the end of the week, Jacob and Thomas had the fence up and rode out to help with the round up. Thomas ended up doing the work of an untrained cowhand, which he was. His riding improved every day but he still could barely rope anything. So he kept the branding fire going and helped with branding and castrating the calves. The smell of the burning hair on the hides when the red hot brands were pressed against the calves rumps gave him a sick feeling. He understood the need for the castration and that someone had to do it, but he would rather dig post holes, which he didn't like to do at all.

Saturday evening, he rode back to the ranch with a message for Jeremiah from Bob, who planned to get the cattle divided and the herd Jeremiah planned to sell moving toward town. The cattle cars needed to be reserved with the railroad. Thomas assumed Bob sent him with the message, because Jeremiah wanted him to stay closer to the main ranch.

Thomas was tired, dirty, and agitated at Harlan and Barney's constant complaining. The time he had spent in the bunkhouse with Harlan and Barney gone had been peaceful. He had to get himself under control to put up with Harlan again.

When he dismounted and unsaddled, Elisha and Joseph ran up and grabbed his legs as they did with their father.

"Hey, Thomas."

"Hey, yourself, Joseph."

"How do you know I'm Joseph?" He stared up at Thomas with a serious frown line between his eyes.

"I'm not sure how I know, but you're Joseph." Thomas turned and tousled the hair of the little boy hanging onto his other leg. "Which makes you Elisha."

"Don't tell anyone how you know. We like to fool people." Elisha's grin revealed a missing front tooth.

"All right, boys. I won't tell, which will be easy as I don't know how I know." He grinned at them. "I'm getting some clean clothes and heading down to the creek before supper. You want to go?"

"We'll ask Mama if we can." They went running into the house.

Thomas let his horse loose into the corral and strolled over to the bunkroom to pick up clean clothes, a towel, and a bar of soap. The boys met him outside the backdoor. They carried their own clean clothes.

Mildred stood in the doorway. "Don't stay too long, boys. Supper will be ready in about thirty minutes." She wiped her hands on her apron. "Welcome back, Thomas. Thanks for taking the boys. They need a bath and we've been busy with the baby and let the boys kind of run wild."

"We'll be back shortly." He waved and then followed the twins to the creek. By the time he caught up with them, they were already jumping into the deep pool that was their swimming hole.

"Hurry up, Thomas." Joseph climbed up on a log and jumped back in the pool.

After shedding his clothes, Thomas jumped in the pool. It surprised him how cool the water was. The fall weather had brought cooler nights and fall was definitely just around the corner. There would soon be a day when he wouldn't want to use the creek for bathing. At least there was the wash-up room with the possibility of hot water that he could use through the winter.

~

It had taken a couple of weeks but Emily was back eating with the family. To him she still appeared fragile and not her lively self. Jeremiah left the round-up and then selling the cattle up to Bob. Thomas didn't question Jeremiah's need to stay close to the ranch house and Emily. If he had a wife like Emily, he knew where he would be, too.

Thomas used his biscuit to sop up the last of the fried eggs, then swallowed the rest of the coffee from his cup. The sound of a horse trotting along the lane from the road got his attention.

Jeremiah looked toward the front of the house. "Wonder who's out this early?" He pushed back his chair and headed toward the front door.

Emily sat holding tiny little Charity. "Thomas, please go see who's there then come back tell me."

He grinned at her. "I'll be glad to satisfy your curiosity." Her giggles followed him into the front room.

Out in the front yard, Jeremiah held the bridle of a big black stallion, shaking hands with the rider. "Elisha Evans, you're a sight for sore eyes!"

The man dismounted and gave Jeremiah a bear hug. "I'm glad to see you, Jeremiah. The herd and the rest of the folks are about three miles behind me. I thought I better warn you."

So this tall man was Elisha Evans, Jeremiah's partner from the mountain ranch. He was older than Thomas had expected. He returned to the kitchen to report to Emily.

"It's Elisha Evans. He said the rest of crew and horses are about three miles behind."

Emily handed him the two-week-old baby and quickly walked to the front room.

Thomas carefully held the tiny bundle of sleeping baby and didn't have any idea what to do. Looking around he saw Mildred and Sally grinning at him.

"Mildred, you want to take this baby before I break her?" He held the pink bundle out toward her as if it was a package.

"Thomas, that's not the way to hold a baby." She came around the table.

Thomas thought she was going to take the baby. Instead, she took little Charity and repositioned her into the fold of his arm with the baby's head up close to his heart. The baby gave a little gurgle and seemed to settle in. The surge of pure protectiveness caught him by surprise.

"Now that's the way to hold a baby. Here, sit down and I'll get you another cup of coffee." Mildred poured the coffee.

Thomas sat and softly rocked little Charity and watched her breathing. The experience of holding this brand new was amazing.

Emily entered the kitchen followed by the man he now knew was Elisha Evans, then Jeremiah. "Oh Thomas. Thank you for looking after Charity for me." She made no move to take the baby, which was just as well as he wasn't sure how to hand the baby off to her.

"Elisha, this is Thomas Black. He came to work here back in April just after you all took the herd to the mountains."

Thomas didn't get up because he was holding baby in his arms but held out his right hand. "I'm proud to meet you, sir. I've heard nothing but good about you and your ranch."

Elisha Evans gave Thomas a firm handshake. "Thanks, it's good to meet you. Let me look at that baby girl." He bent down and ran his finger softly along the soft cheek of the infant. "Let me go wash my hands and then I want to hold that little one."

In a couple of minutes, he was back and expertly took the baby from Thomas. "What a beautiful little girl. Wait until Susana sees you, little one."

Emily leaned forward with an excited grin. "Susana is with you?"

Elisha softly patted the baby's back. "Not only Susana, Joe and Sara, Cookie and Ruth, but also, the children. The riders should have the horse herd here in about an hour."

Jeremiah turned toward Thomas. "Go tell Bob and the other men that the horse herd is here. We'll run them west of the house to the north pasture. Also, when you saddle your horse, saddle one for me. We'll go meet the herd and help drive it on in."

"Yes, sir." Thomas grabbed his hat off the hook by the door and headed toward the back of the barn to find Jacob.

~

It took most of the day to get the horse herd out to the north pasture. Then the buggies and wagons pulled up by the creek poured out a crowd of people. The bedlam that Thomas observed with the children running everywhere, the women talking seemingly without taking a breath, helped him decide it was time for him to keep out of the way.

Supper was served out under the big oak tree. Thomas met Cookie and his wife Ruth, who had been the cook at the Rocking JR Ranch before she married the cook on Elisha Evans' ranch. They were both in their late fifties if not older. It was hard for him to tell. Cookie set up the big chuck wagon between the oak tree and the creek and had three different cooking fires going with big pots on them. One of the cook fires was used for nothing but three big five-gallon coffee pots.

As Thomas stood with the riders from the Rocking ES and the Rocking JR waiting for the call to eat, a rider rode up to the remuda and dismounted. There was something slightly awkward in how he dismounted and as he walked over to them, there was a slight evidence of a limp.

Jeremiah rose from where he was seated on a camp chair talking with Elisha Evans. He turned and looked over at the riders. "Thomas, come over here."

Surprised to be singled out, he pushed off from the tree he had been leaning against with a heel propped up. "Yes, sir."

Jeremiah grinned at him. "Thomas, I want you to meet Joe Weathers. This is Thomas Black. Milburn and Agnes Black are his folks."

Thomas had expected Joe Weathers to be bigger and older from all he had heard about his prowess with horse training. But he was about Thomas' size and only a few years older.

"Glad to meet you, sir." Thomas thrust out his hand.

Joe shook it with a strong grip. "And I'm glad to meet you. Of course, I've known your folks for years. They surely are good people."

"Yes, sir, they are."

"Is this how you're training your hands these days, Jeremiah? You don't have to sir me. I'm just Joe."

Jeremiah waved Joe toward the camp chair. "Sit down here, Joe, and yes, this is how I'm training my cowhands. They all have to sir me." Jeremiah grinned at Thomas. "No, the truth is I've tried to convince Thomas he doesn't have to be so polite, but I think his folks trained him too well."

Thomas ducked his head and didn't know what to say. It hadn't been his folks but the guards at Yuma that had beaten it into him. It was a habit he couldn't seem to break.

He looked up when Elisha Evans spoke in a deep melodious voice. "Leave the man alone. A little manners wouldn't hurt any of us."

"You're right. Thomas, I hear that you work well with the horses." Joe looked up at him from where he sat in the camp chair.

Thomas squatted on his heels and folded his hands across his knees. "Yes, sir. Bob and Jeremiah have been teaching me about the horses. I like working with them. I hear that you are a master trainer."

"Don't know about the master trainer, but horses and I do seem to get along. Maybe you and I can work together while we're here and learn from each other."

Thomas hardly knew what to say. "That would be all right. I'd like that, sir."

"If we are going to be working together, call me Joe." His attention was taken by the sound of women's voices. "Here come the ladies, Thomas. I want you to meet my wife."

Emily came from the house followed by two ladies in their thirties and by Catherine.

Joe stood and walked to meet the women. He gave Emily and Catherine each a hug and kiss on the cheek. Then he turned to one of the most beautiful women Thomas had ever seen and led her over to him.

"Sara, this is Thomas Black, Milburn and Agnes Black's son. He works the horses with Jeremiah."

She looked up at him with the most startling blue eyes. "I'm happy to meet you. Your folks are some of my favorite people." She held out her hand.

Thomas shook her small hand. "Glad to meet you, ma'am. My folks are some of my favorite people too."

Even with the great beauty of Sara Weathers, his eyes couldn't resist Catherine.

She smiled and nodded. "Evening, Thomas."

He smiled back. "Evening, Catherine." He remembered his manners and tipped his hat to Emily and a lovely lady that he assumed was Susana, Elisha Evans' wife. "Ladies."

Emily stood on tiptoes and kissed his cheek. "Susana, Thomas and Jacob rescued the twins when I had Charity. They took them to help build a fence. Of course, you can imagine how much help two five-year-old boys were."

Susana offered her hand. "Reminds me of Joe taking care of Sam and Christine when little Josh was born."

Thomas tucked that comment away to ask about later. He was sure there was a story there. He settled back to just enjoy these people that had such caring for one another. The sound of laughter filled the yard.

~

The next week was busy getting the horse herd situated on the ranch and visiting with everyone. The evenings were especially lively. They sat around the campfires and listened to the stories of these families. Elisha and Susana had been married almost eighteen years. The account of their meeting and marrying was like a storybook. As Elisha told it for the benefit of Catherine and himself around the campfire, Thomas watched the faces of their five children. Then the amazing story of Joe and Sara gave him hope that he could overcome his past. When they talked of meeting Jeremiah ten years earlier there was no mention ever made of where he had come from, or what had been his life before he appeared at Elisha's ranch at age eighteen. Thomas was curious but not about to ask questions.

Thomas was relieved a few days later when they all packed up and headed back to the mountain ranch. The visit had been fun but with so many people about, Thomas was also worn out.

Chapter Nineteen Thomas

Jeremiah called a meeting of everyone working on the ranch after breakfast the next day. They met in the kitchen around the table with coffee and slices of Mildred and Sally's fresh apple cake.

Jeremiah cleared his throat. "I need to tell you all some things and plan the work for the next few months." Jeremiah seemed nervous, but then Thomas realized he always did if he was talking to more than two or three people. "Elisha Evans has made the decision to sell his ranch and move down to the Cedar Ridge area. He and Susana want to be nearer schools for their children and Susana is tired of the winters." Jeremiah took a swallow of his coffee.

Thomas didn't have long to wonder what the move would mean for the work on Jeremiah's ranch.

"He's looking for a ranch to buy and hopes to move by next spring or summer. What it means for us is that the horses that we have here now need to be broke and all but the breeding stock ready by spring to sell to the army. We'll continue to partner. But, we'll cut down on the size of the horse herd, perhaps expand the cattle herd. So, we have the job this winter of getting close to four hundred horses broke and ready to deliver to the army. Joe and a couple of the other riders from the Rocking ES will come back in a month or so and help. If Elisha finds a ranch to buy in the next month, they might move before winter."

Bob leaned forward with his elbows on the table. "I'm assigning Harlan, Barney, and Cal to do the mucking out of the horse barn and to ride herd on the cattle. Jeremiah, Thomas, Jacob, and I will work with breaking the horses."

Thomas could see from Harlan and Barney's faces that they didn't like the assignments. Thomas preferred to work with the horses but would do what Jeremiah or Bob told him to do. It interested him that Cal didn't seem to mind, or at least didn't show any reaction.

Jeremiah asked, "Anyone got any questions?"

Harlan shifted in his chair. "I can rope and ride better than Thomas or Jacob. Why don't you let them work with Barney, and I'll work with the horses?"

Barney threw Harlan a what-do-you-mean-leaving me with the mucking out job.

Thomas almost grinned. Barney just didn't realize Harlan had no loyalty to anyone but himself.

"Bob and I have divided the work the way we think will work best. If I change my mind, I'll reassign people," Jeremiah said in a voice that left no room for arguing.

Bob looked around at each of them as if to make sure they were paying attention. "Sheriff Grant has warned all the ranchers there are small bunches of cattle being rustled. We haven't noticed any specific loss, but I want everyone to be on the lookout for tracks and evidence cattle might have gone missing."

Jeremiah pushed the dishes in front of him toward the center of the table. "Cal, I'm putting you in charge of mucking out the horse barn, looking after the cattle, and anything else I decide you all can get done. Bob, you take Thomas and Jacob and get started with breaking the horses. I've got to go to the bank and will join you later." He stood and surveyed the crew. "All right, let's get to work."

Thomas sauntered over to the bunkroom to grab his jacket and hat. Someone shoved him from behind and he swung around to find Harlan on his heels.

"I know why Jeremiah won't let me work with the horses. He has to keep an eye on you, jailbird. He can't trust you to ride out and look after the cattle."

Thomas grinned at him out of meanness. "You're probably right." Harlan wanted a fight and Thomas agreeing with him didn't make him any happier.

"You know I'm right. I'm of a mind to quit. I've had about as much of that self-righteous gent as I can take." Harlan sounded like he was just getting started.

Grabbing his jacket and hat, Thomas went out by the side door. He wished Harlan would quit his job at the ranch. He was tired of him. However, that was unlikely to happen, as the Rocking JR Ranch was a great place to work.

As Thomas walked up to the corral, Bob was saddling a brown gelding. "Go help Jacob load the wagon. We're going to use the corrals in the north pasture."

"Yes, sir." He headed into the barn where he found Jacob loading branding irons, the shears used for castrating the colts between eight to twelve months old, different sizes of saddles, saddle blankets, ropes, bridles, and bags of sugar cubes and apples into a small ranch wagon.

Thomas helped hitch two horses to the wagon, then climbed up on the wagon seat beside Jacob.

When they got to the north pasture, Thomas could see several hundred horses spread out grazing. Jacob stopped the wagon close to the smaller of the two corrals where they unhitched the horses and then saddled them. Jacob and he rode out to help Bob drive a group of ten horses into the larger corral.

Once they had the horses in the corral, Bob entered the corral on foot carrying his lariat. As they herded the horses in a circle around the big corral Bob studied them and decided which one they would work with. He pointed toward a brown mare with white markings and Jacob and Thomas herded her toward the smaller corral. Bob opened the gate to let the horse through and then quickly closed it behind her.

Bob said, "Thomas, go ride around the corral perimeter and make sure the rails are in place."

"Yes, sir." He checked the fencing that was made up of posts about every five feet with rails up to six feet. It was a well-built corral. When he got back to where Bob was waiting, he found that Jeremiah had arrived.

"Thomas, I want you to just watch for a while." Jeremiah unlatched the gate and entered.

Thomas spent the next four hours watching Jeremiah work with the brown mare. It was an amazing exhibit of his ability to train a horse to respond to him and eventually be willing to be saddled and ridden. Thomas watched and listened as Jeremiah was able to get the mare to follow him in a very short time.

"Think you could do that?" Bob surprised him because Thomas was so intent on watching what Jeremiah was doing he had not heard Bob walk up to him.

"I'm not sure. I'm not totally sure what I just saw."

"That's an honest answer. What do you think you saw?" Bob leaned against the rail fence and kept his eyes on Jeremiah and the mare.

"I saw Jeremiah cooing at the horse but not really looking at it. Then he would walk away, the horse would take a couple of steps toward him, then Jeremiah goes back and does the same thing again. Then the horse walks up to him and nudges him on the shoulder when Jeremiah is ignoring him. Then he gives the horse an apple and rubs its neck and between the eyes. Now, he's putting a hackamore on the horse and then a blanket and walking along side. At this rate, he'll be riding the horse by sundown." He had told Bob what he had seen but why the horse was allowing Jeremiah to get so close, he had no idea.

"I know, you see it but you still don't know how he does it. I can do it now after years of Joe and Jeremiah teaching me. Some men can't seem to do it at all, Harlan being one of them. I think it has to do with the ability to be patient and not wanting to control the horse. It's about letting the horse be in control while you build up trust." Bob reached down, pulled up a sprig of grass, and started chewing on it.

This was a lot for Bob to say at one time. Evidently, he was as intrigued by the process Jeremiah used to break a horse as Thomas was. Before Thomas had come to the ranch he had the idea that a horse was broke by brute strength and manhandling the horse into obedience. Over the last eight months of watching Jeremiah and Bob deal with the horses, Thomas had come to understand their power with the horses was in being gentle and letting the horse choose to be broke. It amazed him.

By the end of the week, Jeremiah had Thomas shadowing him in the corral. Then he backed away and let Thomas work with a horse by himself. When the horse followed him and nudged him on the shoulder, he felt like shouting.

"Now you work with the mare for a while each day over the next couple of weeks. It shouldn't be a problem to finish breaking her." Jeremiah slapped him on the back and returned his grin.

When they got back to the house that evening, Thomas couldn't stop grinning. It felt like a great accomplishment and it felt good.

Chapter Twenty Thomas

Thomas had a hard day followed by a night spent in the horse barn with a mare having a difficult delivery. They had lost the mare and could well lose the foal. Then he endured the next day with Harlan, Barney, and Cal loading the dead mare onto a wagon, driving out to the edge of the back pasture, digging a hole big enough for the big animal, and burying it. It was a difficult task made worse by Harlan and Barney. The dragging behind, trying to do as little work as possible and snide, hateful comments the whole day had left Thomas with his temper barely under control when he got back to the ranch house.

Cal had shoveled and did his share of the work and even snapped at Harlan a couple of times in disgust.

Thomas stuck his head into the kitchen. "Miss Mildred, how long 'til supper?"

She turned from the stove where she was stirring a big skillet of gravy. "I'll have supper on the table in twenty minutes."

"Thanks, that gives me time to go jump into the creek."

"Good, we will all appreciate it." She laughed as he hurried into the bunkroom to grab some clean clothes.

Harlan and Barney were both stretched out on their bunks.

"Mind if I come along to the creek?" Cal threw his towel and clean shirt over his shoulder.

"Naw, we could all use a bath after today's work." The minute Thomas said it, he knew he shouldn't have.

"Are you trying to tell us when we should take a bath now?" Harlan's voice was pure meanness.

"You suit yourself." Thomas left the bunkroom with Cal on his heels.

As they quickly followed the well-worn path from the house to the swimming hole at the creek, Cal spoke up. "You watch yourself. Harlan purely has it in for you."

"Thanks for the warning. What about you? You got it in for me?" Lately Cal seemed to be stepping away from Harlan and Barney.

"Nope, I figure you done your time and besides you're easier to work with than Harlan. You do your share, he don't. I like this job and don't mind the work, but hanging around too close to Harlan could get a man fired."

Thomas glanced at him surprised at the longest conversation he had heard from the thin, balding taciturn cowhand. "Appreciate your viewpoint. I had noticed that you seemed to be a better caliber cowhand than Harlan or Barney but couldn't figure out where you stood with them."

Cal chuckled. "I may seem to go along with Harlan cause I don't like to butt heads with anyone, but I'm not going to let him mess up a good thing here on this ranch. Jeremiah is a good boss and Bob is a fair foreman."

After scrubbing up good, washing his hair in the cold creek water, and putting on clean clothes, Thomas headed to the kitchen for supper just as Mildred rang the supper bell.

Worn out from little sleep the night before and a hard day of shoveling and heaving the horse's carcass, he went to the bunkroom directly after supper. Feeling like he needed to unwind a bit before he could sleep, he opened the book he was reading from Jeremiah's library.

"You shore do smell pretty, Cal. You turning into one of those lily white boys who have to get a bath every other day?" Harlan's voice was sarcastic and whinny. Thomas found it to be more irritating than usual this evening.

"At least I didn't stink up the supper table like a couple of cowhands." Cal's voice was low and soft.

"You've changed lately, Cal. You starting to butter up to the boss and this jail bait here?"

"Maybe I'm just showing better sense than some I know."

Thomas watched the two men as they threw barbs at each other. Maybe he didn't know Cal as well as he thought he did. Cal was showing more strength of character against Harlan than Thomas had seen before. He'd seen men like Cal at Yuma. Ones who held back and let others seemingly take the lead but in reality were walking their own path in their own good time.

Harlan turned his gaze on Thomas, as if not liking the push back from Cal but unsure of what to make of it. "Maybe you've been getting at Cal here, jailbird. You think you're so high and mighty with that gal from the café sniffing around you."

"Shut up, Harlan. We don't talk about ladies like that here." Thomas lowered his book not sure where Harlan was going with such jabs.

"Don't you tell me to shut up. I'm not a rustler that ought to have hung. Any woman that is any good wouldn't hang around the likes of you. What's she getting out of it? Or, does she just like what she gets from a jailbird?"

"I'm telling you for the last time to get your mind out of the gutter and shut up about a decent woman." Thomas put his book down on the bed.

Harlan scraped his chair back and stood. "And you think you can make me. I'll talk about the wh—"

He didn't finish his sentence as Thomas lunged off his bunk. Harlan swung his fist and Thomas took one on the cheek that almost knocked him down. Harlan could throw a punch. Months of anger and frustration at Harlan's constant snide remarks and meanness seemed to congeal into a burning rage within Thomas. He beat and kicked Harlan with every jailhouse-brawler trick he had learned. Other than the one good punch to Thomas' cheek Harlan landed no more solid blows but was trying to defend himself. Grabbing his arm Thomas powered it behind his back and jerked. The sound of the bone cracking and his scream filled the room.

Out of the corner of his eye, Thomas caught the glimpse of Barney's fist just before it landed on his right eye. Sparks of light burst through his head, and he growled as he turned on this new threat. Taking Barney's feet from under him with a sweeping kick, he landed on Barney's leg with his knees and felt something give in the man's knee. For good measure, Thomas backhanded Barney's jaw. Just as Thomas had drawn back his fist to finish him off, he was grabbed by both arms and dragged off him.

"Stop it, Thomas. That's enough." Jeremiah's voice seemed to come from a distance as Thomas gulped for air.

"They're both done for, Thomas. Settle down." Bob's rough voice was in his other ear and his hands had a bruising hold on Thomas' arm.

He nodded. "I hear you." He began to feel the pain of the punches he had received and became aware that blood streamed down his face and dripped onto his clean shirt. Vaguely he wondered if he had another clean one.

Harlan moaned on the floor by the overturned table, holding his right arm as if cradling a baby. Barney didn't seem to be conscious. Thomas noticed that Barney's left knee seemed to be at an odd angle.

"What started this?" Jeremiah still had a tight hold on Thomas' arm.

Cal spoke up. "Harlan wouldn't stop insulting Miss Catherine even after Thomas told him to shut up twice. So, Thomas shut him up. Like always, it was Harlan started it but for once Thomas finished it."

"Sit there on your bunk and don't get up until I tell you," Jeremiah said as he let go of Thomas and Bob propelled him onto his bunk.

Bob knelt on the floor by Barney and tried to straighten his leg. That brought the man awake with a scream.

"His knee is broke." Bob stated the obvious before moving over to Harlan. "Let me see your arm." He gingerly felt along the arm.

Harlan cried out. "Don't touch it!"

Bob nodded to Jeremiah. "His arm is also broke. We better get Doc."

Cal came over to Thomas and handed him a towel to stop the bleeding from the cut on his face.

Jeremiah surveyed the mess of the bunkroom. "Let's get the wagon and we'll take them into Doc. They're going to need mending, and I don't want it to be here." He turned to Thomas. "You need to see Doc, Thomas?"

He shook his head. "No, sir. I'm fine."

"Cal, go hitch up the wagon and then get Jacob. Thomas, you stay in this room until I get back from town, and then I'll decide what to do."

Thomas hung his head and pressed the towel to the cut on his cheek as he grasped what Jeremiah was saying. He couldn't see any way he wasn't going back to Yuma Prison.

Jeremiah had the men put a couple of mattresses into the wagon and then loaded Harlan and Barney for the slow, painful ride to Doc's place.

After they left, Emily and Mildred came in with a basin of hot water and a medicine kit.

"Let me see that cut, Thomas." Emily's voice was soft and warm.

He looked up at her as she took the towel away and began to wash his face. "I'm sorry, Emily."

"Shhhh. Don't talk. I need to put a couple of stitches in that cut. I would say wait and let Doc do it, but he's going to be busy for a while." She took a cloth, soaked it in carbolic acid, and cleaned the cut. Then she took thread she had soaked in the same liquid and a needle she ran through the flame of a candle and sewed up the cut, which was below Thomas' left eye and over the cheekbone.

Thomas managed to stay still through the pain as he realized a worse agony. A moan escaped as he realized what he had done and the effects it was going to have on his folks and Catherine.

Emily laid a clean cloth soaked in carbolic acid on the wound. "I'm sorry, Thomas. It's almost done. Just need to put a bandage on it to keep it clean." Mildred handed Emily a spoonful of honey, which she smeared on the cut after removing the carbolic acid soaked cloth and then a placed a small piece of gauze over the cut. "Don't touch it until I have looked at it again. The honey should help the gauze to stay on if you don't jiggle it."

They straightened the table and chairs and Mildred carried out the basin of water.

"What happened, Thomas? Why the fight this evening? Harlan has poked jabs at you since you got here." She sat down beside him on the bunk.

He glanced at her concerned face. "He insulted Catherine. I can take insults about myself, but when he said those kinds of things about her, I couldn't stop myself."

"Any real man would have done the same. If he had said such things to Jeremiah, he would have been fired on the spot." She placed a small delicate hand over his that rested on the quilt. "I can't speak for Jeremiah, but I'm praying that we can work past this."

He nodded. "Thanks." Even if he had to go back to Yuma, he was glad he had had this chance to get to know people like Jeremiah and Emily.

She patted his hand and stood up. "Why don't you try to get some sleep? It may be hours before Jeremiah is back."

"I'll try." He lay back on his bunk and let the pains from the fight settle into a dull ache. He felt battered and hopeless. To have to return to the torment that was Yuma Prison filled him with misery. What if he never saw Catherine again? There were worse wounds than a cut and a bruised face.

Chapter Twenty-One Thomas

Thomas woke several times through the long night. About midnight he had heard the wagon return, but Jeremiah never came back into the bunkroom. With dawn breaking, he got up and dressed. Cal dressed and left the bunkroom with a sympathetic nod. He knew.

Dread filled Thomas' gut as he thought of the long trip back to Yuma. The next three years were going to be much harder to do after having the near freedom of the ranch, but he saw no way out of Jeremiah sending him back. Maybe if he hadn't hurt Harlan and Barney the way he did. But what was done was done, and he would have to pay the price.

Never far from his thoughts was the image of Catherine. Never to be near her again. Even if he could see her before Jeremiah sent him back to prison, how would she look at him? Someone who was so violent in the midst of her calm world? The longing for her was a hurting that wouldn't stop.

Thomas had been told not to leave the bunkroom and he didn't. After folding up the bedding, he sat on his bunk and waited.

Bob came to the door. "Come on into the kitchen and eat, Thomas."

He made a quick stop by the wash up room and shaved. If he was going back to Yuma today, at least he'd leave clean shaven.

When he made it to the table everyone was there eating. He sat at his usual place without looking up. Forcing himself, he ate breakfast feeling like a condemned man eating his last meal. Even the twins were subdued as if everyone was waiting for something.

Jeremiah finished eating and shoved back from the table. "Thomas, when you're finished, meet me in the front room."

Thomas glanced up at Jeremiah's stern face and nodded. "Yes, sir." After forcing himself to swallow the last of the coffee from his cup, Thomas followed him into the front room feeling as he had when he was seventeen and waited for the judge to pronounce his sentence.

"Take a seat." Jeremiah sat with his elbows on his desk and his fingers steepled. He scrutinized Thomas' face as if searching for something.

Sitting stiff and straight, Thomas waited for the words that would seal his future.

"Tell me what happened and what you were thinking last night."

Not expecting to have a hearing, he took in a deep breath. "I lost my temper. I couldn't let Harlan get away with what he was saying about Catherine. She doesn't deserve that kind of talk."

Jeremiah nodded. "I agree with that but why such force? Why hurt them so bad and especially when you knew the possible cost for yourself?"

"I didn't set out to hurt them so bad, but that's the only way I know to fight. It's no excuse for what I done, but Harlan came at me first and I reacted."

"That's what Cal said. He said you were defending yourself from the two of them. But, they were unprepared for how good a brawler you are." Jeremiah gave a little grin. "And to think I wondered whether you could defend yourself."

"I learned the hard way over the years at Yuma to put a man down so he couldn't come back at you again. Instinct just took over. I didn't set out to hurt them."

"Well, you did. Doc says Harlan will be months before his arm is healed, and Barney will probably never be able to walk without a limp because his knee is so badly broken. I don't regret losing them and probably should have fired them months ago, but this isn't the way I wanted to get them off the ranch." Jeremiah leaned back and gripped the armrest of his office chair. "Now I have to decide what to do about you."

Thomas tried to sit still and stop the trembling in his hands by grasping them tightly. He waited for the words that would seal his return to Yuma Prison. What else could Jeremiah do?

"The sheriff will be out in a little while. Between what Cal will tell him and my word you won't be a future problem, I expect to keep him from taking you into jail. But I need your word that nothing like this will happen again."

Hope flared and Thomas leaned forward. "You're not sending me back to Yuma?"

"No, not unless the judge there demands it. A man should be able to defend himself and to defend those he cares about. I'll inform Yuma of the incident in a week or two. I don't see it would benefit anyone for you to go back to prison. But I need your word."

"You have my word this won't happen again unless .... " He couldn't lie to the man. He'd fight again if it meant protecting Catherine, or even the ranch.

"Unless?" Jeremiah prompted.

"Unless I'm attacked or someone tries to hurt someone I care about." Thomas looked him in the eyes.

"I can live with that. But, if there is a next time, try to come to me and let me handle it."

Thomas knew his own strength and that he could handle any kind of fair fight. He understood Jeremiah was asking him to think whether he should fight before swinging his fist.

"All right, I'll try to remember that."

"This makes it even more important you don't leave the ranch without one of us with you. Maybe for a while you better not leave the ranch except to go to church."

Thomas heard horses coming up the lane and Bob came into the front room. "Boss, the sheriff is here and he has Myles McKinley with him."

Jeremiah stood and crossed to the front door. "You stay where you are, Thomas. Let me do the talking."

The sheriff and McKinley bustled in with scowls on their faces. Thomas felt at a disadvantage sitting in the chair with them bearing down on him.

Sheriff Grant said, "Black, on your feet and turn around. You're under arrest."

Jeremiah placed himself between Thomas and the sheriff. "Whoa there, Grant. You can't arrest a man for defending himself."

"What do you mean? Black here beat up two of your cowhands without provocation."

Jeremiah raised his hands palms out toward the sheriff. "Who told you Harlan and Barney didn't provoke this?"

The sheriff jerked a thumb toward McKinley. "Myles here talked to them and they said that Black here jumped them for no reason."

Jeremiah glared at McKinley. "Well, maybe you want to hear what the witness says before you jump to conclusions. Black was the one jumped, and after he had put up with a lot of guff from both men. I can't fault a man for defending himself, especially from two attackers."

Sheriff Grant frowned and glanced between Jeremiah and McKinley. "Who's the eyewitness? No one told me there was a witness."

"Bob, go get Cal." The foreman left the room and within moments was back with Cal. He must have been in the kitchen waiting.

Jeremiah motioned for Cal to join the men. "Tell the sheriff what you saw yesterday evening. Just tell the truth."

Cal gave Thomas a bland look and then turned his back to him. "Harlan and Barney were ragging on Thomas like always. Thomas was just standing there when Harlan started hitting him and then Barney started in but Thomas was faster and better at fighting than the two put together. Before I knowed what was happening, there they both were on the floor groaning. Thomas didn't have no choice."

Sheriff Grant scratched the back of his neck. "You willing to swear in court Harlan and Barney threw the first punches?"

Myles spoke up. "You can't believe what this cowhand says. Jeremiah probably told him what to say and Cal here wants to keep his job."

Before Jeremiah could respond, Cal took a step toward Myles. "You calling me a liar, McKinley?"

Sheriff Grant stepped between them. "No, he's not. Go get our horses, Myles. We're done here."

With a look of rage at Thomas, Myles stomped out of the house.

The sheriff turned to Thomas and Jeremiah. "I'm going to let this go, but I'm keeping an eye on you, Black. One more problem and you're on your way back to Yuma." Without waiting for a response, he slammed out the front door. Within moments, Thomas heard the sound of horses trotting down the lane.

In the quiet that followed, Jeremiah said, "Thanks, Cal. You two go on and get to work."

Almost giddy with relief, Thomas followed Cal out to the corral and saddled up to go check on the herd. With the loss of both Harlan and Barney, they would have more work to do, but Thomas couldn't say he would miss either of them.

Chapter Twenty-Two Thomas

The next week went by fast with work from dawn to dusk. They were shorthanded and needed more cowhands to replace Harlan and Barney. Jeremiah didn't seem concerned and worked alongside of them with as much effort as he expected from the men who worked on the ranch.

On Sunday, Thomas' folks and Catherine came out after church services as usual, except that a scrawny auburn-haired boy who appeared to be about fourteen years old was trailing along behind the buggy on as sorry a looking horse as Thomas had ever seen. The boy was dressed in clothes as close to rags as one could get, with his boots worn down, and with a piece of the brim of his dirty old straw hat missing. He looked like he hadn't eaten in days and had a wary, anxious glance as his eyes flitted from person to person as if searching for a safe place to land.

Jeremiah, Bob, and Jacob all gathered in the yard behind Thomas.

Pa climbed out of the buggy and offered his hand to Ma while Thomas did the same for Catherine.

"Howdy." As happened so often in her presence, Thomas was tongue-tied.

"Howdy, yourself." She smiled and the sunlight was brighter and the trees greener.

The two women went into the house and Pa turned toward the boy. "Get down, Jethro, and meet these men."

The boy scrambled down off the sway-backed brown mare and stood awkwardly next to Pa. Jethro appeared to make an effort to straighten up to his full height, which came to about shoulder height to Thomas' six feet two inches.

"Jeremiah, this is Jethro Hunter. He's looking for work and I thought maybe you might be needing a hand to help out now that you're shorthanded. This is Jeremiah Rebourn, owner and Bob Fife here is the foreman. This is Jacob Blunfeld and this is my son, Thomas."

The boy ducked his head and mumbled something that might have been a greeting. He looked starved. Although taller than Pa, he was nothing but skin and bone and his tattered clothes looked ready to fall off him. He didn't look as if he'd had a bath in a year and smelled like it also. Where had Pa found this kid?

Jeremiah gave the kid a once over. "Where are you from, Jethro?"

The boy more mumbled that spoke. "Kintuck, mister."

"Where's your family?" Jeremiah frowned.

Shifting his feet in boots that looked like they had been ready to be discarded before the boy was born, he said, "They all dead. Kilt by the cholera four yur ago. I ben on my own."

Jeremiah rubbed the back of his neck. "How old are you?"

"My last birthday I turned fourteen yer old, mister." He seemed to be examining his boots.

Thomas had met some men from the mountains of Tennessee and Kentucky in prison. They had all had the same cadence in their talk as the boy.

Jeremiah put his hands at his waist and stared at the boy. "You interested in a job like Mr. Black here said?"

The boy nodded without looking up. "Yes, mister."

"You think you can follow orders, help muck out a barn, ride fence, and cut wood?" Jeremiah asked.

Lifting his head, the boy stared at Jeremiah with a look that held a hint of hope. "Yes, sir. I kin do that."

"I'll start you out at fifteen dollars for the first month plus room and board. After that we will see how it goes." Jeremiah turned. "Thomas here will show you where to take care of your horse and your bunk. We'll eat dinner in about thirty minutes. That should give you time to wash up a bit."

Thomas hoped the old horse would make it into the barn. He led the way and the boy followed leading his horse. They unsaddled the horse and then put it into a stall with feed and fresh water.

"Grab your bedroll and follow me." Thomas headed for the bunkroom and heard the soft footsteps of the boy behind him. Leading him into the bunkroom, he pointed toward the empty bunks. "Choose one of the empty ones to be your bunk. You got any clean clothes?"

Jethro set his bedroll on the floor by an empty bunk away from both Thomas and Cal's bunks. "No, sir. I's wearing all I got." His voice was soft and sliding into a deep voice of a man but still with the occasional jumps back to a boy's voice.

Thomas glanced around at the clothes hanging on hooks on the wall between the bunks. He noticed a shirt and pair of pants he thought had been Barney's hanging on a hook. They were worn but clean. Barney was about Jethro's height. Thomas tossed them to Jethro.

"Here's some fairly clean clothes. Let me grab a clean set myself and we'll go down to the creek and wash up before dinner." Thomas didn't wait for a reply but as soon as he had gathered his things including a couple of towels and a bar of lye soap, he headed for the creek. Again, the boy softly followed.

Thomas didn't really need a bath but it wouldn't hurt after handling the horses while hitching and unhitching the buggies. And, he decided it was the simplest way to get the boy to bathe. The boy needed a good scrubbing and a quick wash up wouldn't do the job.

When they got to the creek, Thomas pointed to the pool where he usually bathed. "The water is cold but if you get in and out quick, it's not too bad. It's not deep, only up to my chest." Thomas shucked his clothes quick and was into the water before the boy had moved. He scrubbed with the soap with his back to the young man. Looking over his shoulder, he said, "Here, catch the soap."

The boy stood chest deep in the water splashing some up on his chest and shoulders that were painfully thin with all his ribs showing. He caught the soap that Thomas threw.

Thomas went under the water to finish rinsing off and then drudged up onto the bank where he grabbed a towel. He was soon dressed and ready to head to the house. He turned to find Jethro dressed and carrying his ratty old clothes.

"You ready to head in and eat?" Thomas started toward the house even as he asked the question.

"Yes, sir." Jethro walked softly two steps behind. That seemed to be his preferred way.

Thomas led Jethro into the bunkroom through the outside door. He left his dirty clothes in a growing stack at the end of his bunk. "Leave your dirty clothes out where Sally can find them. She'll gather them in the morning. She does laundry for the hands on Monday. If my clothes are too covered in dirt and muck, I'll rinse them out, dry them, and then put them in the dirty clothes pile. Even though someone is paid to do something for you, it doesn't hurt to be considerate and make their job easier. I'm just glad to not have to do my own laundry and want to show appreciation, so when Sally returns your clothes, clean, ironed, and folded, be sure to tell her thank you."

Jethro nodded. "Yes, sir. If'fen it's a problem, I kin warsh my own clothes."

"No, it's not a problem and it's part of Sally's job. Jeremiah wants us out working with the cattle and horses, taking care of the ranch chores, and not spending time doing house chores. Not that there would be anything wrong with us men helping in the house, but it's better use of our time to be doing the heavy work outside." Thomas felt a need to explain things to the boy, as he didn't seem to have had much training. Picking up the rubber comb from the small chest by his bunk, he ran it through his hair hoping it was in some semblance of order. He kept intending to pick up a mirror for the bunkroom when he was in his father's store but kept forgetting.

Pitching the comb at Jethro, he smiled. "Here, see if you can tame that head of hair a bit. You don't want to scare the ladies and look like a wild man." Next time Jacob acted as barber, Thomas hoped he could get Jethro to partake of his service. The boy's thick auburn hair was growing past his shoulders.

Running the comb through his hair, Jethro managed to get a little control of the heavy waves of hair. He pulled it back behind his ears. "That all right, mister?"

Thomas looked the boy over. He looked better after a bath, clean clothes, even if they didn't fit his skinny frame, and an effort to bring the mop of hair under control. "You'll do, Jethro. Follow me and let's go get to the table before the prayer. Once the amen is said, the food disappears real fast."

Jethro nodded and followed close behind Thomas.

All the others were already in their usual places. Thomas pointed to the chair that Barney had usually sat at. "Why don't you sit there next to Jacob?"

Keeping his head down and not making eye contact with anyone, Jethro nodded and sat down at the table, which was laden with the usual roast beef and fixings. Thomas almost laughed at the way the boy's eyes got bigger and he stared at the mounds of food. Then he didn't feel like laughing as he wondered if perhaps the boy was truly starving. After the prayer and the food was passed around the table Thomas watched as Jethro took small helpings and then began to eat hunched over his plate as if to guard what was on it.

Thomas heaped his plate with food and let the conversation flow around him as he ate. A couple of times as the biscuits made their way around the table again after Mildred had replenished them, he noticed the boy slipped a biscuit into his shirt. He would have to talk to Jethro about hoarding food, as there was no need. Emily made sure there was plenty to eat. Shaking his head, Thomas wondered how he had ended up in charge of raising a boy, but it seemed like someone needed to and it might as well be him.

After dinner was over everyone drifted out of the kitchen. Elisha and Joseph edged up to Jethro and Elisha asked, "You want to go see our fort?"

Jethro glanced from the small boys to Thomas. "That be all right, mister?" He towered over the boys who would be six in a few weeks, but he had a look of eagerness at the idea of play. He might be trying to do a man's work, but he was still a boy.

"Sure, Jethro, and call me Thomas. You can do what you want until later this afternoon when we will need to go check on the horses in the horse barn. I'll let you know when."

Jethro glanced at the twins and gave the suggestion of a smile. "I'd be proud to see your'on fort."

"Elisha, Joseph." The boys looked up at Thomas with eager faces. He could tell they were excited to have a new playmate and it would probably be good for Jethro to have some fun. "Boys, I'm making you responsible, and I am encouraging you not to get Jethro into any trouble. You understand?"

Jeremiah walked up next to Thomas. "That's right, boys. Go have fun for the afternoon and show Jethro around but follow the rules."

"Yes, Pa." "All right, Pa," came two voices at once.

"You all go have some fun." Jeremiah pushed the boys toward the door of the kitchen onto the back porch.

Thomas followed Jeremiah into the front room where Pa, Ma, and Catherine had gathered. Emily was nowhere in sight, but Thomas figured she was putting little Charity down for her afternoon nap.

Jeremiah headed for his favorite large oversized stuffed armchair that was angled toward the fireplace. "Thanks, Thomas, for getting Jethro settled. He sure looked and smelled better."

Emily came into the front room after closing the door to her and Jeremiah's bedroom. She sat in the rocking chair across from the lamp table from Jeremiah. Thomas' folks sat on the divan facing the fireplace with Catherine taking the McLean Patent Swing rocker that had arrived by train from Denver the week before. Thomas had no doubt Jacob had examined the rocker and planned to reproduce it with his own designs added in. Thomas grabbed a cane seated sitting chair from against the wall and placed it between the end of the divan and the rocker where Catherine sat.

"Milburn, tell us about Jethro. Where did you find him?" Emily asked.

Thomas suspected Emily asked what she knew Jeremiah wanted to know but hesitated to ask. Emily often started conversations and asked questions that most likely Jeremiah wanted answers to but was too reserved to ask.

"Well, Emily, he came into the store on Friday. At I watched him, as he looked around, I was afraid he would try to steal something." Milburn patted Agnes' knee. "I know, dear, I should be more trusting, but you know there are too many people who will try to take something without paying. Over a period of time it starts eating into any profit."

"I understand, Milburn. But he is just a boy," Agnes replied.

Milburn chuckled. "A hungry boy. He came up to me and asked how many crackers he could buy for a penny. I guess that's all the money he had. I gathered up some crackers from the barrel and wrapped them with brown paper. I wanted to give the crackers to the boy, but I sensed a pride and so I took the penny."

Agnes spoke up. "Yesterday morning he was sitting on the steps of the store when Milburn came down to open up."

"I almost stepped on him. I wonder now if he had slept there. Anyway, he asked real polite if I had any work for him. I didn't really, but I asked him to sweep the back dock and pick up trash along the alleyway to clean up the back of the store a bit. When I paid him a nickel, I told him about the beans Catherine always has available and that he could get a big bowl for a nickel."

Catherine picked up the story. "He must have come right over because he came into the café about eleven. He scooted into a chair at the table in the far corner and never looked up at me when I asked him for his order. He asked for a bowl of beans and placed the nickel on the table as if he thought I would question whether he had the money. He looked so thin and hungry that I added a glass of milk and cornbread to his order. I told him they came together for the same price. You should have seen him eat, as if he hadn't had anything for days."

Milburn smiled at Catherine. "You're as big a push over as I am."

Agnes patted her husband's arm. "Let's hope not or she'll go out of business."

"Now, honey, I'm not that bad. Anyway, he came back yesterday afternoon and asked if I had any other work for him or knew of a job he could apply for. I thought of you all what with Harlan and Barney leaving and so I brought him out today. Agnes said I should have asked the boy to church, but I didn't want to scare him off. And I was afraid that would do it. I could see he needed help, but sometimes you have to do it slow and easy."

Agnes sighed. "I know you are right. I'm too quick to just barge ahead when I think of an idea."

Jeremiah uncrossed his ankles and slouched lower in the chair as if getting comfortable for his Sunday afternoon nap. "I'm glad you brought him out. We do need help and so does he."

Emily stood and turned to Agnes. "You want to see what I've been sewing this week?"

Agnes stood. "Yes, I want to see what you did with that jean material you purchased last week. Was it hard to work with?" She followed Emily toward the sewing room down the hall of the house.

Thomas turned to Catherine. You want to go for a walk?"

"Yes, I would enjoy that. With winter coming soon, we may not get many more Sunday's as pretty as today. Just let me get my shawl and hat."

Chapter Twenty-Three Thomas

Thomas took Catherine's hand as they walked toward the creek. They passed the fort the boys had built out of logs with help from Thomas. It was large enough the boys could be inside it and stand to look out the cracks between the logs and poke their stick rifles out to pretend to shoot the enemies, which today was Jethro. Of course, all of it took place with much yelling and giving of orders from both twins. Thomas noticed Jethro did what the twins told him without much reaction. The boys were so busy with their own imaginations they didn't notice whether Jethro was interacting much. Thomas guessed Jethro had not played much in his life. The twins, on the other hand, were old hands at play and knew how to have a good time.

Catherine laughed and edged closer to Thomas as they walked along the path to the creek. "The twins don't seem to notice that if Jethro wanted he could overcome them in an instant. He's letting them think they are out maneuvering him."

Thomas chuckled. "Yeah, he's letting them have fun. It tells me that he is not a bully if he'll let two little kids run around him like that."

Catherine glanced up at him. "I never thought about that but it's true. Is that why you encouraged him to go play with them?"

"No, I only wanted them to be children and enjoy life. It's a side benefit to observe Jethro has a kind side to him in spite of his hard life."

"Kind of like you." She squeezed his hand as if to emphasize her opinion of him.

It gave him a heady feeling, as he walked a little taller.

~

That evening as Thomas, Cal, and Jethro finished checking on the mares and foals in the horse barn, they walked back to the house together. Thomas noticed Jethro looked pale and his hands shook. They had eaten a good supper before heading to the barn for the last chores of the day, so Thomas knew the boy wasn't hungry.

"Jethro, you feel all right?"

The boy glanced at Thomas and then quickly looked away. "Yes, mister."

Cal gave the boy a scrutinizing look. "He does look a little shaky, Thomas."

Thomas held the door to the bunkroom open. "Go on to bed Jethro. I'll wake you in the morning. We'll go feed the horses in the horse barn and the corral before breakfast. After we eat, we'll ride out and check on the horses in the pastures and on the cattle unless Bob or Jeremiah tells us different."

Jethro stumbled to the bunk made up with sheets, blankets, and a pillow. Either Mildred or Sally had been in and made it up. Thomas noticed that the boy pulled his old boots off, pulled the covers back, and crawled into his bunk with his clothes still on. He seemed to be asleep before his head touched the pillow. How long had it been since the boy had slept in a bed with clean sheets? Thomas felt surprise at protectiveness he felt toward the boy.

Cal chuckled softly. "I don't think we have to worry about him being too noisy. You mind if I leave the lamp on for a while and read? It's still a little early for me."

Thomas sat on his bunk and pulled his boots off. "No, I don't mind. I want to relax and read awhile myself." He was grateful for the peace and calm in the bunkroom now Harlan and Barney were no longer there. He and Cal seemed to get along better and better each day. Pulling his Bible off the small shelf he had put up above his bunk, Thomas settled down to read. After only a few minutes of reading some of the Psalms, Thomas' eyes began to drift shut. He laid the Bible aside, turned down the lamp by his bed, and drifted off to sleep.

Chapter Twenty-Four Thomas

Thomas woke as dawn was breaking and heaved himself out of bed. Stretching and yawning, he glanced over at Jethro. Still in deep sleep, the boy sprawled out on his bunk with his arms and legs going in all directions. Thomas pulled his pants on and grabbed a clean shirt. After he stomped into his boots, he walked over to the bunk where Jethro was softly snoring. Nudging the boy's leg, Thomas softly called. "Jethro, wake up. It's time to start the day."

Jethro came awake and was on his feet ready to swing at Thomas before he could step back. "Whoa, Jethro, it's me, Thomas. You're safe in the bunkroom of the Rocking JR Ranch. Remember?"

Blinking as if trying to get a bearing on what was real and what was nightmares, Jethro went still and stared around the bunkroom. Cal sat on the edge of his bunk pulling on his boots and watching the boy.

Jethro lowered his arms and fisted hands. "Sorry, mister. You surprised me. I don't like no one sneaking up on me."

Thomas nodded. "I understand. I should have spoken to you to wake you up. Get your boots on, grab your towel, and follow me to the wash up room. We'll splash some water on our faces, grab a cup of coffee, and go get the horse barn mucked out. Then we get to eat a big breakfast the ladies will have prepared."

Jethro looked like he might have almost smiled. "Yes, sir." With his hair all tousled and the last relaxation of sleep lingering on his face, he looked younger than his years. He quickly slipped into his shabby old boots and was ready to follow Thomas.

Thomas led the way into the wash up room. Someone had fired up the wood stove and had hot water boiling in the big kettle. He ladled some of the hot water into a metal basin and added some cold water to cool it a bit. Using the bar of soap that set in the bowl by the drain sink, he vigorously scrubbed his face, hands, and arms. After rinsing off, he toweled dry and dumped the soapy water out of the basin into the drain sink. He then ladled more hot water into the basin and set it on the counter in front of the mirror. He reached up and pulled the box with his shaving gear off the top shelf above the counter.

He noticed Jethro followed his example of washing up. "Each of us has a box up on the shelf with our own personal stuff and Mrs. Rebourn lets us leave it in the wash up room. We clean up after ourselves and keep our towels by our bunks. We use the same towel for a week. This morning after I finish shaving, I will put my towel with my dirty clothes as this is Monday and the ladies will gather the wash. By evening, we'll have clean clothes and a clean towel. If something happens and you need a clean towel before the week is up, grab one out of the closet in the hallway. Just don't ever leave wet things lying on the floor. There are plenty of hooks in the bunkroom to hang your stuff up."

Jethro nodded and frowned as if he was trying to remember all the instructions. Thomas figured it was better to tell the boy straight out what was expected of him. When Thomas had arrived at the ranch, it had been Jacob who had given him the hints of how to live at peace in the ranch community. Now, it was Thomas' turn to pass the information on to Jethro.

After he finished shaving, dumped the water from the basin, and wiped it down with the towel, he put his shaving things into his box and set it back on the upper shelf. "Ready to get to work?" he asked Jethro who looked more awake now.

"Yes, sir." Jethro followed Thomas back to the bunkroom where they left their towels and grabbed their jackets and hats.

Thomas reached up on a shelf and pulled down a worn pair of gloves. He pitched them to Jethro. "You can keep these for your use. You might as well save your hands from blisters. But you're responsible for keeping up with them." Thomas pulled on his own gloves and headed across the hallway with Jethro following behind him. After a stop in the kitchen for a quick cup of coffee, they headed for the horse barn.

It was a clear, cool November morning with a hint of frost. Winter was on its way and the birds seemed to be chattering more than usual. Thomas scanned the sky for indications the weather was about to change. He was four years old when his folks had transplanted the family to Arizona, and he didn't remember a winter in Colorado. He wondered how difficult the snow and cold would be. One thing for sure, both he and Jethro had to have a coat. Thomas hated to ask for anything, but he would need to ask Bob or Jeremiah about getting some kind of winter clothes. He could ask his folks for himself using the money they had given him, but wasn't sure what to do about Jethro.

When they entered the horse barn, they found Bob and Jacob at work. After exchanging morning greetings, Bob leaned on the pitchfork he was using and regarded Jethro. "You ever do much work around horses?"

"Yes, sir. I worked in the livery stable fore and helped on some ranches for a time." The boy spoke so softly that Thomas had to strain to hear him.

"Good. All these horses are breeding mares and their newborn foals. We work quietly and gently around them. The stalls need to be mucked out, fresh hay put in the stalls, water and feed put out. That will be your job. Thomas and I will check the mares, especially those about to foal and the ones who have just delivered a foal. Then we'll help you and Cal finish up. Thomas will be in charge and you can direct any questions to him. Do what he tells you to do. You have any questions for now?"

Jethro shook his head. "No, mister."

Thomas glanced at the boy. "Come over here and grab a wheelbarrow and a pitchfork. Muck out a stall carefully and completely. If a mare has a foal with her, keep away. Bob and I will lead the mares out into the corral to check on them and while we have them out of the barn, you and Cal need to get the stalls cleaned out and fresh hay scattered in it. Also, put out some oats and a bucket of fresh water. Let's go to work."

Bob opened a stall and attached a bridle on the mare. He gently led her out of the stall and barn and into the large corral. Thomas went to the next stall and did the same with the mare that was there, only this mare had a small foal following along behind.

Thomas walked the mare around and watched how she moved. The little foal trotted around investigating the corral.

Bob also watched. "She seems to be doing fine after giving birth last night. Let's keep her and the foal in the barn and the corral here for a few more days and then we'll turn them out into the east pasture."

Thomas nodded. "Sounds good." He checked the hooves of the mare and ran his hands over her to make sure she hadn't started a fever. He then checked the little foal who scampered about, but each time he got too many steps from his mother, he quickly came back to nuzzle her as if to reassure himself that she was still there. Thomas then led the mare followed by the foal back into the barn to the clean stall Jethro had mucked out. After Thomas had her and her baby back in the stall, he checked that she had water and some oats, as well as the clean hay. As the mare ate oats in the feedbag, the foal nursed.

For the next several days, Thomas kept busy with normal work around the ranch and in instructing Jethro in his duties. The boy seemed eager to learn and without complaint set about any task Thomas gave him. In fact, he didn't say much of anything. However, Thomas noticed that the boy intently watched everything going on around him.

They were finishing breakfast when Jeremiah cleared his throat. When he had everyone's attention, he said, "Jethro, I want you to go into town today with Jacob. We need to send in two wagons to pick up supplies that are coming in on the train and what we need to pick up at the mercantile. If anyone needs something from town, give your list to Jacob. Thomas, you and Cal go check on the north herd and if they're drifting too far north, start them back toward the ranch. Pack a lunch with you but be back before dark." He took time to sip from his coffee cup before he continued. "Bob and I will work with the horses. Any questions?"

Emily stood and smiled. "You forgot to mention Mildred and Sally will be cooking and cleaning. You also forgot to mention that I'll be taking care of three children. Any questions?"

Jeremiah sat and looked at his wife as if he couldn't figure out what she was going on about. Thomas decided to get out of the kitchen before he started laughing. Cal, Jacob, and Jethro were close behind him.

Once in the bunkroom, grabbing his jacket and gloves, he started chuckling and Cal and Jacob joined in.

Cal took his coat from the hook by his bunk. "You reckon Jeremiah will figure out what Mrs. Emily was trying to tell him?"

Thomas shook his head. "No, I don't think he has a clue, but I'm going to go back to the kitchen after we get the horses saddled and get a few sandwiches and maybe a couple of apples for our lunch. When I do, I'm thanking Mildred and Sally for their hard work. I got the message."

Cal nodded. "Me, too."

Jethro looked from one man to the other with a frown. "What message?"

Thomas glanced at the boy as he gathered his gloves and put on his hat and jacket. "Mrs. Emily was trying to remind Jeremiah that the women on the ranch would be working today as well as the men. Jeremiah is so focused on the ranch work he must be overlooking what Mrs. Emily, Mildred, and Sally are doing to keep things going. I know he appreciates their work but even the women like to hear someone say, 'Good job'. Just like us men do."

Jethro was still frowning. "Like saying thank ya for a good breakfast?"

Thomas slapped him on the back as he headed toward the outside door. "Yep. I don't know about you, but I appreciate coming in after a hard day in the saddle and having clean clothes, the bunkroom swept, and a hot meal on the table. Could you imagine if we didn't have Mildred and

Sally helping out? Why Jeremiah would have us helping Mrs. Emily wash diapers."

The look on Jethro's face at the idea of washing diapers had both Cal and Thomas laughing as they headed to the corral to catch up a horse to ride for the day. Jethro went into the barn to help Jacob push the two wagons out and to gather the harness necessary to hitch up the horses for the trip to town.

"Cal, I'll go get some food for today if you'll fill the canteens." Thomas tied the big gray gelding to the corral fence and proceeded to saddle the horse. After he finished, he made his way back to the kitchen. The wind was starting to pick up and clouds were moving in with a definite chill in the air. His light jacket wasn't much protection.

He went into the kitchen and noticed Mildred making sandwiches with leftover roast beef. "Miss Mildred, what will it take for me to get about four of those sandwiches, some cake if any is left from last evening, and some apples?"

Mildred looked up from her task and smiled. "The chance is good as that is what Emily told me to prepare for you and Cal to take for your dinner. I'll have it ready soon and put it in this flour sack. Be sure to bring the flour sack back. The last time you forgot and threw it away."

Properly chastised, Thomas gave her a peck on the cheek. "Yes, ma'am, and thank you."

Looking slightly flustered, Mildred gave a wave of the hand. "You're welcome, Thomas. Now get going."

Thomas looked toward the front room. "Jeremiah still here?"

"Yes, he just got another cup of coffee and is at his desk."

Thomas walked into the front room and toward the cherry desk behind which sat Jeremiah.

"Something I can do for you, Thomas?"

"Yes, sir. I have a question about Jethro. The boy only has one set of clothes. I gave him an old shirt and pants of Barney's, but they are too big for him and they're worn out. Also, he doesn't have any winter clothes, no coat, and his boots are falling off his feet."

Emily had come to the front room from her bedroom carrying little Charity. "Thomas, thanks for reminding us. I have been so busy I didn't pay attention."

Thomas looked from Jeremiah to Emily. "After you wrote the judge and he said it was alright for my folks to give me some money, they have given me ten dollars a month. I can give you that to help get the boy some clothes."

Jeremiah shook his head. "Keep your money, Thomas. I appreciate the offer but the ranch will provide the boy with some clothes. I'll have Jacob shop for him while they're in town today."

Emily sat in the overstuffed chair in front of Jeremiah's desk. "What about you Thomas? Your clothes are starting to look awfully worn and that jacket you have on isn't going to be warm enough even for today."

Thomas looked at the floor. He could feel his neck and face getting warm with embarrassment. "I'll use the money from my folks for a coat. I don't want to ask them for more clothes."

Jeremiah gave Thomas a long slow look and then he nodded. "Make a list of what you think Jethro needs and what you need. Give it to Jacob. I'd send you into town to shop for yourself, but I think we still need to avoid you being seen much off the ranch, except for church."

"I understand. I'll get the list ready." Jeremiah was right, but Thomas hated the reminder of his status as a prisoner.

Emily got up and gave the baby to Jeremiah. She came over to Thomas and kissed him on the cheek. "Thank you for being so thoughtful of Jethro. I know he appreciates it, but he is just a boy and probably won't think to thank you."

Thomas shuffled his feet. "You're welcome, ma'am." Turning to Jeremiah, Thomas said, "Cal and I are heading out. We plan to ride to the north fence and will spend most of today hazing cattle back south. We'll keep an eye on the weather as I suspect it's about to change."

"Good, that's exactly what I want you to do."

Quickly as the morning was well started, Thomas grabbed the flour sack of food and after putting it into his saddlebag walked into the barn where Jacob was getting harness for the second wagon.

"Jacob, Jeremiah wants you to get the kid some clothes while you're in town today. You need me to write a list?"

"What do you want me to get?"

Thomas glanced around to make sure Jethro was still out harnessing the horses to the first wagon. "He needs about three sets of clothes, a coat, and new boots. You might want to get him a union suit while you're at it. Also, a heavy duster or rain gear. Winter is coming fast and the boy doesn't have any clothes for the harsh weather. In addition, here's some money for you to pick up a couple of union suits for me, a winter coat, and some heavy boots. My pa will know the size. If you have enough get me a couple of pairs of worsted wool pants and a couple of heavy shirts." He held out the twenty dollars he had managed to save.

Jacob took the money with a thoughtful look. "Don't worry. I'll take care of getting clothing."

Chapter Twenty-Five Thomas

Thomas and Cal made it to the north fence by noon. They had passed the cattle in order to reach the fence and check it out. They would haze the cattle south on their way back. As they rode the split rail fence, they came to a section with the rails scattered about which left a twenty-foot break in the fence.

Cal dismounted first and examined the downed fence section. "This didn't come down by itself, and look at the cattle tracks."

Thomas nodded grimly. "We've got a rustler problem. How many head do you think went through here? And how long ago do you think it happened?" Cal was a much better tracker than he was.

Cal took off his hat and slapped it against the leg of his pants. "The tracks look to be about two days old. From how churned up the ground is, I would say about a hundred head were driven though. Look here at the horse tracks on top of the cattle tracks. Maybe three horses came along behind the cattle." Cal stood looking north at the high hills that led into the mountains. "They are probably long gone, but they might have driven them north into a canyon and be holding them. Only way to know is follow them."

Thomas gave a sigh. "Let's repair this fence and start hazing the cattle back toward the main ranch. Jeremiah will have to decide what to do about tracking the cattle, even if you could after this long a time."

"You're right. There's not much chance to get those cattle back. Let's get busy repairing the fence. It's going to take a while and I doubt if we make it home before dark."

Thomas knew Cal was right. It was going to be a long day of hard work. This was the first time Thomas had been on the side of the rancher who lost his cattle to thieves. He didn't like it. He and all the other men on the ranch had worked hard to brand and herd those cattle. That someone thought they had a right to waltz onto the ranch and steal their hard work, offended him. How he had concluded almost thirteen years ago, that it was all right for him to steal another man's property was mystery to him now.

They hurried, but it still took them two hours to get the rails back up and nailed in place. Fortunately, they both had brought a hammer and enough nails in their saddlebags. They often had to repair a fence, but normally it was only the top rail or so and easily nailed back in place. A whole gap in the fence took more doing to get it back into place. By the time they finished and took ten minutes to eat, it was early afternoon.

"Come on, Cal, let's get started back south and do what we can before dark. It's going to be a long afternoon."

Cal mounted the brown mare and watched Thomas climb up on the big gray gelding. "You got that right, but we had to get the fence repaired. I don't look forward to telling Jeremiah. At least, no one can accuse you of rustling the cattle. You haven't been off by yourself long enough for days."

Thomas grinned. "You're right, but that won't stop folks from talking."

Working their horses and themselves hard they got most of the herd drifting south and made it back to the ranch house well after dark. Both men and horses were exhausted and hungry.

Cal caught the reins of Thomas' horse. "I'll tend to the horses if you'll report to Jeremiah."

"All right but if he gets mad at me, I'm taking it out on your hide." Thomas untied his saddlebags and headed toward the ranch house.

"Better you than me." Cal shouted after him.

Thomas enjoyed the banter, but he didn't like the news he had to give his boss. The whole day they had worked well together. Not having to put up with Harlan and Barney was a relief.

As he entered the bunkroom, he found Jethro asleep in his bunk on top of the covers with his boots still on. Thomas guessed it was Jethro who had lit the box stove and had the logs burning brightly warming the bunkroom. Thomas had been chilled most of the day except when they had worked on the fence. All afternoon the temperature had dropped while the wind increased.

There were brown paper wrapped packages on his bunk he assumed were clothes for Jethro and maybe some for himself. He hung his hat and his jacket hooks and placed his gloves on a shelf above the hooks. He took a minute to stand by the stove and rub his cold hands together in the warmth emanating from the cast iron stove. Hearing his stomach growl reminded him there was food and a warm stove in the kitchen.

After stopping in the wash up room to get some of the dirt off his hands and face, Thomas headed into the kitchen. He could hear the twins in the front room and the men's lower voices. He assumed everyone else was there.

Mildred was kneading bread on the kitchen work counter. "Come on in and sit down. I've got plates warming for you and Cal. Is he far behind you?" She went to the warm up oven at the top of the big Windsor cook stove and pulled out a plate of fried chicken and potatoes. She sat the plate in front of Thomas and then took a pan half-full of biscuits out of the warm up oven and slid it onto the table.

"I've got some gravy heating up. Won't take but a minute. Go ahead and get started with your supper."

"Thanks, Miss Mildred. Cal should be here in a few minutes."

Jeremiah came into the kitchen from the front room, followed by Bob and Jacob. "I thought I heard your voice. You boys got home pretty late." The three men sat around the table.

Thomas took a swig of coffee from the cup Mildred sat down on the table for him. "Yes, sir. It was a long day. When we got to the north fence we found about a twenty-foot section down and evidence that a bunch of cattle had been driven through."

Thomas paused to take another sip of coffee, Cal came in from the hallway. He sat across from Thomas. Mildred placed a plate of food in front of him. Thomas picked up his fork and pointed at Cal. "I'll let you tell what you read in the tracks."

Cal looked at Jeremiah. "A bunch of cattle had gone through the break in the fence followed by at least three men on horses. It was probably two days ago from the way the tracks had caved in on the sides. I'm guessing maybe a hundred head of cattle from the look of the tracks."

Thomas took up the telling. "Cal and I decided that we wouldn't be able to catch whoever had done it and needed to get back here to let you know. We spent a couple of hours rebuilding the downed section of fence. As we rode back, we hazed as many cattle south as we could. When it got dark we decided we had done as much as we could for today and headed on in."

Jeremiah sat calm and quiet for a moment and then said, "You handled it right. Bob, where do you think someone might run a bunch of cattle to the north?"

Bob rubbed his chin that showed a need for a shave. With his thick dark beard, he could shave twice a day and still show a shadowy beard. It gave his thin face a rough look. "It's hard to guess where they might be trying to get to because there's not much north of the ranch except hills and canyons. The nearest ranch is over to the east and that would be Ackerstone's place."

Thomas waited for Jeremiah to comment and he held up his cup for Mildred to replenish it as she made the round of the table with the coffeepot. "Thanks, Mildred."

"Cal, I want you and Bob to go back up there tomorrow prepared to spend some time following those cattle. See what you can find out and then get back here. Don't confront the rustlers. Those cattle aren't worth getting into a gun fight over, but I'd like to know where they're being taken. I want to find out who is behind the rustling and try to put a stop to it with the help of the sheriff."

Bob raised an eyebrow at Jeremiah. "What are you going to be doing, boss?"

"I'm going to talk to the sheriff, and then I'm going to try to find out if anyone is selling cattle. Maybe see if anyone is ordering cattle cars at any of the stops along the rail line. In fact, I may hire an investigator out of Denver to do some real sniffing around."

Thomas listened to Jeremiah and Bob. Jeremiah took the rustling seriously but not foolishly. He had half expected Jeremiah would have all the hands grab a horse and ride after the rustlers. But, that would have been foolish considering the rustlers would soon have a three day start. No, Jeremiah was going about it in a wise way.

Jeremiah spoke and broke into Thomas' thoughts. "You boys go ahead and get some sleep. Tomorrow, Thomas, I want you to work here close to the house with Jacob. We've got to be sure that you are where you need to be and with a witness that you are here on the ranch. So, stay close to Jacob. Hope you don't mind my saying that, but people want to blame someone and right now you're the easiest target."

Bob nodded. "You and Jacob can take care of the horses and work at chopping wood. Also, someone needs to be here watching over the women and children."

Both men were right, but Thomas still wished he were free to go help locate the cattle.

Cal spoke up. "You might want to consider sending Jethro with Bob and me. I've talked to him, and he's done a lot of hunting. He may be able to follow the trail better than Bob or me."

"You may be right. It wouldn't hurt, and we'll keep him out of trouble," Bob said.

Jeremiah looked at the men then pushed back from table. "Bob, if you think Jethro will be useful, ask him to go. If he seems reluctant leave him here." He placed his cup in the dry sink and turned to Mildred who waited for the dishes still on the table. "Mildred, you and Sally make up a pack of food for three men to last a week on the trail please."

"Yes, Jeremiah. We'll have it ready for the boys in the morning."

Thomas placed his dirty dishes in the basin of water in the sink and headed to the bunkroom. There would be no reading tonight. He was too tired. First, he had to open the packages on his bunk before he could fall into it. He noticed Jethro's name written on several and the rest had his name. He carried the ones with Jethro's name over to the boy who sat on his bunk pulling off his shabby boots.

"Here, Jethro, open these and see if they fit."

Jethro picked up one of the packages as if he didn't know what to do with it and started untying the string that held it together.

Thomas opened the packages on his bunk. A large warm coat with sheering lining, three pairs of wool worsted pants, three heavy wool shirts, socks, union suits, and fur-lined gloves were soon spread out on Thomas' bunk. He opened the last package and found a pair of heavy calf high, low-heeled boots and a pair of wool felt boot liners. He could see Ma's hand in the amount and choices of clothing. Thomas hadn't given Jacob enough money for all these clothes. What had Jacob told his parents? Not that he didn't appreciate the warm clothes. He hated to still be depending on his folks for his basic needs.

"Thomas?" Jethro's voice sounded like the boy he was.

Looking up Thomas saw Jethro holding a thigh-length heavy winter coat with a sheering lining. "Hey, that's like mine. It'll keep you warm in the coldest weather."

"But where did all this stuff come from? I got no money to pay for it." Jethro waved his hand over the clothes and boots spread out on his bunk.

Cal spoke up. "You don't have to pay for it. Jeremiah and Emily provide it as part of your pay. Just make sure the sizes are all right. Jacob can take them back into the store and exchange them if you haven't worn them." He pointed to the heavy coat hanging on a hook by his bunk. "Jeremiah gave me that coat last year. I'm hoping it will last a couple more years."

Jethro looked at the stuff on his bunk. "You mean I kin keep all these here clothes? Even the boots?"

Thomas heard the wonder in the boy's voice and hurt for him. He guessed the boy had never been given much in the past. God only knew the barren life the boy had had before landing at the Rocking JR Ranch.

After trying on his coat, Thomas hung it on a hook by his bunk. He then sat down and tried on the boots, which also fit perfectly.

"Try your clothes on, and if they fit hang them up on the hooks. Don't worry if they are a little big. I suspect my ma picked them out and would have gotten yours a size or two too big so you can grow into them."

Thomas held the pants up and tried on one of the shirts. They fit perfect. Ma knew his sizes. He then hung all his new clothes on the hooks by his bunk.

Before he would let himself collapse onto his bunk, Thomas went out to the hallway and into the big storage room. He found Bob there. "I wanted to see if there was a sleeping bag or blankets for a bedroll for Jethro."

Bob nodded. "That's a good idea. I'm just grabbing one myself. They're here on this shelf. Jeremiah keeps several on hand. One of his rules is during winter you don't ride out without one in case you get caught out in the weather. Does Jethro have saddlebags or a pommel rain slicker?"

Thomas pulled a rolled up sleeping bag off the shelf and an oilcloth to use to spread out on the ground under the sleeping bag. "You can assume Jethro doesn't have anything."

Bob added a pair of saddlebags, a canteen, and a pommel rain slicker to the sleeping bag. "In the morning, you help Jethro get his gear packed and tied onto his horse. I'm going to let him ride with a rifle. I quizzed him pretty hard, and he talks as if he can handle a rifle, but he's never had a revolver."

Thomas gathered everything up and stepped into the hallway. "Bob, you think it's a good idea to take Jethro?"

Bob took a moment to answer. "Whether I do or not, Jeremiah has decided. I know you would like to take his place, but you can't. It's just how it is."

"I know you and Jeremiah are right, but it doesn't feel as if I'm holding up my end of the work and responsibilities around here."

"You make sure everything keeps going and make sure the women and children are safe. You and Jacob may be the only men on the ranch for a few days."

"Jacob and I will take care of things. Just be safe yourself." Thomas went into the bunkroom and off loaded onto the table. After undressing, he crawled into bed. Cal and Jethro were already asleep. Thomas turned down the lamp until it flickered out.

Chapter Twenty-Six Thomas

Thomas stood with Jeremiah and Jacob to watch Bob, Cal, and Jethro ride out with each man trailing an extra horse. Jeremiah had his horse saddled and was ready to ride to town to see what he could learn of possible cattle shipments.

"Keep an eye on the twins and make sure the women have anything they need. I'm depending on you two to keep everything going here. I should be back in about three days or sooner depending on what I find out." Jeremiah had already said his good-byes to Emily and the children. He mounted his horse and with a wave of his hand started down the lane toward the road.

Thomas turned to Jacob. "The horse barn first?"

"*Ja*, we do first, and then start to chop the wood."

"Yesterday, Cal and I saw some downed trees to the north. We can take a wagon and chop the wood there, or, I can take a couple of horses and drag the trees back here."

Jacob scratched his head. "Maybe better to do chopping close to ranch house so we can watch out for women and children."

Thomas nodded. "I reckon that is best."

By mid-morning, Thomas had tied ropes to several of the larger branches of the downed trees and then tied the other end around the pommel of his saddle. He snaked several good-sized trees close to the house before he had enough for several days of chopping firewood.

Jacob spent the time sharpening several axes to a fine edge. He also sharpened the two-man saw for use in cutting the tree trunks into manageable sizes.

The next three days fell into the same pattern of Jacob and Thomas caring for the horses and then chopping wood. By evening, all Thomas wanted to do was heat water for a hot bath and then fall into his bunk. Muscles he didn't even know he had hurt after six to eight hours of chopping wood. But, now the stacks of cut wood extended along two sides of the house. They also cut and stacked wood under the overhang by the door to Jacob's woodshop so he would have easy access to firewood through the winter. They had only made a beginning on the amount of firewood needed through the cold snowy weather to come but it was a good start.

The morning of the fourth day after the other men being gone was cloudy with a stiff chilly north breeze. Thomas was glad to pull on his new heavy coat and boots. After taking care of the horses in the horse barn, he saddled a horse to go snake a couple of more fallen trees close to the house when he heard riders coming up the lane.

Jacob came out of his workshop dressed for the cold.

Sheriff Grant rode a big black gelding followed by Deputy Fred Miller on a brown mare into the yard between the house and the barn. "Where's Rebourn? I need to talk to him."

Thomas didn't know whether or not to tell the sheriff that Jeremiah was gone. He breathed a sigh of relief when Jacob stepped forward to take the lead. But, before he could say anything Emily stepped out of the house and onto the porch.

"Sheriff, deputy, come in for some hot coffee and fresh baked cinnamon rolls. Jacob, you and Thomas come in also." She turned and entered the house as if there was no need to wait for the invite to be accepted.

Thomas took the reins from the two men and tied the horses to the top rail of the corral. He assumed they would not be staying long enough to need the horses further cared for.

He followed the men into the kitchen where Mildred was lifting a large pan of cinnamon rolls out of the oven and onto the middle of the table.

"Sally, pour these gentlemen each a cup of coffee." Emily distributed plates and forks around the table as Sally poured a cup of coffee for each man. "Set here Sheriff and tell me what brings you out from town. We don't see much of you this far out."

Sheriff Grant seemed a little uncertain as he sat at the table and watched as Mildred dished up a couple of hot cinnamon rolls onto the plate in front of him. "Is Jeremiah around, Mrs. Rebourn?"

Emily accepted a cup of coffee from Sally and smiled. "No, he's on a business trip."

Thomas watched Sheriff Grant struggle to swallow the large bite of cinnamon roll he had taken.

After taking a swig of coffee, the man said, "When will he be back?"

"I'm not really sure. In the next couple of days."

Grant glared at Thomas and Jacob. "When did he leave?"

After taking a sip of coffee, Emily daintily patted the corners of her mouth with the napkin that had appeared by her plate. "He's been gone for three days."

Finishing the cinnamon rolls in great bites, Grant washed them down with the last of the coffee in his cup. "Black, you got anyway to prove where you've been the last couple of nights?"

Jacob shifted in his chair. "Why you ask that, Sheriff? Something has happened?"

The sheriff shifted his eyes to Jacob. "I'm asking Black here a simple question."

Thomas didn't see any reason not to answer and he didn't want Jacob to get into a confrontation with the sheriff. "I've been here in my bunk."

Sheriff Grant spoke in a rough accusatory voice. "I'll ask you again. You got any proof of your where abouts in the last couple of days and nights?"

Jacob spoke sharply. "I can testify Thomas has not left the ranch since last Sunday morning and then he was with us at church."

Emily raised her eyebrows. "I can also speak for Thomas. Jeremiah instructed him to stay close to the house and work on taking care of the horses in the horse barn and to help Jacob chop wood for this winter. Thomas has not left the ranch."

Still with a suspicious tone, Grant asked, "What were you going to do with that saddled horse?"

Jacob responded before Thomas could speak. "He is getting ready for us to go snake some dead trees closer to the house so we can chop more winter wood."

Grant looked from Jacob to Thomas. "I only saw one horse saddled."

Jacob nodded. "*Ja*, I am slow this morning. I hope maybe Thomas saddle for me, but it not work. I must saddle my own horse."

Thomas laughed. "Jacob, all you have to do is ask. I don't mind saddling a horse for you, but you have to tell me which horse you want to ride."

"Okay, I want the brown mare I rode yesterday. She is gentle but strong."

Sheriff Grant shoved back his plate in frustration. "I don't care if you saddle your own horse or not. But I do need to know if you have been away from the ranch for several hours at a time, Black."

Emily shook her head. "No, he hasn't. With all the rustling and accusations going around, Jeremiah thought it was wiser for Thomas not to leave the ranch except to go to church. We haven't even let him go to town or the mercantile. If there has been more rustling going on, then Thomas is not your thief. You need to look elsewhere for the one guilty of any crimes."

Jacob also agreed, "*Ja*, I watch because Jeremiah ask. Thomas has not left the ranch."

Grant gave a mirthless laugh. "So Rebourn doesn't really trust Black here and set someone to watching him."

Emily shook her head again and stood. "You have it all wrong, Sheriff. Jeremiah trusts Thomas but he also knows how people are. He wants to protect him. False accusations can be difficult to disprove at times and Jeremiah doesn't want to take any chances. Is there anything else you needed to know, Sheriff?"

Evidently, Grant knew he was being dismissed and rose from the table. "Not for now but I'm going to continue to keep an eye on you, Black. So watch yourself. It would be a good idea for you to continue to stay here at the ranch."

Thomas had no problem with doing that, as long as his folks and Catherine kept coming out on Sundays. "I'll take your advice, Sheriff, and stay close to Jacob and Emily until Jeremiah gets back."

"Thanks for the coffee and cinnamon rolls, ladies." Grant left the house followed by his deputy.

Jacob struggled back into his coat and grabbed his hat. "You stay here, Thomas. I see they leave." He followed the sheriff and his deputy out of the house.

Thomas turned to Emily. "Thanks for speaking up for me."

She smiled. "Of course I'll speak up for you. You're family. Just be careful not to get too far from the ranch house. I think it might be a good idea if you and Jacob work close together until Jeremiah gets back."

He had to agree with her. It was obvious he was Sheriff Grant's chief suspect. He might feel the same if he were in Grant's position. The other ranchers must be putting a lot of pressure on Grant. Thomas would be glad when Jeremiah and the other men got back.

~

Thomas had just gotten out of the tub from his bath after supper when he heard someone riding up the lane. He hurried to dry off and dress. By the time he entered the kitchen, Jeremiah came through the back door and into the hallway.

Emily ran up to Jeremiah and gave him a welcome home kiss as Thomas stood there not knowing what to do.

"I'm so glad your home, sweetheart. Let me have your coat and hat. Mildred has food ready."

Jeremiah handed his hat and coat to Emily. "I'm glad to be home. I've been gone a couple of days longer than I planned."

Two little boys ran into the hallway yelling. "Papa, you're home." "Papa, you're back."

Laughing, Jeremiah grabbed a boy with each arm and held them like sacks of potatoes. "Yes, I'm home. You boys behaved yourself while I've been gone?"

Giggling, they yelled, "Yes, sir!"

Jeremiah deposited them on their feet and herded his family toward the kitchen. "Everything all right here, Thomas? Any problems?"

"No, sir. Jacob and I looked after the horses and chopped wood. We didn't get far from the house. I would have liked to have looked over the herd but Jacob felt it was wiser to stay close."

Jeremiah nodded. "That's exactly what I wanted you all to do." After washing his hands at the sink, he sat down at the head of the table and Mildred set a plate of hot food and a cup of coffee in front of him.

Emily sat down next to him with a small boy leaning on each side watching their father as he bowed his head and silently prayed.

Thomas sat down at the table and took the cup of coffee Sally handed to him. "Thanks, Sally."

Emily took a cup of tea from Mildred. "Thank you, Mildred."

Jacob entered the kitchen. "I rub your horse down good, Jeremiah. He is tired horse."

"Yes, I've ridden him hard the last few days, all the way to Denver and back." He glanced around as if looking for someone. "No word from Bob and the fellows?"

Emily shook her head. "No word from anyone, except Sheriff Grant who was out questioning Thomas."

Jeremiah looked up as if startled. "What do you mean questioning Thomas? What about?"

Thomas decided to join the conversation. "He never said why he was questioning me. He wanted to know if I had left the ranch at any time in the last few days. Fortunately, because of your concern, we were careful, and Jacob or Emily had known where I was at all times. Beyond that I don't know anything about the reasons for Sheriff Gran'ts visit."

"I may have a clue to what he wanted. Several other ranches have lost cattle in the last two weeks just as we have. Pressure is on Grant to find the rustlers and put a stop to it. You're an easy target, and even I heard some men questioning whether you could be a part of it." Jeremiah lifted his cup for a refill of the hot coffee. "I found no evidence of any unusual cattle sales, and the railroad has had no orders for cattle cars in this area.

I've hired a range detective from Denver. I'm hopeful he can come up with something. I hoped Bob, Cal, and Jethro would be back with news."

Jacob scratched his head. "They only took food for five days and that will be tomorrow. Maybe they come home then."

Jeremiah frowned as he accepted a piece of apple cake from Mildred. "If they haven't had some success then we are going to have to start systematically searching the hills and canyons north and west of here. I have the feeling all the rustled cattle are still in the area and being held somewhere, a hidden canyon or secluded valley."

Thomas had to agree with Jeremiah. It frustrated him any search beyond the ranch would probably be done without him. Sighing, he guessed he would be left at the ranch again to watch the women and children. He looked up as Jeremiah was speaking.

"Jacob, you and Thomas go look over the north herd tomorrow. I'll check on the cattle we're holding in the eastern pastures. Keep an eye out for tracks and movement of cattle that indicate someone is trying to bunch them. They should be scattered with no one from the ranch working them for the last week. If you do see any unusual tracks, don't follow them but report back to me as soon as possible."

"Ja, we do it. On way back we will snake some more fallen trees to cut for firewood."

Emily laughed. "You can save those for Jeremiah. Cutting firewood is one of his favorite things."

Jeremiah gave his wife a stern look. "We do not even joke about cutting firewood. It is an awful chore that must be done. That's why I have ranch hands, so I don't have to do."

Thomas and Jacob both grinned. It was seldom that Jeremiah joked around. Although, Thomas wasn't sure Jeremiah was joking.

~

Thomas pulled the collar of his heavy coat up and tugged his hat on snug as the wind picked up and snow fell from the dull sky in the late afternoon. He worried about Bob, Cal, and Jethro. They had now been gone six days. As he approached the house in anticipation of supper, after having spent the day caring for sick horses and chopping more firewood, he heard the sound of several horses moving up the lane and walked around to the front of the house.

Recognizing the big sorrel gelding Bob rode, Thomas yelled his greeting. "Welcome back fellows."

Jeremiah came out onto the porch struggling into his heavy coat. He stepped next to Thomas as the three cowhands walked their weary mounts up to the house with their extra mounts trailing behind.

Bob pulled the bandana down from around his face. "Hey, Boss. Thomas."

Jeremiah gave Bob, Cal, and Jethro a long look. "You all look done in. Let's get your horses taken care of, eat some supper, and then we'll talk."

~

Thomas and Jacob joined the three returning riders in the front room after the supper was done. Jeremiah sat in his familiar place by the fireplace and the others pulled up chairs and sprawled on the two couches.

Jeremiah pointed his chin toward Bob. "You want to start?"

Bob nodded as he hooked an ankle over his knee and settled into the overstuffed armchair, as if he planned to be there a while. "We followed the trail of the cattle taken from the north pasture for about five miles and then we lost them in that area of shale. We kept trailing back and forth, spread out like, and Jethro picked up the trail of another herd. We were able to follow that trail a ways and then lost it in a rocky trail close to a creek. Keeping on in the general direction, we would get small sections of trail and then they would peter out. But, all seemed to be heading north by northwest."

"It takes some good drovers to hide the trail of several hundred head of cattle," Jeremiah commented.

Cal glanced at Bob and then picked up the story. "Bob figured they were headed towards a canyon, maybe a high meadow somewhere in those foothills to the northwest. I've been through that area a couple of times, and it's full of box canyons. As you get to the higher elevations there are some large basins between hills that would be easy places to hold a herd. Course the problem with the higher elevations is the winter weather is coming. Even though we rode into a lot of box canyons and such, that's where I think we will find a herd of cattle that has been gathered from several of the ranches in this area."

Bob took up the report. "We combed the foothills for three days but couldn't locate where the cattle are being held, but I agree with Cal, I think that's where we'll find our cattle."

Jeremiah glanced at Jethro. "You look like you got something to say. Speak up, you have done your share of the work, you get to put in your two cents worth."

Jethro seemed to look anywhere except directly at Jeremiah. His face was red from embarrassment at being singled out. He straightened his shoulders and met Jeremiah's gaze. "Yes, sir. I got something to add. We ran 'cross tracks of four small herd of cattle counting our'ons. Yur cattle done got took by three hombres. By paying attention to the horse tracks, I'd say they was a total of five different riders. But not all five at one time."

"So, Jethro, you're saying we are looking for five rustlers."

"Yes, sir. That's the ones took the cattle. Maybe a couple of other gents who tell them what to do." Jethro glanced at his boots as if he had said too much.

Bob grunted. "Yeah, I have to agree with Jethro. He's really good at tracking and reading what the tracks mean. If we had kept looking, we might have found out more. But we were running out of food. The weather turned colder and I figured we were about to see our first real snow of the season. So I made the decision to get on back to the ranch."

Jeremiah nodded. "You did right. With the snow coming I doubt much will be left of what tracks there was and I will predict the cattle will be held where they are. Come spring we have to be ready to find them before they can get them sold off. For now you men get some well-deserved rest. Then we'll get work done around here. But, come the first major break in the weather toward spring we will hit the trail again until we solve this. In the meantime, we need to keep a close watch on the herds in case I'm wrong and they try to take more cattle even with the snow."

As the men filed out of the front room and headed to the bunkroom, Thomas was impressed with Jeremiah's ability to step back and look at the big picture. Thomas wanted to go after the rustlers until they caught them, but with the weather closing in and with how good the thieves had been at hiding their trail, Jeremiah's decision to wait was a wise one.

Chapter Twenty-Seven Catherine

Catherine looked across the kitchen table at Thomas after Milburn concluded the prayer for the meal. It had been a question whether she, Milburn, and Agnes would make it to the ranch after church. It had snowed some through the night, but the roads were still passable. Winter was about to descend with a vengeance and this storm had been a warning. Catherine regretted that she and Thomas would no longer be taking leisurely walks down to the creek to watch the twins play in the water and that the weather would soon prevent trips to the ranch altogether. She looked forward to the few hours at the ranch and especially the time spent with Thomas.

"Aunt Catherine, will you play a game with us this afternoon?" Joseph asked with a hopeful look.

"Please, Aunt Catherine. If you play, Thomas will play for sure." Elisha added.

She almost smiled as Thomas' face turned red. He gazed at his plate of fried chicken, potatoes, and a couple of biscuits smothered with hot gravy. The boy was right.

Catherine couldn't stop the giggle that escaped from the look on Thomas' face. "I'll be happy to play a game with you all. We must start right after we finish eating, as we will need to head back to town before it gets late. With this weather, we don't want to be traveling after dark." She glanced at Milburn who nodded in agreement. "Maybe you would like to play with us, Jethro?"

The boy jerked his head up from where he was intent on shoveling food into his mouth as fast as possible. "Ma'am?"

"I'm asking you to play a board game with us after lunch." Catherine looked over at Jeremiah. "Will that be all right, Jeremiah, unless Jethro has chores to do?"

"Sure, Jethro, you can play a game with the twins and Miss Catherine. Other than the horse barn, which we took care of this morning, there is nothing you need to do today since it's Sunday. Relax, get some rest. Tomorrow morning we'll all be up early to start moving all the animals closer to the ranch house. It's likely we'll have more bad weather in the next few weeks and need to be prepared. We'll meet for breakfast and talk about what we need to get done."

After helping clear the table, Catherine went to the bookshelves by the fireplace and picked out a game. *Across the Continent* was the game she had received for her birthday. She had left it at the ranch knowing that was where it was likely to be played. She handed the game to Elisha who placed it on the kitchen table and began to set it up for play.

Joseph grabbed Jeremiah's hand. "Pa, please play with us. I'll be your partner. It's an easy game, and I'll help you."

"You think I'll need your help with the game?" Jeremiah's eyes twinkled as he regarded his son.

"Well, Pa, you're not too good at games. You can't guess what the other players are going to do."

Ruffling his son's hair, Jeremiah laughed. "You're absolutely right. I need a good partner and you're it."

Elisha pointed to Thomas. "I want you as my partner. You always win at games."

Thomas grinned at the boy. "All right, you and I will partner, but don't blame me if we lose. I don't always win."

Catherine smiled at the boys, Jeremiah, and Thomas. "Well I want Jethro to be my partner. Don't worry. The game is easy. You'll catch on quick."

They took their places around the kitchen table and across from their partner. Catherine explained how to play the game. Elisha and Thomas won the toss to go first. Soon, it was Catherine and Jethro's turn.

"Toss the dice to find out how far we get to move." Catherine slid the two dice toward Jethro.

He cautiously rolled them out on the table. They came up with a double five. Catherine moved their piece forward.

"We get to pick up a card. I hope it is not a punishment card." Catherine sighed. She waited for Jethro to pick one from the pile but he sat with his head down and his eyes covered by the long auburn hair falling across his brow. She reached for the top card on the pile.

As the game continued, Catherine began to suspect Jethro's lack of interaction during the game was due to not being able to read. Each time they moved or needed to pick and read a card, he left it to her. She glanced at Thomas and saw his intent gaze on Jethro. Did he also suspect Jethro couldn't read?

The game ended with Thomas and Elisha winning, as the boy had predicted. "Yahoo! We won!" Elisha shouted.

"Quiet down. Your mother has just gotten your sister to sleep," Jeremiah cautioned.

"Sorry, Pa. I'm glad we won. It was fun."

Jeremiah stood and grabbed a giggling boy under each arm. "Let's go see what's going on in the front room."

Jethro stood. "Thanks for letting me play the game. I never played no game fore."

Thomas lightly thumped Jethro on the back. "You did well for your first game. You can go to the front room and sit around with everyone, or, if you would rather, go to the bunkroom and take a nap. I'll call you when we need to go check on the horses."

Jethro nodded and headed toward the bunkroom.

Catherine smiled. "He's a growing boy who probably can eat or sleep whenever he gets a chance. I like him."

"He's real quiet and not a big talker, but he's proved to be a good worker for his age." Thomas laughed and ran his fingers through his hair. "He's a better cowhand than I am. Much better at riding and roping than I've ever been."

"I'm glad to hear that, but I think he has a difficulty you may be able to help him with, Thomas."

"Yes? What's that?" He stood with his head cocked to the side as he waited for her response.

"I don't think he can read. He did his best to follow the game but whenever it was necessary to read a card, he seemed to try to hide." Catherine wasn't sure what Thomas would or could do for the boy. But, not being able to read would be a hindrance for the rest of his life.

Thomas looked thoughtful. "He's a little old to go to school to learn to read. I don't think that would be workable."

"No, you're right. It would be too hard on his pride to sit in a schoolhouse with six year olds learning to read."

"You think I could teach him? In the evenings, especially with winter we will have more time." Thomas frowned, as if not sure it was a good idea.

"I think that would be a perfect solution. You could do it in the privacy of the bunkroom." Catherine smiled and laid her hand on top of his. "That would be a Christian kindness you could do for him."

Catherine wanted to smile at how red Thomas became, but he didn't remove his hand from under hers. Instead, he grasped her hand and began to rub her inner wrist in circles with his thumb as he asked, "How do I go about teaching someone to read? I've never done that."

Catherine wanted to keep the warmth of Thomas' touch as long as possible. She had never had a man hold her hand so gently and mesmerize her with such a simple touch. She was feeling a little breathless as she responded. "I'll ask Mr. Pritchard, the school teacher in town, what books he uses to get the little ones started on reading and maybe some writing, too. Your pa will order what is needed, and I can bring it out to you. You should start by teaching him the ABCs, both to write and recognize."

Catherine felt the pull of Thomas' gaze as he kept his eyes focused on hers. Listening to the sound of his deep mellow voice, she almost missed what he said next.

"I'd appreciate that but we don't want to let anyone else know what we are doing. I don't want to see Jethro teased. I don't think he had his folks for very long and has been on his own since. I doubt he got much chance to go to school. I got through eight years of schooling because Ma was determined I would do it. Looking back I wonder why I protested so much."

"That's why this is a great gift you can give him. With Christmas in just a few weeks, you could offer lessons as a Christmas gift. Of course, we are assuming he wants to learn to read." Catherine felt a longing as she continued to gaze at Thomas. Only a good man would be willing to do something like this for a stray boy. If only Thomas wasn't a prisoner and was free. She heard footsteps coming toward the kitchen from the front room.

With a sigh, Thomas squeezed her hand. "I don't plan to give him a choice. We'll have lessons. Course, like you say he has to decide to learn."

Milburn and Agnes came into the kitchen with Jeremiah and Emily following.

Catherine retrieved her hand from Thomas' and slid it into her lap. The loss of warmth from his big hand left her wanting to return her hand to the safety of his grasp. But, she didn't want to give an appearance of getting too close to Thomas. She wasn't sure what Jeremiah would say about Thomas, still a prisoner, getting too close to a girl.

Milburn went over by the backdoor and took down his coat and hat. "Catherine, I'm sorry to cut our visit short today, but with the weather looking more and more like it's about to descend, we should head back to town."

Thomas stood and headed toward the bunkroom. "I'll grab my coat and hat and help you hitch up."

Emily stood with Jeremiah's arm around her shoulders. She glanced with apology at Catherine. "I'm sorry we didn't get more time to visit, but thanks for playing with the twins. It makes a long afternoon when it's too cold and windy for them to play outside."

Catherine pulled on her coat, scarf, hat, and gloves. "That is one thing I don't like about our winters. It makes our visits too short and too long in between. Hopefully, the weather will clear by next Sunday."

Jeremiah nodded. "We can hope and with Christmas only two weeks away Emily wants to get into town and do more shopping, which she needs to do to be sure to have enough gifts for me." He gave his wife a wink.

Emily gave her husband a light slap on the arm. "You can hope, but it's more likely I'm shopping for the children."

Catherine drank in their sense of love and liking. It made her long for a time when she could have that and the person she envisioned providing it was Thomas. The two and half years left on his sentence seemed to stretch forever.

When Catherine walked outside, she immediately felt the sharp sting of the cold wind and realized the temperature had dropped. The sky was a dull grey. Occasional snow flurries floated by. Thomas and his pa had the horse hitched to the buggy.

Thomas took his mother's hand and guided her to the buggy seat. He then turned to Catherine. "I suggest you sit up here on the front seat with Pa and Ma. It will be a little warmer and you can share the lap robes."

"Brrr. I didn't realize it was getting so cold." Catherine squeezed in beside Agnes and enjoyed the close view of Thomas' face as he leaned in front of her to tuck a couple of lap robes around his mother and then around Catherine.

He grasped her hand and smiled. "Have a good week and stay out of the weather. I hope you can make it out next Sunday."

Squeezing his large warm callused hand, she responded, "I'll miss you and keep you in my prayers."

As Milburn settled on the buggy seat and picked up the reins, Thomas released her hand and stepped back. "I need all the prayers I can get. Take care, Pa, Ma. It was good to be with you all today."

As the horse pulled the buggy down the lane to the road, Catherine smiled with contentment at the time she had spent with Thomas. She had begun to depend on the weekly visits to the ranch.

Chapter Twenty-Eight Thomas

Thomas rode out with Cal the next morning to work with the horses. It was cold and cloudy but the heavy snow hadn't arrived, as he had expected. Keeping an eye on the weather, he worked with the horses Cal herded into the smaller corrals. Three geldings that had similar brown coats already were gentled to where they could be ridden. Thomas worked at getting them used to a rider and to respond to his signals. He worked the horses to a point where other riders could be secure.

At the noon break, he and Cal huddled in the lee of several small boulders that blocked the wind. They made coffee to go with the sandwiches Mildred had sent with them.

Cal sipped on the hot, strong coffee and searched the sky. "That wind feels icy. I suggest we let the horses in the corral go and head back to the ranch house. I got me a feeling."

Thomas settled his hat on more securely against the rising wind. Even with the protection of the rocks, it cut through his layers of clothing. "I got the same feeling. I'm surprised the snow has held off this long. We don't want to get caught in a white out this far from the barn."

Cal began to gather up the coffee pot and cups while Thomas put out the fire. They mounted their horses, turned out the ones they had been working into the large pasture, and headed back toward the ranch house. Flurries of snow swirled in the wind and both men urged their horses to a faster pace. By the time they rode into the barn behind the house, the snow was falling so heavily they could barely see the ranch house.

Thomas put his horse into a stall, unsaddled, and put out feed and water. He took the time to wipe his horse down with a burlap feed sack. Then he put his saddle and bridle away in the tack room with Cal behind him doing the same. Thomas turned to the barn door when he heard a pounding. Looking out he saw Jeremiah nailing a rope into a wooden t-bar.

Jeremiah looked up from his work and spotted Thomas. "Glad you boys rode on in. It feels like a big one is moving in. I wanted to get this rope up in case there's a white out and we need to follow it from the house to the barn."

Thomas nodded. "I'd rather it be there and not be needed than to chance getting lost in a snowstorm."

Jeremiah stood back and examined his handiwork. "I know this is your first Colorado winter. Cal and I will try to remember that and give you proper directions on how to deal with the cold and snow. We'll show you the extra work we need to do with the horses. If you men are ready, let's grab Jethro and head up to the horse barn to check on the mares I herded there this morning."

Thomas nodded and followed Jeremiah toward the house as Cal closed the barn doors. Thomas appreciated the rope that was stretched between the ranch house and house barn. Since Jacob lived in the workshop in the back of the barn, would he stay there through the winter storms or move into the ranch house? As the three men walked through the deepening snow, Jethro came out of the bunkroom tying a scarf around his neck. Thomas recognized the scarf as one Emily had been knitting.

Jeremiah stopped in the blowing snow, as Thomas, Cal, and Jethro gathered around him. "I don't want anyone going off to work by himself when the weather gets like this. One of the reasons I built the fence between the two barns was to offer a guide when the snow gets deep and is blowing. Even if you can see the way when you start out, always go by the fence. If it gets so thick you can't see, you'll have the fence to guide you. Let's go get the horses in the horse barn taken care of. Then we'll head in for supper and not have to go out again this evening. Jacob is feeding the chickens, pigs, and milking the cows. Any questions?"

Thomas and the others shook their heads and followed Jeremiah along the rail fence to the horse barn. The horses standing in their stalls added their warmth to the inside of the horse barn and with the break from the wind, it felt warm to Thomas. He took his gloves off to rub his cold hands together to get some feeling going Putting his gloves back on Thomas grabbed a pitchfork, climbed to the loft of the barn, and started to pitch clean hay down so the others would have it to put into the stalls. By the time they had the work done, dusk was setting in and over a foot of snow had accumulated.. The presence of the other men and the guide of the fence were welcome as Thomas kept his head down to shield his face as best he could from the sting of the blowing snow.

Emily came out of the wash up room as the men stomped into the hallway between the bunkroom and the kitchen. "I'm glad you all are back. I've got the stove going in the wash up room and water heating if anyone wants a hot bath before supper."

Thomas grinned at Emily. "Thank you, Mrs. Emily. I'll take you up on that. I haven't been warm since this morning. A hot bath will do the trick."

She pulled a small rug over to where they stood by the backdoor, pulling their snow covered boots off. "Put your boots on this rug and don't worry about the snow melting. We'll clean up the rug later. I'm afraid you are going to be cold a lot, Thomas. The first winter in this country is always the most difficult. I remember my first winter here. Even though I had been through several Boston winters, it wasn't the same as a mountain winter."

Jeremiah walked in his stocking feet to take his wife's hand. "Come on, sweetheart, let these men get out of their wet clothes and get warmed up."

Thomas watched the smile and bright eyes that Emily turned on Jeremiah as she grabbed his hand with both of hers and started rubbing the cold out. They disappeared through the door to the kitchen on their way to the bedroom and bath in the other end of the house. Through the summer, Jeremiah had built a bigger bedroom with a full bath off the hall just outside the new bedroom. It had a water source and drains so hot water could be available to fill the big claw foot bathtub.

Looking from Cal to Jethro, Thomas asked. "Who wants a hot bath first?"

Jethro frowned. "I took a bath on Saturday. I'se don't need no bath today."

Cal shook his head. "You may not need a bath to get clean, but you're shivering with cold right now. A bath will warm you up quicker than anything."

Thomas wanted to go get into the hot bath to get his feet warm. He wasn't sure they would be warm again until next spring. But, Cal was right, the boy was shivering with cold. "You go get into that tub of hot water and soak until you get warm. No arguments." He gave the boy a gentle shove toward the wash up room. "I'll go get you some dry clothes and set them in the room."

Jethro gave the two men a glare. "I'll go get into the tub to get warm but I don't need no bath to get clean. A man shouldn't take a bath more'en once a month. It ain't healthy."

After the boy had entered the wash up room, Thomas and Cal went into the bunkroom. Thomas walked over to the box wood stove that was putting out a hot heat warming the large room against the winter cold. Sitting on one of the two burners was a pot of coffee that smelled as if it had just been brewed. "That Mrs. Emily, she did this, not wanting us to come into a cold room."

Cal spread his hands toward the stove to get them to warming. "She's a kind lady. This is a good spread to work on. I'm glad Harlan and Barney didn't mess it up for me."

"You didn't let them. You're too good a man to be influenced by the likes of them." Thomas grabbed a clean shirt, pants, socks, and union suit for Jethro. "You want the bath after the kid?"

Cal pulled a chair up to the stove, sat down, and pulled two pairs of wet socks off. "No, I want to drink some coffee and rest a bit. You go next. Since we're back to the house early, we got time before supper. I sure am glad Jeremiah don't expect us to go out into the storm again this evening." He poured himself a mug of coffee, took a sip, and leaned back stretching his bare feet toward the warmth of the stove. "Ahhh. This is the life."

Thomas grabbed clean, dry clothes for himself along with his towel. Taking the clothes for Jethro and himself, he stepped back into the hallway that was notably cooler that the bunkroom. He put the clothes for Jethro in the wash up room and stepped back into the hallway to give the boy his privacy. "Hurry up, Jethro," Thomas yelled through the door. "As soon as you're warm enough, get out of the tub so Cal and I can get warmed up."

"Yes sir. I'm about done," Jethro yelled back.

Thomas turned to the backdoor as it seemed to blow open and a blast of cold air slammed into the hallway. Jacob hurried in and kicked the door closed against the blowing snow that followed him in. Snow stuck to his hat and coat and was caked on his boots. He carried a basket of eggs and a covered five-gallon bucket of warm milk.

"Thomas, you are back. It is good. Too cold to stay out." He set the basket of eggs and bucket of milk on the floor.

Thomas took the heavy coat from Jacob and hung it on one of the many hooks in the wall by the door. It hung alongside about ten other coats of various sizes.

Jacob stomped out of his boots and slipped into a pair of slippers that had been on a shelf of boots and shoes. "My place, it is warm, but the good food is here."

"Jeremiah had us come on in early after we got the horse barn done. I see you got the milking done. You finished with taking care of the animals?"

"Ja, is all done. No more work today. Let it snow. We be warm, eat good food, and rest." He picked up the bucket of milk and basket of eggs and headed for the kitchen.

~

Thomas lingered at the supper table, as did the others. After his hot bath, dry clothes, and three bowls of hot stew and cornbread, he was as relaxed as he ever got. As he looked about the table at the friendly, kind faces of his friends, he could only silently thank God for being where he was, even if he was still a prisoner. The window over the kitchen sink rattled as another gust of wind hit the house. The sound of the wind could be heard continually above the talk that was going on around the kitchen table. Thomas couldn't imagine the snowdrifts that were building outside the snug house.

Jeremiah cleared his throat, and the murmuring of conversation settled as everyone gave him their attention. "Since we're all together and this is Thomas' first big storm, I'd like to talk a little about the winter work."

As Mildred poured more coffee into the cups of those who wanted it, Emily turned her gaze on Jethro. "What about you, Jethro? Have you been through a northern mountain winter?"

The boy, who had slicked his long hair back behind his ears after his bath, shook his head. "No, ma'am. I'se seen the winter time in them hills back in Kintuck, but I suspect they's lots more snow and cold here'un."

Thomas noticed that he was understanding Jethro's accent better. This early evening might be the right time to spend some time seeing how much he knew about his letters and writing. Hearing Jeremiah start talking he turned in his chair to face toward his boss.

"The work in winter is different from the rest of the year. It's more work to survive than it is to develop the land or the herds. We need to spend time getting more firewood. Through the summer as you know, we snaked dead and fallen trees from the hills to the pasture to the west. Now is when we really start bringing those dead trees up to the house and chop them up for firewood. We have a good amount of firewood already but we have to keep at it to last the winter. We also need to keep the cattle we herded closer toward the ranch house bunched and if need be, we chop ice out of the ponds and creek so they can get to water. When snow is covering the ground, we have to start taking hay out to the herd. A cow needs about twenty pounds of feed a day, more if they're carrying a calf. One of the reasons I keep each herd to five hundred or less. If you have too many cattle, it becomes too hard to feed them in winter."

Jeremiah stopped talking long enough to drink the last of the coffee in his cup. "The breeding horses need about the same amount of hay. The workhorses will need more grain added to their hay. If you ride a horse for half a day, feed it a half to two pounds of grain per hour of work. If you ride a horse all day then you may need to add up to two and half pounds of grain per hour of work. When it gets cold like this, we may need to add more feed as horses and cattle burn up more fat to stay warm."

Emily laid a hand on Jeremiah's arm. "Honey, can the men learn more on another day?"

Jeremiah looked around and grinned. "Yes, we can continue more lessons on ranching at another time. For now, let me tell each of you what I want done tomorrow if the storm lets up enough. Thomas and Cal, I want you to ride out and check on the horse herd. Be on the lookout for any wolves coming down out of the mountains. Jacob and I will check the cattle. Jethro, I want you to take care of the horses in the two barns. If you see any problems, let me know. Then the day after tomorrow, if it doesn't warm up, we will take hay to the herds. But, I'm hoping this storm will pass through quickly and we will have a few warm days before the next one. If we have to start taking hay to the herd this early, I'll have to buy more before winter is over. Any questions?"

Thomas wanted to ask Jeremiah how he could keep training the horses with the winter weather. He decided to wait until they were alone. His ignorance of ranching was bad enough without parading it in front of the other men. He wished Bob were here because he felt more comfortable asking him questions. But, the ranch foreman was down in New Mexico looking at a stallion Jeremiah was interested in buying to add to the breeding program of the ranch. Bob wasn't due back for a month or two, as he was also planning to visit his folks in Texas over Christmas. Thomas couldn't begrudge the man the time off, as it was his first trip home in several years.

Jeremiah stood up from the kitchen table indicating he was through with his instructions. "Anyone who wants can gather in the front room. I plan to enjoy having a long evening in front of the fireplace."

Mildred and Sally began to clear the table and do the dishes. Emily picked up baby Charity from her wicker basket baby carriage in the corner of the kitchen and carried her toward the bedroom. In Jacob's workshop Thomas had spotted the baby highchair Jacob was working on for the little baby girl even though they still had the two he had made for the twins. Thomas suspected the one for little Charity would have flowers carved on as decorations.

Jeremiah gathered the boys and guided them toward the front room with Jacob and Cal trailing along behind. Thomas signaled to Jethro to follow him to the bunkroom.

Grabbing the pad of paper and a pencil, Thomas indicated for Jethro to sit at the little table in front of the box woodstove. "Let me put more wood in the stove, and then I want to show you something."

Feeling unsure of himself and what he was about to do, Thomas took his time adding wood to the stove and adjusting the damper. Then he settled into a chair at the little table across from Jethro. "I don't want to get into your business as I respect a man's right to his privacy. But I'd like to ask you a question."

Jethro looked at him with a frown and brushed his hair back behind his ears. "Sure."

Thomas cleared his throat. This was harder than he had expected. He didn't want to embarrass the boy. Maybe just saying straight out was best. "Can you read and write?"

Ducking his head and letting his long hair fall around his face, Jethro slowly shook his head and softly said, "No, sir. I can't. I'se never bin to school."

"Would you like to learn how to read?"

Raising his head as if startled by the question, he looked at Thomas. "Yes, sir. I purely would like to learn, but I'se too old for to go to school. Sides, I got to work."

Thomas nodded his understanding. "I agree about you being too old to go to school but you're just the right age to learn to read. I'm willing to try and teach you if you're willing."

The boy's eyes opened wide. "You do that for me?"

"Sure, Jethro. It will take some work. But, on evenings like this, we have time, and we could work at it every day. By spring you could be reading and writing."

"How do we do it?"

"Well, I thought this evening we could start with you learning to write the ABCs. Everything about reading and writing comes from that. Then in a few days, we'll start with learning to write words. Here let me show you." Thomas took the paper and pencil and made a capital A and a small a. "Now hold the pencil like this and copy these each five times. Sound out the letter as you copy them."

Jethro took hold of the pencil as if it was a hot stick. Thomas helped him position the pencil in his hand and then watched him struggle to copy the letter. After he had copied it five times, he looked up at Thomas.

"Good job, you have just done the first step toward learning to read and write." Thomas grinned at the boy and relaxed a bit. Maybe teaching

Jethro how to read and write wouldn't be so hard after all. "Now copy this one, B."

Licking his lip and frowning deeply, Jethro attacked the coping of the letter B, as if it was a spring calf he was trying to deliver.

An hour later Thomas wrote the letter M for Jethro to copy, he noticed the boy's hand trembled slightly from gripping the pencil so tightly. The effort Jethro put in to form the letters had made Thomas tired, so he could image how exhausted the boy was.

"Let's stop for this evening. Here, I've written out the entire ABCs while you worked. If you have any free time, I want you to copy each of these letters ten times from A to M and then tomorrow evening we'll do the rest of the alphabet. As you copy them try to memorize them in order."

"Yes, sir. And thanks, Thomas."

"You're welcome. I'm just teaching you what Ma taught me."

Cal came into the bunkroom from the hallway. "What are you fellows doing?"

Knowing Cal would figure it out, Thomas decided to be honest. "Jethro and I are working on some school work. I'm helping him improve his reading and writing over the winter, as he didn't get much schooling."

Jethro ducked his head and let his hair flow around his face as if embarrassed.

Cal sat on his bunk and started unbuttoning his shirt. "That's great, Thomas. Wish I had a friend like you when I was Jethro's age. I didn't find anyone to teach me until I was twenty years old. Schooling was hard to get living out on the prairie two hours from town. Neither of my folks could read or write. Us kids had to make do best we could."

Jethro looked at Cal with a surprised expression. "But I seen yu'uns reading all the time."

Hanging his shirt on a hook, Cal laughed. "Now you see me reading but you should have been around when old man Snodgrass tried to teach me. Then I found a schoolmarm, who in exchange for me cutting wood for the schoolhouse, taught me some more. It took a couple of years, but I soon read anything I wanted. It sure helps pass the cold winter evenings to be able to read."

~

Sunday started out as a bright, sunny, cold winter day. Thomas rode to church with Jethro. He liked that Jeremiah let him ride a horse instead of the buggy. This was Jethro's first Sunday. He seemed nervous.

"You been to church much, Jethro?"

"No, I's never been to no church fore." The boy glanced over at Thomas and then at his horse's head.

"Just follow me and do what I do. It's really a good thing." Thomas slowed his horse a bit and let the buggy carrying the family move ahead "You believe in God, Jethro?"

The boy was quiet for a couple of moments. "Yes, sir, I do. Don't understand much about Him, but I knows he's there."

Thomas nodded. "That's sort of where I was last year before I started to read my Bible and go to church."

Jethro looked up at Thomas. "You think I's can learnt them words so I's can read that there Bible?"

"I know you can. It will take us a few months of hard work but my hope is by summer you will be reading your own Bible."

"Aint that sumpthin' to do." Jethro's voice was full of wonder.

Thomas smiled. "In the meantime, I will read the Bible to you if you want. There's a bunch of good stories all through the Bible."

"Why are ya doing this for me?"

"Because it is a good thing and makes me feel good." Thomas was surprised at just how good it did make him feel. He sat a little straighter in his saddle.

After the services, Catherine and Thomas' folks came out to the ranch for dinner. They brought a packet wrapped in brown paper and tied with twine.

Catherine handed it to Thomas. "These are books to help teach Jethro. There's a McGuffey's primer for reading, Osgood's spelling book, and Spencer's book on penmanship. Mildred also added a slate, slate pencil, and a couple of paper tablets."

"Thanks, I'll put them into the bunkroom for now." Thomas wanted to keep the studying as private as possible.

"Have you started lessons?" Catherine asked.

Thomas nodded. "On Monday evening we started with the ABCs. Jethro has a good memory and has already learned them. He can say them and print them. I think he will make good progress now I have these books to help us."

Catherine smiled. "And that he has someone to teach him. Can you imagine not being able to read your Bible? What a wonderful gift you are giving him."

Thomas looked away. He wanted her approval and it felt good to hear Catherine say such flattering things.

Chapter Twenty-Nine Thomas

The snow had not lingered after the first snowstorm. It warmed up enough for everything to melt within two days, leaving behind a lot of mud. Thomas, Jeremiah, and Cal worked most days breaking horses. The couple of weeks before Christmas, Jeremiah returned from town after getting supplies with a letter from Elisha.

After everyone had finished eating supper, Jeremiah cleared his throat, which was his general signal he had something to say to the group. Thomas scooted his chair slightly so he could pay more attention to Jeremiah.

Jeremiah pulled a letter out of his shirt pocket. "Elisha has written about some of his plans. Joe, Sara, Jim Finely, Santo, and his wife Mara with their baby will be here the week or so after Christmas. We'll work at getting the horses ready to sell to the Army by the end of the spring. We'll keep the breeding program going with the mares and sell all the others except for five stallions of various ages. We have room here in the house for Joe and Sara and for Santo, Mara, and their little one. Jim will stay in the bunkroom. Elisha is selling his cattle and most of his horses come spring and plans to move down here by next summer. He even has a possible buyer for his ranch."

Jeremiah paused to sip on his coffee. "I also got a telegraph from Bob. His pa broke his leg, and Bob plans to stay at his folks' ranch through the winter to help his brothers out. Therefore, with Bob gone, I'm going to put you, Cal, in charge of the cattle. Jacob and Jethro will mainly work with you. When you need help, you ask for it. Otherwise, the rest of us will be working with the horses. I'm going to put Joe in charge of the horses we're breaking. Thomas, you'll be working with Joe, Jim, and Santo. I will work where needed, but mainly I'll be taking care of the breeding mares. Right now, we have over two hundred mares scheduled to drop their foals through the spring and summer. Any questions?"

Jacob shifted in his chair. "*Ja*, does Elisha have a ranch in mind where to move?"

Jeremiah shook his head. "Not that I'm aware of except to say he plans to look for land around Cedar Ridge."

Thomas wondered what it would mean to have the other riders and the two women on the ranch. The extra hands to help with the work would be welcome. They had been working shorthanded for weeks. How would Joe Weathers be to work with? Did he know that Thomas was a prisoner? At least they had a few more weeks to get ready for them to arrive.

Jacob was speaking again. "How they get out of valley after Christmas? Pass gets blocked with snow early up in mountains."

Jeremiah pointed to the letter lying on the table. "Elisha writes that so far they aren't snowed in and plan to keep the pass open until after Joe and them head our way. Hopefully, the heavier snows will hold off until middle of January."

Emily rose from the table to pick up the baby who had begun to fuss. "Does everyone know that we have invited Thomas' family to spend Christmas here?"

Thomas glanced quickly from Emily to Jeremiah. "I didn't know. Does that include my sisters, Bessie and Hope, and their families? Last I heard they were coming from their ranches in Wyoming by train to stay a few days at Christmas."

Emily patted little Charity on her diapered bottom and smiled at Thomas. "Don't worry. They're still coming. You know your folks don't have room for everyone to stay in their place."

Thomas did know the space over the store was too small for everyone. And by staying out at the ranch, he would be able to visit with his sisters and their families more. Maybe Jeremiah and Emily had been thinking of that when they invited them.

"Like I said, don't worry, Thomas. I've got it all worked out. We have plenty of room for everyone to stay and it will be fun to have all the family here with the children. Your folks are closing the mercantile on Christmas Day. Your sisters plan to arrive on Wednesday, the 24th, and your folks will come out to the ranch with them and spend the night. I've also invited Catherine to come out."

Thomas barely kept himself from grinning at that news. It was sure going to be a different Christmas than he had experienced since he was a kid. He had already been working with Jacob on some Christmas gifts. Between his regular work, teaching Jethro, and getting ready for Christmas, the next few weeks would be busy.

Charity started fussing again and Emily turned to head for the bedroom. Stopping at the door from the kitchen to the front room, she said, "By the way, be looking for the perfect Christmas tree. We will cut it and bring it into the house on the 24th so we can have it decorated by the time everyone arrives."

Thomas had no idea what a perfect Christmas tree was. Why cut down a tree and bring it into the house? He must have looked puzzled because Jeremiah began to explain.

"Years ago when Jacob and I worked at the Lazy ES, he introduced us to the German custom of bringing an evergreen tree into the front room and decorating it. We liked how it brightened up the house, so we have continued it. Emily was aware of the tradition from her years back east as a schoolgirl. So look for a cedar or fir tree that has a good round shape, not too wide and tall enough to fit into the front room without touching the ceiling."

Jacob laughed. "*Ja*, do not worry, Thomas. I find perfect tree for Mrs. Emily. You be ready to chop it down and bring back to the house."

"Okay, if that is what she wants. Just seems strange to me." Thomas shook his head. Strange as these new customs were he couldn't help but feel the beginnings of a delightful anticipation for the festivities ahead.

~

He spent the next few weeks doing the ranch work and teaching Jethro in the evenings. Thomas was proud of the boy's hard work and at his progress. They quickly worked their way through the first two McGuffey's Readers. Jethro could read simple sentences and both his writing and figuring was coming along. Each evening after working on his schoolwork, Jethro listened to either Thomas or Cal read from the Bible.

Thomas woke early on the morning of the 24th with the thought that today he would see his sisters for the first time in over twelve years. He would meet two brothers-in-law and five nieces and nephews. This morning, they would work in the horse barn and then bring the big Douglas-fir tree down from the hills to put into the front room.

Sighing, he swung his legs out of the warm bed and planted his feet on the cold floor. He lit the lamp on his bed stand. Grabbing his wool shirt and wool worsted pants off the hooks on the wall he dressed quickly. Then he put on two pairs of wool socks and pulled on his boots.

Shaking Jethro awake, he said, "Come on sleepy head. We got work to do."

"It ain't morning yet. Look at that dark out the windor." Jethro pulled the covers over his head.

Thomas remembered mornings when he was Jethro's age and stifled a laugh. Taking pity on the boy, he left him to get a few more minutes of snoozing and went to the box stove to build up the fire. Soon he had it blazing with several logs. Then, he went to the wash up room and did the same thing with the stove there. After filling a pot with water from the well room next door, he placed it on the stove to start heating to have hot water for washing up and shaving. He had bathed the evening before and had made Jethro do the same in preparation for the arrival of company in the late afternoon. He had Emily cut his hair the day before. Glancing in the mirror in the wash up room, Thomas was grateful Jacob and Emily could cut hair since he could not go to the barber in town. And, besides that, they didn't charge him for haircuts. He used cold water to wash his face, which helped to wake him up, but was happy for the hot water to shave. After cleaning his teeth, he went back to the bunkroom to wake Jethro.

Cal pulled on his vest over his wool shirt. "Morning, Thomas. You're up early."

Thomas glanced toward the pocket watch Cal carried. "Morning, Cal. Did I get up too early and wake you?"

"No, I was ready to get up. I'm hungry for breakfast and we got a lot to do today before all the company gets here." Cal grinned. "Maybe Miss Mildred is going to let us eat some of the goodies the ladies have been a'baking the last week. I haven't ever seen so many cakes, pies, cookies, and bread in one kitchen."

"We can only hope so. It's been hard to smell all that food baking and not to get any."

Jethro stuck his head out from under the covers. "Somebody say sump'n bout food? My stomach done got acquainted with my backbone."

"I'm smelling bacon, so would guess breakfast will soon be ready. Get dressed and washed up." Thomas couldn't resist ruffling Jethro's wild looking hair. "And comb this out good. Why you won't let Mrs. Emily cut your hair, I don't know."

"It's you'ren fault it looks all wild, having to bath and warsh it out and then go stright to bed. It ain't natural. And, why do I need to wash up again. I done took a bath last night." Jethro's grumbling followed him as he walked out the door into the hall.

Thomas watched him go. "That boy is changing. And, for the better. It's healthy for a boy that age to grumble about getting up and having to bathe so often. When he first came, he wouldn't have spoken up like that."

Cal straightened his covers on his bunk. "Yep. He trusts us to say what he's thinking and that's good."

"I think he keeps his hair long so he can hide behind it."

Cal rubbed his jaw. "Now that you mention it, I think that is exactly what he's doing. I bet when he feels okay about being here, it gets cut."

Thomas nodded. "As he's learning to read and write and being told he's a good worker, he walking talller, not shuffling so much like he was when he got here."

"We need to keep being patient with him and give him time. He's still just a boy doing a man's job. I know what that's like as I had to do it myself."

Thomas wondered about Cal's background. The man hardly ever mentioned anything about his life before coming to work at the Rocking JR. Cal was a good man, a hard worker, and patient with Jethro and the twins.

~

All the men pitched in to get the horse barn cleaned out and the other animals taken care of. Then they headed to the house for breakfast. After the blessing and as the fried eggs, bacon, gravy, and biscuits had been passed around, Thomas noticed that everyone seemed to be talking and there was more laughter.

Young Elisha was almost bouncing in his seat. "Jacob, when do we go get the Christmas tree?"

Jacob, with a smile that even sparkled in his eyes, said, "Why? Do you think maybe you get presents under the tree?"

"Yes!" shouted both twins.

"Then we go get tree. Jeremiah, Thomas, and Jethro must come with Elisha and Joseph and me to chop down tree and bring to house. We go now." Jacob left the table and headed toward the hallway to grab his coat, hat, and gloves.

Thomas put on his heavy coat, hat, and gloves, then followed the others out to the corral. The morning was clear and the air was below freezing. With a lot of joshing and laughter, they caught up their horses and saddled them. Leading a packhorse, Jacob led the way toward the hills to the north of the ranch house. After thirty minutes of riding, he led the group to a stand of Douglas-fir trees.

Pointing to a well-shaped tree about eight feet tall, Jacob dismounted. "This is perfect tree."

Jeremiah rubbed his chin. "You sure, Jacob? Maybe that little one over there would be better."

Joseph quickly ran up to the one Jacob had pointed out. "No, Papa. Can't you see? This one is much better."

"But son, think how much easier that little bitty one would be to cut down and get back to the house."

Thomas realized Jeremiah was teasing the boys. He decided to join in. "Now, I don't want to disagree with you and Jacob, but don't you think that tall one over there would be better?" He pointed to an old giant of a tree.

Elisha was shaking his head. "No, no, no. It has to be this one. It's perfect."

Jacob removed his hat and scratched the back of his head. "Jethro, what do you think is perfect tree."

The boy looked from the twins to Jeremiah and Thomas. "I ain't never chopped no tree to brang into a house. But it seemed if'en yur goin' to do it you get that one." He pointed to the tree Jacob had picked out.

Jeremiah let out a big sigh. "Well, Thomas, I guess we have been out voted. We will just have to chop that one down."

"Yeaaaa!" Elisha and Joseph yelled and danced around their choice.

Thomas walked up to the tree carrying the ax he had brought. "Boys, go stand back by the horses while I chop this tree down. I don't want any flying wood chips to hit you."

The boys moved back and Jeremiah went to stand behind them, putting a hand on the shoulder of each one.

The tree was soon ready to fall with just a few more whacks of the ax. Jacob laid out a canvas with rope lying under it where he estimated the tree would fall.

Thomas aimed a few more good swings at the base of the tree and it slowly fell onto the canvas. He grinned when everyone yelled as if it was some tremendous feat to have chopped down the tree. Jeremiah laughed as he hugged the twins and then helped Thomas and Jacob roll the tree up in the canvas and tie it. Then, as Jethro held the horse still, they lifted the tree onto the pack and secured it.

Jacob rubbed his hands together. "*Gut*. That is first part. Now we go to house and put up in front room."

Thomas examined the bottom of the tree trunk where he had chopped it down. "How do you expect it to stand up?" It wasn't going to stand up on the rugged base that he could see.

Jeremiah swung up into the saddle for the ride back to the ranch house. "Don't worry about it. Jacob already has a base put together for us to stand the tree on. When we get to the house, we'll offload the tree onto the front porch, saw the base of the trunk flat, and attach the stand."

Thomas nodded his understanding. Of course, Jacob and Jeremiah had it planned. He still wasn't sure what they would do with it after they had the tree standing in the front room of the house.

An hour later, they had the tree standing where Emily wanted it. "Thank you all for getting this tree. Now, you men go get some coffee and cake in the kitchen. Jethro, after you and the twins have had your treat come on back here to help decorate the tree."

Relieved that he was not expected to be involved in decorating the tree, Thomas followed Jeremiah and Jacob into the kitchen with the boys following. Sitting on the kitchen table were a couple of cakes and a plate of cookies.

Mildred set cups around the table as everyone grabbed a seat at the table. "I assume you men want coffee. How about milk for you boys?"

Jeremiah winked at Mildred. "I think you better get them milk as that's what I've heard helps the bones to grow. We got to grow these boys tall so they can do a lot of ranch work."

Elisha nodded. "Milk and cookies and cake will make us as tall as you, Papa."

"Or, taller like Uncle Elisha." Joseph added.

"Well, Jethro, you may want to grow some more so I guess it is milk for you, too." Thomas wanted to draw Jethro into the good-natured conversation. Jethro grinned. "I expect I might grow some more. And I like milk and cake."

Mildred cut a big wedge of an applesauce cake and put it on a plate for Jethro. "Then this will get you started."

Thomas spent the rest of the day helping get ready for the visitors. He carried wood into the house to make sure the woodstoves and fireplaces had plenty. Then he refilled all of the water reserves both in the bathroom, wash up room, and kitchen. While he was busy helping wherever he could, he kept an eye out on the lane. He was anxious to see his sisters and their families, but mostly he kept watching for the buggy that would bring Catherine.

As the shadows of the late afternoon fell across the lane, Thomas went into the front room carrying several brown paper wrapped packages. He stood and stared at the tree transformed by colorful ribbons, paper chains, and wooden ornaments all painted in different bright colors. There were small wooden carvings of horses, cows, sheep, and other animals, as well as little log cabins, wagons, and even a train engine. Obviously, Jacob had made these ornaments, as he was the only one Thomas knew who could carve such intricate figures. On the top of the tree was what looked like a silver star. Arranged around the room on bookcases and the mantle were boughs of cedar and holly berries. The whole front room was transformed into a holiday delight. Thomas had never seen anything like it.

He laid gifts he had prepared under the tree with several others already placed. With Jacob's help he had made little keepsake boxes for all the children. Jacob had carved flowers and butterflies on the ones for the girls and horses on the ones for the boys. For his sisters, Emily, and his mother he had made wooden photo albums they could add to and tie together with leather binding. For all the men, including Jethro, he had made boxes to hold their shaving gear. He had used scraps from Jacob's woodpile and had varnished them so that they gleamed. As he looked at the pile of gifts, he was wishful that he could have had the money to buy something special for everyone. But, on his limited funds, he had done the best he could. He built an open-face corner cabinet for the front room for Emily in exchange for her knitting a bright red shawl, which he intended to give to Catherine for Christmas.

Just before dark, horses could be heard coming up the lane. Thomas grabbed his coat, hat, and gloves and made his way to the front porch. Looking down the lane, he saw two buggies approaching filled with laughing, waving adults and children. As they pulled up in front of the house, he saw two women that could only be his sisters, Bessie and Hope. They scrambled out of the buggies and caught him up in embraces so tight he felt that his ribs might crack.

"Thomas, oh, Thomas. Is it really you?" Bessie pushed his hat back from his forehead and stared up at him. "Yes, it is but so grown up."

"Remember me, big brother?" Hope looked up with tears in her eyes.

"Hey, Bessie, Hope, it is really good to see you all after such a long time." Thomas saw the tears running down their faces and felt a stinging behind his eyes. Blinking to keep from crying in front of everyone, he hugged his sisters to him.

Bessie pulled away and turned to the man who had walked up behind her. "This is my husband, Hank Smith. The best man that ever was."

Thomas shook his brother-in-law's hand. "Good to meet you, sir."

"It's just Hank. I'm glad to meet you. Bessie and Hope have talked about you so much I feel as if I know you."

Another man came up to them He introduced himself. "I'm Bill Oliver, Hope's husband."

Thomas shook his hand and looked at the two couples. Both men could have been brothers. They had the weather-worn faces of men who worked outdoors. "I'm really glad to meet you both and to see my sisters again. Thanks for bringing them so far."

His ma moved toward them surrounded by children. "Thomas, meet your nieces and nephews." She tapped them each on the shoulder as she said, "This is Henry, age 10; this is John, age 8; this is Randall, age 6; and, this is Hope Ann, age 4. These are Bessie and Hank's four children."

Thomas shook each of their hands as they politely said, "Hello, Uncle Thomas."

Turning to two other children, Ma said, "An these are Hope's three children, Billy, Jr., age 8; and George, age 6; and the little one your pa is holding is Mary, age 2."

Thomas shook hands with the two boys. "Hello, Billy, George."

"Hello, Uncle Thomas."

Pa came over carrying a beaming little girl with black curly hair. "Mary, this is your Uncle Thomas."

Mary waved her pudgy little hand and then stuck a couple of fingers into her mouth. "Un Tom."

Emily stepped off the porch and put her arm around Mildred. "Welcome, everyone. Bessie, Hank, Hope, Bill, it's good to see you all again. Come on in. The men will take care of getting your things in and putting up the horses." She led the way up the steps to the porch and into the house with everyone following.

Bessie and Hope each had Thomas by an arm as if afraid to let go. He looked down the lane just before entering the house. Where was Catherine?

Emily directed everyone where they would be sleeping. "Rest a while, or come back into the front room to visit after you get settled." She turned to the twins who had come in from the kitchen with their wraps still on. "Boys, you remember Henry, John, Randall, Billy, and George? If it's okay with your mothers, why don't you boys go on out back and play. Elisha and Joseph have a great fort to play in."

With yells, stumbling over each other, and general stampeding out the door, the boys all disappeared before their parents had a chance to say anything.

"God bless you, Emily. The boys have been cooped up in the train and then the buggies. Running around outside is exactly what they need." Bessie helped four-year-old Hope Ann take off her coat, scarf, and gloves. "But this one needs to lie down before supper or she will fall asleep at the table."

Emily smiled at the little girl who stepped behind her mother's skirt and then peeked back. "The boys have about an hour before it's full dark and by then supper will be ready. You all go rest a bit and if you need anything let me know. Jeremiah is up at the horse barn and should be in shortly."

Thomas wasn't sure what to do. Did he need to go help Jeremiah or visit with his family?

"Thomas, while I settle everyone, will you please get some coffee for your pa? By the way, Jeremiah doesn't expect you to do anymore work today. Enjoy your family. Their visit is going to be too short as it is."

"Thanks, Emily. Ma, you want some coffee?"

His ma sat down in one of the overstuffed chairs by the fireplace and extended her hands toward the blazing fire. "That would be lovely. I did get a little chilled on the ride here. I wish Catherine could have come out with us, but she's keeping the café open through an early supper hour. It will be well after dark before she gets here."

Thomas glanced at his folks. "How is she coming?"

Pa shifted as he sat in the chair across from Ma. "She has rented a buggy from the livery for tonight and tomorrow. That way she can go back and forth."

The image of Catherine driving a buggy in the dark alone made Thomas feel uneasy and angry at himself. He couldn't even go help Catherine to drive out to the ranch. But what could he do?

 Thomas went to the kitchen and found Mildred preparing a tray with cups, saucers, cream, sugar, and a large china coffee pot. She moved back from the table and let Thomas pick up the large wooden tray and carry it into the front room.

Bessie and Hope had come back into the front room.

Thomas set the tray on the side table and his mother came over and began serving those who wanted coffee.

Thomas said, "You all excuse me. I need to take care of something. I'll be back shortly."

He went out to the barn and found Cal putting away harness. "I need a favor, Cal. Would you ride into town and drive Catherine out. She'll close the café in about thirty minutes and it'll be dark by then. I would go but you know…."

Cal gave him a solemn look. "You go visit with your folks. I'll go take care of it. No need for her to drive out here alone in the dark."

"Thanks, Cal. I owe you. Which horse do you want to take? I'll help you saddle up."

"The dapple in the stall there shouldn't be too tired for a ride to town. On the way back I'll just tie her up to the back of the buggy."

By the time Thomas walked across the yard to the backdoor of the house, Cal rode down the lane toward the road to town. Thomas had not bothered to put on his coat when he went to look for Cal and shivered as he entered the hallway between the bunkroom and the kitchen. He walked through the kitchen and Mildred gave him a little smile and a nod as if she knew what he had done. He nodded back to her and walked into the front room to sit on the couch between his two sisters.

Mildred rang the bell for supper, and they gathered in the kitchen.

Looking around, Jeremiah asked, "Where's Cal?"

Thomas answered, "He rode into town to drive Catherine out since it will be dark."

"Good, I'm glad he did that." Jeremiah cleared his throat and everyone quieted down. "Let's hold hands and have the blessing. Then Emily will tell us where to sit." He waited until they had all grabbed someone's hand. "Heavenly Father, thank you for the safe arrival of everyone. Bless each one here from the richest of your blessings. We thank you for the bounty we have to eat, the warm home, and that all are well. Be with Catherine and Cal as they make their way here. In the name of Jesus, the Christ. Amen."

Before everyone could start talking, Emily spoke up. "I want all the little boys to eat at the table set up in the hallway between the kitchen and the bunkroom. And Jethro, may I ask that you oversee the boys and make sure they don't get into mischief?"

Jethro gave her a startled look. "Uh, yes, ma'am."

Thomas almost laughed, as he was sure Jethro had never been in charge of children before and wasn't much older than they were. It was a good arrangement and he appreciated Emily's thoughtfulness in helping Jethro feel needed while at the same time giving him an opportunity to be a kid. The boys all wandered out to the hallway where a wooden folding table with folding chairs had been set up.

"Now, if all the adults will gather here in the kitchen. Just sit where you want but leave a couple of places for Cal and Catherine."

Thomas sat in his usual place at the end of the side facing the main part of the kitchen. He liked to have the wall at his back. He leaned a chair at the end, next to him, toward the table reserved for Catherine.

Mildred and Sally kept putting platters and bowls on the two tables until Thomas was afraid the table legs would bend. It was a crowded table but the sense of family and companionship filled Thomas as much as the

222 A J Hawke

anticipation of roast beef, ham, and all the other side dishes and desserts. Just as they started passing the food, Cal and Catherine came in with a blast of cold air. A tightness that had been growing in Thomas' jaw relaxed, as he stood and seated Catherine at the table.

Chapter Thirty Thomas

Thomas was back at breaking horses the week after Christmas. The holiday week had gone by so quickly it was almost like a dream. He rode out on Friday with Jeremiah and Jethro to work with the horses that would be sold to the Army. It had felt good to become acquainted with Bessie and Hope and their families now that he was an adult. His sisters and their husbands were good people, and they were raising good children, which made him proud. But, at the same time, he ached to have a family of his own.

"What the matter, Thomas? That's the third sigh since we left the house." Jeremiah guided the black gelding to ride along side of the palomino mare that Thomas rode. Jethro was ahead a ways on the trail to the corrals.

"I was thinking about last week and how great it was to see my sisters and their families."

"Why does that make you sad?"

Thomas glanced over at Jeremiah. "I didn't realize I was sad but I guess I am a bit. I almost envy them for their families and normal lives. I don't know that I'm really envious or just wishing my life had been different."

"I can understand that. I would encourage you to think with hope. You've already been here for nine months. This first year will be over before you know it. You have time in your life for a home and family. Make wise decisions, and you'll get there." Jeremiah had kept his voice low and more personal than usual.

"Thanks, Jeremiah. I needed that reminder. I guess we always want what we want now. Waiting is no easier for me as a grown man than when I was a kid."

Jeremiah chuckled. "I know what you mean. I hate to wait sometimes, but the waiting can make the reward even sweeter. Think what you would have missed if you had been released from Yuma a year ago, without a parole."

The thought of what he would have missed caused his chest to tighten. He would have missed Catherine, because without the parole he probably would not have returned to Cedar Ridge. "Maybe waiting isn't so bad. I feel better looking at it that way."

Jeremiah prodded the gelding to canter toward the corral that was now in sight. He waved his hand as he shouted. "Good!"

The air was cold with a smell of snow. The clouds increased through the day. When Jeremiah finally decided to saddle up for the ride back to the ranch house, Thomas was ready. The full day of work with the horses left him both physically and mentally exhausted. They had been working the horses every day for a week since his sisters and their families had caught the train for Cheyenne.

The barnyard was full of people, a buggy, and two wagons. Joe and the others from the mountain ranch had arrived. Keeping control of his horse amid the yell of greetings and the running around of the twins took all of Thomas' attention. He dismounted and caught up the reins from Jeremiah's horse as his boss dismounted and hurried forward to grab Joe in a bear hug.

"Glad you made it and with fairly good weather." Jeremiah turned and shook hands with Santo and Jim.

"We were fortunate to get out of the valley before the next big snow. Elisha had the fellows work at keeping the pass clear so we could get out. Sara, and I'll admit me too, wanted to spend the last Christmas at the Rocking ES." Joe walked with Jeremiah toward the back of the wagons where Jacob, Jim, and Santo were unloading trunks, boxes, and valises.

Jeremiah hefted one end of a large trunk while Joe grabbed the other end. "Emily has your rooms all ready. We might as well unload everything now as later."

Joe nodded as he gripped the bottom of the trunk. "This trunk is Sara's things. We only brought what we will need until spring when we'll go back to the Rocking ES and bring the rest of our things. By then, I hope to have found a place for us to move to. The other wagon is mostly tack and such for working with the horses. Elisha has started cleaning and sorting out the contents of the barns."

As Jeremiah maneuvered up the couple of steps onto the back porch, he nodded toward Thomas. "After you get our horses taken care of, I need you and Jethro to see what you can do about making room in the tack room. We may need to move some stuff to the loft of the barn. As soon as we get this wagon unloaded, we'll come help get the other one emptied out."

Thomas walked his and Jeremiah's horse into the barn and unsaddled them. Thinking of how to make room for a wagonload of tack, he thanked God that he wasn't responsible for making the move from the mountains. Elisha had two large homes, four cabins, and three barns, not to mention close to twenty people to get ready to move. And there was still the question of where they were all moving to.

After getting the horses rubbed down, fed, and watered, Thomas went into the tack room with Jethro following him. When he had first come to the ranch, he had thought Jeremiah was a little over zealous about keeping the tack room in good order, but now it would pay off.

"Jethro, I'm going to start putting some things outside the tack room and you can take them up to the loft. There are shelves in the southwest corner. We have extra horse blankets, bridles, and even a few saddles that no one is using. Then we'll see what they brought down from the Rocking ES."

"Yu'uns want me to put canvas on the floor iffen them shelves get plum full?" Jethro didn't often offer suggestions.

"That's a good idea. The animals usually keep the barn warm enough that the cold won't affect the leather but there's no need to get everything all dirty and dusty. We can get Jacob to build more shelves and saddle racks. This is sure going to be an interesting year with all the changes."

Thomas had the tack room mostly rearranged by the time that Jeremiah and Joe came into the barn. Jim Finely and Santo Real had finished taking care of the horses they had brought to the ranch. Thomas admired the quality of horseflesh, the rsult of Elisha's 20-year breeding program.

As Thomas and Jethro carried various bits of tack to the loft, Jeremiah showed Joe and the other men where to store the tack brought from the mountains. An hour before dark, they had the wagons unloaded and stowed behind the barn.

Joe lightly slapped Jeremiah on the back. "Okay, tell us what to do next. You're the boss here."

Jeremiah gave a little grin. "Is that right, Joe?"

"Yes, it is. We came to work, but you got to tell us what to do." Joe stood with most of his weight on his left leg and leaning against the barn wall.

Jim grinned and Santo gravely nodded.

Jeremiah rubbed his hand across the back of his neck. "All right then, who doesn't mind helping Jacob with the farm animals, raise your hand." All of them raised their hands, including Thomas, Cal, and Jethro.

Laughing, Jeremiah pointed at Joe and Thomas. "You two help get the farm animals taken care of with Jacob in charge. The rest of us will go get the horse barn work done. We usually have supper right about dark."

Thomas was surprised Jeremiah had designated Joe for the chores of taking care of the farm animals, instead of the horses. But, he soon realized that it was easier work. It took about thirty minutes to feed the pigs, feed the chickens, gather eggs, and milk the three milk cows.

Joe reminisced with Jacob, who he had known since their first cattle drive together up from Texas. He turned to Thomas. "I'm going in to find a hot bath before supper. I think that's one of the reasons Jeremiah assigned me such easy work. After traveling for two days, I'm needing one."

Thomas chuckled along with Jacob. "Jeremiah has a subtle way of getting what he wants. You probably remember where the wash up room is in case the new bath is in use. Get you some clean clothes, and I'll get some water heating for a hot bath."

Joe walked in step with Thomas toward the house. "Thanks, Thomas, that's considerate of you. I'm glad for the opportunity to work some horses with you."

Thomas glanced over at the man who wasn't far from his own age. "Me too. I expect to learn a lot from you."

"Don't know about that, but it'll be interesting to see what the two of us together can do to maybe break and train some horses faster than one man alone."

After they entered the hallway between the kitchen and bunkroom, Thomas showed Joe where to hang his hat and coat. "We take our boots off and put on these slippers for here in the house. Mrs. Emily wants the tracking in of mud and stuff to be limited to this hallway."

Joe started toeing off his boots. "Smart lady. I guess that means you use this entrance most of the time."

Thomas nodded. "Unless I'm going directly into the bunkroom. But, if my boots are muddy I come in this way. And come to think of it, my boots are usually muddy."

"I'll go get some clean clothes. And, just so we are clear about the work with the horses. Jeremiah told me he was putting me in charge of that part of the ranch work. But what I expect is that we work as partners."

"Sounds good to me though I don't mind you being in charge. Jeremiah lets me work the horses in my own way, but I'm open to learning and improving, so just tell me what to do."

"I like your attitude, Thomas. We're going to work together just fine."

~

Joe and the others had been at the Rocking JR for six weeks. They would have the horse herd ready for sell in another month. They had been able to work most days except for a few breaks when snowstorms kept them close to the ranch house. As winters went, it was almost a mild one, and spring was arriving early.

Thomas and Cal had continued to read a couple of chapters out of the Bible each evening with Jethro an avid listener. They read the Book of John and then the Book of Acts. Jethro rarely said much. but it was obvious that he hungered for more Bible stories. His reading improved daily.

On Easter Sunday, Jeremiah and company rode to church in new outfits, which was Emily's doing. She insisted that everyone on the ranch wear new Sunday clothes. Thomas felt stiff in a new black suit his folks had given him. It was the first suit he had ever owned. The service wasn't any different than usual. The sermon was on the importance of worship. But at the invitation song, Jethro went forward to the front and talked to the preacher while the congregation kept singing, Thomas watched intently.

James Quinn motioned for everyone to be seated. "I'm happy to announce that Jethro Hunter of the Rocking JR has come asking to be baptized for the forgiveness of his sins. He tells me that he has been reading the Bible with Cal and Thomas and has come to an understanding of some needs in his life." The preacher motioned to Jethro for him to stand and face the congregation. He looked a little pale.

"Now, Jethro, tell these good people why you have come forward this morning." Brother Quinn had his hand on Jethro's shoulder, as if to give him support.

Straightening his shoulders and looking at the congregation, Jethro said, "I knowed I done sinned. But Jesus loves me and God wants to forgive me. We'uns read in that there book of Acts what God wants us'uns to do to be saved. So, I wants to do what God wants. I'm sorry I sinned and done told God I'd try not to sin no more." Jethro glanced down and then straightened up again, looking at Thomas. "I's going to try, can't promise no more. So I asks the preacher to help get baptized to warsh away my sins, get saved, and have Jesus on my side." He turned and looked at the preacher with a look of question.

James Quinn smiled at Jethro and patted his shoulder. "That's a great statement of faith, and we will now all gather at the river at two o'clock this afternoon for the baptism. Let's pray.

"Our heavenly Father, bless this fine young man, who has come today to repent of his sins, acknowledge you as his God, and express his belief in the saving power of your Son, Jesus the Christ. As he becomes our brother in Christ and is added to this church, the family of God, help us to be what Jethro needs to live faithful to You. Bless Cal and Thomas for being willing to teach this young man and share their faith. We ask these things in the name of Jesus the Christ. Amen."

Thomas made his way up to the front of the small church building and waited his turn to speak to Jethro, as everyone gave him a handshake or a hug and expressed delight at his decision.

Taking Jethro's hand and holding on tight, Thomas had difficulty speaking. "Jethro, I don't know what to say, except you're making a mighty fine decision today. And one that took courage. I'm proud of you."

"Thanks, Thomas. Kin I ask you something?"

"Sure."

"Would you baptize me?"

Thomas took a deep breath. "I'd be honored to baptize you."

With the baptism scheduled for just a couple of hours later, Jeremiah offered to pay for lunch for everyone at the hotel dining room. Later, Thomas couldn't remember if he ate much or not. The time passed quickly and soon they were riding down to a spot by the river where baptisms usually took place.

Spotting James Quinn in the growing crowd of people, Thomas strolled over and got his attention. "Brother Quinn, I've never baptized anyone. Can you tell me what to do?" Thomas wanted to be the one to help usher Jethro into the kingdom of God but was fearful of doing something wrong.

James Quinn put his hand on Thomas' shoulder and spoke softly telling him what to do. He ended his instructions by saying, "Remember that you are only helping Jethro be obedient to God's command to be baptized, God is the one washing away his sins with the blood of Christ. Think you can remember all of that?"

Thomas nodded. "I'll do my best."

The preacher nodded. "You'll do fine. Now, let's go find Jethro."

After Thomas and Jethro had taken their boots off, they wadded into the slow flowing river until Jethro had water up to his chest. The water was cold but not freezing.

Thomas raised his hand to get the attention of the crowd standing on the river bank. "Jethro, do you believe that Jesus is the Son of God and will be your savior?"

Jethro's voice was strong and sure. "Yes, sir, I do."

Thomas quietly said, "Fold your arms across your chest and hold your nose. When I start to tip you back into the water just lay back on my arm and trust me to bring you back up."

Jethro followed Thomas' directions and then Thomas said in a strong voice. "I baptize you into the name of the Father, the Son, and the Holy Spirit for the forgiveness of your sins and so that you may receive the gift of the Holy Spirit."

Thomas tipped Jethro back into the water until he was completely submersed and brought him back up out of the water.

Jethro emerged from the water with a whoop and a grin. Thomas pulled him into a bear hug disregarding the water dripping off Jethro. "You know now we're brothers in Christ?"

Jethro's grin got bigger if that were possible. "Then you'd best be a good'un."

Thomas thumped him on the shoulders in a manly hug. "I'll do my best." He released him as they made their way to the shore of the river and the rest of the congregation greeted Jethro as the newest member of the family of God.

Catherine handed Thomas a towel. "You did that so well, as if you have baptized others."

Thomas smiled at her. "I know that God guided me through it, because I was so scared I'd mess it up. I can't describe how good that makes me feel knowing I had a hand in someone becoming a Christian. I'm humbled, too. Jethro is the one who showed real courage by going before the church this morning. I had no idea he was thinking about doing such a thing. Of course, I should have guessed from all the questions he asked the last week."

Catherine took his arm as they walked up the slope from the river to the waiting buggies and horses.

~

A week later, Thomas looked across the corral out in the pasture where they trained the horses and watched Joe finish schooling a horse that he had been working with for several days. The big sorrel gelding had been a challenge but was finally coming along. It had been a sunny day but with a bite in the air from the breeze that blew down from the north. Thomas searched the skies for an indication of what the weather would do.

Joe turned the horse he was working over to Santo and walked to where Thomas leaned against the corral fence. "By my count that makes four hundred ready for sale to the Army. I know we're early but they will probably take delivery. We still have others to work with but at least that contract can be met."

"Jeremiah would know more about that than me. It wouldn't hurt to get the herd sold. The horses are ready now and the longer we wait, the more we have to school them and feed them."

Joe took a long swig of water out of his canteen. "I want to spend more time fixing up our new place. Once the herd is delivered, I'll have some time before we head back to the mountains. Elisha is going to need all the help he can get preparing for his move."

Thomas kicked at a small rock partially buried in the ground and then glanced up at Joe. "I'd like to go with you to the Rocking ES. I've never seen that part of the country." He sighed deeply and then said it. "But with my status as a prisoner here, I can't leave the ranch."

"I'm sorry about that. You'd be a big help. It's only two more years. Then you can go where you like. I'm just glad you're here helping with the horses. You've made a big difference."

"Thanks, Joe. In another six weeks, it will have been a year since I arrived here. It's hard for me to believe how much I have learned and can do now." He tugged off his hat and ran his fingers through his hair. "Jethro, as young as he is, still knows more than I do about ranching."

Joe met his gaze with a serious expression. "And yet you have been able to give him an invaluable gift. You've taught him how to read and write and you're catching up to him in your ranching knowledge."

"Teaching him to read and write was easy. The boy is so starved for learning; he drinks it in. I have to tell him to turn off the lamp and go to bed so he'll have energy to work the next day. He's reading that Mark Twain book, *Adventures of Huckleberry Finn*, again."

How did Joe know he was teaching Jethro? They had kept their study to the bunkroom. It must have been Jim Finely who told Joe. Jim had not made any comments about the hours of study time Thomas and Jethro spent during the evenings sitting close to the box stove to keep warm with snow falling outside.

"Well, you're making a difference in that boy's life. Even his speech has changed in the last few weeks. I think he tries to mimic you and Jeremiah."

Thomas was surprised Joe had noticed. What he said was true. Jethro was speaking in more conventional English. Catherine had even mentioned she missed hearing the lilting mountain cadence.

Joe put away his canteen and picked up his saddle blanket and saddle. "Let's saddle up and head back to the ranch house. We've done enough for today." He whistled toward Jim and Santo and they responded with a wave.

Thomas saddled up his palomino mare. It wasn't really his, it belonged to the ranch, but he was the only one who rode the horse that he called Mandy. He liked her even temperament and gait of the horse.

Jeremiah rode up as the four men started toward the ranch house. He had spent the afternoon riding a circuit of the western part of the ranch keeping an eye out for downed fencing or unusual tracks. The five men rode the twenty minutes back toward the ranch house with few comments, tired at the end of a good day of work.

Two horses that didn't belong to the ranch were in the barn. Thomas had a bad feeling and a chill ran up his spine as he sensed danger. He looked around but couldn't see anything that indicated a problem.

Jeremiah was also eyeing the two horses. "Thomas, you and Jim take care of our horses. I'm going to the house to see who is here. After you get the horses taken care of, go to Jacob's workshop and stay until I send for you. Jim, you come into the house after you finish in case I need to send you after Thomas."

Thomas and Jim had the horses unsaddled, rubbed down, fed, and watered in record time. He watched Jim head for the house and he walked around to the back of the barn and entered Jacob's workshop. The workshop stove had a bright fire burning and was warm. Jacob wasn't in the workshop. Thomas was curious about who had come and Jeremiah's odd request for him to stay in the workshop until sent for. He decided to sweep out the workshop while he waited.

Soon Jim appeared at the door. "Jeremiah wants to speak with you in the front room." Frowning, he added. "Sheriff Grant and his deputy are here."

Thomas put the broom away and followed Jim to the house. Why was the sheriff here? What did he think Thomas had done now? He sighed. Would his past always follow him?

He stepped into the front room in the midst of an argument between the sheriff and Jeremiah.

"I'm telling you there is no way Thomas Black was out rustling cattle last night. He hasn't left the ranch and hasn't been alone for days. I've made sure of that." Jeremiah stood next to his desk with his face like stone.

Sheriff Grant's voice was loud and harsh. "Well, all I know is someone matching his description was spotted out at Arkenstone's ranch as a bunch of cattle were driven off."

Jeremiah's voice was not as loud but had a level of hardness in it. "Isn't that just a little suspicious? Don't you find it strange rustlers would be so open and obvious, stealing cattle so close to his ranch house and so early in the evening? As if they wanted to be seen and the only one Arkenstone can describe is one that resembles Thomas?"

"All I know is I have an eye witness accusing Thomas Black. Now I'm taking him in until Judge Yeakley gets here and then let him decide what to do. You or any of the ranch hands try to stop me, and you'll be under arrest along with Black." The man looked ready to pull his gun and his deputy was standing behind him carrying a rifle.

Thomas didn't want to go with the sheriff. Jail was not where he wanted to be. But, he couldn't let Jeremiah put himself or anyone else on the ranch in danger. "I'll go with you, Sheriff. Let me get my coat and hat and saddle up a horse."

Jeremiah stepped toward Thomas. "You shouldn't have to go. We can prove you were here at the Rocking JR."

"I know and that's why I'm not worried about going with the sheriff. But there's no point to making a fuss and take a chance on someone being hurt."

Sheriff Grant nodded. "He's showing some sense. If he's innocent, then let Judge Yeakley decide."

Jeremiah shrugged his shoulders as if giving in. "Then a couple of the boys, and I are going to ride in with you."

"Suit yourself, but there's no need. If you are riding with us, get your horses saddled. Smith, you go with Black to get his hat and coat and meet us at the barn." Sheriff Grant turned to Thomas. "You're not going to give us any trouble are you?"

Thomas shook his head. "No, sir."

~

The ride into town was embarrassing to Thomas. Sheriff Grant had insisted on tying his hands. Fortunately, he didn't tie them behind his back so Thomas could ride easier. But, it bothered him to be tied up as a prisoner. He was a prisoner on the ranch, but no one treated him as one. It had been easy to forget the sting of humiliation. As they entered town, Thomas kept his eyes on his horse's head. He hoped neither his folks nor Catherine saw them ride up to the sheriff's office. Soon, he was locked into one of the small, cells that smelled like unwashed bodies, alcohol and mold.

Jeremiah stood outside the cell. "Don't worry. We'll be back tomorrow for the hearing with the judge. We'll all be ready to testify for you."

"Thanks. Would you mind seeing my folks and Catherine before you go back to the ranch? I don't want them to hear about this from the gossip mill." Thomas didn't want them to know at all, but that was impossible in a small town like Cedar Ridge.

Jeremiah put his hand between the bars and grabbed him by the shoulder. "Try to relax and get some rest. I'll take care of it."

After Jeremiah and the others left, Thomas sat on the small cot when his first of several visitors arrived. First, his father came with a concerned look, then James Quinn, the preacher, came by to promise prayers by the church members, and then toward suppertime Catherine arrived carrying a big basket of hot food.

Thomas hated she was seeing him behind bars but he couldn't have told her to stay away. He wanted to see her beautiful, friendly smile too much.

"Oh, Thomas, I'm so sorry this is happening. I know there is no way you can be guilty. People are so quick to condemn." Her loving look of concern almost made being put in jail worth it.

"Hopefully, Jeremiah will be able to sort it out tomorrow with the judge. Don't worry. What have you got in the basket?" He might be able to relieve her mind, but he was still worried.

Catherine uncovered the basket and passed a jar of hot stew with some cornbread through the bars. "I asked the deputy to unlock the cell so I could give you your supper but he said he couldn't without Sheriff Grant's permission. He doesn't know when the sheriff will be back. I wanted you to have this still warm. Here's a spoon." She passed the spoon between the bars.

As Thomas took it, he also took her hand and held it. "Can you stay a bit? Just while I eat, and then you can take your things back."

Catherine set the basket down by the bars and pulled up a rickety wooden chair that was by the wall. "I can stay a while. After you eat the stew and cornbread, I have dried apple pie for you baked fresh this afternoon." She searched around in the basket, brought out a jar of coffee, and passed it between the bars. "I'm sorry it's not real hot. I didn't have anything to carry it in to keep it hot."

Thomas smiled. "Thanks, this is great. At Yuma when they gave us coffee, they didn't worry whether it was hot or not. I got used to drinking it room temperature. This is still plenty warm." He opened the jar and took a long swallow.

"The sheriff told Jeremiah the man they thought was you was riding a palomino and had a black hat like yours. Do you think someone is deliberately trying to throw blame on you?"

Thomas paused in his eating of the stew into which he had crumbled the cornbread. "I didn't know about the horse or the hat. It does sound like someone is trying to throw blame on me. Whether it is someone who wants to get rid of me or to divert the sheriff from looking in another direction, I don't know. But don't worry. Jeremiah and the other men on the Rocking JR can testify I haven't left the ranch except for church in weeks. Jeremiah has made sure I never worked alone."

"What about at night? Could you have snuck out with no one knowing? Not that I think you did, but folks will ask."

"No, that would have been impossible. Both Jim Finely and Jethro sleep with one eye open. You turn over, and they are awake watching. No way I could have gotten out of the bunkroom and ridden out without them knowing. And, they wouldn't lie for me either."

"I'm glad. I mean I'm glad you have witnesses to your whereabouts. I care too much what happens to you." The soft glow of Catherine's eyes and the sweet smile left a jolt in Thomas' chest.

His voice was low and husky. "You care what happens to me?"

Catherine reached between the bars and Thomas took her hand. "You know that I care deeply for you. You're my best friend."

Thomas ran his thumb in a circle around the spot on her wrist where he could feel her pulse. "Could I ever be more than a friend?" He had no right to ask such a thing in this setting, but he wanted to know.

Catherine gazed into his eyes and slowly nodded her head. "I think you already are."

Thomas took a deep breath to keep his breathing going. Just the sight of her took his breath. "You mean everything to me, Catherine. But I have no right to declare it, not standing here on this side of these bars. I won't have the right to declare it until I can walk down the street a free man."

She smiled. "I still like hearing it. We have no choice but to take it slow. Perhaps that's a good thing. We can be friends for now and get to know each other. And when the timing is right, with God's help we will know the next step to take."

He lifted her hand and kissed it. "Then I will find ways to say it, sweet Catherine." Hearing the door from the office opening, he dropped her hand and stepped back from the bars. "Thank you, for supper, Miss O'Malley."

Sheriff Grant looked into the cell section of his jail. "Miss Catherine, you shouldn't be here."

Catherine looked up at him with her normal gentle smile. "I'm waiting for Mr. Black to finish eating, so I can take my things back to the café."

"All right, but as soon as he is done, you need to leave."

"Yes, sir," she said as he withdrew back into his office.

Thomas almost laughed at the sweet, innocent voice with which she spoke. No one would guess from her look and voice that she had just declared that she cared for him. Such a feeling of joy bubbled up in his being that he wanted to shout it out to the world. Instead, he kept his gaze on her hands as she passed him a large piece of dried apple pie wrapped in brown paper.

"I want to save this for later. The evening is going to be a long one." Thomas set the piece of pie on the narrow cot that took up most of the space in the small cell.

"I'd best go before Sheriff Grant gets upset and won't let me come back. I'll bring breakfast in the morning. Now I'm off to visit with your mother. She wanted to come but your pa won't let her. We'll be praying for you and thinking about you."

Thomas reached between the bars and stroked her cheek. "Goodnight, sweet Catherine. I'll also be thinking of you and praying God's blessings on you. Give my love to Ma. I'm glad Pa won't let her come to see me in jail. I wish you didn't have to see me here."

Catherine pressed her hand to his as he caressed her face, then she pulled back, picked up her basket, and headed into the office of the jail.

Thomas pressed his forehead against the bars in an all too familiar way. The cell was suddenly dark and colder. He shivered as he thought of being sent back to Yuma. Then, he remembered the most powerful thing a man can do. He closed his eyes and prayed for deliverance.

Chapter Thirty-One: Catherine

Catherine held back tears as she left the jail and crossed the street to walk up the block to the mercantile. How she hated to see Thomas behind bars. He was innocent of the charges, of that she was sure, but being innocent might not protect him. She nibbled on her lower lip as she entered the mercantile. Could Myles McKinley be behind this? He was the only person she knew who disliked Thomas enough to want him sent back to prison.

"Catherine, are you all right?" Milburn stood behind the counter at the back of the store.

She sighed. "I'm fine although concerned for Thomas. I just left the jail after taking him a hot supper."

"Yes, his mother and I are also concerned. He can't seem to get a break. Go up and talk to Agnes. I'm about to close up for the night. We can talk and pray together and put it into God's hands."

"Thanks, Milburn. I need to be reminded we have access to help outside of ourselves." Catherine smiled weakly at Thomas' father. He was such a good, grounded man. "I'll go on up to Agnes. I'm sure she is distressed by all of this."

Catherine climbed the stairs to the living quarters above the store. Knocking on the door and pushing it open, she called out, "Agnes, it's me."

Agnes walked into the front room from the kitchen. She pulled Catherine into a hug. "I'm glad you came. I'm needing someone to talk to."

Catherine hugged Agnes back and then pulled back to sit her basket down. "I've come from the jail. I took Thomas a hot meal. I have a contract with the town to feed the prisoners. Of course, this prisoner got a nicer supper than I usually prepare."

"Thank you for watching out for Thomas. I hate to think of him back behind bars. I'm so worried." Agnes waved Catherine to sit next to her on the couch. "How did Thomas seem? Did they hurt him any when they arrested him?"

"No, he's fine. Jeremiah told me there was no resistance when Sheriff Grant came to the ranch. Thomas went with the sheriff and his deputy willingly, because he didn't want to put anyone at the ranch in danger."

Agnes took Catherine's hand and held it. "What did you take him to eat?"

Catherine smiled. "Agnes, you are such a mother hen."

"Well, he's still my youngest child even if he is a man grown."

"Yes, I can see that. Well, I took fresh made stew and cornbread, hot coffee, and a large piece of dried apple pie. He ate everything except the pie, which he saved to have something to eat later." Catherine found it strange to be talking about what Thomas had eaten for supper when the next day a judge would decide his fate. Rustling was a hanging offense. Sending Thomas back to Yuma Prison might be the better outcome.

Milburn came in and joined them. They talked over the situation every way possible. But, it changed nothing. Catherine was still worried.

Finally, Milburn said, "Let's pray and then try to get a good night of sleep. We want to be rested for whatever comes tomorrow."

They stood and joined hands. Milburn led the prayer of petition for Thomas' release from the charges and for strength for all of them for whatever was to come.

After the prayer, Catherine squeezed both their hands. "Thanks Milburn. I'll try to not worry and leave the outcome in God's hands. Now, I'm going home and let you all get some rest. I'll take breakfast to Thomas in the morning."

Milburn nodded. "Jeremiah suggested I go over to the jail in the morning with shaving gear and clean clothes. I'll insist the sheriff let Thomas shave and put on clean clothes so he can make as good an appearance before the judge as possible. The northbound train will arrive at 2:30 tomorrow afternoon. Jeremiah thinks the judge will start court by three, which is what he usually does. The judge will want to get done in a couple of days, so he can go on to his next stop."

Catherine had never paid much attention to the judge's schedule, as she had never had to be in the court sessions. However, she planned to be at the one the next afternoon. After giving Milburn and Agnes hugs and grabbing her basket, she made her way to her room at the back of the café. Sleep was hard to achieve, but finally she was able to drop off for a few hours.

~

The next morning the café seemed busier than usual with talk of Thomas' arrest and the ongoing problem of cattle rustling in the area. She had asked Beryl to come in early so Catherine could take Thomas' breakfast over to the jail. He seemed quiet and pensive but not particularly worried. Sheriff Grant let her stay and visit with Thomas while he ate.

She was back at the jail at noon with dinner for Thomas. Catherine watched him eat the three pieces of fried chicken, mashed potatoes, gravy, green beans, and rolls. "Your appetite doesn't seem to be affected."

Thomas looked up at her from where he was mopping up gravy with a roll. "Well, these may be the last good meals I get for a while. No point in not enjoying what I have at the moment, good food and pleasant company."

Catherine refused to let the tears fall that gathered behind her eyes. The thought of Thomas being so far away was crushing, but the fear they might hang him if the judge found him guilty was something she fought to keep at bay. "You feel confident that the judge will listen to Jeremiah and the other men?"

"I have to, Catherine. There's no reason to think the judge won't be fair and just. Jeremiah has hired the lawyer, Mr. Pickering, to represent me. The lawyer came by this morning and asked me questions he thinks the judge will ask. He didn't seem to see a problem, as he knows the judge." Thomas ate the last bite of fried chicken and handed the narrow bowl back through the bars to Catherine. "He did ask questions about who might want to set me up and throw the blame for the rustling on me."

"What did you tell him?"

"I told him the only enemy I knew of was possibly Myles McKinley. But Mr. Pickering couldn't figure out a reason why McKinley would be involved in rustling."

"What do you think?"

"Well, when I was a kid and involved in rustling, I think folks would have said the same thing about me. There was no logical reason for me to have been that dishonest, but I was." Thomas' voice had gone soft and serious.

Catherine nodded. "The face we put forth is not always the real one. How can we find out who the real rustlers are?"

Thomas smiled. "*We* are not going to find out. You stay out of this. Jeremiah is working on it with others."

"Well, if I hear anything at the café, I'll let Jeremiah know. I need to get back to help Beryl with the dinner crowd, and then we are closing the café for the judge's hearing." Catherine packed her basket and stood to leave.

Thomas reached between the bars and took her hand. "I'd rather you not come to the hearing. But, I suspect I can't keep you away."

"No, you cannot. I'll be there in your support. And I'll be praying. Most of the congregation will be there plus all the men from the Rocking JR Ranch. You're liked and respected and people want to show you their support."

Thomas smiled. "Thanks for your support and your prayers. I'm trying to think positively about this and remember that God is with me. You are such a good person, Catherine. I know God is hearing your prayers."

When Catherine got back to the café, the only topic of conversation seemed to be the hearing later that afternoon. At two o'clock Jeremiah and the hands from the Rocking JR came into the café.

"You have any pie and coffee?" Jeremiah asked.

Catherine nodded. "All you men want pie and coffee? It's chess pie today."

Various grunts, yeahs, and yes, ma'ams indicated everyone wanted pie and coffee. Beryl and Catherine quickly served them, and then Catherine poured herself a cup of coffee and sat at the table with Jeremiah, Joe, and Cal.

"Emily stayed at home with the children?" Catherine asked.

Jeremiah nodded. "She wanted to come for the hearing, but I convinced her that if she came I would have to leave one of the men at the house. So, she stayed home." He took a sip of coffee and glanced at Catherine. "Are you staying home for the hearing?"

Catherine shook her head. "No, Milburn and Agnes will be there and I plan to sit with them in support."

He nodded. "That is thoughtful of you. I'm hopeful they won't need much support. If the judge is open to our testimony this should be quick and Thomas back at the ranch by supper time."

"Oh, Jeremiah, I hope so."

After the men from the Rocking JR left the café, Catherine and Beryl cleaned the tables and washed up the last of the dishes from the noon meal. Hearing the tinkle of the bell over the door, Catherine stepped back into the dining room of the café. Myles McKinley was setting down at a table.

Catherine wiped her hands on a dishcloth. "We were just closing up, Myles. I can get you a cup of coffee but we're not serving food just now."

"Coffee will be fine." He watched her as she poured a cup of coffee and set it on the table in front of him. "You going over to the hearing for Black?"

Catherine stepped back from the table. "Yes, I'm going over to the mercantile and walk over with Milburn and Agnes."

Myles looked at her over the rim of the cup as he sipped on the hot coffee. "You know Black is going to get sent back to Yuma Prison at the very least and maybe even convicted again of rustling."

"I don't know any such thing. He has witnesses that will testify as to his movements over the last few weeks." Catherine tried to keep her tone neutral but even she heard the hostility in her voice.

"You mean those riders from the Rocking JR that are willing to lie for him? The judge will see through that. Black was seen and he will pay." Myles looked at Catherine with a hard and mean expression on his face. His voice was not his usual suave tone.

Catherine understood now the depth of Myles' hatred and jealousy of Thomas. People liked Thomas, even if he was a prisoner paroled to Jeremiah. But, she couldn't think of one person who had expressed a liking for Myles

Beryl came into the dining room and took the now empty cup in front of Myles. "I'll just wash this cup and then we can be on our way. Afternoon, Myles. You ready to head out so we can close up?"

Catherine refrained from laughing at the frustrated expression Myles gave Beryl. However, he got up, dropped a coin on the table for the coffee, and left.

"Thanks, Beryl. I didn't know how to get rid of him."

"Well, I couldn't help but overhear what he said. What he has against Thomas, I don't know. But, he obviously wants Thomas to be found guilty." Beryl placed the washed and dried cup back on the shelf. "Let's get out of here before anyone else shows up."

Catherine put on her hat, gloves, and shawl. Out in the wind it was still a cool day. Full spring was a few weeks away even though today was warm enough to leave off her heavy coat. She let Beryl leave the café. She turned the sign to show closed and locked the door. Crossing the street to the mercantile, she looked toward the schoolhouse where the judge would listen to cases for the next two days. Several horses and wagons were in front of the building and other people were walking toward it from the town. Catherine met Milburn and Agnes as they stepped out of the mercantile, and Milburn locked the door behind them.

Putting her arm around Agnes' elbow, Catherine said, "We better go quickly as I'm afraid there is going to be a crowd at the schoolhouse. We want to get seats close enough up front to hear everything."

"My yes, come on Milburn. Let's hurry."

Milburn scurried along behind them as Agnes set a fast pace. When they entered the schoolhouse, they quickly found seats a couple of rows from the front and off to the right. Catherine glanced around at those already seated and saw Jeremiah and the other men from the Rocking JR. She spotted Myles at the back. Then Judge Yeakley strolled in with Sheriff Grant behind him. Thomas walked behind the sheriff with the deputy bringing up the rear. Thomas' hands were handcuffed in front of him. He spotted her and smiled as if he were out for a stroll. Catherine didn't know how he could be so calm. She found herself breathing too fast and trembling.

Judge Yeakley sat down at the teacher's desk at the front of the schoolroom. He carried a gavel and a black leather folder. Sheriff Grant pointed Thomas to a chair next to Mr. Pickering. The deputy stood off to the side as the sheriff went and said something quietly to the judge.

Picking up the gavel, Judge Yeakley pounded it on the desk. "This court is in session. The first case to be heard is Thomas Black and the charge is rustling. How does the defendant plea?"

Mr. Pickering stood. "The defendant pleas not guilty your honor."

Judge Yeakley looked sharply at Thomas. "Not guilty? Then I guess we have to hear witnesses."

Catherine couldn't believe what she heard. Of course, they would hear witnesses, even if she had to stomp up to the judge and demand it.

The judge pointed his gavel at the sheriff. "Grant, you got any witnesses?"

"Yes, Judge, John Arkenstone and a couple of his riders." Sheriff Grant indicated the rancher and a couple of cowboys seated off to the left.

"Well, let's hear them," said the judge in an impatient voice.

Catherine felt Agnes grab her hand and hold on tight. She didn't feel very confident about the proceedings either. Glancing over at Jeremiah, she could have sworn he looked bored as if nothing that would be said was anything to worry about. Taking a deep breath, she whispered to Agnes, "Look at Jeremiah. He's not a bit worried. Let's pray and believe that God has it under control."

Agnes squeezed Catherine's hand and whispered back. "Thank you, my dear. I'm just so concerned about Thomas."

Arkenstone stood in front of the desk before the judge. Sheriff Grant held a Bible out to him, on which he laid his hand. "Do you swear to tell the truth, the whole truth, so help you God?"

The rancher cleared his throat and with a deep bass voice said, "I do."

As they had no prosecutor, the judge asked the questions. "What happened out at your place the other night?"

Arkenstone glanced around the schoolhouse full of his friends and neighbors. "Well, about nine o'clock as I was about to head to bed. Jack here ran into the house and said some riders were after the cattle we had gathered up close to the ranch house. I grabbed my rifle and ran out into the barnyard yelling for the hands to get me a horse saddled. In no time at all, we rode out for the herd. Me and five of my men. They was four riders out by the herd. The moon was out and you could see some but not much. I saw four riders trying to bunch up my herd and get them moving. One of them was riding a palomino and an old black hat like Black wears. The riders took off, and we gave chase but they was too far ahead. I sent a rider for the sheriff and told him what I had seen. He said it might have been Black here by the description. That's all I know except this is third time rustlers have gotten after my cattle. The first two times they got away with a couple hundred head."

The judge looked from Thomas to the rancher. "Do you believe Thomas Black tried to rustle your cattle Mr. Arkenstone? Can you swear it was him for sure?"

The man fiddled with his hat, which he held in his hands. Then he looked at Thomas and said, "No, Judge Yeakley. I can't swear to it. I want it to be someone so we can get this rustling stopped, but I can't swear it was him positively. But, the horse looked like his and so did the hat."

"Thank you, Mr. Arkenstone. Let's hear from your riders."

Catherine was pleased when both of the riders' testimony was basically the same as their boss. No one had seen the rustler close enough to swear it was Thomas. With feeling running high against the rustlers, people wanted it to be Thomas to put an end to it.

The judge, after dismissing the last of the riders, turned to the sheriff. "You got any other witnesses?"

"No, your honor."

"What about you Mr. Pickering? You got any witnesses for your client?" The judge pointed his gavel at the lawyer.

"Yes, sir. I do. I call Jeremiah Rebourn to the stand." The lawyer pushed his spectacles up his nose and turned to Jeremiah.

After the sheriff swore him in, the judge asked Jeremiah to give his testimony.

Jeremiah looked around at people gathered in the schoolhouse. "Thomas Black has been a paroled prisoner at my ranch since last April. That means that he is serving out his sentence working for me, and I am responsible for him to the courts. He is not allowed to leave the ranch without someone with him. And, I don't allow him to work alone on the ranch. In other words, Thomas Black is never alone. My men are under orders to keep him in their sight day and night. Mr. Arkenstone says that a man resembling Thomas rode out at his place about nine that night. At that time, I had finished having a cup of coffee with some of the hands in the kitchen. Thomas was with me at that time. I've asked all the men involved to be here this afternoon for you to question them. No way was Thomas off the ranch that night, nor any other night."

The judge stared at Jeremiah and then banged his gavel on the desk. "Since we have no witnesses that can swear to Thomas Black being at the Arkenstone ranch and we have witnesses swearing he was at the Rocking JR, I see no reason to waste the court's time." He lifted his gavel as if to pound it on the desk and then stopped its downward swing. "Thomas Black, please stand up."

Thomas stood and quietly waited.

The judge continued. "You're a convicted rustler serving out your sentence. It's understandable why your neighbors would be distrustful of you. You have two more years, as I understand it, to serve out your sentence. I could order you back to Yuma and relieve your neighbors' minds."

Catherine caught her breath. Oh no, even if innocent, Thomas could be sent back to Yuma. The pain in her chest grew as the fear radiated through her system. She couldn't lose Thomas.

After what seemed an eternity of waiting, the judge cleared his throat and said, "But I'm not going to do that. I'm turning you back over to Rebourn to finish working out your sentence. And, Sheriff Grant, quit trying to blame this rustling on one of the best guarded men in the county and find the real rustlers. Case dismissed." This time the gavel came down hard on the desk.

The judge stood and spoke to the sheriff. "Get these folks cleared out and call the next case. I don't have a lot of time."

Even though Catherine wanted to run up to Thomas and give him a big hug and kiss, she sedately walked out of the schoolhouse with Milburn and Agnes.

Agnes looked anxiously at Milburn. "What now?"

Milburn patted her shoulder. "We go home and wait. Jeremiah said that if it was possible he would bring Thomas by on their way back to the ranch. But, he said if the crowd was not accepting of the judge's decision he would get Thomas back to the ranch, to safety."

Agnes nodded. "Come on, Catherine. Let's get back to the store. Milburn can open up and we'll put on coffee in case Jeremiah and Thomas come by."

They had coffee made and cake sliced by the time Jeremiah, Thomas, Joe, Jim, Jacob, Jethro, and Cal came through the back door of the mercantile.

Thomas hugged his parents and then Catherine. "All that worry for nothing."

Catherine kept close by Thomas as the other men crowded around the table to get coffee and cake.

Jeremiah took a cup of coffee. "When I saw Judge Yeakley, I didn't believe for a minute he wouldn't rule fair. If it had been another judge that could have been bought, the outcome wouldn't have been so sure." He turned to Agnes. "I hope you don't mind I brought all the fellows. I want them all here until I get Thomas back to the ranch. Whoever set Thomas up is still out there."

Agnes gave Jeremiah a kiss on the cheek. "Thank you, Jeremiah, for believing in our boy. Your men are always welcome."

Thomas held his hand out to Jeremiah who took it in a solid handshake. "My thanks also, boss."

"How about you, Thomas? I didn't see you even ruffle a feather walking in." Jeremiah seemed curious.

"I can't explain it. A feeling of peacefulness came over me last night while I was in jail. Somehow I knew I was going to come through all of this okay. Guess it's because I turned it over to God.

Jeremiah nodded and smiled. "Well, we need to ride out to the ranch. Emily will be anxious."

Catherine stepped forward and gave Jeremiah another kiss on his cheek. "You tell her we'll be out Sunday, and I'll bring fresh baked bread and pies."

As the men started leaving, Catherine took the opportunity to give Thomas a kiss on the cheek. "I'm so glad about the outcome, my more than a friend. I would have been awfully unhappy if you had gone back to Yuma."

Thomas grinned and gave her a hug. "Me, too."

Chapter Thirty-Two: Thomas

Two weeks after the trail,, Thomas sat on his horse, Mandy, and watched the squad of ten soldiers from Fort Lyon drive the horse herd from the ranch and toward the south. Jeremiah and Joe had been awarded the contract the year before to deliver four hundred horses ready to ride to the US Army by summer. They were several months early in fulfilling the contract but the Army was eager to get the horses.

Though proud of the work he and the other men had done to get the huge herd of horses ready, Thomas was relieved the Army came for them. The ranch hands would not be responsible for driving the herd to Fort Lyon. Now, work could turn toward repairing fences, branding cattle, and caring for mares in foal. Later in the summer, the haying would begin. Thomas regretted he wouldn't be able to help with moving Elisha and the others from the mountain to the Cedar Ridge area.

Joe rode up and pulled his horse alongside of Thomas. "Feels good to have that many horses broke and ready for the Army. Not that I'm boasting, but we sure put in some hard work to get to this day."

Thomas nodded. "When I got here last year, I had no thought I would be involved in such a work."

"Well, you learned fast and have done a good job. Now we need to get some things caught up around here, and Jim and I will go back to the Rocking ES to help with the move. Sara will stay here and get the new place ready for our stuff to arrive."

"I like that old ranch house you're redoing. How many acres do you have there?"

"We have five hundred acres with an option to buy more. We don't really need a big place since we're so close to Jeremiah's land. We plan to continue to partner with Elisha with the horse breeding. The ranch house is almost finished. Those new kitchen cabinets you and Jacob built look good in that big kitchen. We should be able to move in as soon as our stuff from the mountains gets here. Sara and Emily are making curtains, cushions, and such like. I thought the place looked pretty good, but then the women starting finding all sorts of things that needed done." Joe shook his head. "When I came up the trail from Texas with Cookie, Bob, and Jacob from Texas, all I had was a valise and three sets of clothes. Now, I'm hoping three big wagons will hold all of the goods we own. You'll find out how much more complicated your life gets when you take a wife."

"I'm glad you like the kitchen cabinets. They were fun to build. We included Jethro on that job and he's turned out to be handy with woodworking."

Hearing a horse coming across the pasture toward them, Thomas looked toward the ranch house and saw Bob riding toward them. It had been good to see the ranch foreman return from several months spent in Texas on his family's ranch. Thomas liked the man and the way he led the work on the ranch.

Joe reined his horse around as Bob rode up at a gallop and pulled up his horse in a scatter of dust and dirt. "What's wrong, Bob?"

"Jeremiah wants you all back at the house. We got trouble. While the horse herd was being rounded up and driven out, rustlers took a couple of hundred head of cattle from the north pasture."

"Let's go, Thomas. Good thing the horses are on their way to Fort Lyons. That frees us up to go after the rustlers." Joe and Bob led the way with Thomas quick to follow.

As they rode into the yard between the ranch house and the barn, Jethro and Cal were tightening the cinches on their horses that were tied up at the rail of the corral with Jacob doing the same thing to the big gray gelding Jeremiah often rode. Thomas spotted rifles in the scabbards and bedrolls tied to the back of the saddles.

Jeremiah came out of the back door with his rifle and saddlebags slung over his shoulder. Emily followed behind him carrying a couple of tow sacks. Jeremiah handed the rifle and saddlebags to Jacob. "Put these on my horse, and you men gather around."

Thomas dismounted and dropped the reins. Mandy stood still as he had trained the horse to do. Bob and Joe did the same, and all the men gathered around Jeremiah to await instructions.

Jeremiah glanced from man to man and nodded. "Jacob, you stay here at the ranch house and make sure the women and children are safe. I want you to meet Sheriff Grant if he should shows up. Elmer Smith was passing by on his way to town, and I sent a note to the sherif. That doesn't mean he'll come out. You tell him we started out while the trail was still fresh with the intent to get the cattle back. We'll try to do it without a fight if we can, but if not, then we'll do what we have to do. I figure we are about three hours behind the rustlers and they won't be able to move too fast with several hundred head of cattle."

Jacob nodded. "Do not worry, Jeremiah. I watch and the families will be safe."

"I know that, Jacob, and I appreciate your willingness to stay behind and be the keeper of the stuff, as it says in the Bible. Bob, I want you to take Cal and angle north and east. Head toward the gap in the hills near Panther Creek. Joe, you take Jethro and follow the tracks left by the cattle. Thomas and I will head toward the pass up over Fletcher's Ridge. It shouldn't take more than a couple of hours of riding to know which direction they're taking the cattle." Jeremiah turned and glanced at each man. "This is dangerous and should be the sheriff's job, but it can't wait. This is our best chance to find out who is stealing cattle. Ride careful and if you do come upon the rustlers, hold back until the rest of us get there. I don't want anyone to get hurt. We will try to do this without bloodshed. For now, I just want the cattle back and to learn who the rustlers are. I'm willing to leave capturing them to the authorities. Any questions?"

Bob shook his head. "No questions, just an observation. I think Cal and me will be able to tell if they are heading for the pass quickly and should be able to join Joe and Jethro. I'm thinking they'll try for the trail through the valley along the ridge."

Jeremiah frowned. "I suspect you're right. Just remember not to engage them until we are all together. Now, if you need a fresh horse, get saddled and let's head out."

Thomas went into the bunkroom and grabbed his gear, including a rifle of Jeremiah's that he had Thomas carrying in case he needed one out on the range. Not knowing how long they would be gone, he stuffed saddlebags with a set of clothes, matches in a tin box, extra bullets for the rifle, and his jacket. Then he rolled up his blankets to make a bedroll and got a sheet of treated canvas from the storage room to have as a ground cover to lay his bedroll on. He passed through the kitchen to see if Mildred had any extra biscuits he could take along.

When Thomas entered the kitchen, Mildred handed him a couple of gunnysacks. "Here's food for a couple of days. Give this sack to Bob. I put in a coffee pot and some tin cups. Emily has already carried food out to Jeremiah and Jethro. She said you were riding with Jeremiah and he has a coffee pot and cups in his saddlebags, too. Anything else you boys need?" She waited for his answer with a worried frown.

"No, ma'am. This will do fine. Just pray for us and don't worry." Thomas kissed the older woman on the cheek. He liked Mildred and her plainspoken ways. Without a lot of fuss, she took care of everyone on the ranch.

~

It took Jeremiah and Thomas a couple of hours of hard riding to get to the ridge. Thomas was not sure if they were still on Jeremiah's land, but the countryside had gotten wilder and more heavily forested as they rode. The big pastures of the Rocking RS were left behind. They climbed steadily. Jeremiah led the way through the forest and seemed to know where he was going. Without a trail, Thomas was soon unsure exactly where they were but he trusted Jeremiah. It was late afternoon when they guided the horses along the top of the ridge. Thomas could see for miles in the direction of the ranch house.

Jeremiah pulled a pair of binoculars out of his saddlebag and began to examine the land south and east of the ridge. Thomas dismounted to give his horse a rest. He pulled up fresh spring grass and fed it to Jeremiah's horse but let his own horse graze. Sitting on his horse gave Jeremiah a few more feet of height from which to survey the land.

"I think I see them off to the east and they are headed the way Bob figured. Here take a look." Jeremiah handed the binoculars to Thomas.

After searching through binoculars in the direction Jeremiah pointed, Thomas spotted the faint cloud of dust. It had to be the herd to kick up that much dust. Even a herd of elk wouldn't raise that much.

He handed the binoculars back to Jeremiah. "How long do you think it will take us to reach Joe and Jethro? I'm assuming you think they're close behind the herd by now."

Jeremiah returned the binoculars to the saddlebags. "They're on the trail, but how close I'm not sure. However, by the time we get there, they should be right on them. One of the advantages to us coming up here and looking, I'm fairly sure I know the route they're taking with the herd. We'll head out on a trajectory to meet up with them not long after dark. The rustlers are going to be skirting the heaviest of the forest so as to make good time. And, I suspect they will stop for the night and make a camp. They probably have no idea we're so close behind them. They'll have a fire and cook some food. We have to be careful not to ride up too close before we see them. The mooing of the cattle should alert us along with the smell of the campfire." Jeremiah looked around at the area where they had stopped. "Let's make a small fire under those fir trees, have some coffee, and eat. The horses need a little longer to rest. After we eat, we'll ride until we find Joe and Jethro, or, at least the herd. By dark we should be out from the heavy forest. We'll have a full moon tonight."

Thomas watched Jeremiah make a small fire that was almost smokeless. The branches of the trees helped defuse what little smoke there was. From a distance, he didn't think anyone would be able to spot it. While waiting for the coffee to brew, they ate a couple of the roast beef sandwiches Mildred had sent. She had even included some sugar cookies. As soon as the coffee water boiled, Jeremiah slowly poured some Arbuckle coffee into the pot and let it boil another minute. He then poured the hot liquid into the two tin cups he had pulled from his saddlebag.

"Careful, that is strong and hot."

Thomas carefully took the tin cup and started blowing on the hot coffee. "This looks strong enough to help stay alert for a while. Can I ask you something, Jeremiah?"

"Sure." Jeremiah took a small sip of coffee.

"How do you know so much about making do on the trail and even finding the herd?" Was he being too nosey? Jeremiah didn't seem to be someone who wanted people asking personal questions.

"How much do you know about my background before I started work for Elisha?" Jeremiah asked.

Thomas shook his head. "Nothing. No one has said anything about your life before the ranch and your marriage to Ms. Emily."

Jeremiah smiled. "Actually that's good because, that's when my life really began on my arrival at Elisha's ranch when I was eighteen. Before that, I had lived and ridden with a bunch of outlaws. My pa was an outlaw. He was killed in a robbery when I was twelve. After that, I stayed with the gang until I was sixteen when we were all arrested or killed. I spent the next two years in a sort of prison. When I was freed, I found Elisha and Joe and the others at the ranch. They took me in and raised me."

"You spent two years in prison? No wonder you seemed to understand."

Jeremiah looked out across the land. "It's an experience that stays with you. You just don't let it hold you back."

Thomas didn't know exactly what to say. Jeremiah had had a much rougher life than he had. Yet, look at what a great man he was. "Thanks for telling me that. I want you to know you can trust me to keep your story private. It gives me hope I can move beyond my problems like you have done."

"That's why I told you. I don't talk much about that time of my life because I have moved on and let it go. Now I have the Lord, my beautiful wife, and three amazing children. In addition, I have friends who care about me. It's all because I made the decision to make right choices no matter how hard they are. You have the opportunity to do the same thing. Start over and do it right. Every man has that choice in his life. Now let's get mounted and go find some rustlers."

When full dark descended they stopped the horses to let them rest and to wait for the moon to rise to give them enough light to move forward.

Jeremiah raised his hand and quietly said, "Listen. You hear that?"

Thomas strained to hear what Jeremiah was hearing. The faint sounds of mooing, bellowing, snorting, and grunting cattle carried on the light evening breeze. "I hear it. They sound stressed and evidently a few cows have been separated from their calves. I recognize that bellowing. How far away are they?"

Jeremiah rubbed the neck of his horse as the horse grazed with him holding the reins. "Let keep our voices real quiet from now on and try to keep your horse from whinnying. It sounds as if they are less than a mile away. Joe and I have a signal that we use when hunting." Jeremiah chirped like a cricket. "Listen for that sound and we should be able to find Joe and Cal somewhere south of the herd."

They mounted up and Thomas followed Jeremiah as he rode sitting straight in the saddle as if he hadn't been riding through rough country for the last twelve hours. Thomas' back and thighs were aching from the hours in the saddle, but he wasn't about to say anything. Jeremiah had to be as tired as he was. Every few minutes, he heard Jeremiah making the sound of a cricket. He was actually very good at imitating the small creature. Finally, Thomas heard an answering chirp off to their right. Jeremiah pulled his horse over toward the right and slowed to a slow walk as he again made the sound.

Soon a deep voice whispered, "Jeremiah, that you?"

"Here, Joe." Jeremiah whispered back.

Thomas could make out several men standing at the heads of their horses. He quickly dismounted and made sure his horse didn't try to give a greeting. Jeremiah did the same.

Joe's voice came again. "We're all here and the herd is just over that small ridge."

Thomas could barely hear Jeremiah when he asked, "How many rustlers are there?"

"Jethro was able to get real close and he counted six riders," Joe answered. "What do you want to do?"

"Where is the camp?"

Jethro answered in a quiet voice. "They's camped just off to the left of the herd. Is you planning to stampede the herd?"

The boy's grammar had gotten better the last couple of months, but Thomas figured Jethro was under a bit of stress this night. What would Jeremiah do? A gun battle with six rustlers was not something Thomas wanted to be a part of in the dark.

Thomas strained to hear as Jeremiah answered, "We wait until after midnight. All but a couple of the rustlers should be asleep. We'll hit the herd from three sides and start them running toward home. Try to avoid getting shot and try not to shoot anyone. All we want to do is get the herd back, and then we'll let the sheriff round up the rustlers. Try to get a look at any of them that you can and any horses with special markings. If we get separated, just head for the ranch house. Thomas, you're with me on the east; Bob and Cal, you take the back of the herd; and, Joe and Jethro take the west. Jethro, you think you can sneak in and let their horses loose?"

"I kin do that."

"All right. Let's stay quiet, let your horse graze, and get some rest. We will head out in about two hours. Any questions?"

He hated to sound so ignorant, but Thomas had a question. "How do we get the cattle to start running?"

Joe softly chuckled. "That's a good question. Jeremiah, you want to answer it?"

"You got a watch Bob? When it's midnight you and Cal start firing your rifles into the air and yelling. That should get most of the cattle going. As soon as Thomas and I hear that, we will do the same. Joe, you and Jethro use your judgment. You're going to be the closest to the camp and in the most danger. If it's safer, you all ride with the herd until you're well past the camp and then keep what cattle you can moving with yelling and swinging your ropes. We ride out in two hours."

~

Thomas hoped the moonlight wasn't exposing him and his horse as much as it was Jeremiah. As they slowly walked their horses toward the east side of the herd, the moonlight was almost like a beacon. The low mooing of the cattle hid the sound of their horses. Jeremiah stopped his horse just below a moraine of land that would have exposed them to any rider doing nighthawk duty around the herd. Thomas heard the click of Jeremiah's pocket watch being opened and then closed. Jeremiah had checked the time by opening the face of the watch.

In a barely discernible whisper Jeremiah said, "It's time. Get ready."

Thomas shifted in the saddle and grasped the reins tighter. Every nerve in his body seemed to be more alert. He jerked as he heard the rifle shots and yells from Bob and Cal and then Jeremiah was riding toward the herd yelling and firing his rifle. Thomas kicked his horse into a gallop to follow Jeremiah, and he grabbed the stock of his rifle. But,he didn't pull it free.

As they rode within sight of the running herd, he spotted a rider at a distance. If he could see the rider, the rustler could see them. The noise from several hundred bellowing, stampeding cattle made it difficult to hear anything else but Thomas could hear the popping sounds of gunfire. He and Jeremiah galloped alongside of the herd.

Thomas felt a blow to his thigh and then an agony of pain took over his leg. He kept riding. To stop meant either another bullet or hooves of the cattle. Wetness ran down his leg and into his boot.

Fighting the pain, he searched for Jeremiah who had gotten ahead of him. Just when he spotted him, Jeremiah jerked sideways in the saddle and then righted himself. He pulled away from the herd and Thomas followed him. Soon they had left the herd behind and the night became quieter. Jeremiah's horse slowed to a walk and then stopped and Jeremiah slumped forward. Thomas rode up beside him. As he did, he saw the splotch of something on Jeremiah's back. He had also been shot.

"Jeremiah, can you hear me?"

"Yes, I can hear you. Get us away from the herd. Ride east. About five miles from here there's a cabin and water. I'll try to stay in the saddle. We have to get away from the rustlers before I collapse." His voice was raspy and rough, as if he was in a lot of pain.

Thomas opened up his saddlebag and pulled out the extra shirt he had. He wrapped it around the wound in his leg and tied it off as tight as he could stand it. He then pulled out the extra pair of trousers he had and urged his horse over close to where Jeremiah sat slumped on his horse.

"Jeremiah, do you have a wound in your chest?"

"No, just my back. I can feel blood flowing down my back but I don't seem to have an exit wound. Not good."

"All right, I'm going to try to make a rough bandage using these trousers. We need to stop the bleeding." He bunched up the top of the pants over the back wound and used the pants legs to tie around Jeremiah's chest. It was a crude bandage but the best Thomas could do for the moment.

Jeremiah sucked in his breath sharply and groaned softly.

Thomas unscrewed the cap of his canteen and held it to Jeremiah's mouth. He drank several swallows and then shook his head. "Thanks."

~

Daylight had come when Thomas pulled the horses to a stop and looked down into a valley and saw a cabin in the distance next to a waterfall. He glanced over at Jeremiah whom he had tied on to his horse during the night. When Jeremiah had lost consciousness, he wasn't sure but Jeremiah hadn't made a sound for several hours. Keeping the horses at a slow walk, he tugged on the reins of Jeremiah's horse and led the way toward the cabin. The sooner he found a bed for Jeremiah and looked at both their wounds, the better.

Thomas' own wound was now easy to see in the daylight. A bullet had gored a groove through his outer right thigh. Fortunately, it hit no bone, but it had bled copiously. Thomas gritted his teeth at the pain at every footfall of his horse.

The cabin didn't look abandoned, but there was no indication that anyone was around. Not far from the cabin was a corral with a shed that would hold the horses. The amount of grass growing in the corral was another indicator no one had spent time at the cabin lately. Thomas dismounted and groaned at the pain of putting weight on his leg. Carefully he stepped to the porch testing whether his leg would hold him. It was shaky but it bore his weight. The door to the cabin was unlocked but stiff to open. Once he was inside he saw a large, one-room cabin with a double bed, a table with four chairs, a couple of overstuffed easy chairs, a box stove that was both a cook stove and a heat source. On shelves and in the one cabinet were pots, pans, and dishes. One shelf held canned goods. On the box stove set a coffee pot and a large pot for cooking or boiling water. Although dusty, the cabin was relatively clean and free of evidence of varmints. He also had noted the wood stacked up on the porch.

Thomas went back out to the horses and grabbed his bedroll. Jeremiah was still unmoving from where he lay on the neck of his horse. Thomas went back into the cabin and pulled the bedding back on the bed. It was relatively clean like the rest of the cabin. He spread the oilcloth canvas sheet over the mattress.

Now, he had the task of carrying Jeremiah into the cabin and onto the bed. Untying Jeremiah from the saddle, he let the unconscious man fall across his shoulder. Maneuvering the step up onto the porch was the hardest part of getting Jeremiah into the cabin, because of the protest from his leg. He was finally able to dump Jeremiah onto the bed, and he was still breathing. Thomas wiped the sweat from his forehead with a shaking hand.

Wanting only to lay down on the bed himself, he kept pushing, bringing in the saddlebags, Jeremiah's bedroll, and the two rifles. He then brought in several armloads of wood and started the fire going in the small box stove. He picked up the bucket he found by the cabinet and walked down to the creek just down the hill from the cabin. The waterfall was a constant cascade of sound in the cool clear air. Rinsing out the bucket in the cold water, he filled it and returned to the cabin. When he entered, he noted that Jeremiah had not moved but was still breathing. Filling the coffee pot and the big pot after rinsing them, he set them on the stove. While waiting for the water to heat, he went out and unsaddled both horses, setting the saddles in a corner in the cabin. Leading the horses down to the creek, he let them drink and then led them into the corral. With grass almost to his knees, the horses had plenty to graze on within the corral. Thomas was in no mood to let the horses roam and have to round them up.

Inside the cabin he found Jeremiah thrashing about and mumbling. When he put his hand on Jeremiah's forehead, he felt the fever that the wound was causing. He spent the next hour getting Jeremiah undressed, cooled down with cloths soaked in the cold water of the creek, and the shirt unstuck from the wound where it had dried after being soaked in blood. The wound was red and angry looking, but it wasn't bleeding much.

Thomas took a deep breath and tried to think. The bullet needed to come out but he had no experience at doing such a thing. Both he and Jeremiah carried knifes, but for the delicate job of poking into a wound trying to retrieve a bullet, they would be difficult to use. With shaking hands, he washed the area around the wound, and with a shirt he found in Jeremiah's saddlebags, he bandaged it. That was the best he could do for the present. Feeling light headed and feverish himself, he ate the last of the sandwiches that Mildred had prepared for them and drank some of the coffee. Securing the door with the dropdown pole, he spread out his bedroll on the floor, sat and pulled off his boots, then using his saddlebags as a pillow he let himself drift into a troubled sleep.

Chapter Thirty-Three Catherine

Catherine glanced up from sweeping the boardwalk in front of the café and watched as Sheriff Grant with several men riding behind him rode down the road. All of the men were dressed for a long ride and had bedrolls and saddlebags tied onto the back of their saddles.

Herman Jones, who owned and ran the wagon yard crossed the dusty, rutted road behind the riders and stepped up on the boardwalk. "You got any coffee left?"

Catherine lifted her eyebrows. "When have you known me not to have coffee ready to serve?"

With a chuckle, Herman stood next to Catherine, and took his hat off. "Actually, never."

Pointing toward the group of riders disappearing around the curve of the road out of town, she asked, "What's going on? Where is Grant going with what looks like a posse?"

"That exactly what it is, a posse. Jeremiah Rebourn sent word they had a bunch of cattle stolen last night and he was going to follow the trail. Grant got some deputies together and is going out to see what he can see. I don't expect much since he hasn't done anything about the rustlers up to now. But I guess he has to make a show of it."

Catherine looked sharply at Herman. "You saying you don't think he's really made an effort to catch whoever has been behind the rustling that's been going on over the last year?"

Herman shook his head. "I'm not saying that at all. I'm saying I don't think he knows how to catch them. We need to call a marshal in or even ask the Colorado Cattlemen's Association to send in a range detective. I told Grant as much, but he won't listen to anyone except that McKinley. Grant keeps wanting it to be Thomas Black. But, that doesn't make sense. Jeremiah has Thomas under observation too much for him to be involved in something like this."

"Absolutely, it's not Thomas. You think the sheriff is going out to the Rocking JR to arrest Thomas?"

"I wouldn't put it past him. I think Grant is honest, but he has no imagination. He only sees things one way, and when he gets an idea in his mind, he ignores facts that might indicate a different way. That can be dangerous." Herman put his hat back on. "Well, I'm ready for some coffee, and then I need to get back to the wagon yard."

"Go on in, Beryl is in the kitchen and will serve anything you want." Catherine finished sweeping the boardwalk in front of the café and then stood staring down the empty road toward the Rocking JR. Making up her mind, she went back into the café and through to the kitchen.

Beryl was busy making bread for the dinner and supper crowd. "What's put that frown on your face, Catherine?"

After putting the broom away, Catherine reached for her shawl and hat. "Beryl, I've got a bad feeling that something is wrong out at the Rocking JR. I'm going over to talk to Milburn. Can you handle the café today? If Milburn decides to go out there, I want to go with him."

"Sure, honey, you do whatever you feel like you must. I can take care of things here. This is usually one of our lightest days of the week."

Catherine gave the older woman a hug. "Thanks, Beryl, I appreciate you more than you know."

Milburn was behind the counter at the back of the store when Catherine walked in. "Catherine, what brings you here this morning? Did you forget something you need?"

"No, I don't need any supplies." Not sure she wasn't overreacting, she hesitated. "Milburn, did you hear that Sheriff Grant just left with a posse and going out to the Rocking JR?"

Milburn took his reading glasses off and stuck them on the top of his head. "No, I didn't hear. What's going on?"

"They had cattle rustled last night and Jeremiah and the cowhands have started out on the trail. Sheriff Grant, evidently, is sure that Thomas is involved someway. I have a bad feeling about it."

"You think we need to go out there?"

"I would like to make sure everything is all right. I could rent a buggy to drive myself."

Milburn took off his bib work apron. "Agnes is upstairs. You go get her. I'll close up the store and go hitch up my buggy. Now I've got a bad feeling, too."

~

As Milburn guided the buggy up in front of the ranch house, Catherine spotted the men and horses of the posse out by the corral fence. The corral seemed to be empty of the usual number of horses and, except for the posse, she had a sense of unusual quiet around the barn and house.

Catherine hurried into the house with Agnes behind her. Milburn headed to the barn to leave the horse and buggy.

Emily stood in the front room facing Sheriff Grant. "I will say it again. Thomas is with the men from the ranch, including Jeremiah. They left last night to trail the rustlers, and I have not received any word. Thomas could not have been involved with the rustling. He hasn't been off the ranch, and he left with Jeremiah."

"Which way did they go?" Grant asked.

Emily pointed north. "The cattle taken were in the far north pasture. You will have to go out there to see where the trail led. I have no idea."

"Fine, that what we'll do, but if Jeremiah comes back tell him to wait here for me. He has no business trying to go after a gang of rustlers."

"Well, someone had to, and the cattle that were stolen are from this ranch." Emily's voice was full of sarcasm. Catherine was not used to Emily showing her feelings toward the sheriff or anyone except with sweetness and patience. Evidently, she was running out of patience with the sheriff.

Sheriff Grant stomped past Catherine and Agnes without a word and let the front door bang shut behind him.

"Oh, Catherine, Agnes. It's good to see you, but I didn't want you all to be worrying. Is Milburn with you?" Emily led the way into the bright, warm kitchen where Mildred was busy at the stove with several pots going. Catherine and Agnes removed their wraps and placed them on the pegs by the outside door.

Catherine gave Emily a hug. "I heard about the rustling and asked Milburn and Agnes to drive me out. I had a bad feeling." She then turned to the silent Sara who stood to the side. "Honey, you all right?"

"Yes, Catherine. Just worried." Her voice was soft. Sara always seemed to be in the background with Joe taking the lead. But, she was always helpful and the children were often in her lap, especially little Charity.

Emily gave Agnes a hug. "Well, we all have a bad feeling. I've been worried ever since the men left to go after the herd. Since no one has come back to the house, I can only surmise they are following the trail of the rustlers. Sit down and I'll get us some coffee, or would you rather have tea?"

Catherine responded. "I'll take tea."

Agnes sat at the table. "Me too, I prefer tea if you have it handy."

Milburn walked into the kitchen followed by Jacob. "I'll have coffee, please." He had evidently heard Emily's question as he and Jacob came in from the hallway.

Emily gave the older man a hug. "I'm glad you came out. I was feeling a little lonely as I worried about the men being gone overnight."

Milburn and Jacob sat down at the table with Catherine and Agnes. "Jacob told me about the rustling and the men heading out to track the herd yesterday morning."

Emily poured coffee for the men and tea for the women. Sara set a small pitcher of cream on the table next to the bowl of sugar.

Emily shook her head. "I can't believe the stubbornness of Sheriff Grant. He's still determined Thomas is behind the rustling. It doesn't make sense."

Jacob spooned several teaspoons of sugar into his coffee. "*Ja.* He not think beyond one thing. But is foolish."

Milburn nodded. "Yes, by concentrating on Thomas, Grant isn't focusing on the real rustlers."

Catherine stirred her tea. "Maybe that's easier than trying to find the real thieves."

Emily set her teacup down a little hard and the porcelain cup made a sharp sound on the saucer. "I wish Jeremiah would get back or send someone with word. I hate this waiting." She cocked her head. "Excuse me, I hear Charity stirring. I'll be back as soon as I take care of her." She quickly left the kitchen.

Agnes stood and replenished the tea. "You men ready for another cup?"

Milburn pushed his cup forward. "Just half full and then I'll go with you Jacob and help out. I know you're shorthanded with all the men gone."

"*Ja,* I must go check on some mares close to foaling."

Agnes looked around the kitchen. "Mildred, what can we do to help? I need to do something while we wait for word."

"Well, I was about to go change the beds and start the laundry. I have Sally out back getting the washtub full of water and the fire started under it. Sara was about to make bread for us."

Catherine stood. "Then we'll help with the laundry. You and Sara continue with the preparation for dinner and supper."

Mildred nodded. "All right. I want to have food ready when the men do get back. They'll be hungry. I also want the laundry done as I suspect they'll get back covered in dirt, and we'll have a bunch more laundry to do."

Catherine went to Emily's bedroom to gather laundry. She found Emily nursing little Charity as she sat in the rocking chair by the fireplace. "I thought I would find you here. I've come for the laundry. Where are the boys?"

"Jacob has them in the workshop working on lessons. They'll listen to him, and they're fine there for a while." Emily settled the light blanket she had over the nursing baby and across her shoulder. "I must say again how glad I am you came out. I have prayed and know God is watching over Jeremiah and the men, but I can't help but be concerned."

"Until you have everyone back safe at home, it's normal to be uneasy. We are all praying and know that all will work out in God's timing." Catherine reassured Emily and herself.

The day passed slowly with everyone trying to keep busy but often looking toward the north where the men had gone. Catherine swept the porch so she could look toward the north, hoping to see riders coming back from the chase.

Elisha and Joseph seemed to be the only ones hungry as they sat at the supper table. Catherine pushed the mashed potatoes around with her fork. "I keep wondering what's happening. I really expected word by now."

Milburn nodded. "Me too. We need to head back into town soon."

Catherine heard the sound of riders coming from the back of the house. She jumped up with Emily and hurried over to the window over the sink. Looking out she saw several riders, but the one she really wanted to see wasn't there.

Emily stood on toes to peer out toward the pasture. "Jeremiah and Thomas don't seem to be with them." She turned toward Mildred. "Let's get the table cleared and reset for the men. After they get the horses cared for they'll be coming in hungry for supper."

Milburn and Jacob were already heading toward the kitchen door. "We'll go out and help with the horses."

Elisha and Joseph crammed their mouths full and started to leave the table.

Emily shook her head. "Now, you boys sit back down and finish eating proper. We'll wait here for the men to bring the news."

"Ah, Mama." Two voices in tune sounded out the protest of having to wait.

"Be calm and do as you're told. We have enough strain for now. I don't need to worry about you boys." Emily's voice held an unusual sternness. It told Catherine of her friend's concern about her missing husband.

"Yes, ma'am." The twins replied in quiet voices.

Catherine took pity on the two little boys. "Miss Mildred has a butter pound cake for dessert. If you sit quiet, you can listen to the men when they talk over their supper and then have a piece of cake with them."

Both boys' faces brightened and they grinned at Catherine. One day she wanted to have children that would fill her heart, as did these two little scamps. Even with her concern about Thomas, she had to return their grins.

By the time the women had cleared most of the table and set places for the four men, Catherine heard them coming into the hallway between the kitchen and bunkroom. Soon Bob, Cal, Joe, and Jethro came into the kitchen with Jacob and Milburn following. They had left their boots by the outside door in the hallway and their entrance was relatively quiet as they walked in their sock covered feet.

After the men were seated, Bob bowed his head and said a blessing, which included a prayer for safety for Jeremiah and Thomas. Catherine swallowed her fear and could barely sit still waiting for Bob to tell them what had happened.

Emily gave the men a few minutes to fill their plates and start eating before asking, "Bob, where are Jeremiah and Thomas?"

Bob glanced up at her with a guilty look and then returned his gaze to his plate of food. "I don't know, Mrs. Emily." Raising his head, he met her intense glare. "Cal and me found the herd just before dark yesterday afternoon, and then Joe and Jethro found us. Not long after dark, Jeremiah and Thomas rode up. Jeremiah decided we would wait until after midnight and then stampede the herd back toward the ranch. He told us to keep the cattle moving and we would meet up back here at the ranch if we got separated. We did as he said, and there were a lot of shots fired." He ducked his head down, staring at his plate.

Joe spoke up, "We couldn't see much even with the moonlight and kept chasing the cattle. When dawn came, we realized Jeremiah and Thomas weren't with us. By then we were closer to the ranch than where we found the herd. I made the decision for us to keep the cattle moving toward home and hope Jeremiah and Thomas had somehow ridden ahead of us."

Emily stood and put her hands on her hips. "Joe Storm Weathers, are you telling me that my husband could be lying hurt or dead out there and you worried about a bunch of cows?"

Joe stood and put his arm around her shoulders. "Emily, we did what Jeremiah told us to do. As soon as we have eaten and rested a couple of hours, we plan to go searching for them. We haven't slept for thirty-six hours or more. We'll do better searching with a bit of rest. All of us are going out, and will stay out, until we find them."

Emily covered her face with her hands and her shoulders shook but she made no sound. Catherine not knowing what had happened to Thomas and Jeremiah was so frustrated she could scream. It wouldn't help the situation though. Instead, she went to Emily and gathered her into a hug.

Turning to Bob, she asked, "What do we need to do to help you men be ready to ride out again?"

Bob rubbed the back of his neck. "While we get a little shuteye if Milburn and Jacob could saddle us fresh horses that would help. In addition, Mildred, if you and the ladies could pack us enough vittles for two or three days. Also, someone could fill all our canteens with fresh water."

Emily straightened. "You men go get some rest. We'll get things ready for you to ride back out."

Joe and Sara walked toward the front room and their room on beyond. Joe stopped and turned back. "What about the sheriff? Did he come out?"

Emily nodded. "He came with a posse several hours after you left. They headed north. I'm surprised you didn't run into them."

Bob shrugged his shoulders. "I doubt if he stayed out all night. He probably rode back into town. Maybe he'll come back out in the next day or so. We can't spare anyone to ride in to tell him what is going on, and besides I'm not sure he would help."

"Not that I think it will matter much, but if the sheriff is in town, I will tell him what is going on," Milburn said.

Catherine had to agree with him. She watched as the men got up from the table and headed toward the bunkroom with no talking. They were a weary bunch. She sighed and turned to Mildred. "What can I do to help?"

"Why don't you cut some bread. Agnes, you can wrap up some ham and biscuits. Sally, you fill up the canteens after Milburn goes and collects them. Is that all right with you, Milburn?"

"Sure and I'll take these two little fellows as helpers. Come on men. We got to find all the canteens and water bags and fill them. Then we'll help Jacob with the horses. You two can fill some tow sacks with feed for the men to take." Milburn left the kitchen followed by two six-year-olds filling the air with questions.

Emily stood in the middle of the kitchen looking lost. "I'm going to go make up a pack with bandages and things to treat wounds, just in case."

Catherine felt lightheaded. No, Thomas and Jeremiah couldn't be wounded. They had to be all right, please God.

Two hours later the men climbed back into their saddles and rode out even though it was only an hour from dark. Catherine watched with her hand pushed to her chest, as if she could push away the fear gathering there.

Milburn touched her arm. "Catherine, we need to get back to town. You can stay or you can come back with us tomorrow."

Catherine shuddered as if waking from a bad dream. "I'll ride back with you all. I need to serve breakfast in the morning at the café. What time will you come back out?"

He scratched his head. "Unless we know something different, I'll keep the store open until about two in the afternoon and then close up until Monday morning. We should know something, one way, or another, by then."

Chapter Thirty-Four Thomas

Thomas went back into the cabin after tending to the horses. As he approached the bed, he saw that Jeremiah's eyes were open for the first time since they had arrived at the cabin two days before. "You awake?"

Jeremiah whispered in a husky voice, "Water?"

Thomas grabbed the canteen from the table and lifting Jeremiah's head slightly, held the canteen to his lips. After a two sips, he pulled it away. "Don't want you to drink too much too soon. You can have some more in a few minutes."

"How long we been here?" Jeremiah looked around but didn't move.

Thomas pulled a chair up to the bed. "We got here day before yesterday. You couldn't go any further. I saw the cabin and decided to stop. I've not seen anyone around since we've been here."

Jeremiah sighed softly. "Hopefully none of the rustlers know about it and the boys have gotten the herd back to the ranch. How bad am I hurt?"

"It's bad. The bullet is still in there. I've been afraid to try to take it out. You've been very feverish for the last two days."

"I feel weak as a day old calf."

Thomas leaned forward. "I've been thinking about it. We need to try to get you back to the ranch and the doctor. You can't ride. I can make a travois, and your horse could drag you. We can leave in the morning at first light. How far do you figure it is to the ranch?"

Jeremiah frowned. "I'd rather not move from how I'm feeling, but you're right. We need to get to the ranch. Emily will be worried sick. And I'm concerned about the men, whether or not others were wounded. Did you get hurt?"

"I got a chunk gored out on the outside of my right thigh. Other than that, I don't know what happened to the herd or to the men. I couldn't see anyone else and I thought it best to get you away from there."

"You did good, getting me here. This cabin and land belong to me. I bought it for Emily and me. The week we spent here right after our wedding she called our wedding trip."

Thomas looked around with his eyebrows raised. "Not a fancy place for a wedding trip."

Jeremiah chuckled and then groaned. "Don't make me laugh, it hurts. All Emily and I wanted after the wedding was privacy. The ranch house is only about ten miles southeast of here."

"We could probably make it in about three to four hours. You think you could make that?" Thomas didn't like to think about what the trip would be for Jeremiah. But he needed to be where Thomas could get better help. And, if he told the truth, his leg needed some attention. He didn't know what to do but keep it clean and try not put too much pressure on it.

"Jeremiah, you think you can eat something? I found some tins of beef and made a soup."

"I'll try. Don't rightly feel hungry, but I need to get my strength back." Jeremiah plucked at the edge of the blanket covering him. Thomas didn't like how pale the man looked.

After Thomas fed some of the beef broth to him, Jeremiah drifted back to sleep. Laying his hand on Jeremiah's forehead Thomas could feel the fever. Grabbing the hand ax, Thomas went outside to find a couple of tree limbs he could trim into poles to make the travois. He had never made one before but had seen one. When he was a kid, he had seen some Indians traveling through the country. He figured he could make one and tie it onto the saddle of Jeremiah's horse. Fortunately, Jeremiah was riding a calm brown mare and not his big black stallion. That animal wouldn't have stood still for a travois.

Thomas was roused several times in the night from the groans that Jeremiah made. He didn't seem to be conscious though he mumbled something about keeping the lamp lit. Since Thomas wasn't getting much sleep anyway, he was up and getting things ready to go before daylight. When he was ready to get Jeremiah loaded on the travois hitched to the brown mare, he went into the cabin.

He gently shook Jeremiah's shoulder. "Wake up, it's time to go."

"What?" Jeremiah looked around groggily, as if it was hard to focus.

"We need to get going back to the ranch. If I help you, can you try to walk out to the horse?"

"Just help me sit up and pull my legs to the side of the bed. Sorry to be so weak this morning."

It took all of Thomas' strength to get Jeremiah onto his feet and walk him the short distance out to the waiting horse with the man leaning most of his weight against him. As Thomas lowered Jeremiah down onto the blankets he had used to make the travois, Jeremiah let out a deep groan and broke into a sweat.

"I'm sorry, Jeremiah. I know you're in pain. We got to do this." Thomas quickly wrapped Jeremiah up in the blankets from his own bedroll. "I'll go easy, but we need to keep going until we get there. You want me to stop, you holler."

Jeremiah nodded and closed his eyes as if the act of getting to the travois had taken the last of his energy. Thomas bit his lower lip as he tried to think of anything he could do to make the trip easier. There wasn't anything to do but try to get to the ranch as soon as possible. A fine layer of clouds hung low and they began to glow with the colors of the dawn. Sunrise would be upon them by the time they topped the ridge above the cabin. Keeping the horses at a slow walk, Thomas started toward the ranch.

After couple of hours, Thomas pulled the horses up and stepped down from his with a groan that matched the ones Jeremiah was making whenever they crossed a rough bit of ground. Grabbing the canteen, Thomas dropped to his knees beside the travois.

"Jeremiah, can you hear me? You need to drink some water." Placing his palm on Jeremiah's forehead, he felt the heat of the fever. Lifting Jeremiah's head, he put the canteen next to his lips. "Drink some water!" He commanded wanting to penetrate through the fevered mind.

Jeremiah groaned and his eyes fluttered open, but there was no recognition. Thomas tipped the canteen, and Jeremiah swallowed a couple of swigs of water. After drinking several swallows of water himself, he put the cap back on the canteen. Looking out over the trees and pasture of the sunlit land, Thomas climbed back into his saddle. *Lord, help me get Jeremiah back to the ranch alive. Don't let me get there with a dead man. Please, Lord.*

Thomas twisted in the saddle to look back and check on Jeremiah. He saw a piece of bark fly off a tree behind them as he heard the CRACK-BOOM of a rifle. Not waiting to locate the shooter, he kicked his horse in the flank and hung onto the reins of Jeremiah's horse. He headed toward the bottom of a ridge and into a bunch of tall boulders large enough to shield both men and horses. Grabbing his rifle, he dismounted and tied the horses to a tree. Glancing at Jeremiah, he wanted to check on him but his first priority was the shooter or shooters. Was it the rustlers?

Peering between two of the taller boulders, Thomas searched in the direction the sound of the rifle fire had come from, but could spot nothing out of the ordinary. Just as he pulled back to find another angle to look from, several bullets hit the rocks and sharp bits of the boulder flew out pelting Thomas' cheek and neck. He felt blood trickling down his face and neck from the cuts of the shards of rock. Glancing around he searched for a way out of the entrapment of the boulders but saw nowhere to go that wouldn't expose them to the shooters.

Thomas lifted the rifle and sighted across the meadow and toward the tree line. He fired three rounds into the copse of trees without much hope of hitting anything. He just wanted to slow the shooters down and hope he could figure a way to get Jeremiah out of danger. Several answering shots were fired at them. He jerked back behind the protection of the large boulders. Glancing at the sun, Thomas figured they had only traveled a couple of more hours and had most of the day to wait for the protection of darkness. He wished they were closer to the ranch house so maybe someone would hear the rifle fire, but wishing wouldn't make it so.

"Thomas?" Jeremiah's voice was weak and low.

Thomas took another glance between the boulders before he hunched down and moved over to Jeremiah, still wrapped in the blankets on the travois. "I'm here."

"Who you firing at and how many are there?" Jeremiah's pale face was twisted into a frown of concern.

"I don't know the answer to either question. I haven't seen anyone, but it does seem like more than one shooter. I'm assuming it's the rustlers."

"Any way to get out of here without getting shot?"

"Not till dark and that may be chancy, but we'll have to make a try." Thomas uncapped a canteen. He raised Jeremiah's head and held the canteen to his lips.

Jeremiah only took a couple of sips and then pushed the canteen away. "How much water do we have?"

"We have two canteens almost full. They should last until tomorrow if we're careful." He put the cap back on the canteen without drinking any water himself. He could wait and Jeremiah needed it worse than he did.

The day finally came to a close. Jeremiah was either unconscious or sleeping. Thomas couldn't tell for sure and didn't want to disturb him as it didn't make any difference. It would be dark in another couple of hours. Thomas planned to melt quietly into the shadows and try to get Jeremiah to the ranch house. Taking a quick look around Thomas then went to the horses to make sure they were ready to go. He tightened the cinches he had loosened earlier.

Kneeling, he felt Jeremiah's forehead and could feel the fever.

Jeremiah opened his eyes. A look of pain grimaced across his face before he got control. "Is it time to try to leave?" His voice was a weak whisper.

Thomas offered the canteen again and Jeremiah swallowed some of the tepid water. This time Thomas also allowed himself a couple of swallows. As he put the cap back on the canteen, he answered Jeremiah. "We will try to leave in an hour or two. We have got to be real quiet, and I know starting out again is going to hurt bad."

"You need to gag me, Thomas. When the pain gets to a certain point I can't help but groan. You gag me."

Thomas stared at his boss. He hated to think what the next few hours would bring. Jeremiah was right, he needed to gag the man. "Thanks for understanding. I'm going to lead the horses for a while. If we make it away from here without any trouble, I'll mount up and try to get us to the ranch house as quick as possible. It's going to be rough."

"I know, Thomas. Just do the best you can, and if you have to leave me somewhere to save yourself, you do it. You can always bring back help."

"I'm not going to leave you. Don't even think that. We're getting back to the ranch and then you'll get tended by Emily and the doctor. Everything is going to work out," Thomas told Jeremiah in an insistent whisper. "You make sure you hang on."

Jeremiah managed to grin. "Yes, sir, I'll do that."

"Well, see that you do."

"Keep praying Thomas. That's our biggest weapon."

"I have been and plan to continue."

"Just give me a little warning before we start out so I can get prepared."

Thomas nodded and then tied the canteen back on his saddle. Stepping over to the slit in the rocks he had discovered had the best view of the meadow and trees beyond, he searched for any sign that anyone was still there, but all was quiet.

Once it was full dark and before the moon rose on the horizon, Thomas tied Jeremiah's bandana around his mouth to gag him. "We're leaving now before the moon comes up," he whispered.

Taking the reins of the two horses Thomas began to walk slowly out from the shelter of the large boulders and headed southeast toward the ranch house. Shivers ran up his spine as he hunched his shoulders waiting for rifle fire. As he stepped carefully guiding the horse, he began to breathe easier as they moved away from the boulders and among the trees. He had been walking for a while and watching the moon come up in the eastern sky, when he heard something off to the side. He stopped the horses and stood still. He heard the sounds of horses walking through the underbrush parallel to their path.

Thomas spotted a glimmer of light just ahead and then made out a campfire. Not knowing who the riders were or who was camped ahead, he tied the horses to the branches of a tree and hoped the horses would stay quiet. Creeping through the brush, he edged his way toward the campfire while listening for the riders off to his right. With a sigh of relief, he recognized the horses tied to a rope just beyond the campfire and then men including Joe, Bob, Cal, and Jethro. Just as he was about to step out into the light he caught sight of someone to his right leveling a rifle at the men seated on logs around the campfire.

Letting out a yell he swung his rifle around and fired at the rifle. He then fell flat to the ground as the men around the campfire dived for protection and brought their own guns up. As general gunfire broke out both from the camp and the trees, Thomas rolled to his left and crawled around the perimeter of the camp. Hugging the earth, he spotted Jethro crawling a few feet away from him.

"Hey, Jethro," he whispered.

Jethro swung around and raised his rifle. "Who's there?"

Thomas was glad he was asking rather than shooting. "It's me, Thomas. Don't shoot."

Jethro grinned. "Stay put while I go help with them yahoos shooting at us." The boy continued to crawl until he disappeared behind the shooter.

Thomas waited and the shooting stopped.

A few minutes later Jethro hollered. "Somebody bring me some rope. I got me some critters to tie up."

Cautiously Thomas stood and walked into the light of the campfire. "You boys got any coffee made?"

"Thomas, is that you?" Bob stood from behind the log where he had been concealed.

"Where's Jeremiah?" Joe called from the other side of the camp.

"You fellows want to jaw with Thomas later. I need some help here," Jethro's plaintive call came.

The men quickly helped Jethro tie up the three men he had knocked out. When the men were brought into the fire light, Thomas was surprised to see Myles McKinley was one of them.

Cal handed Thomas a cup of coffee. "Nice to see you in one piece."

"Thanks, Cal." He swigged down the coffee like the thirsty man he was. "I need your help. I got Jeremiah hidden back a ways. He's hurt bad and we need to get him to the ranch house as soon as possible."

Bob pointed to Thomas' blood stained pants leg. "It looks like you got hurt too."

"I got a furrow along the side of my thigh. It bled a lot but I'm doing okay for now. However, Jeremiah was shot in the back and the bullet is still in him. He has been feverish for days."

Joe turned to Jethro. "Think you can handle these men while we go get Jeremiah?"

Jethro glared at the three rustlers. "Sure, let me finish tying their legs and they'em not be going nowhere."

"Lead the way Thomas," Bob said as he picked up a lantern.

Thomas led them at a fast pace back to where he had left the horses and Jeremiah still on the travois.

Joe knelt down by the wounded man. "Why is he gagged?"

"I knew the rustlers were close by and he's been groaning and moaning. I had to keep him quiet." Thomas quickly removed the gag. "Feel his forehead and you'll feel the fever. He's not sleeping, but is unconscious."

Joe stood. "Let's get him to camp and see what is best to do to help him. Cal, you and Bob grab that end of the travois, and we'll let the horse carry the other end. That way it's not so rough. You lead the horses Thomas."

Thomas was relieved to have someone else directing the care of Jeremiah. He didn't feel like he had done too good a job so far.

After they got Jeremiah back to the camp, Joe looked at his wound and shook his head. "I don't like the look of this. I had thought maybe we could wait till morning and get a wagon here but now I think it's better if we break camp and head toward the ranch house. We can be there by morning. There's enough moonlight to see to travel and we can use these lanterns to light our way."

Bob asked, "What's the best way to carry him? That travois is a rugged way to travel with a bullet in your back."

Cal scratched the back of his neck. "Why can't we do what we just did? We're only about four miles from the ranch house. By taking turns we can get there in about an hour or so."

"I think that might be best. Thomas, you ride the horse. With your injured leg you should be riding rather than walking anyway. Jethro, can you bring our guests? Wish we had their horses."

"I kin get them horses. I knowed where they is."

Joe nodded. "Go get them while we break camp and get our own horses saddled. I want to get back to the ranch house as soon as possible."

Thomas watched the boy head into the forest. His speech reverted to his hillbilly vernacular as the stress of the night continued.

Soon they had everything packed on the horses. Jethro returned in a short while with three horses. They forced the silent outlaws onto their horses and tied their hands to the pommel and their feet together under their horses' bellies.

Thomas took the canteen and tried to give Jeremiah some water but he was unresponsive. Thomas wet a bandana and wiped Jeremiah's face and neck. He didn't know what else to do for him.

"You did good, Thomas, getting Jeremiah this far. Was he shot that first night of the stampede?" Joe asked.

"Yes, and then I found a cabin where we stayed for a couple of days. Jeremiah wasn't getting any better, and I had to try to get him home. About four hours after we left the cabin we got pinned down by rifle fire. I would bet my boots it was them three galoots. After dark, we started out again, and then I saw the campfire. You all are sure a good sight to see."

"It's amazing you made it this far. Let's get going and finish the job."

~

Daylight was breaking by the time the weary men made it to the ranch yard. Thomas was beyond exhausted and was barely hanging on to the pommel. The other men had rotated carrying the end of the travois and Joe and Bob gently placed it on the ground. Jethro and Cal untied the travois from the horse and then Joe and Bob lifted it again. Just as the four men started toward the back door Emily, followed by Sara, and Mildred came hurrying out of the door. Jacob came running up from the barn.

"Joe, is it Jeremiah?" Emily asked as she ran to the side of the travois.

"Yes, and he's bad hurt. We got to get him into bed and go for the doctor and the sheriff," Joe responded.

Jethro lifted his head to look at Emily. "Ma'am. Let me hand this off to Jacob and go saddle a fresh horse. I'll get the doctor and the sheriff out here."

Jacob stepped in and took the pole Jethro had been lifting. "Ja, I got Jeremiah. You go get doctor."

"You want to rest up a bit and eat something before you go?" Bob asked.

"Nah. I'll eat when I get back." Jethro turned toward the corral and by the time they had Jeremiah to the bedroom the sound of a horse galloping away could be heard.

After Jeremiah was safely moved onto his bed, Thomas exited the crowded room and went back into the backyard. He gathered the reins of the horses and led them to the barn. It was all he could do to lift one foot in front of the other the fatigue was hitting him so hard. Bob and Joe could handle the rustlers that Thomas left still tied to their horses by the corral fence. Thomas just wanted to get the horses taken care of and find his bunk.

Bob and Cal came into the barn. Bob took the saddle Thomas was holding. "Go on into the house Thomas. You look like you're about to fall over. Go on into the kitchen. Mildred is preparing breakfast. Eat something and then go to bed."

Thomas didn't argue. "What are you going to do with these fellows?" Thomas pointed toward the rustlers sitting drooped in their saddles.

"Jethro is getting the sheriff as well as the doctor. We'll let the sheriff decide what to do with them."

Thomas staggered into the house, too tired to eat. He made it to his bunk, took off his boots and hat, and collapsed in his clothes onto his bunk, asleep before his head touched the pillow.

Chapter Thirty-Five Catherine

Catherine had tried to sleep again but for the fourth straight night since the men went after the rustlers, she had tossed and turned and woke every hour or two. This morning she was tired down to her bones.

Beryl came into the café back door and put her things on the hooks. Getting a clean apron out of the cupboard, she turned and looked closely at Catherine standing by the stove stirring gravy for the sausage and gravy they would serve for breakfast along with eggs, ham, and biscuits. At the back of the stove was a large pot of oatmeal.

"By gravy, you look a mess, girl. Haven't you been sleeping at all?" Beryl asked.

Catherine chuckled. "Thanks Beryl. A girl always likes to be told she looks a mess. I did comb my hair."

Beryl patted her on the shoulder. "But it doesn't hide the fact that you aren't sleeping."

Catherine sighed. "How can I when Jeremiah and Thomas are missing? I'm praying and trying not to worry, but it has been four days now."

The older woman gave Catherine a hug. "We just have to wait and see. Hopefully they're all right."

Catherine fought tears. The longer Thomas was missing, the more Catherine realized how involved her heart was. She had fallen in love with Thomas, and the thought of something happening to him was like a fist squeezing her heart.

Someone banged on the front door of the café.

Catherine moved the sausage and gravy off the burner. "I'll go unlock the door. Probably a cowhand wanting an early cup of coffee." She hurried to the door. "Hold your horses, I'll open up."

Opening the door, she found Jethro covered in mud and dust, and yes, with the beginnings of a mustache on his face. "Jethro! Has something happened? Do you know anything about Jeremiah and Thomas?"

Jethro swept his hat off his sweaty, matted hair. "Yes'em. They's back. Jeremiah is shot real bad, and Thomas' leg is hurt. I thought you would like to know. We'uns just got back this morning."

"Have you told Milburn and Agnes?" She held onto the doorframe with relief that the men were home.

"Not yet, ma'am. Just you, Doc, and the sheriff. We brung three rustlers back to the ranch."

"Come on in and I'll tell Beryl to feed you breakfast. I'll go over to the Mercantile and tell Milburn and Agnes." She stepped back to allow Jethro to enter the café.

"I guess that would be all right. You got biscuits?" The hope in his voice was almost comical.

Catherine nodded as she headed toward the kitchen. "Biscuits, sausage and gravy, eggs, ham, and coffee, that do you till noon?"

Jethro tentatively sat at a table and placed his hat brim up on the floor under his chair. "Yes'um. That there will do."

Catherine looked back and caught the grin on the boy's face. "Beryl, would you get Jethro a full breakfast. And, can you take over here? Jeremiah and Thomas are back at the Rocking JR and I'm going out there."

"Sure, you go do what you need to do. I can take care of the café. We already have the noon meal cooked with that big roast and vegetables. I'll make tea and more biscuits."

"Thanks, I'm not sure when I'll get back. Jethro said the men were hurt." Catherine went into her room at the back of the café and packed a small valise with her night things and a change of clothes.

~

Doc's buggy and the sheriff's gray gelding were in front of the barn when Milburn maneuvered his buggy alongside of Doc's. It had taken Milburn and Agnes only minutes to leave for the ranch..

Entering the kitchen from the backdoor, Catherine heard a loud shout, almost a scream. She found Mildred and Sally in the kitchen with tears streaming down their faces.

Taking Mildred into her arms for a hug, Catherine pushed the fear away enough to ask, "What is happening?"

Mildred dried her tears with her apron. "Doc is having to cut Jeremiah to get the bullet and open him up to let the infection out. He couldn't get Jeremiah awake enough to take some laudanum and that's him you hear. The pain must be awful."

Catherine felt the tears gathering in her own eyes to think of Jeremiah suffering so. "What about Thomas?"

Mildred pointed toward the bunkroom. "He came in so tired he didn't even stop to eat or undress. He just fell across his bed asleep. Doc said to let him sleep until he can take care of Jeremiah, and then he will look at the bullet wound in Thomas' leg."

Catherine started for the bunkroom. "I'll just check on him."

Milburn put his hand on Agnes' arm. "Let Catherine check. We don't all need to go barging into the bunkroom."

Agnes sighed. "You're right." She turned to Mildred. "What can I do?"

"Could you go check on little Charity? Emily is in with Jeremiah and Jacob has the twins over in the workshop. Charity was taking a nap, but with Jeremiah's cries of pain she may be awake and Emily doesn't need to hear her crying."

"Oh, bless her heart. Of course, I'll go take care of the baby. If she's awake I'll bring her in here."

Catherine set her things down and quietly crossed the hallway to the door leading into the bunkroom. She slowly pushed it open and saw it was empty except for Thomas lying on his bunk. He was unshaved and wearing filthy clothes. She could see the pant leg stained with dried blood and wanted to see the wound. But, the doctor needed to deal with that.

Thomas looked peaceful and didn't seem to be in any pain nor distress, just tired looking. Catherine brushed some hair back from his forehead, which was cool, and silently said a prayer of thanksgiving. What if she had lost him? One year was almost gone. With the thought of not having Thomas in her life at all, the next two years did not seem that long anymore. She could wait for him. Looking around she saw no water in the room and that was something she could remedy.

Feeling more at ease about Thomas but still very concerned for Jeremiah, she made her way back to the kitchen. Agnes came in from the front room carrying little eight-month-old Charity. The baby was babbling baby talk and pulling at Agnes' dress collar that had a border of lace. Agnes looked at Catherine with anxious eyes.

Wanting to reassure her, Catherine quickly said, "He seems to be all right. Just exhausted and sleeping. He has a wound in his leg, but it seems only along the side of the thigh, like a graze. Doc will need to look at it when he can. For now, I think Thomas needs to sleep."

"Oh, thank the Lord. It could have been much worse, and maybe for Jeremiah it is." Agnes bounced the baby in her arms and nuzzled her little soft curls.

Bob came into the kitchen from the front room. "We need some more bandages and hot water."

Mildred lifted a pot off the stove using a hot pad. "Here, take this and we'll get some more bandages." As she handed the pot off to Bob, she asked in a hesitant voice. "How is he?"

Bob shook his head. "It's bad. Doc has the bullet out but now has to stop the bleeding. Jeremiah doesn't seem in as much pain as when Doc was digging for the bullet, but he is one sick man."

Catherine put her arm around Mildred's shoulder and said to Bob, "Go on with the hot water. I'll be there in a minute with some more bandages."

After Bob left, Catherine went to the linen closet in the hallway and pulled out two clean sheets. She returned to the kitchen and Sally handed her a pair of scissors. Catherine quickly cut the sheets up into wide strips that would make clean bandages. Mildred and Sally helped fold them into rolls.

Catherine took down a basket and gathered the rolls of bandages into it. "I'll take this to the bedroom. You all listen for Thomas, please."

She walked into the large bedroom hating the smell of medicine and blood. Jeremiah was on the bed with his shirt and pants off and a sheet lying over the lower half of his body. His chest was covered with bloody cloths and the floor had even more bloody cloths scattered about as if hastily thrown there. Emily sat on the bed by Jeremiah's head, stroking his brow. Cal and Bob were holding Jeremiah's legs still and Joe was holding his shoulders down.

"Oh, good. More bandages. Can you clear some of these bloody ones out of here?" Doc asked.

"Sure. We can roll more bandages. Just let us know." Catherine set the basket of clean bandages on a chair pulled up to the bed and gathered the soiled bandages from the floor and around Jeremiah.

Emily glanced up, with a look of fatigue and anxiousness. "Oh, Catherine, you're here." She sounded like a lost little girl.

"Yes, and Milburn and Agnes. She has Charity, so you can take care of Jeremiah."

Emily stared down at her husband. "Thank you."

Doc pointed toward the bloody pieces of cloth Catherine had gathered. "Wash those in boiling water and put them somewhere clean to dry. We're going to need more bandages before Jeremiah is well."

Catherine dared to ask, "He will get well?"

Doc peered at her from where he wrapped a bandage around Jeremiah's chest. "He has a good chance now the bullet is out. We need to pray his body can fight off the fever from the infection. But, he is strong and healthy otherwise."

"I'll take care of these bandages, and we have more sheets we can cut up if needed."

Catherine kept busy the rest of the day trying to help anywhere she could. Supper was a somber affair with everyone busy with their own thoughts. Even the twins were unusually silent. Catherine searched for a way to reassure the little boys.

"Elisha, Joseph, you know your papa is being taken care of by your mama and the doctor?" Catherine asked.

Elisha responded first as he often did. "Is Papa going to die, Aunt Catherine?" Both boys stared at her as if holding their breath.

"There is that chance, but the doctor doesn't think so. Now, that he has the bullet out and the bleeding stopped, he thinks your papa has a good chance of being all right. We need to keep praying for him. You boys can help by being quiet in the house, playing with your little sister, and bringing in wood and water."

Both boys nodded, and Joseph spoke up. "We can do that. When can we see Papa?"

Jacob answered with a smile. "We let your papa rest, and when he is feeling better, we see him. Maybe a day or two."

Catherine stood and started clearing the table. After setting the dishes by the dry sink, she crossed the hallway to the bunkroom. Agnes sat by Thomas' bed watching her son sleep.

Placing her hand on Agnes' shoulder, Catherine asked in a whisper, "Has he stirred at all?"

"Not much. I keep thinking he will wake soon. How is Jeremiah?"

Catherine sighed, "Doc says it is just waiting now. Jeremiah's fever is high, and he's still unconscious."

"Catherine, would you mind sitting here for a while? I'd like see what I can do to help Emily. She has been by Jeremiah's side all day. She must eat something. I would tell her to rest, but until he's better I doubt if she will."

"I'll be glad to sit awhile with Thomas. You go on and see what you can do for Emily." After watching Agnes leave the bunkroom, Catherine sat in the chair next to Thomas' bed. She reached over and felt of his brow. It was cool.

Thomas turned toward Catherine and opened his eyes.

"Hello, how are you feeling?" Catherine asked as Thomas took her hand.

"Like something the cat drug in. Is there any water?" His voice was husky from his exhausted sleep.

Catherine rose, picked up the pitcher of water, and filled a glass. Sitting down, she slid her hand behind his head and raised it while she guided the glass to his mouth. He drank deeply until the glass was empty.

As she lowered his head, he took hold of her hand. "Thanks."

Catherine was a little embarrassed to be so close to Thomas in his bedroom. "Do you want more water?"

"No, I'm fine. How is Jeremiah?"

"Doc got the bullet out and stopped most of the bleeding. Jeremiah is running a high fever. Doc is hoping the fever will break, and then he says Jeremiah should be on the road to recovery. Right now the fever is the danger."

"I should get up and do something. What time is it getting to be?"

Catherine shook her head. "No, you need to rest and take care of your own wound. Doc said to come get him when you woke so he could look at your leg."

Thomas sighed wearily. "I guess I might as well let him. All I really want is a bath and something to eat. Then, I think I could go back to sleep."

Letting go of his hand that had recaptured hers, she moved toward the door. "I'll be back shortly."

When she informed Doc that Thomas was awake, he grabbed his bag and followed her.

"Does he seem to be in pain or feverish?"

"No, he just wants to take a bath, eat, and go back to sleep. Let me know what I can do to help."

As Doc crossed the kitchen on the way to the bunkroom, he turned to Catherine. "I need a pan of hot water and a bunch of bandages. I'm probably going to have to soak the pants away from the wound. I hope it hasn't gotten infected from not being attended to. Jeremiah's wounds were so much worse."

Catherine gave the older man a hug. "What a choice to have to make. You choose wisely. Thomas didn't seem to be in any pain, and his forehead was cool a few minutes ago."

"You're right, I hardly had a choice, but Jeremiah is stabilized and we need to wait. Mildred, after I take care of Thomas can you have me a plate of food ready?"

Mildred wiped her hands on her dishtowel. "Anytime, Doc."

Doc stopped where Agnes was rocking the baby. "Agnes, why don't you give the baby to Catherine, and you and Milburn come help me take care of Thomas' wound? We will have to undress him." Doc looked at Catherine and winked.

She could feel her face turning red with embarrassment. She had been so concerned with helping Thomas the propriety of the situation had not even entered her mind. "Of course, I'll take Charity."

Agnes gave the baby to Catherine, then followed Doc toward the bunkroom. Milburn took the pot of hot water from Sally and hurried behind them. Patting the diapered bottom of little Charity, Catherine sat in the rocker. Stifling her impatience, she waited for her chance to go and care for Thomas. Until they could marry, she had no right to Thomas. He cared for her, she knew he did, but he was careful not to promise what he might not be able to fulfill.

It seemed like hours before Doc came back into the kitchen and sat at the table. Mildred took a plate of food out of the warming oven and set it in front of him. "You want tea or coffee, Doc?" she asked.

"I'll take tea. I've drank so much coffee in the last twenty four hours that tea will make a nice change." He began to eat like a man who often had his meals interrupted.

Catherine rose and put the sleeping baby into the crib in the corner of the kitchen. She gave Doc time to eat, but as soon as Mildred served him a slice of apple pie, she asked softly, "How is Thomas, Doc?"

He looked over at Catherine and smiled. "You've been very patient, Catherine. Thomas is fine. He does have a serious graze along the side of his upper thigh. And it looks a little red and angry, so we are going to have to change the bandage often, and keep it clean and dry. He's a strong man and should heal quickly. That's not to say, he won't be in some pain and shouldn't put too much strain on the muscles around the wound. I don't want him on a horse for a couple of days, but whether he will listen to me or not is a question." He scraped the last of the apple pie from his plate and after licking the spoon, patted his stomach, and sighed. "Miss Mildred, you have outdone yourself. That was the best pie I've ever eaten. Now, I better go check on Jeremiah. Miss Catherine, why don't you go sit with Thomas for a while. I'd like Milburn and Agnes to see if they can get Emily to eat something and then rest a bit. She's going to be sick if she keeps on as she's going."

Mildred put a bowl of hot stew and cornbread on a tray and added a glass of tea. "Catherine, this is for Thomas"

Catherine nodded and turned toward the bunkroom. Milburn and Agnes had a better chance of getting Emily to listen than anyone else on the ranch.

Thomas was lying flat on his bunk with a sheet over his legs and a clean undershirt on. He looked even paler than before the doc had seen him. His bloody, dirty clothes lay in a pile on the floor at the end of the bunk. Agnes was wiping his face with a wet cloth. Milburn sat on the next bunk.

Catherine set the tray on the table by Thomas' bunk. "Doc suggested you all go talk Emily into eating something and then lying down to rest. She won't listen to Doc. He hopes she'll listen to you."

Thomas gently pushed away his mother's hand holding the wet cloth. "Ma, I'm fine. Catherine has brought me something to eat and can stay. Emily needs you now."

"You're sure, son?" Agnes asked.

"I'm sure." He looked up at Catherine. "You don't mind staying a bit do you?"

Catherine smiled. "Not at all."

Milburn held out his hand to Agnes. "Come on, love. Let's go help Emily."

After they walked out of the bunkroom, Catherine helped Thomas sit up and plumped up some pillows for him to lean against. "Stew and cornbread all right?"

Thomas grinned. "Anything will do. I'm hungry enough to eat an old boot."

Catherine laughed. "That won't be necessary." She set the tray across Thomas' legs and then lifted it again as she saw him wince. "I'm sorry. I didn't think about your wound."

He took the tray from her hands and positioned it more comfortably on his lap. "It's just a tad sore is all. A little discomfort is worth it to get some of Mildred's stew. Sit down and visit while I eat. Doc didn't say much when I asked about Jeremiah. How is he?"

She sat in the chair that Agnes had just vacated. "He hasn't come to yet and his fever is high. Doc keeps reassuring us Jeremiah will probably be fine. He's still very ill and it's going to take weeks for him to be back on his feet."

Thomas crumbled cornbread into his stew. "I feel bad I couldn't do more to help him and to get him back here sooner."

"Don't you know you saved his life? What if he had been alone? He'd be somewhere out on the range dead by now. You don't have anything to feel bad about."

"Thanks for saying that. I felt responsible while we were out there and couldn't stand the thought of returning to the ranch with him dead. I couldn't have faced Emily and the boys."

Catherine nodded. "I can only imagine what it was like. Hopefully, it's over with the arrest of the three men. Do you think Mckinley was behind all of this from the beginning?"

Looking thoughtful, Thomas nodded. "It looks like it.You know he was one of the rustlers we brought in. I hope there is enough evidence to convict him. We caught them sneaking up on the fellows but we didn't catch them actually rustling the cattle."

Catherine chuckled. "You haven't heard then. Milburn told me the two men with Myles confessed all and placed the blame on him. Myles may not have confessed but with the testimony of those two men, he will be brought to justice."

Thomas looked relieved. "Well, that's a load off my mind. I was afraid he was going to get away with it again."

Catherine shook her head. "Not this time. He will have to pay the piper. The bank is also closed, and the state is sending in an examiner to sort out his books. Everyone who has had cattle stolen is placing claims on Myles' money and ranch." She took the tray with the empty dishes and set it on the table.

Thomas rubbed his leg. "Maybe now I won't have to feel like everyone is watching and judging me."

"Oh, I hope so too." Catherine let Thomas take one of her hands.

He began to rub his thumb again her palm. "You know that this week is an anniversary."

Catherine felt a tingle clear to her toes and made no move to pull back her hand. "What anniversary?"

Thomas locked his gaze with hers. "It was exactly a year ago today that we met. A third of my time as a prisoner here is done. I only have two more years."

"That is a great anniversary. I know the year has been hard in some ways, but the next two will go by fast."

"I don't have the right to ask you to make any kind of promise to me, but do you think you could consider waiting for me?"

Catherine couldn't stop the smile. "I think I might consider that, if that is what you want."

Thomas tightened his hold on her hand. "That is what I want, more than anything. I care deeply about you Catherine. More than I have ever felt for anyone in my life. I don't ask that you commit to caring for me. Just let me try to show you how much I care."

"Oh, Thomas, if you only knew. My life revolves around when I will be with you. I'm so glad Jeremiah and Emily don't mind me coming out here so often. I suspect they know my motivation."

"You come just to see me?" Thomas asked with a tone of wonder in his voice.

"Of course."

"Catherine, would you think it too forward of me to ask for a kiss?"

"Not if you don't think it's too forward of me to give you a kiss." Catherine could feel the heat rising on her cheeks and knew she was blushing like a young schoolgirl.

Thomas placed his hand on the back of her neck and pulled her gently toward him.

Catherine closed her eyes and then felt the soft sweet pressure of his lips on hers. He pulled back a bit and then kissed her again before pulling away.

"We best not do that too often. You're so beautiful and too tempting." Thomas eyes sparkled even though his voice was somber.

"We best not. I could get addicted to that," Catherine confessed.

"Maybe we could try it just one more time?" Thomas asked hopefully.

"Well, maybe ..." Catherine stopped and looked toward the bunkroom door as Cal and Jethro came in.

Thomas let go of her hand and Catherine pressed her palms across her skirt as if to rubbing out winkles.

Cal grinned. "Hey, Thomas. How are you feeling?"

"Hey, yourself. I'm feeling much better since getting some sleep and now some food. Just sore and still weary from all the excitement."

Cal nodded. "Yeah, it was kinda exciting. Different from taking care of the horses and building fences. But getting shot isn't my idea of fun."

Catherine stood and picked up the tray of dirty dishes. "I'll take this back to the kitchen. Is there anything you need Thomas?"

Thomas grinned at her. "No, I've everything a man could want."

Hoping she wasn't blushing too much, Catherine turned and left the bunkroom. She heard Cal asking Thomas how long until he could ride again. Neither Cal nor Jethro had seemed to notice the moment of intimacy between herself and Thomas. Holding the tray with one arm, she touched her lips with her fingers almost in wonder. It was the first time she had ever been kissed, and it couldn't have been sweeter.

Chapter Thirty-Six Thomas

Thomas' leg was almost healed two weeks later when the sheriff sent word that he wanted to see Thomas in town at the jail.

Bob wasn't pleased with the request. "What now? We've got work to do. I can't have Thomas off in jail for some stupid reason. Not with Jeremiah still laid up."

Thomas didn't want to go into town either, especially without Jeremiah. "When do you expect Jeremiah will be back on his feet?"

"He's barely moving about in the house. He won't be back riding for a couple more weeks if even then," Bob said.

"I don't suppose we can wait for that before going into town?" Thomas knew the answer but wanted to ask anyway.

Bob took off his hat and beat it against the side of his leg, a sure sign of frustration. "No, we can't wait for another two weeks before responding to the sheriff. Go saddle up a couple of horses, and I'll go in and tell Jeremiah."

Thomas dragged his feet as he made his way over to the corral. He chose a couple of mares and soon had the saddles on. Just when things seemed to be getting back to normal, the sheriff was going to stir things up. By the time Bob came back out of the house, Thomas had the two horses ready to go.

It only took about thirty minutes to reach town, keeping the horses at a lope. Having to pay attention to his riding helped Thomas not to have to think too deeply while they were in town. The main street was mostly empty in the middle of the afternoon. Thomas looked toward the café hoping to see Catherine, but it appeared empty.

Bob turned his horse toward the livery stable. "I don't know how long we'll be here so we might as well have the horses rubbed down and watered."

After they dismounted they handed off the reins to the livery owner and walked the short distance to the jail. Before entering, Thomas looked up and down the street. He hoped no one was watching and wondering why he was at the jail again.

Sheriff Grant sat behind his battered old desk with a bunch of wanted poster stuck haphazardly on the wall behind him. "Howdy, boys. Have a sit. Glad you came on in so quickly."

Bob pushed his hat back on his head. "What's this all about, Grant?"

"Hold your horses Bob. I'll get to it. First, how is Jeremiah doing?"

"He getting better every day, but he still has a ways to go. That bullet in his back was bad enough, but then it took three days to get him to the doctor. It will take some time. Doc says he should be his old self by late summer."

Thomas sat in the hard wooden chair and felt the sweat trickling down his back. He didn't think he would ever feel at ease in a jail.

Grant took a deep breath and glanced at some papers in front of him. He picked one up and handed it to Thomas. "The governor was so impressed with your going after the rustlers and keeping Jeremiah safe, even with being wounded yourself, that he has sent you an official commendation."

Thomas looked over the piece of paper. Sure enough, it was an official commendation of valor from the governor himself. "I'm real surprised to get this. Who would have thought the governor himself would be aware of what happened and my part in it."

Grant nodded. "I wondered that myself until I heard that a few of the citizens around town had talked about it to a newspaper man from Denver. I guess the governor read about it and decided it was an opportunity to be gracious."

Bob grinned at Thomas. "So do I need to call you Mr. Black now?"

Thomas grinned back with a shake of his head. "It's just a piece of paper."

Grant picked up another piece of paper. "It's more than that, but before I tell you what else I have here, I want to say something."

"Yes, sir?" Thomas wasn't real sure what was going on, but the sheriff was making him nervous.

"I want to apologize for my suspicions. I admit they were being fed by Myles McKinley. I didn't bother to think in any other direction but the one he kept pointing to, namely you Thomas. I should have done my job better, and then you and Jeremiah and the other hands out at the Rocking JR would not have had to do it for me. You have been without blame this whole year. All I could see was that you got convicted once and so you were guilty again. Will you accept my apology?" Grant held his hand out to Thomas.

Thomas shook the sheriff's hand. "I do accept your apology. I've tried hard this year to just do what was expected of me and to obey the rules of the parole."

"I know you have, and now I know who was really behind all the problems here. Now that we have that out of the way I have one more thing to tell you. Judge Yeakley, when he was here last week and sentencing those three rustlers to long terms in the penitentiary, was intrigued with your story, Thomas. He felt you should have some reward for what you did in saving Jeremiah." Grant slowly handed Thomas the piece of paper he had been holding. "Read this and tell me what you see."

Thomas took the piece of paper and began to read. The first word that caught his attention was Arizona. He couldn't breathe as he realized that he held in his hands a full pardon. He glanced up at the sheriff. "This is what I think it is?"

The sheriff nodded as he grinned. "Yes, sir, it is. A full pardon."

Bob sat up in his chair. "A what?"

Grant chucked. " Judge Yeakley got in touch with the judge in Arizona and recommended that Thomas be rewarded with a pardon. The judge set aside the conviction as if it had never happened. Thomas, you also get to split the rewards for the rustlers. Even though McKinley offered part of the reward that was really for his own capture, the bank was the one officially offering the reward, and so it will be paid."

Thomas continued to stare at the sheriff trying to take in what it meant. He was free at last. After thirteen years, for the first time in his adult life he was free.

Bob slapped him on the back and held out his hand. "I'm real glad for you, Thomas. You deserve it."

Thomas, still in a fog took Bob's hand. "Thanks, Bob. I can hardly believe it."

"I haven't told anyone. I thought you might like to tell your folks and a certain pretty young lady." Sheriff Grant looked ten years younger as he gleefully shared about the pardon with Thomas. "You get to tell Jeremiah he's lost a free laborer."

Thomas frowned. Would he have to leave the Rocking JR?

Bob spoke up. "You may not be a free laborer anymore, Thomas, but if you want a paying job I'm sure Jeremiah will offer it. You've become a real good horse wrangler."

Peering at the official pardon, Thomas read it over again. "It doesn't say that I have to go back to Arizona, and it seems to be official as of yesterday."

Grant nodded. "It is official. You don't have to do anything. You're a free man although I would keep that pardon in a safe place. Unless you particularly want to, you don't have to ever go back to Arizona."

Thomas felt like he was coming out from under a nightmare. Now he only wanted to get to Catherine and let her know. And his folks after all they had gone through with him being their son, deserved the happiness the pardon would bring them. Thomas fought tears as he thought of how steadfast they had been all of the years since his conviction. And now to have a pardon as if it had never happened. .

Bob stood up and shook hands with Sheriff Grant. "Thanks for this. I have a feeling you gave a recommendation as well."

Grant turned a little red. "Well, the judge did ask me what I thought about it, and I did tell him I thought it was the right thing to do."

Thomas didn't know what to say. He held out his hand and shook the sheriff's hand again. "My thanks don't seem to be enough. You've helped get me back my life."

Grant smiled. "Well, just make sure that from now on the only thing we have to talk about is the weather."

Bob led the way out of the jail. "Go on, Thomas. Go tell your girl and then your folks. I'll wait for you and ride back to the ranch together. Until people know about this, you don't want to give anyone a reason to think you're breaking parole. Also, you need to let Jeremiah know as soon as possible. You owe him and Emily that respect."

"You're right, Bob. Just let me go tell Catherine and my folks and then we will head back to the ranch."

Thomas wanted to run down the street whooping and hollering. As he began to believe that he was really free, a joy bubbled up in his being as he had never experienced before. The café was closed for the afternoon and he went around to the back door and knocked.

Catherine opened the door with a look of puzzlement. "Something wrong, Thomas? Why are you in town in the middle of the week? Who is with you?"

Thomas gently pushed her back into her little apartment and closed the door. "Is anyone else here?"

"No." Catherine's look of puzzlement was increasing.

Not wanting to hold back from her any longer, Thomas pulled her into his arms and gave her the kiss that he had been wanting to give her for the last year. He pulled back and Catherine seemed to have lost her breath.

"Thomas, what is going on?"

"I have something I want you to read." He pulled the pardon out of his coat pocket and handed it to her.

Catherine started reading it and then gasped. "Oh, Thomas, is this what I think it is?"

He pulled her back into his arms. "It's a full pardon. I'm done as a prisoner. After thirteen years I'm free."

Tears gathered in Catherine's eyes and spilled down her cheeks. "A pardon, how, why, who?"

Thomas handed her his handkerchief. "Hey, don't cry. It's a good thing."

She laughed. "I know it's a good thing. These are tears of joy. God has answered my prayers."

"And mine."

"But Thomas, how?"

"Sheriff Grant and Judge Yeakley petitioned Arizona to grant it as a reward for helping catch the rustlers and helping save Jeremiah. Catherine, it's a full pardon. It's as if I had never been convicted."

"Just as God pardons us, as if we had never sinned."

Thomas solemnly nodded. "I hadn't thought about it like that, but it's same idea isn't it?"

"Now what will you do? Will you go to work with your pa? Or, continue to work for Jeremiah?"

Thomas rubbed the back of his neck. "I haven't really had time to think yet. I just found out. And, I still need to let my folks and Jeremiah know. As much as I love Pa, I really don't like the idea of working in the store. I've learned a lot in the last year and have come to love ranching. If Jeremiah will have me, that's what I'd rather do."

Catherine placed her palms on each side of his face and gazed into his eyes. "I'm sure Jeremiah will want you to stay there. And, I'm also sure your folks will understand. Shouldn't we go tell them?"

Thomas pulled her close and kissed her. "Yes, we need to go tell them."

When they entered the store, Milburn was finishing up with a customer and Agnes was nowhere in sight.

Catherine let go of Thomas' hand and softly whispered. "I'll go find your ma. She must be upstairs. You close up the store when your pa finishes with this customer. Then bring him upstairs."

Thomas smiled at her. It seemed to be the only thing he wanted to do. "All right, we'll meet you upstairs."

He waited as the customer slowly left the mercantile. Then he walked over and locked the door and turned the sign in the window to closed.

"Thomas, what are you doing?"

"Pa, don't question me. Just follow me upstairs. I'll tell you and Ma at the same time what's going on."

Pa looked befuddled but followed him up the stairs and into the front room of the upstairs apartment.

Catherine was seated on the couch with his mother in her usual place. Thomas sat down next to Catherine and Pa took his usual chair.

"Now, Thomas, what is going on?" His mother's voice held the tone he had experienced as a child when she had caught him doing some mischief.

Thomas drew out the pardon again and handed it to Pa. "Read this and tell me what it sounds like, please."

Pa started reading and then sat up on the edge of his chair. "No! It can't be. Is this true, Thomas?"

Agnes twisted the handkerchief she was holding. "What Milburn? What is that piece of paper saying? Is it bad news? Are they sending you back, Thomas?"

Thomas left his seat and knelt in front of his mother. "No, Ma, they are not sending me back. In fact, that is a pardon from the territory of Arizona. I'm free."

"What is he saying, Milburn? I don't understand." She looked on the edge of panic.

Thomas took her into his arms and hugged her. "It's all right, Ma. Judge Yeakley and Sheriff Grant petitioned the judge in Arizona and got me a pardon. That takes away the conviction for rustling. I am no longer being held accountable for what I did thirteen years ago. I don't have to serve that last two years of my sentence. I'm free, Ma. Free."

"Oh, my son, thank God. It's an answer to our prayers." His mother dissolved into tears.

Milburn stood and walked over to his wife and son. Thomas stood and accepted the hug from his father. "I'm so glad for you, son. You have earned this."

"No, Pa, I haven't earned it any more than I've earned the pardon of God. I was guilty. And now I am freed from that guilt by grace and mercy. God's grace and mercy, and the mercy of a judge in Arizona."

"You're right, son. We can't earn a pardon when we are guilty, but we are all pardoned by the blood of Christ."

"All I know is that I don't have to keep having the nightmare of you being sent back to that terrible place. That is what this means?" Agnes asked with a trembling voice.

Catherine took her hand. "Yes, Agnes, that what it means. Thomas can now stay here with us."

Thomas smiled. "And you're not going to get rid of me. But, until I've told Jeremiah and the word has gotten around, I need to be cautious. Bob is waiting for me, and we need to ride back to the ranch."

"Will you keep working on the ranch, son?" Milburn asked softly.

"That's what I'd like to do," Thomas answered.

"You know you could always work here if there is ever a need, but I don't want you feeling any obligation. I want you to do the work you want to do. You're not a store man like me. You're a rancher like Jeremiah. I have seen that clearly for the last year."

"Thanks Pa, for understanding. If Jeremiah doesn't want me to stay, I will look around at getting hired on by another ranch."

"Oh, don't worry about that. I have a feeling that Jeremiah will want you to stay." Pa nodded.

"That's what Bob told me, too." With both men seeing it the same perhaps it would be true.

Catherine put her arm around Thomas' arm. "Go on back to the ranch and tell Jeremiah and Emily what has happened. We'll come on out later for supper if that's all right. We need to celebrate."

Thomas patted her arm and held it tight against him. "That would be great." He turned to his folks. "That all right with you all?"

"Go on, son. We'll see you after while." His pa held out his hand for his son to shake.

Thomas kissed his mother on the cheek and then Catherine. "I'll see you all out at the ranch."

~

As Bob and Thomas rode up to the barn at the back of the house, Jacob and Cal came out of the barn.

Bob dismounted and handed his reins to Cal. "If you fellows don't mind, take care of our horses. We need to see Jeremiah about something. Come on Thomas, no use waiting."

Thomas dismounted and handed his reins to Jacob. "Thanks fellows. I got to follow Bob."

Quickly Bob led the way into the house, through the kitchen and into the front room. Jeremiah was seated in his big leather chair close to the fireplace.

"Boys, I see you're back from town. What's going on?" Jeremiah sat back comfortably in his big armchair. He still looked pale and like a man recovering from a gunshot in the back.

Thomas pulled up a chair facing Jeremiah and pulled the pardon out of his coat pocket. "Sheriff Grant wanted me to come into town so he could give me this." It was hard, but he kept from grinning. Until he knew Jeremiah's response to the pardon, he couldn't fully celebrate.

Jeremiah took the piece of paper and glanced from Thomas to Bob. He began to read it. Slowly he laid it on the table next to his chair. "I couldn't be more surprised or more glad. A pardon, I wanted you to be paroled early and have your freedom, but a complete pardon. Thank God. Do your folks and Catherine know?"

Thomas grinned. "Yes, I told them first while we were in town. They are coming out for supper and to help celebrate if that is all right."

Jeremiah slowly stood pushing himself up by his arms like an old man. A reminder to Thomas that Jeremiah was not fully healed. Jeremiah held out his hand and Thomas took it to shake. But, Jeremiah pulled him into a hug. "I'm really very glad."

"Thanks, Jeremiah. I'd like to tell everyone at supper." Thomas was not sure now was the time, but he went ahead. "I'd like to keep working for you. At least until I can make some plans. I can always work for Pa at the mercantile, but that's not what I want to do. He understands that I much prefer working on a ranch."

Jeremiah nodded. "I'm pleased you like working here. You've done a good job. I've seen you learn a lot and you're a hard worker. How about we start you at thirty dollars a month?"

Thomas felt a relief and released a breath he had been holding. He wasn't ready to leave the Rocking JR yet. However, someday he would and it would be to go to Catherine, wherever she wanted to be.

Emily came into the front room from the hallway to the children's bedrooms. "Well, you men look pleased with yourselves."

Jeremiah walked slowly over to her. "Thomas and Bob were in town and invited Catherine and Thomas' folks for supper this evening. Hope that is all right."

Emily glanced around at Thomas and Bob and turned back to Jeremiah. "Something is going on, but you will tell me when you're ready. Of course, they're welcome for supper. I'll go tell Mildred, so she can be sure we have enough food."

"Good and before you tell me, dear wife. I'm going to go lie down for a while and rest up for company." Jeremiah kissed his wife on the cheek, gave a wave to Thomas and Bob, and slowly made his way to their bedroom.

Emily stood and watched him go, shaking her head. "Well, I surely do not know what is going on, but for Jeremiah to go rest without a fuss. Well, I never."

Thomas smiled at her and gave her a peck on the cheek. "Strange things are happening, Mrs. Emily. Very strange."

He headed out through the kitchen and into the bunkroom. "I'm going to shave and clean up. Maybe put my best shirt on. I feel like celebrating."

Bob laughed. "I can imagine that you do. Guess I'll go out and warn the fellows that we're having guests for supper."

After Bob left the bunkroom, Thomas sat on his bunk and stared at the wall. He was free. He could ride into town without an escort and call on his girl. He could make plans. Wiping his eyes, he couldn't understand why he felt like weeping.

~

Thomas met Catherine and his folks as Pa's buggy pulled up. He told them that only Jeremiah and Bob knew and the others on the ranch would be told after supper.

Every time Thomas made eye contact with Catherine, his ma, pa, and Bob , they smiled at him, and he had to smile back. Finally, when everyone had finished their peach cobbler and those who wanted it had been served coffee, Jeremiah tapped his cup with his spoon, signaling everyone he had something to say.

He stood and inclined his head. "This is really Thomas' news to tell."

Thomas shook his head. "You tell it, Jeremiah. You're better at speaking than me."

"All right, I'll tell it. This afternoon Thomas went into town and spoke with Sheriff Grant. Judge Yeakley and Sheriff Grant, were able to do something for Thomas." He stopped and looked around at everyone at the table. "All of you are Thomas' friends and will want to celebrate with him the fact that the judge in Arizona who had sentenced Thomas has granted him a full pardon. Our Thomas is a free man this evening."

Jethro let out a loud and long "Yeehaw!" And, for several minutes it was bedlam and congratulations. Thomas feared his ribs would crack from the hugs, especially those from Joe, Cal, Jacob, and Jethro. Even Elisha and Joseph lined up to give Thomas a hug. Then Emily, Mildred, and even Sally congratulated him. Then Elisha and Joseph enthusiastically gave Thomas a hug wearing big grins.

Joseph looked up at Thomas from where he had an arm around his waist. "I don't know what a pardon is but it must be good. Even Pa is grinning."

Thomas ruffled the boy's hair. "You're right it is a very good thing and I'm glad to see your pa grinning."

He looked over at Jeremiah who lifted his cup of coffee up in a salute.

Emily and Sara were hugging Catherine and Agnes.

"Did you know?" Emily asked.

Catherine wiped her eyes. "He told us this afternoon right after he found out. It's so wonderful. I still can hardly believe it."

Elisha tugged on Thomas' arm. "Does this mean you're going to leave us?"

Thomas knelt down and gathered a little boy into each arm. "No, I'm not going to leave you. It just means I'm not a prisoner anymore and can go to town when I want. And, it means that your pa will start paying me for my work."

Joseph cocked his head and looked at Thomas with a questioning eye. "I knew you were a prisoner because Pa told me but I never understood why."

Emily stepped up. "Now boys, Let's not be bothering Thomas."

Thomas shook his head. "They deserve to know and understand."

Emily looked down the table at Jeremiah who nodded his head. "All right, Thomas. Help them understand."

Thomas took a moment to think what to say to these two precious children. "When I was younger, I didn't listen to my pa, and I did some bad things. The law caught me and sent me to prison for 15 years. I had done wrong, and it was right that I go to prison. Then the judge said I could come here and spend the last three years of sentence working for your pa."

Elisha nodded. "That was a good thing."

"Yes, it was." Thomas agreed. "But, yesterday, the judge did something even better. He decided he would forgive me for doing wrong and showed me mercy. He forgave my wrong and wiped it out as if I had never broken the law. Yesterday, I was still a prisoner, but this evening I'm a free man."

Joseph looked up at Thomas with eyes wide and his mouth an oval. "Just like God the Father forgives the sinners."

Thomas swallowed to keep from weeping that this child understood what a pardon was for both a prisoner of the state and a prisoner of sin.

"Amen." Jeremiah stood. "Come on boys. Walk me back to the front room and I'll read you a story before your bedtime."

Elisha and Joseph quickly moved to each side of their father and took his arm to help him back to his comfortable chair in the front room. Thomas smiled at the way Jeremiah was letting the boys think they were helping him. Jeremiah didn't need their help but the boys needed to feel like they were helping their father.

Thomas looked at Catherine. She was so beautiful, both outwardly and inwardly. It was hard to take in all of his blessings. "Would you like to stroll a ways with me. It's a full moon."

Catherine blushed and lowered her eyes. "I'd like that."

Thomas took her arm and guided her to the outside door. Holding it open, she brushed against him as she passed through to the backyard. Taking her hand Thomas led her down the path that followed the creek. Thomas didn't feel like talking much. He just wanted to be near her. When they had gone far enough, he stopped and pulled her to him.

"What are you doing, Thomas?" she asked in a coy voice.

"I'm thinking about kissing you. I'm sort of getting the hang of it, but still need more practice."

"Oh, you do, do you? It seemed to me that you were doing very well at it," she giggled.

Thomas chuckled. "How about one as a goodnight kiss? We can practice again some other day."

"All right. Just one." She leaned toward him.

Thomas took his time and kissed her tenderly. It was a promise of what was to come.

Catherine laid her head on his chest and rested comfortably in the safety of his arms. "We best head back. Your folks will be ready to head back to town. We have to be up in the morning for work."

"You're right. I just don't want the evening to end. It's been a blessed time." Thomas held her for a moment longer and then started back toward the house.

~

The next couple of weeks were fun times for Thomas as people heard about the pardon and so many friends from town and from church expressed their pleasure. No one seemed to resent or question that he had been pardoned. Every night Thomas went to bed with a prayer of thankfulness to God for the blessing of his freedom and every morning he woke to a fresh day filled with enjoyment.

After breakfast on a Friday morning, Jeremiah asked Thomas to meet him in the front room.

Thomas was puzzled but sat in the chair facing Jeremiah.

"Bob came to me yesterday with some news. You know he's from Texas and his family has a ranch there. It's a large family and Bob came up the trail with Elisha and Jacob and stayed on to work with Elisha. However, his folks are getting older, and he's missing seeing his family. He's decided to go back to Texas."

Thomas was more than surprised. Bob was a permanent fixture at the ranch. More than that he supervised much of the work, especially now while Jeremiah was slowed down from his wound.

Jeremiah leaned forward. "I've thought about this carefully and prayed about it. Bob will be here another month, then he will leave. He and I talked, and I want to ask you to step in as my foreman when Bob leaves. It's twice the pay, and if you and Catherine decide to marry you can either live here at the house or we will build you one."

Thomas struggled to get control of his breathing. Foreman! "What about Joe? Or even Jacob? They know more about ranching than I do. Not that I'm not flattered to be asked, but I'm not sure I'm ready to be foreman."

Jeremiah steepled his fingers as he regarded Thomas. "Neither Joe nor Jacob want the responsibility of being foreman. Joe plans to work some for us and some for Elisha. Jacob has his furniture building business. Cal isn't interested either, and Jethro is too young. So, either you step in or I will have to hire from outside the ranch, and I'd rather not do that. I realize you're new to ranching. But, based upon what you have learned in the last year, I am completely convinced you are capable of doing the job. And, you have already shown an ability to draw men to you. All of the men have said they would have no problem with you being my secunda. If after a few years you decide you want your own place, I'll help you get one."

"I'd be foolish to turn down such an opportunity. How about we say I'll work for a year and then you'll reconsider whether I'm doing the work well enough or not?"

Jeremiah nodded. "That would be more than fair. I know how you work. I know what you know and don't know. I'm not asking blindly."

"All right then. If you're willing to take a chance on me, I'm willing to try." Thomas could feel his heart beating in his neck. Was he getting in over his head? Could he do it? All he could do was give it his best.

"Are we agreed then? You'll be the foreman of the Rocking JR?"

"All right Jeremiah, you have yourself a new foreman. I hope you know what you're doing."

"Trust me, I do."

Jeremiah stood and held out his hand. Thomas took it.

After the afternoon work was done, Thomas borrowed the small buggy and drove into town. He stopped at the back of the café and knocked on the door.

Catherine opened it and smiled her welcome. "Thomas."

"Can you pack a quick picnic? I have the buggy as you see and we can go for a ride and have a picnic." Thomas cocked his head and raised his eyebrows.

"Yes, we can have a picnic. Give me a couple of minutes to get it together. Beryl can handle the evening crowd if she leaves the dishes for me to clear up later."

"Sounds good. I can help do the dishes with you." Thomas offered.

"You wash buckets of dishes? This I must see." Catherine made up some roast beef sandwiches, added apple pie, and a couple of jars of tea. Within minutes she had a picnic put together. She stepped into the dining room where Beryl was wiping the table and chairs. "I'm going out with Thomas. Please leave the dishes, and I'll do them when we get back."

"Sure and go on with you. Have a nice time. And, don't you worry about the café. I'll handle everything."

Thomas put the basket with their meal on the floor of the buggy and helped Catherine step up. Once they were situated, he looked at her with fondness. "You look lovely this evening."

"Thank you. You always make me feel lovely."

Thomas wanted to take her into his arms and kiss her for the next hour, but that would not do in the middle of town. Just their riding in a buggy together would start tongues wagging. Thomas started the team and drove out to little river that made its meandering way through the countryside. That was one thing about living in a small town Thomas decided. You could be in the countryside looking toward the high mountains within minutes of leaving town. He found the spot he wanted and pulled the team to a stop. After tying up the team, he helped Catherine down from the buggy. Picking up the basket and a couple of blankets, he led the way down to a little meadow that ended at the river's edge.

"This all right?" Thomas asked.

"This is perfect." Catherine twilled in a circle with her arms out and laughed. "What a lovely spot for a picnic. How did you know it was here?"

Thomas grinned. "I looked for it. I knew that along the river there must be a nice place for a picnic." He spread the blankets on the grass and placed the basket by the edge.

Catherine gracefully sat on the blanket with her feet tucked under her skirt. "Let's eat. I'm hungry, and I would guess you are too."

Thomas sat down beside her. "I could eat."

Catherine laughed. "I've noticed that you are always ready to eat. It must be all the hard work you do. But seriously, you eat more than two men, yet you don't put on weight."

"I've always had a problem keeping my weight. I do work hard but I eat a lot. But nothing turns to fat."

"You're blessed that way. Some people just look at food and gain weight."

"Like my ma. She doesn't eat near what Pa and I eat and she is constantly fighting her weight. She tells us that it is completely not fair." Thomas reached out and brushed a strand of soft hair back behind Catherine's ear.

Catherine looked at him with serious eyes. "Thomas, where are we going with this?"

He didn't pretend that he didn't know what she was asking. He had asked himself that very thing. "I'd like to think we are going forward together. I'd like for us to."

Catherine shook her head. "You have to do better than that. How do you want us to move forward together?"

Thomas took a deep breath. "I love you Catherine and I want to spend the rest of my life with you. You walk into a room and it's brighter and the colors are stronger. We walk in the moonlight and it glows only for you. You're all I think about and all I can see in my future."

"Oh, Thomas. That's lovely. I love you, too. I think I started falling in love with you from hearing Agnes and Milburn talk about you with such love in their hearts. I feel so safe when I'm with you and I do want to be with you. I want to bear your children and grow old together."

"Catherine, will you marry me? I'm just a cowhand and won't ever be rich even though Bob is leaving the Rocking JR and Jeremiah has asked me to be foreman. It means more pay and possibly a small house. I may be employed by Jeremiah but I'm really working for you and will do my best to provide for you all the rest of my days."

Catherine met his gaze with a look of pure love. "Yes, I'll marry you."

Thomas gently and lovingly took her in his arms. Gazing into her eyes that held such love, he thanked God for the blessings He continued to give him. He was free to love and share his life with this beautiful woman who loved him.

About A J Hawke

If you enjoy the feel of the wind on your face, and the open sky before you, join me here to find the romance and flavor of the West. I, too, enjoy those things, but, most of all, I love that our loving and living God, created it all for our pleasure. I love how He works out His plans in the realm of human events. I have been blessed with a gift: a compulsion to write historical and present-day novels set in the American West that demonstrates His power to transform ordinary people into true heroes and heroines. I am just a scribe really, who finds the joy of participating in the creation of inspirational fiction indescribable.

May our Lord Jesus Christ receive all of the credit and be glorified.

The study of history is an ongoing fascination for me. In college, I studied American History taught by Dr. Raymond Muncy. He saw the study of Western Expansion in American History as the examination of people and their times. How did their decisions affect their own lives and the lives of those around them? As I look at the way people lived and worked, it reveals the thinking that shaped their lives. Work, housing, food, family, and religion are fundamentals for people at any time.

Visit my blog at AJHawke.com/Blog where I will share the day-to-day lives of people of the West in the 1800s. Although I also tell stories of the contemporary lives of the people of the West, most of my novels are placed in the 1800s. I love that time of our history, especially the romanticized view of it. It was a land of larger than life men and the women who stood by them, who braved harsh elements and hard work. I write so you, too, may be a part of that time and place, of the great American West.

Born in Spur, Texas into a multi-generational Texas family, I have lived and traveled throughout the American West as well as other parts of the world and now make my home in the Dallas area. Some of what I enjoy doing is reading, writing, and visiting with friends, and family. More than anything else in my life, I take great joy and comfort in my Christian life.

To learn of new titles as they come available sign up for my Newsletter on AJHawke.com. Also, follow me on my blog at AJHawke.com/Blog.

Find me on: http://Facebook.com/AJHawkeBooks
http://Twitter.com/AJHawkeAuthor
http://AJHawke.com
AJHawkebooks@gmail.com

Books by A J Hawke

Available on AMAZON in Paperback and through AMAZON KINDLE

Cedar Ridge Chronicles

CABIN ON PINTO, Book 1, By A J Hawke Inspirational historical western romance

Overview:

Elisha Evans is out of luck. By the age of twenty-five, he'd planned to have his own ranch. Instead, he's forced to beg for a job, destroying his dreams of having a family he can provide for and protect. Betrayal and loss bring him to a cabin on Pinto Creek in the high Colorado Rockies. Just before winter hits, he finds a broken-down wagon in the snow with precious cargo inside. Perhaps, his luck is about to change.

Susana Jamison does not feel so lucky. Despite being rescued by Elisha, she is challenged to the limit of her strength, both physically and spiritually, when faced with the brutal conditions of frontier living and the dangers she encounters. Can she hold on to her faith in the midst of this desperate situation, especially when she's forced to marry a man she's doesn't love?

JOE STORM NO LONGER A COWBOY, Book 2, By A J Hawke Inspirational Historical Western Romance

If a cowhand can't ride, what can he do? Joe Storm can no longer ride a horse—and that hurts a lot more than his injured hip. Swallowing his pride, he takes a job as cook's helper on a trail drive. There he meets the daughter of the owner of the trail herd. In spite of the opposition of her father, Sara befriends Joe. When the herd is sold to a rancher in Colorado Joe wonders if there will be a place on the ranch for a man who can't ride. And he has to watch Sara and her father head for California and out of his life. Facing life without the woman he has come to love, Joe must also confront his past when his father, whom he hasn't seen in twelve years, arrives at the ranch. As Joe struggles to build a place for himself on the ranch, he longs to go to Sara in search of a happy forever. Only with the help of God and friends will Joe be able to achieve his dream

COLORADO MORNING SKY Book 3, By A J Hawke Inspirational Historical Western Romance

Overview:

Swift Justice in the American West. At age 16, a guilty verdict hurls Jeremiah Rebourn across a hot Arizona desert in a prison wagon on his way to Yuma Territorial Prison. The year is 1876. Left for dead after an Apache attack on the wagon, Jeremiah alone survives. He wakes to find himself blindfolded, shackled, and enslaved to a cruel, mute taskmaster. His only companion becomes the ever-present noose around his neck that forces him to do its bidding. He labors hard in a gold mine for days, months, years. He awakes one day to discover his irons and blindfold gone...and an unexpected message. Now equipped with uncommon strength and a deep distrust of his fellow man, he sets out to begin a life. Balm from a Gentle and Quiet Spirit. Emily Johnson, at finishing school in Boston, is summoned west to Colorado by her ailing grandmother. She arrives in Cedar Ridge and soon attracts the attention of Jeremiah. This strong, silent rancher draws Emily's interest as no other man has ever done. Will her love break the chains that enslave his heart? Will Jeremiah grasp that God is using the evil done to him and his present trials for a grander purpose?

Stand-Alone Novels Available on AMAZON/AMAZON KINDLE

MOUNTAIN JOURNEY HOME By A J Hawke

An Inspirational Historical Western Romance
Overview:

A man's word is a man's life. Rock Corner, Texas. 1877. Life couldn't get much better for Dave Kimbrough. He has a beautiful wife in Jenny, a fine young son in Jonathan, and a small ranch with which to build their future. But, when Jenny suddenly dies, the heartache is more than Dave can bear, so he leaves his son with his wife's family and rides off into the rugged Texas country alone. After several years, Dave is wrongly accused of murder, and when he sets out to find the man who can clear his name, he runs instead into a posse that has set out to kill him. Wounded, he holes up for the winter in a cave. It is not time wasted however, as he is given time to contemplate the mistake he made in abandoning his son. Once spring arrives, Dave returns to make things in his life right. Things rarely go as planned, however, and Dave's plans are no different. Beset by a trip to jail, Jenny's spirited sister Rachel, and the heartache of taking away the only life and family his son really knows, Kimbrough makes a promise he thinks is the right thing to do. But, a fateful winter followed by a deadly spring storm changes the course of their lives in ways that no one—least of all Dave—could have ever imagined.

CAUGHT BETWEEN TWO WORLDS: COWBOY BOOTS AND HIGH HEELS By A J Hawke Inspirational Contemporary Western Romance
Overview:

Single parent Flint Tucker had no intention of leaving his small daughter on the ranch in Colorado with his parents. Not even for the dark haired beauty found on a mountain trail. So how did he end up in New York working for Stephanie Wellbourne?

Stephanie Wellbourne needs help to save her position as CEO of her corporation. She's sure Flint Tucker is just the man for the job if she can get him to stay in New York. Why is he not enticed by her wealth and position?

How can a man from a ranch in Colorado and an Upper Manhattan career woman find love when they are **CAUGHT BETWEEN TWO WORLDS: COWBOY BOOTS AND HIGH HEELS?**

36978127R00168

Made in the USA
Middletown, DE
20 November 2016